MURDER ON A SCHOOL NIGHT

MURDER
ON A
SCHOOL
NIGHT

KATE WESTON

KATHERINE TEGEN BOOKS
An Imprint of HarperCollins Publishers

Katherine Tegen Books is an imprint of HarperCollins Publishers.

Murder on a School Night

Library of Congress Control Number: 2023930369
ISBN 978-0-06-326027-6

Typography by Carla Weise
23 24 25 26 27 LBC 5 4 3 2 1

First Edition

For Chloe Seager
the actual best
<3

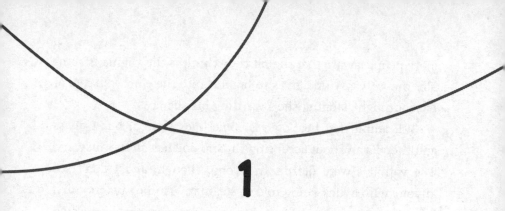

1

"Body positivity influencer Winona Philips says she recites this prayer to her vagina every morning!" Annie shouts across at me as the two of us cycle side by side.

It wouldn't be so weird that she was shouting the word "vagina" across the street if it weren't for the fact that she's riding her six-year-old sister's bicycle. Complete with streamers, glitter, and an old Paw Patrol reflector. It's our first day of junior year—where we'd committed to a more sophisticated way of life—and yet a broken chain on Annie's bike hath shat upon all our poise.

"If Winona Philips is so body positive, then why does she also say that she steams her vagina once a week over a pot of boiling chickpea water?" I question, rolling my eyes. "If you ask me, that sounds like a recipe for thrush."

Winona Philips brings both joy and confusion to our lives. Sometimes what she says is so spot-on (that you don't have to have a vagina to be a woman) and other times it's just confusingly wild (Chickpea vajacials? No thank you). The prayer is meant to attack taboos around vaginas and vulvas and make

1

more people aware that the bit they think is the vagina is actually the vulva. Annie loves to howl it into the empty streets of Barbourough claiming she's warding off shame.

"I'll admit that her logic is sometimes flawed, but I guess adulthood's all about accepting that no one has *all* the answers. The vajacials were definitely wrong, though, and I don't see anyone with a dick being told to steam it," Annie says proudly, her sweet, heart-shaped face, big eyes, and rosy cheeks making the word "dick" seem adorable.

As we ride around the quiet, tree-lined residential streets of Barbourough, the sun shines through the leaves, offering a feeling of peace and light. We fly past houses with their windows left open to let in the late-summer breeze, the occupants completely unaware of the words that Annie is about to spew into their early morning world.

Like me, Annie's five foot one. Small and mighty. She looks like a cherub but has a mouth like a dirty sewer, and I love her.

I can't wait until we're two old ladies, hanging together in our rocking chairs, Annie reciting poetry to her vagina, me taking my teeth out so I won't be expected to join in.

I'm not a prude. Just, I guess, more of an introvert.

"I'm starting the prayer right now, Kerry, and you can't stop me!" she shouts, looking down at her crotch area while I focus on the road ahead.

"Oh god." I blush, trying to cycle into the wind so that the words get lost.

As people in the houses and driveways around us get their kids ready for school, some of them taking pictures of first uniforms or waiting on porches for slower younger siblings, I doubt anyone's bargained on Annie's poetry joining the chatter of birdsong from the trees. We cycle past other Juniors getting into each other's cars, and I keep my head down, focusing on getting past them ASAP, or at least before she gets to the last line.

"I am strong and empowered, the patriarchy is but shit upon my shoe, good morning to all, and a very . . ."

Annie strings this last bit out as we reach old Mrs. Robbins's, who's putting out the garbage in her hairnet, as she does every morning at this time.

"GOOD VULVA TO YOU!" Annie screams into the wind as we pass, making poor Mrs. R drop her bag of trash to the floor. She starts shaking her fist wildly at us.

This has become a daily ritual for the two of them, Annie shocking and appalling Mrs. Robbins with what she calls Annie's "loose language." It's an experience that she definitely enjoys more than Mrs. R.

"Annabel! I should tell your mother, the way you fling these dirty words around!"

"Chill out, Mrs. R, babe. Vulva's not a swear word. They exist and they matter. Go stick a mirror between your legs and free yourself from the ancient shame that binds you!" Annie tries to cycle away as fast as she can, her knees knocking into her elbows with every pedal rotation. She looks like a little *Mario Kart* character on speed, streamers dancing in the breeze behind her.

"Sorry, Mrs. R," I stop, and mutter.

"I fronted women's lib back in the day, you know! And I NEVER had to use such language!" She shakes her head as she shuffles back indoors, her dog, Herbert, giving me a final side-eye.

I catch up with Annie in two casual pedal rotations, while she's powering away furiously next to me. Her legs are racing around, trying to generate some kind of speed, but she's getting nowhere. Those tiny wheels are in no rush.

"Poor Mrs. R," I say.

"My sleuthing skills tell me that she wouldn't come out here every day at the same time if she didn't want me to shout 'vulva' at her. She must love it, really, or she'd just come out five minutes later," Annie says, trying to keep up with me as I cycle next to her.

I can't fault her logic, even though Annie only decided that it was her destiny to be a detective this summer after reading ten Agatha Christie books. Since then, she's been trying to find mysteries everywhere she can, which in a village this size is hard. She's manifesting drama in a place where the highlight is the annual village jam competition.

Her latest investigation arose when she realized that the pigeons close to the village green seem to be lusher of feather and claw than the ones that hang out near the school. She believes someone to be feeding the pigeons by the village green. It's hardly a Nancy Drew mystery. She code-named her investigation "Operation Plumage."

"Dude, you look hilarious trying to go fast on that tricycle," I say, noticing the beads of sweat on her furrowed brow, eyes set in steely determination.

"How *dare* you! I think I look very sophisticated," she says, red-faced. "Either way, in two weeks, this cycling hell will be over for both of us because you'll have your license!"

"My permit. I still can't drive us with that," I say.

Just the thought of driving makes me anxious. Last year,

I was diagnosed with anxiety after I started having panic attacks. I'd start worrying about something, and before I knew it, it would control all my thoughts and make focusing on anything else completely impossible. I'm on medication now, and I had therapy, but I still find myself anxious a fair bit. It's not something that just goes away.

"Whatever," Annie protests. "Everyone knows that there are two ways to become popular. Either being one of the first in your year to get your license or being on a reality TV show. And until I solve Operation Plumage and go viral"—I snort at this—"you're our only chance. GRASP IT WITH BOTH HANDS. DO IT FOR US!" Annie squeals to a halt in front of me, drifting her trike perpendicular so she can stop me and plead from her tiny chariot.

"Always with the obsession to be popular. What *is* it that makes you want it so much? Aren't I enough for you?" I ask.

"Of course you are, but wouldn't it be nice if people carried stuff for us and moved out of the way in the corridor like they do for Heather, though? Pretty badass, no?"

"Uhhh, that's not popularity that you're craving; that's a dictatorship," I say as she puts her little finger up to her lips, mock-supervillain style.

"Oh! My bad." She stares at me sideways in a sketchy manner.

Previously, due to Annie's obsession, we've made several attempts at popularity. I don't need to explain that these were unsuccessful.

Firstly, we started the CSI Coders club in seventh grade having watched too much *Pretty Little Liars*. We thought we'd need to hack into things and perform various sleuthings in our teenage years to prevent dark crimes from being committed and be revered by our classmates. Totally cool and normal. Sadly, hacking was harder than we anticipated and shockingly has never actually been necessary in a village where most people consider contactless card payments to be a form of technological witchcraft and proclaim they "don't trust it."

Then, in ninth grade, despite neither of us having any musical talent or skill, we decided to start a band and compete in the school talent show. We were an a cappella group singing songs about the struggles of loving Harry Styles, when he'll never know who we are (it felt relatable at the time). Not only did we come in last, but during some very active dancing, Annie fell off the stage and twisted her ankle. Poor Annie had to do the hop of shame around school for six weeks after that.

Sophomore year, we attempted to throw a party for our joint birthdays. Three people came, two of them were related to us. The other was a two-year-old Annie's mum was babysitting. It's hard to get people to come to your party when the only time they've noticed your existence you made a holy show of yourself by falling off a stage.

Mostly I feel bad for Annie because she really tries, her spirit never faltering in her belief that one day she will be popular. Whereas I resigned myself a long time ago to not being a popular person—sometime around age three when we were thrown out of a playhouse for not being cool enough. Instead, I resolved to find success elsewhere and decided I'm going to be a journalist. An investigative journalist who reads lots of books and never has to face the prospect of rejection from her peers again.

We pull up in front of the school, and I marvel at Annie's commitment to the tiny bicycle. Getting off and proudly rolling it through the gates in front of everyone, gold helmet still in situ. People give the bike a funny look as we pass through the parking lot to the bike rack, but mostly they're busy catching up in their cliques.

We don't have a clique. I like to think of the two of us as our own self-contained clique. It's more badass to be on your own path. But Annie's told me that saying "badass" immediately makes me less badass. Also, in the high school hierarchy of cliques, I'd say if ours really was a clique, it's quite far down the list. In short, we're less cool than a hairnet-wearing cafeteria lady.

I'm just fixing my helmet hair, attempting to give my mid-length mousy-brown mop some kind of volume despite it being plastered to my head with sweat, when the noise of Lizzo and a sense of impending doom fills the air.

Right on cue, an imposing black Jeep with tinted windows comes careering around the corner as the parking lot parts like the Red Sea. Within the Jeep's tanklike shell sit the current monarchy, the monsters on the throne that Annie so desperately wants.

Les Populaires.

It's not so much that people in this school want to be friends with Les Populaires; it's that they want to *be* them. Everywhere they go, people move out of their way. If they wear something, most of the school will be wearing it the next week. Rumor has it that Heather, Head Populaire, has brand sponsorship from all the major fashion houses and makeup brands, and she's constantly posting #PR and #AD content on Instagram to her thousands of followers.

"I mean, that could be us soon, when you get your permit," Annie says, gesturing as the Jeep—driven by Heather's parent's driver—zooms toward us. Unfortunately, she takes her eyes off the Jeep for a moment and doesn't notice a coffee cup come flying out of the window from the unmistakable bejeweled hand of Heather's best friend Selena, smacking Annie square in the tits.

For a while, Annie doesn't move; she's just staring eerily ahead with her mouth open. It's as if she's been frozen in time, forever stuck in the moment before her white top was stained with what smells distinctly like a mocha latte, and then she springs into action. Ten thousand emotions cross her face all at once as she looks down at her soiled T-shirt, before finally settling on rage.

"FUCKING SHITBAGS!" she screams at the top of her lungs as the Jeep comes to a standstill in the parking lot, sprawled across three spaces.

Like Miranda in *The Devil Wears Prada* arriving to the magazine office, Heather's entry to the parking lot is the event of the day. As the passenger door of the Jeep opens, her Louboutin boots signify the start of her junior-year style. The rest of her follows as groups around the lot raise their iPhones to take unsubtle pictures. She looks around her, aloof, disinterested, savage, tossing her long auburn hair behind her pale, freckled shoulders.

She's followed by Heather Junior, otherwise known as Selena. Selena's more dangerous to us than Heather because she actually knows who we are. Fresh from her coffee-throwing violence, Selena swings her long, tanned legs out of the Jeep.

Luscious straight dark hair swishes behind her, her huge brown eyes concealed behind big black sunglasses, lips pursed in constant duck pout so as to accentuate her cheekbones, and tiny, pointed nose. She smooths down her dry, unstained dress and straightens her prim black headband. To an untrained eye, she looks innocent, but we know she's evil.

And last come the twins, Colin and Audrey. The double threat. Between the two of them, they've more secrets than MI5. They're both incredibly poised, and beautiful, and their outfits always complement each other. Today Audrey wears a short white sundress, with her perfectly long, dark brown legs accentuated by a pair of white-and-gold cork wedge heels. Meanwhile, Colin wears a white shirt and beige trousers. Audrey's makeup is, as ever, perfect: bright red lipstick and contour on point. Colin and Audrey come as a pair; they share everything except men. You cross one, you cross the other.

You never cross one.

The four of them line up in sequence, legs moving in unison as they walk in an unbreakable line toward the common room. The two of us jump out of the way before they flatten us. Our peasanty existence not even in their line of vision.

"I'm sorry for your loss," I say once they've passed, gesturing to Annie's white T-shirt but pleased that for once it doesn't seem to have actually gotten on me as well.

"I'm sorry, too," Annie says sadly dabbing at her boobs with an old Pret napkin from the bottom of her bag. "That I will have to kill them all and end up in prison before we've even really started the term."

It's interesting that despite all her interactions with Les Populaires ending like this, Annie still wants to be popular. I guess it's a bit of "if you can't beat them, join them."

"Completely understandable. No one would convict you after a second in their company," I say as we grab our bags and walk toward the safety of school.

And that's when I smell him.

Adam Devers.

He shines like the sun.

He sparkles like the stars.

He is the moon, the planets, and the universe.

I'm stopped in my tracks by his beauty and take a deep breath trying to inhale his scent as he passes, my tongue breaking forth from my mouth as if to taste it. If I can lick a drop of his sweat, I'm sure it will cure me of my virginity. Not that, you know, I'm ashamed or anything. (No one must ever know that the closest I have ever come to a sexual experience is accidentally sitting on my phone when I got a text.)

"Je canNOT," Annie whispers, her hand still on her coffee-soaked tit as she dabs at it with her Pret napkin, looking like a bit of a perv actually.

He is the dictionary definition of the phrase "pants feelings." It speaks volumes of his hotness that even Annie sees it when she normally proclaims lusting after people to be a waste of time.

I compose myself and stare pointedly at Annie's boob-dabbing hand. It's as if she's sucking up all the moisture from her top, she's so thirsty for him.

"Oh, how the mighty feminist hath fallen." I shake my head at her.

"Sorry, Your Honor, it's not me, it's my vagina." Annie continues staring.

I can't talk; I'm staring at Adam Devers's arms as he climbs the stairs with the football captain, high-fiving everyone on their way, other boys from the football team trailing behind. It's like watching Justin Bieber interacting with the front row at one of his concerts, only sexier. He even takes the glory from the captain, outshining him with his beauty. Every person he walks past gushes in his presence. He's flustered more women than I've had periods, and I started menstruating in sixth grade.

"I don't think we're supposed to objectify people," Annie whispers right in my ear, the feeling of hot air hitting my ear canal making me jump out of my arm-focused trance.

I'm not sure how she got so close to my face without me realizing, and I love her, but I hope she never ever does that again.

The two of us follow in Adam's footsteps up the stairs and into school. The musk of abandoned gym bags, hormones, and rejection hits me right in the nose and instantly kills my lady boner.

Sadly, Adam's been betrothed to Heather the Horror since seventh grade. They apparently lost their virginities to each other freshman year using a sandwich bag as contraception. I don't believe it and don't believe sandwich bags are an effective form of contraception, and I will die on both of those hills.

We head for the common room, the MOST exciting thing about being juniors. We can FINALLY just stroll into that regal ground and be those people we've long admired who sit on the comfy padded seats, drinking tea, playing music, and wearing clothes that aren't uniform. Only upperclassmen allowed. Like a senior lounge, except better. Because juniors are allowed, too.

Two long years of watching others enter the sacred space, dreaming of when we eventually get to do it, and that day is finally here.

2

The sound of music and boiling kettles spills out into the corridor as the doors swing open. Heather's already pinned Adam up against the fridge, sucking his face off, turning the kitchen into a sex zoo, and making it desperately unsanitary in there. More importantly, they're preventing anyone from getting to the milk, and there's a queue of five people backed up and waiting, angrily clutching mugs of black coffee and tea.

Close to the lockers are the IT nerds, the only people who were excited when we embarked on CSI Coders. They're more fun than people think, and they've got hearts of gold, but Annie got annoyed when she discovered their coding skills were way above hers and refuses to engage with them. And over by the speakers are the musicians—they're in a band. They wear their own unintentional jeans-and-leather-jacketed uniform. Another group that—especially after our one and only gig in freshman year—Annie and I weren't cool enough to join. Much like the jocks, although their love of sports makes us instantly uninterested in them. And then there are the witches. They wear all black, mostly crushed velvet, and are never far from a pack of tarot cards. We love the witches, but they eye us with a suspicion that makes me scared for my future. What can they see that makes them look at me like that? The witches are NEVER to be confused with the Goths, who also wear black but definitely don't practice magic.

We walk through the room, heads held high, shoulders back, emboldened by at least being allowed in here to be honest. We pick two seats right at the edge away from everyone, near the bathroom, and settle down just as the bell rings for homeroom.

We're first to homeroom after perilously running the corridor gauntlet and sit right at the front, watching the rest of the class file in at a normal speed, getting less-good seats. Losers. Heather and her squad, Selena, Audrey, Colin, and of course Adam, come in two seconds before Mr. Cronin crosses the threshold, and run straight to the back of the class.

"Welcome back, fellas. Relieved to be starting the year on a Friday," Mr. Cronin shouts, skulking into the classroom.

Straight-out sexism with the "fellas" there. He looks over at Annie and me with our eyebrows knitted together in fury already. He does stuff like this on purpose to rile us. Mr. C's only been at the school for a year or so, and all it took was a week for us to assess that he was a real douche.

He places his bag on the desk and takes out an apple before slumping down onto his chair and kicking his feet up. There's an arrogance to him as he tosses the apple into the air. I really hope it smacks him in the head.

"So, we've been joined this morning by the newest member

of the junior class. Team, meet Scott," Mr. C says, pointing to the back of the room. We all turn to follow his finger.

At the back of the room, a dark-haired guy with dimples wearing a Sonic Youth T-shirt and a leather jacket raises his hand awkwardly in greeting. He looks like he wants the ground to swallow him up. My interest is immediately piqued, though, because Sonic Youth is my absolute favorite retro band and the only other person I know who has heard of them is Annie, and that's only because I'm always talking about them. I assess him in a way most un-feminist. He's not Adam Devers, but he's got stubble (A beard? What hormone heaven is this? Dear puberty, with this un-sculpted facial hair you are really spoiling us), I feel a stirring in my stomach that lets me know I'm in trouble. Do I . . . ? I think I might . . . ? Is he hot? (I can't know for sure until I smell him, you know?) It's probably just the T-shirt.

"I was going to ask Scott to stand up and tell us a bit about himself. But that feels boring, so instead I'm going to ask you all to stand up and tell Scott what you got up to over the summer. A little I-know-what-you-did-last-summer game and a nice way of introducing yourselves. *And* I get to sit and watch you all squirm with embarrassment while judging you. But please, let's keep it interesting. Ladies, I don't want to hear about all the hours you spent on TikTok perfecting your makeup," Mr. C says, smirking as the room does a collective groan, except for Annie, who's rising above his sexist comment because she's been *waiting* for someone to ask what she got up to. She was born for this moment.

"Any volunteers?" He's barely finished asking before Annie's hand shoots up and she climbs onto her desk to address the class.

"I guess we'll start with you, then, Annie. You could, of course, just do it sitting down. I was hoping for a one-liner, not a presidential address. But come on, then, let's hear what absolute snoozefest you spent your summer doing." Mr. C sighs.

Annie ignores him and takes a deep breath before beginning. "I'm Annie!" She addresses this pointedly to Scott, and I cringe so hard I fear my body may turn inside out. "I started the summer crocheting hats for refugee babies, and then I went to a comedy workshop, where I learned to tell the perfect joke and perform with confidence." Annie keeps standing as if she's waiting for applause or something.

"Fascinating. Tell us a joke," Mr. C presses.

Suddenly all of Annie's poise and confidence falls out of her and she looks panic-stricken.

"Too slow, we all know women aren't funny, hey, guys? Better luck next time, Tina Fey!" God, he is brutal, and Annie looks gutted. I hate him so much. "Next!"

I stay seated and stare at my desk willing this moment to be over ASAP.

"Um. So, I'm Kerry, I went to a talk by the journalist that uncovered a ring of money launderers working at a top international bank. Then I also crocheted hats for refugee babies, and um, I went to another talk by this psychologist who's working with prisoners to reform them so that they can become members of society again," I say, still staring at the desk. I feel like I'm having a hot flash. It sounds silly saying it aloud, but I want to be an investigative journalist and I just wanted to use the summer to work on my future career.

"How does he know he's reformed them and hasn't just let a load of serial killers out to merrily kill again?" my

15

ever-unsupportive teacher drawls. I look up at Mr. Cronin's questioning face and feel an urge to commit extreme violence.

"It's actually a SHE, sir. And *she* has tests and markers to note the changes. They were monitored very closely."

"Sorry, Kerry, Mr. Misogyny over here." Mr. Cronin raises his hands, trying to be cool and funny while Annie and I sit glaring at him with our heads tilted to one side.

My eyes fully glaze over listening to stories of holidays and parties until something catches my attention. He's gotten to Selena from Les Populaires at the back—aka the Heathertron—and yet instead of what I expected her to say, which was that she spent the summer perfecting how to be even more of a narcissistic horror show, she's said something even scarier. She's tossing her long hair as she speaks, looking like the same Heather-bot she's always been but the words she's saying suggest otherwise.

"So, I went to work with my dad most days at the *Times*. At the start, he spent a lot of time at the BBC in Manchester in meetings about something to do with a gender pay gap or something; whatever that means. Anyway, Daddy said I have great journalistic instincts, so by the end of the summer, I was working on the news desk helping check and edit the new stories as they were coming in and I even got to help on some investigative work with the reporters."

How is it fair that Selena gets an opportunity like that when the only thing she's ever read is Instagram? And even then, she complains when the captions are too long. She once compared Jekyll and Hyde to the Kardashians before and after surgery in English class for Christ's sake. Which, if nothing else, just makes her a terrible human. I've wanted to be an investigative journalist ever since I found out what one was. This is BEYOND unfair. It's criminal. Why is it the biggest assholes get the biggest opportunities?

"What. The. HELL?!" I hear Annie muttering next to me, her eyes flitting rapidly from side to side in solidarity with me. She knows that would have been my dream internship. I even applied for one at the BBC last year but didn't get it because they said someone who fit into the team more got it. Was that who it was? Selena?

I notice that Mr. Cronin is looking at us, and I realize that I've accidentally tutted out loud. He's so clearly smirking at me, enjoying every second. Not only that, but Heather's annoyed, too, and she and Selena are glaring over at me and Annie like we're about to get our second coffee of the day. Fortunately, the bell rings just as I'm ready for my chair to turn into a Venus flytrap, and everyone rushes to leave.

"Ew, is that tie-dye?" Selena says, breezing past us and pointing to the coffee stain on Annie's top. "The nineteen-nineties called; they want their ugly shirt back."

"YOU KNOW IT'S NOT TIE-DYE!" Annie rages, her tiny face struggling to contain all the anger, but Selena's already breezed out the door into the corridor, Annie's fury probably not even reaching her ears.

I grasp Annie's shoulders with my hands and look her straight in the eyes.

"Repeat after me: Selena Munroe is not worth a rage blackout," I say, even though right now I'm pretty raging at the clearly unfair opportunity she's been given. Annie does a deep inhale and exhale, blowing her morning breath right in my face as she calms down.

* * *

17

"It's straight-up nepotism!" Annie screeches, slamming the door of the toilet stall before doing what I can only describe as an angry pee—a stream so fierce it could crack the toilet.

She's been texting me her fury throughout first and second period, and it looks like even though she used capital letters and endless murder-and-flames-style GIFs, she has not yet fully expressed herself.

Now she's pissing pure rage.

"I know, but we'll get our chance," I say sadly because I'm starting to wonder if really we ever will.

"BUT WHEN, KERRY?! I mean, do we actually have to make actual friends with Selena Shitbag Munroe for you to work at a newspaper or for me to investigate anything actually investigate-able? Because I WON'T!" I hear her viciously tearing the toilet paper before slamming her hand on the flush. "Is that tie-dye?" She mimics Selena's voice.

I don't want to interrupt, but I also highly doubt that Selena Shitbag Munroe would EVER be friends with us, either.

The stall door swings back open, and her face hasn't softened even a tiny bit since she went in there.

As she begins the process of exasperated handwashing, the main door opens, and the two of us look up silently in the mirror, freezing when we see Heather's face. She's completely alone, which I don't think I've ever seen before, and she's staring directly at us, which definitely doesn't bode well.

She walks so silently over to us that I wonder if she's doing charades and we have to guess what on earth she could possibly want.

She's finally made it over to the sink and is just standing, glaring at us. I don't know where to look.

"It's you two, isn't it?" She stares at us in fury but gives absolutely no context as to what on earth she's talking about.

The silence in the bathroom is punctuated only by the fact that I'm pretty sure I can read Annie's thoughts, and right now all she's thinking is "Queen of Les Populaires knows I exist!"

"It's what? What is?" Annie takes a while getting the words out, probably in shock, and looks around her trying to fathom what the hell's going on. I'm just trying my hardest not to be present in this moment, whatever it is.

"I heard you two grumbling during homeroom. You've been sending me the messages? Pretending to be my dad?" She's definitely starting to lose confidence in her accusation, and I still have no idea what she's talking about.

"Um . . . no?" Annie says, and I can tell this is not how she thought Heather would finally notice her existence.

"This!" Heather looks exasperated and thrusts her phone in our faces.

On the screen is an Instagram profile. The picture and name are that of her dad, her dad who died last year in a speedboat accident while on a business trip in the Bahamas. The profile was made a month ago, so unless they have Instagram in the afterlife, it's unlikely it was actually made by him.

There are pictures of him on the grid, pictures of him with Heather as a baby, and pictures of him from old newspaper articles about his company, V-Lyte, the revolutionary period product manufacturer, who aimed to make periods more discreet with their compact goods.

My least favorite thing is when people tell us we should be quieter and smaller about periods, so I have personally never used a V-Lyte product as a matter of principle. Although now that Heather's mum has taken over the business after his death, they've fortunately started to drop this line.

Heather's mum was always the real businessperson in the relationship anyway; she has her own successful lifestyle business. They live on a huge estate on the fringes of Barbourough that used to be a farm. There's not a single animal on it now—instead it's just acres and acres of land used as a symbol of their extreme wealth.

"What? That's so weird," Annie mutters, staring at the phone propped in Heather's furious hands. "Who would do that?"

"Are you seriously telling me this isn't you?" Heather says, pressing the messages symbol to display a stream of DMs from the account.

"Definitely not!" Annie says, while I'm still rendered speechless at this entire interaction. "This is twisted. It's gross!"

She's not wrong. The messages displayed are pretty haunting to be honest.

> **Mr. Stevens:** I know a secret. I don't think things will be so rosy when everyone else does too.

> **Mr. Stevens:** Secrets catch up with you in the end, and if secrets don't, I will.

> **Mr. Stevens:** You can't keep me quiet, soon enough everyone will know. Your days are numbered.

Mr. Stevens: Tampons can't solve everything.

"I've got no idea what they're talking about, but it's super creepy and I hate it," Heather says matter-of-factly, barely looking either of us in the eye.

"So you don't know what they mean about the secret?" Annie asks, looking suspicious.

"NO, I already said that, didn't I?" Heather looks frustrated by us once more.

"You know . . ." Annie says, her eyes flashing in a way I've come to realize is always dangerous. Oh no . . . "We used to have a club in seventh grade, CSI Coders. We could easily figure out who this is for you. Can I take a look?" Annie's holding out her hand for Heather's phone.

I feel my eye twitch at the mention of the club out loud, in public, and I start to wonder if it's possible to flush yourself down the toilet. Heather looks suspicious but hands the phone over to Annie so she can take a closer look.

"Oh yes," she says after a quick scroll. "We can do this no problem. The thing about this sort of stuff is that it's usually someone you know. So, we need to be able to observe the people you're friends with. Really get *close* to everyone in your world."

I have a deep and impenetrable sense of impending doom right now.

"I'm having a party tonight?" Heather looks slightly baffled as to what's happening, and for the first time in my life, I feel like I'm on the same page as her. What the hell is Annie doing?

Annie passes the phone over to me, and there are hundreds of these messages. She must be receiving about ten a day. The latest message is from a few minutes ago and says You're not as smart as you think you are.

"Perfect! Why don't we come, and we can watch and work out who it is?" Annie's now beaming from ear to ear. Why am *I* being dragged into this? Why, Annie? WHHHYYY?

I watch Heather regain her composure and take her phone back from Annie. She stares between us both as if she's trying to suss us out. Whatever it is she wants from us, I'm not sure I'm helping. The best my face has to offer is a kind of constipated, pensive look. Annie smiles at her hopefully, and she sighs deeply.

"Okay, fine, but don't talk to me in front of anyone." She looks furious at the very thought.

"Deal, and we'll need access to your Instagram account so we can look at the messages in more detail," Annie says.

"Are you joking?" Heather looks at her like she's just said she's going to need to lick her eyeballs, and I think Annie's probably pushed too far.

"We need to be able to analyze the messages, and this way we can see exactly when you receive new ones while we watch everyone at the party. There's more chance of us catching whoever it is red-handed if we can see it all happening in real time!" Annie states excitedly.

Heather's eyes once again drift over me suspiciously before she appears to relent.

"Fine, but post anything or do any weird shit with it and I swear to god you will never breathe fresh air in this town again." Heather looks deadly serious about this, and I actually wonder if she's ever killed before.

I watch her quickly clear messages from her inbox and anything that might be personal. Then she logs in to her profile on Annie's phone.

When she's done, the two of them stare at each other, eyebrows arched in understanding, and I already hate all of this. I feel like I'm on the sidelines at a tennis match with no idea of the rules or even what the game is.

Annie's going to make me go to that party with her, and then bang goes my evening of watching retro nineties teen movies. I don't understand how she thinks she's going to actually solve this when her experience extends to watching five and a half episodes of CSI, reading ten Agatha Christie novels, and researching the eating habits of the town's pigeons.

"Fine," Annie says in agreement as I feel anxiety take hold in my bowels.

"You have until Monday. If you don't find out who did it, I'm changing the password on my account and telling everyone you're a pair of losers." With that, she turns on her heel and walks out.

So generous.

After checking that the coast's clear outside, Heather flounces out into the hall, and the two of us are left in the bathroom, wondering if that even just really happened.

"OMG, a PARTY invite," Annie says, eyeballing me at practically the same time. "An ACTUAL party invite! WE ARE SO GOING!"

I stare at Annie, furious that I wasn't consulted about any

of this AND because I've no idea how she actually thinks she's going to find out who's doing it.

"Oh yeah? But at what cost? How are you going to work out who's trolling her?" I ask, already dreading how much Annie thinks I will need to be involved. "And if you can't work it out? What will she do to us, then? She already seems pretty furious."

I grab my bag off the side and get ready to follow out in the direction that Heather just left and check my ever-flattening hair in the mirror on my way to the door.

"This is valuable detecting work experience, and there's no way we won't work out who did it by Monday. We're the greatest minds in this school. Between the two of us, we can do this in no time. Especially if it's someone she knows," Annie says, holding the toilet door open for me as we slink back into the corridor.

"You only think it's someone she knows because of all the Miss Marples where it's someone the victim knows! This is *real* life." I'm starting to get pretty exasperated with her. This feels like another scheme to get us popular, and those usually make us even less popular than we were to begin with.

"*Trust* me, I got this," Annie says, and then catches my unsure expression out of the corner of her eye as we walk down the narrow hall. "What? You want Selena Shitbag Munroe to be the only person who gets a chance at investigative journalism around here? Think what you could do with it once you work out who it is."

"Oh yeah, I'm sure Heather would love that," I say, rolling my eyes at her as I adjust my backpack, trying to avoid a group of asshat freshman throwing a ball around. Why do people do that in an enclosed space? And how do they always seem to find Annie and me to do it around?

"Duh, we'd be popular by then; it wouldn't even matter." Annie raises her hands at me in a shrug as I duck, narrowly avoiding being walloped in the face by said ball.

"Urgh," I say, straightening myself up and getting my composure back after my near miss, as we round the corner. "I'm premenstrual and crabby; please don't make me go," I say, looking back at Annie and realizing my error too late as I walk square into something hard, tall, and . . .

"Whoa," the square, hard, and tall something exclaims, stepping back to look and see who's just clumsily stumbled into them. I look up, feeling my cheeks flush.

The Sonic Youth T-shirt comes into focus as they move back, and I feel a sinking in the pit of my stomach as all my spidey-senses literally tingle.

"Orghk." The involuntary noise seems to come out of my nose quite without my say-so as I look up into the most handsome green eyes I've ever seen, making eye contact with the new guy, Scott.

"Um, are you, er, okay?" Scott asks, his cheeks slightly pink, too. I come to, realizing I'm staring and leaning slightly too much toward him—a very bad combination—and I still haven't said anything. He looks kind of scared.

A guy I recognize from sophomore year who's in a band is standing next to him, adding to my feeling of total dweeb-ness.

"Yes, she's just got very low blood sugar right now. Don't worry, I'll take care of her; thanks for your concern, er, what was your name again?" Annie takes my hand and pretends that she doesn't remember Scott from before.

"Scott." His lips almost touch my nose as he talks because I am far too close to him, and he may now wish to take out a restraining order on my face.

"Scott, great. Lovely to meet you, Scott," Annie says, and gently escorts me around him.

We're drifting up the corridor, I suppose we're walking, but really, we could be flying for all I'm aware of right now.

"Did you like the pretty man, Kerry? Is that why you've become a mime? Are you okay? Or am I going to have to revive you like the time that you thought you saw Harry Styles in a parking lot, but it was actually just a random senior? Am I to get some smelling salts?"

"Mmmmmm," I say, slightly annoyed that she's brought up the whole Harry Styles thing when I'm trying to fantasize somehow getting to kiss Scott without having to make any potentially awkward and stressful social interactions with him first.

"You know where he'll definitely be later, don't you?" I hate where she's going with this, and I hate her smugness. "The party!"

I groan because I know she's not going to let up, and she's right: he probably is going to be there. But I'm not going to go to some hellish party just because he's there. Am I?

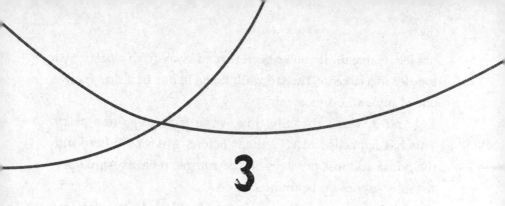

3

We pull into my front yard and get off our bikes. I was hoping I could slink off alone after school and once I got in just not move, thus meaning I did not have to go to the party. Unfortunately, Annie's not stopped talking about the party the whole way home, and now she's tracking me to my front door, showing no sign of letting up whatsoever.

"Look, all I'm saying is we go to the party—our FIRST PARTY—and we find out what's going on," Annie says. She looks at me with pleading eyes as I put my key in the lock.

"Yes, it's the first party that we've been *invited* to, but let's be honest, it's not the first time we've tried to go to one, is it?" I ask, even though I hate myself for bringing it up in the first place.

"Look, that was one time," Annie says, knowing exactly what I'm referring to. "And I still say I could have taken out Heather's cousin when he denied us entry."

"Annie, he was two years old!"

We tried to go to a party at Heather's house in eighth grade, and her small cousin was on the door as a "bouncer." You've not felt shame until you've been turned away from a party by a toddler in a tuxedo. The sad walk home in our best dresses was one of my darkest moments.

"And it wasn't the only time we've tried to go to a party. This has happened MANY times before. MANY!" I head into the house and toss my keys on the console table as Annie persistently carries on behind me.

"Don't you want to know what the inside of Heather's house looks like?" Annie throws puppy eyes at me.

"Not really, no. I imagine it's something like the tenth circle of hell?" I head over to the counter between the kitchen and the living room area where I can see that Mum's been unpacking the freebies she gets sent for her job.

My mother's a kind of doctor, but not a sore-throats-and-headaches kind of doctor, more of an older people's health and sex doctor. She specializes in things like HRT, vaginal lubricants, and, my personal favorite, incontinence pads. She's well respected in her field and I'm proud of her for the things that she speaks out about, but it just gets a bit icky for me sometimes.

"Look, how am I going to become a detective if I don't jump at this most basic of chances? I need to go to that party so I can solve Heather's mystery, thus actually *starting* my career," Annie reasons, except I know that as much as she says it's about detecting, it's still about being popular.

I don't know why she wants it so much when I can remember every single shitty and embarrassing thing that Heather and her crew (mostly Selena) have done.

A few years back, they found an article Mum had written about sex after fifty and read it aloud every time I entered a classroom. There isn't enough therapy in the world to deal with the things I've heard read aloud about my father's penis. As a good feminist, I wholeheartedly support what she's doing, and I marvel at the way that most of what paid for our house is her honesty and TED Talks about how she wet herself regularly after I ruined her pelvic floor. As her daughter, though, I wish she'd use words like "erection" less.

I head around the counter to get a glass of water, wondering why Mum's left such a mess; she's normally super tidy. Annie follows me with her puppy eyes still working their magic.

"Pllleeeassseee come with me?"

I try to ignore the pleading and focus on other things. Annie hates it when I intentionally ignore something she wants to do because I just want to hide away.

A large part of me does still want to go because I might see Scott there, but the anxious part of me feels sweaty and dizzy at the thought of it. My stomach flip-flops at the possibility that I might make a fool of myself in front of him again. Maybe it'll be even worse than my silent mime act earlier. If I was a "normal" person, I'd go to the party, I'd flirt with him with a level of competency and brace myself for the consequences. Instead, when I imagine talking to him, it's like I can hear the sea rushing in my ears, giant waves of anxiety rendering me speechless as all the blood rushes to my cheeks. No, it's far safer if I stay under the duvet and watch rom-coms where the shy girl gets the guy instead.

"You can go. I just don't know that I'm really a party person," I say, trying to scramble together more reasons why I can't while putting a glass of water in front of Annie. She must be thirsty with all that talking.

"But I can't go without you?! Oh, dude, what is this?" Annie asks, picking up an open, fancy-looking velvet box from the counter.

Against my better judgment, I take a sip of water and look over at what Annie's holding while she carries on talking about "the investigation" and what we'll wear to the party, and how I'm going whether I like it or not.

My blood runs cold, and I choke, the sip of water flying out of my mouth and onto the PR note attached to the empty box. I realize with alarm as I take the box from Annie why this packaging mess has been left with my parents nowhere in sight. I drop the box almost immediately, nausea overtaking my whole body. Even in my wildest nightmares, I never imagined anything so disturbing could happen in this house.

The PR note floats to the floor, staring up at me, detailing "the enclosed whip and handcuffs set."

"Fine, we're going," I cut Annie off midsentence while she continues to ramble on about her one big shot at a detective career, completely unaware of the trauma I'm going through. Even a party at Heather's house has to be better than staying around here knowing what's going on just a thin floor away, surely. And maybe seeing Scott again wouldn't be the worst thing that ever happened. As long as I try to control myself this time. Best to just not say anything and try to stay a respectable distance away. "We'll get ready at yours, but I have to be back home by ten."

"Why ten?" Annie eyes me suspiciously, not even noticing my green face or disgust in her excitement.

"Because . . . that's the time my retainer goes in," I whisper.

"FUCK YOUR RETAINER!" Annie shouts at me. "Do you think fucking Emmeline Pankhurst was all 'I'd love to protest but I have to put my retainer in'? NO! SHE WAS NOT!"

Before Annie has the chance to continue her rant to me about historical feminists who are much braver than I am, I push her out of the front door and away from my parents' dirty afternoon.

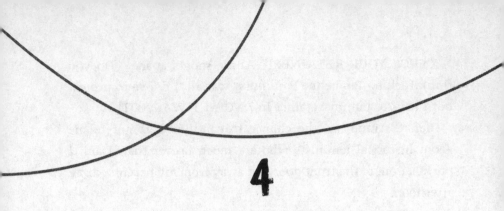

4

Annie has somehow got me wearing a sequined miniskirt, false eyelashes (I can't tell if they're even on right; it just feels like something's pressing down on my eyes while fluttering about up there), lipstick (which has definitely migrated to my teeth), and heels (what fresh hell is this because now I am Bambi on ice?!). She calls these our "disguises" to blend in. Apparently this discomfort I'm feeling right now is an important part of the detecting process. Meanwhile Annie's got on a sequined catsuit, which she wore to Halloween several years ago when she simply decided she wanted to go as "magic." She looks like a disco ball and yet is still more agile than me.

I don't exactly feel dressed for solving a cybercrime. I feel like a toddler in her mum's clothes.

The way to Rose Hill Farm is down a series of winding lanes that we bump over on our bikes. Annie's besequined limbs have to work their hardest to keep the tiny bike upright over the potholes and lumps along the track. The Paw Patrol reflector is catching the light from her sequins and the evening sunlight while we bravely continue down the deserted dirt tracks, taking us farther and farther away from civilization and closer to something I fear will be a bit *Lord of the Flies*.

As the farmhouse looms around a curve, it reminds me of a creepy-looking sprawling Edwardian manor, something from an Edgar Allan Poe novel or perhaps every single horror movie I've ever watched.

"Does Heather's house look kind of sinister to you?" Annie asks just as I'm trying to push my scaredy-cat tendencies down.

"We could just go back to yours instead?" I suggest hopefully, seeing Annie gulp at the sight ahead of her.

Before we have time to contemplate saving ourselves, the unmistakable noise of a car approaching faster than we can move out of the way fills the lane. I can now be completely certain that this is where we're going to die.

There's nowhere to go. The road's too narrow and completely surrounded by brambles.

I turn behind me to see Annie furiously speeding up, glancing back over her shoulder in panic at the encroaching headlights. My heart's racing, but the rest of me is moving in slow motion as I try to work out a way to save my own life. Annie catches up with me, swerves, and takes us both deep into a patch of thorny bushes to the right of the lane. The Jeep rolls past while I hyperventilate into some thorns, and Selena leans out the window, her perfect brown hair blowing in the wind.

"OUT OF THE WAY, BICYCLE BITCHES!" she shouts as they pass, her cackles getting caught in the wind and blown all the way back to us, echoing down the already *Blair Witch*–y lanes.

I feel the moisture hitting my bare arm in a thin stream before I see the water gun, held by Colin, and being fired directly at us. The water arches upward from the pistol before falling back down and showering our arms and legs.

"Right," I say, standing open-mouthed as they drive off, our legs and arms scratched and any effort to look sophisticated now drenched. "This is why we don't come to parties."

"At least it's just water," Annie says as my nose starts to twitch, and I register the smell and amber-ish color.

"Or piss," I say, staring angrily at Annie, sniffing the air and thinking about the nice clean, relaxing bath I could be having right now.

"Oh my god." Annie's eyes widen, and she starts to sniff, too. I can see her brain already whirring around, getting to its logical conclusion. "WHAT IF THE WEE IS DISEASED AND IT GOES IN THE SCRATCHES AND ENTERS MY BLOOD-STREAM?" She glares at me, her eyes wild like a hunting cat in the dark.

"Bit dramatic." I blink at her and take another sniff of my wet hand again. "My bad, I think it's probably just beer."

Annie's face relaxes, and she licks her hand.

"Yeah, you're right, it's beer. ONWARD!" She gets back on her tiny bike, and the two of us continue our perilous journey.

"Urgh, I already want to go home," I say, feeling disgusting.

"You know what? This is all part of the experience! We've just been soiled earlier in the night than I thought we would be, but honestly, soiled at a party is on my bucket list." Annie's trying really hard to prevent the inevitable: me turning back before this night gets any worse. "Do you think the intrepid and fearless explorer and journalist Nellie Bly ever shied away from an experience because she got a bit of beer on her?! NO! We'll get you cleaned up, and then we'll get loose. Have a drink

34

or twelve and it'll be like it never happened. Everything smells like beer at a party anyway."

I start to think she's probably right. She knows how to play me, and a reference to my hero Nellie Bly would do it. I've come this far, and in the back of my mind, not that I've been thinking about it at all, I guess, is Scott.

"Urgh, fine," I say, cycling on toward the farm.

"And if we come back in body bags, at least we lived. For one night only." Annie gulps looking at the mansion ahead of us.

> *Dear Lord,*
>
> *Please protect me from whatever madness will occur here. Especially if, with it being Heather's house, it turns into a scene from the Blair Bitch Project. Thank you, dearest high priestess.*
>
> *P.S. Sorry I was never christened and have never spoken with you before. I know it might seem like I haven't believed in you all this time, but really any port in a storm. I'm sure you can understand. And if I do die, please let the record show I did sort of half start believing in you before my demise.*

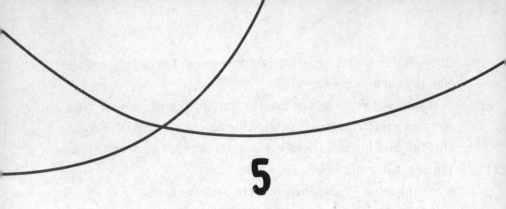

5

The party is fucking feral. This house is wild, not to mention the driveway, which has bushes all trimmed into different topiary animals. There are people EVERYWHERE. I was wrong with my *Lord of the Flies* prediction; this isn't nearly as civilized as that.

Plus, on the inside, everything is a sensory hell. Gothic meets pink PVC. There's a suit of armor next to a fuchsia pleather sofa. I squint at it and tilt my head to the side.

"Does that sofa look like . . . ?" I start.

"A vulva?" Annie finishes, making a shrugging gesture. "I guess with her dad's job it was a comfortable choice."

The next thing I notice, which assures me the end is nigh (after the yonic sofa), are the swords over the fireplace. If there are swords right there in the middle of the living room, imagine how many other things there are that could potentially maim a teenager around this hell mansion.

"Congratulations, you've brought us to our death," I say, gesturing to the medieval weapons. "At least we know which room to stay out of when the Hunger Games begin later."

Everyone's wasted, the place is getting trashed, and Heather's nowhere in sight. At least the tuxedoed toddler isn't here this time, though.

So, this is what it's like being at a party? I'd say I don't recognize three-quarters of the people here, but that would shock no one.

There are people downing beer and spilling it all over the place while shouting at each other, about three different kinds of music playing, people making out and half-naked, and in the corner are the cool nerds who used to do CSI Coders with us, clustered around a table that seems to have old artifacts on it. Things that I think might have been on display around the house, such as an old helmet from a suit of armor and a codpiece that seem to be missing the rest of their suit.

I do a double take. Was literally everyone invited to this party except us?

"We need to find Colin, Audrey, Selena, and Adam. They're our prime suspects," Annie says, looking around the carnage to try and find them. "They know her best—they're in her house and her space the most, so they've far more chance of finding out her secrets. We just have to put ourselves in their mindset." She breaks off to sigh. "If we knew *what* the secret was, it would make it a hundred times easier."

"Do you really believe Heather doesn't know what they're talking about?" I ask before seeing one of the jocks out of the corner of my eye heading over to the swords to try and pry them off the wall, heightening my sense of danger.

Do you know what? I think I will drink, after all. If I'm

37

going to die here, I've got a lot of stuff to tick off my bucket list first—starting with drinking warm alcohol of questionable authenticity.

From the movies I've seen, I know that at parties you drink from red cups and there are kegs. There doesn't seem to be either of those things in this kitchen. Instead, the counter's covered in warm, cheap, stolen booze: odds and ends from liquor cabinets, warm supermarket store-brand beers, and a bowl of something which I assume is punch but looks as murky as swamp water.

"You only live once. I'm going in," Annie says, taking a ladle of said murky punch to a plastic cup.

There are two things wrong with this:

1. Annie drinking from a plastic cup is like the king eating at McDonald's. This doesn't happen. Usually, she would have stood on a chair and given everyone at this party an hour-long speech about climate change and the damage that one small plastic cup can have on the earth. She calls plastic bottles "destruction vessels." (She's right.)

2. Everyone knows that the punch at a party is laced with pubes and whatever else people have thrown in there.

"Are you okay?" I ask, watching her down a whole cup of pube punch.

"Yeah, look, we're here! We've made it to the inner sanctum! I intend to enjoy every single second of it!" She helps herself to another ladle of the punch.

"You don't have to be wasted to enjoy it?" I suggest, looking for something that's not two-thirds pocket lint and one-third ethanol.

"Yes, but I want to fit in, don't I?" she asks, gesturing at the mayhem around her, and I have to say, I can't fault her logic. Everyone here *is* wasted.

I grab a beer from the side like I know what I'm doing, take a sip, gag, and put it back down. Vile. No wonder I assumed it was piss when they squirted it at us earlier.

"Ohhhkay, *Euphoria*, maybe slow down a little bit," I say, watching Annie power through her third glass.

She slams it down on the counter like she's doing shots in a Western, and while I'm sure there was some tequila in there, I'm also sure it was not alone. Maybe she's got the right idea, though. I feel so out of whack here I wonder about climbing into one of the kitchen cupboards and just waiting until it's over.

"Ooop, dizzy," Annie gasps, her eyes wide, while she grabs the counter.

I take hold of her shoulders and direct her toward some French windows where I can already hear people outside.

"Come on, party queen, let's get you some fresh air," I say, shuffling her toward the mild evening breeze, weaving our way through crowds of people.

As we head outside, I'm relieved for the air, but it's already obvious that this isn't just any normal backyard. This is a mega yard. There are acres of land and a *pool*. I always knew that the farm stretches for miles around, even hitting the boundary of the village and bordering onto the next village over. But to see it all like this, laid out? You could disappear here for days—especially as it's a five-minute drive from the village center—and no one would find you. My idea of heaven, really.

"A POOL! A FUCKING POOL?!" Annie shouts. "We're not

in LA! It rains three hundred and sixty days of the year in this village! When do they even use that thing?"

But it's not just the pool that's piqued my attention. Scott's here. I mean, I knew he'd be here and obviously I'd thought a couple of times in my head (not much) about how he'd be here. But now he's HERE. He's here; I'm here. I just need to remember that in order for me to stand any chance with him, I need to stay far away from him and not talk to him. Yep, that is the most sensible way to get a guy to like me. Instead, I'm just going to continue staring at him by the looks of things, because that's not weird at all, Kerry.

I know Annie's talking, but I can't understand any of the words she's saying because all I can focus on right now is him. I could stare like this my whole life. I never want it to end . . . oh my god, he's coming over here. He's on his way over. Is he coming to talk to *me*? Maybe *I* don't need to avoid talking to him. Maybe he *wants* to talk to *me*.

"IloveSonicYouth!" I whisper into his face while he passes right by me. My face goes bright red as I realize that he wasn't coming to talk to me at all, and I've just broken all my rules. I grab Annie's hand, bolting from the scene as fast as possible, like the little pervert I am.

I don't even look back to see if he heard what I said. The best I can hope for is that he didn't and that, despite everything I've done today, he hasn't even noticed my existence.

"WHERE ARE WE GOING?" Annie complains like a toddler while I drag her through the kitchen. I don't answer. I'm busy wondering if I could just run all the way back to this morning and start the day again.

In the kitchen, there are people doing shots and chanting

loudly. I feel like I've come from one hell to another as a girl I don't recognize with bright purple lipstick around her face like a clown and the kind of drunken eyes my mum gets after a night out turns to me, shot glass in hand.

As soon as she notices me, everyone else does, too, and pretty soon five strangers are all shouting "SHOTS!" in my face while I try and struggle my way through them without having to drink a thimble of paint stripper.

I've always suspected, but now I really *know*, it's Annie who wants the hustle and bustle of being popular, really all I want is peace. People scare me.

I rush through the shots crowd, headed for the bathroom I spotted off the kitchen earlier. The door's closed but not locked, and I hurriedly open it, ready to fling myself and Annie in there and hide, but I'm greeted with the sight of a guy on his knees, his head in someone's crotch.

"MY EYES!" Annie screams next to me.

"Oh, shit, sorry," I say, covering my eyes and backing out, closing the door before I slink against the wall.

"What exactly are we running from?" Annie asks.

"Scott," I say—just as I see him entering the living room with Selena, the two of them looking chatty.

"But you like him?" Annie asks.

"Correct," I say, blush rising on my cheeks just at the sight of him.

"Okay, how exactly are we supposed to investigate if you're just running away from him all the time, dragging us from room to room?" Annie asks as her phone beeps. "It's another message to Heather's account."

She angles her phone toward me so I can see it.

Mr. Stevens: Maybe you should be more careful about who gets in your house.

It's a picture of a room with a desk and a globe, a portrait of Heather's dad on the wall, and the products from his company littered around the desk. It wouldn't take a genius to work out that it must be his study. A chill runs up my spine.

"We need to find where the study is," Annie says. "But look cool; no one needs to know that we're here on official business. We need to fit in so we don't arouse suspicion."

In her sequined jumpsuit, leaning slightly against the wall, Annie starts nodding her head along to the hip-hop playing from the living room. Getting taken by the rhythm, she relaxes her knees and does a kind of bounce, shifting her shoulders from side to side, shimmying along the wall. She takes a pause to push her glasses up like she means business and nods to me. This continues, Annie bopping and glaring right at me, until I copy her movement.

Please, God, let me pray to you twice in one night. May Scott never witness this.

The two of us continue, on the fringes of the party shimmying against the kitchen wall. Annie's really into it now, swaying her head in time, swinging her arms; I have never wanted to be invisible more in my entire life.

I focus on looking ahead and trying to work out where the study might be.

"It's got to be down here somewhere. Maybe over there." Annie points while still dancing over to a darkened corridor.

"Over there." I raise my finger in the same direction.

I didn't see him coming; I don't know how I missed him.

Last time I saw him he was in the living room, and yet somehow, I've smacked into Scott for a second time today. This time literally, as my hand connects with his nose.

"Uhrghsorry," I mutter over the sound of blood rushing to my head, which fills my ears and makes me dizzy.

"Sorry," he says at the same time, looking as embarrassed as I am.

"No, I'm sorry," I say again while a drunk football player comes hurtling through as if from nowhere, knocking me off balance so I stumble against the wall, and pours beer all down my top.

That's enough for me. More than enough. My face is burning, embarrassed hives spreading down my neck and chest. I need to get out of here. I turn on my heel and head completely the other way, walking fast through the living room, and head for the stairs. There has to be somewhere I can just have a minute to myself.

"Where are you going?" I can hear Annie calling behind me as I push my way up the stairs, past about ten thousand couples, all at different stages of fornication. It's like they're trolling me. Annie's still in hot pursuit while I look for somewhere to escape. Thankfully Scott seems frozen to the spot where I bodychecked him.

Upstairs I nervously peer into rooms for somewhere I can sit with my head in my hands or maybe at least clean up the beer with no one around so I can complete my existential crisis. Sadly, every time I open a door, I'm greeted by scenes from terrible pornos. There are rooms I don't even bother to enter because in one you could hear whoever's in there faking an orgasm from Mars. From another one of the rooms, I can hear

Journey's "Don't Stop Believin'" playing, which I've heard is the song that the football captain has sex to. Gross.

I finally find an open room and run in, but I don't feel far enough away, so keep going until I've climbed into a wardrobe. There's a sliver of light; Annie follows, having caught up, and swings the door closed behind her. We crouch in the darkness, muffled music floating up from downstairs the only sound.

"How long do we need to stay here?" Annie asks as I wait for my breathing to slow down.

"Forever," I say reasonably.

"Ooohkay." Annie stretches out her legs and gets comfy, lying among the clothes like a cat, and I slink further and further down my shame spiral. "I'd just like to point out that we were about to uncover our suspect."

I raise my head from my knees and glare at Annie for such a long period of time that I think my eyeballs are going to crack. Is that really all she can think about right now, in my hour of need?

"Fine, if we're going to be here awhile, I'm going to have a party moment," Annie says from her spot on the wardrobe floor, rolling around among someone's clothes. "Please, leave me to express myself in a way fit for a party montage scene."

"You're doing snow angels in someone's underwear." I point to the bra behind her. "Can we just go home? I just want to die of embarrassment in peace. We're never going to find out who it was. There are too many possibilities."

"Nope, we're not giving up just because you got beer poured on you," Annie says, analyzing the clothes littered around her.

I'm clutching the retainer in my pocket for comfort and safety. Who brings a retainer to a party? Someone who stares at their crush for an uncomfortably long time and then runs away, that's who.

"FINE." Annie sits up eyeing me suspiciously and pulls her phone out of her pocket, scrolling to Heather's profile to see if there are any new messages.

Mr. Stevens: Maybe you should have hidden the weapons before I got here.

There's a picture of the swords over Heather's fireplace underneath the message. I feel all my internal organs freeze.

"Great, they've found the weapons!" I mutter sarcastically, thinking of the night that could have been. Right about now in my film watching, the school introvert would be having her makeover even though she looked great before.

We're staring at each other like owls, eyes wide, petrified that both we and Heather have underestimated this.

The sound of the bedroom door opening and closing makes us both jump so much we nearly fall out of the wardrobe, and it takes a second before we muster up the composure to peer through a crack in the door and see who it is. I've already done so many weird things tonight; I'm not adverse to just jumping out of this wardrobe and running out of here—but it depends on who it is. I can't see them, though, so they must be by the door.

"You don't think anyone saw us come in?" It's a girl's voice I vaguely recognize . . . but it's like they've made it deeper, like they're trying to be sexier?

"Nah, they were all too busy hooking up." A guy's voice that sounds like . . . It can't be . . .

"Adam!" Annie mouths to me, eyes like saucers as whoever it is moves into view before falling on the bed in a passionate embrace (I loved *Bridgerton*, can you tell?).

45

But that did NOT sound like Heather. Is he with someone else at his girlfriend's HOUSE? Annie gets her phone out of her pocket and types a note to me.

THAT'S NOT HEATHER!

He's cheating on her! What if it's him sending the messages as well? I type back.

Dude, he's too hot to be sending serial killer vibes like that last message, Annie types, rolling her eyes at me.

Don't make me google world's hottest serial killers for you again, I type, although I think I still have that tab open in my phone.

We both watch intently, not because we're creepy, but because we're *investigating*, and we need to know *who* is under Adam right now.

We nearly miss the great unveiling because at the moment he pulls away from his mystery companion, Adam also takes his shirt off. I have to work pretty hard to stay focused on the task at hand, but what is unveiled shocks both of us to our very core.

SELENA! Annie types out to me as the two of us stare at each other, open-mouthed, almost (but not quite) too shook to pay much attention to the fact that the sexiest guy in school is naked about a yard away from us.

I always thought if I ever saw Adam Devers naked, it would be the most distracting thing in the room. It turns out it's not.

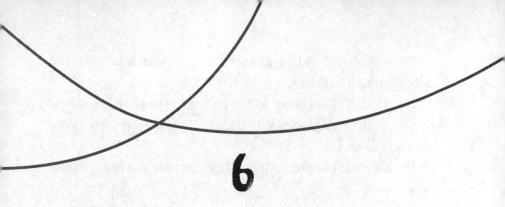

6

How can no one know that they're cheating when they're taking this long about it? Annie writes, rolling her eyes.

We need to escape. We could do a commando style crawl across the floor while they're distracted? she types again, and I shake my head.

Too many commandos in one room, I write back, trying to shake a cramp out of my right leg.

We're both wearing several items of clothing wrapped around our heads to protect our eyes and ears now. When I wrapped the fourth sweater around, I finally stopped being able to hear the feral mating sounds.

Wait! Annie sits bolt upright and takes some clothes off her head. I think they've finished, she types.

I unwrap the sweaters from my head and listen before looking through the crack in the door. The two of them are up from their horizontal position, and Selena's got her phone out typing something. Just as she puts her phone away, Annie's vibrates—threatening to uncover our whereabouts—and the two of us freeze.

"You go first." Adam gestures, and Selena heads out the door closing it behind her.

Annie and I look down at her phone to see what the vibration was. It was a message to Heather's Instagram. From the troll account.

Mr. Stevens: I can uncover it all tonight. Are you ready to talk now?

Annie's so shocked that I have to stop her from falling out of the wardrobe and onto Adam's feet as he heads for the door.

"It's SELENA!" she mouths at me, pointing from the phone to the door. "She did the . . . and then this went bing . . . and IT'S SELENA!"

Annie's practically shouting as the two of us topple out of the wardrobe into the empty bedroom and the scene of many crimes.

"We need to find her and tell her," Annie says as we untangle ourselves on the floor.

"She told us NOT to talk to her in front of anyone," I say.

"Dude, her best friend is hooking up with her boyfriend *and* trolling her. I think we NEED to tell her in person. Besides, I want the glory—please let me have the glory?" She knows how to play me. I'd feel mean taking that moment away from her.

"Fine, let's find Heather, tell her who her mystery messages are coming from, and get the hell out of here," I say.

We're back in the kitchen, right in the eye of the party, trying to spot Heather. I'm on high alert in case I accidentally smash into Scott again. I've had three run-ins with him now, all of increasing embarrassment. A fourth would send me into a permanent state of beet.

"Look, she's over there," Annie says. She makes a beeline to where Heather's dancing with Audrey and Colin. Selena's nowhere to be found, which is probably a good thing at this point.

"Yo, Heather!" Annie waves over at her, and Heather looks like she might vomit.

She shuffles over to us quickly, looking furious, and ushers us into a toilet off the side of the kitchen.

"What *is* your damage? I said NOT to talk to me in front of people!" she hisses, closing the door.

"We solved your mystery. It's Selena," Annie says, clearly a bit pissed off by the way Heather's dismissing her. "Oh, and she's hooking up with Adam."

Oh my god, Annie. I hope that Annie never becomes a nurse or someone in the caring profession if that's how she delivers bad news.

"WHAT?" Heather looks murderous, and I worry I'm going to have to step between the two of them.

"We saw them together upstairs, and then she sent something from her phone, at the same time you received a DM from the fake profile," I say. Hopefully that provides enough evidence before she kicks off at Annie.

Heather's standing completely still, just staring. She's either in shock or trying to burn a hole in the wall with her eyes. For a minute, I wonder if I need to check her pulse, and then it happens. She turns on her heel, flings the toilet door open, and hurls herself out into the kitchen.

"SELENA FUCKING SLUT MUNROE, WHERE THE FUCK ARE YOU?" she screams, silencing the party around her before marching off.

"Never the guy that gets in trouble or called a slut first, is it?" Annie asks, crossing her arms over her chest.

"Feminism's got a long way to go," I agree. "Can we go home now?"

"Jesus, party animal. Can't we at least take two seconds to see if she kills her? Also, what if in the fight Selena unveils what the secret actually is?!"

We stand and watch for a little while as Heather heads to find Selena, but she's quickly out of sight. We've done what we came here to do, and the party's carrying on around us, back in full flow. I just want to go now. I clutch my retainer in my pocket. Soon, my pretty.

"Do you think we're in now? I mean, I've solved her drama," Annie asks.

"I don't know. Do you really want to be 'in' with people like Heather and Selena?" I ask, but Annie's already back over by the punch bowl. "I guess we're not leaving after all, then," I mutter to myself, watching her take a straw to the bowl of lint and ethanol.

"Want some?" she asks cheerfully.

"Nah, I'm good," I say, looking around me for something else that's a little less full-on.

I turn around and feel my head collide with someone else's.

"Oh god, sorry. That was me that time," Scott's voice says, and I can already feel my cheeks flushing, but when I open my eyes his are, too.

50

"No, my fault, I should have looked where I was going," I say, clutching my head.

"Oh no, are you okay?" He rubs his head and looks at mine. "I didn't leave a bump or anything, did I?"

I touch my forehead where the contact was made, but it seems okay.

"It's okay," I say, impressed with myself for actual words coming out of my mouth. Maybe the bang to the head helped a bit.

I scan down his face up close: the nose—cute—the cheeks—still dimpled—and the lips . . . They're magnetic, drawing me in. I genuinely think I might be falling onto his face. Is it bad if I just run my hand through his hair a little bit?

Why, yes, I do read a lot of romance novels. What made you ask?

"Want a drink?" he asks. It brings me back to earth and helps me realize I'm just staring at him. This is mortifying.

It also dawns on me that I've just stood with my mouth open and my hands posed in front of me, slightly bent at the wrist, like an excited puppy. Suddenly I don't know what to do with my limbs.

"Oh, I'll just . . . just some water," I say, wondering if I can be trusted to get it myself while I'm feeling so . . . lusty.

"I'll get it," he says, and I watch as he gets the glass of water like a normal human being and passes it to me. His warm, manly hand brushes against mine.

A man is giving me things.

A hot man is giving me things.

I DON'T NEED MEN TO GIVE ME THINGS. I CAN GET THEM MYSELF.

But this is nice.

"Thanku," I mutter, my eyes firmly on the water, and the proximity of his hand to mine right now.

I suddenly feel hot and dizzy. I try and keep myself calm; he must think I'm really chaotic after everything I've done so far. Why does he even want to talk to me?

"So, you like Sonic Youth, too, huh? I don't think I've ever met another fan before."

I just nod at him because I feel SHAME that he actually heard me say that.

"I'm Scott. I feel like we never actually did the proper introductions. . . ."

Oh, don't you worry, I remember your name, Scott. In my head, I've already put our two names together to create Scerry.

". . . Kerry," I say as if it's the first time anyone's ever asked me my own name. I'm back to the first day of kindergarten. In a few minutes, I'm going to start crawling on the floor doing finger painting.

"Nice to meet you, Kerry," he says, and we lock eyes. "I, err . . . found what you said in homeroom really interesting earlier," he says, his cheeks blushing slightly. "The thing about the psychologist working to help criminals back into society from prison. True crime and things like that are kinda my, errr, my jam. What kind of crimes had they committed?"

"Oh, like a mixture," I say, feeling my confidence grow. It's so much easier talking to someone when you're talking about stuff you're both into. "Some small crimes, but they were just kinda stuck in a loop. There was one case study she talked about with an actual murderer." And then my confidence slides back again. *Actual* murderer? That was so not the cool, relaxed vibe I was going for.

I stare straight ahead; I should have stuck to not talking. Although one of us is going to have to say something now because the silence between us is so loud that I'm almost grateful for the noise of Heather's screaming, still trying to find Selena in the background.

"Where did you move from?" I blurt out, finally taking a gasp of air after.

"Oh, Manchester," he says, and I kind of hoped for more than that. I'm going to have to speak again.

"How come?" I feel like an interviewer, a really intense one that keeps staring at his hand around the beer bottle, his fingers peeling at the label.

"My mum was sick. We just need to be somewhere a bit quieter while she recovers," he says, staring solely at the beer bottle.

"Oh, I'm sorry," I say, and now I'm back to awkward again.

"It's okay; she's much better now. I had to care for her for a while, but it's cool. It's just the two of us anyway. We're a unit." The way he talks about his mum is so caring and sensitive. A tight, plain silver bracelet on his wrist catches the light as he plays with it. "It was a bit touch-and-go, but she made it."

"Oh," I say really awkwardly because this sensitivity has made him even hotter to me and now I can't get words out again.

"So is this what you guys do for fun around here?" He gestures at the room full of people drunk off their faces. "I've only been in town for a few weeks, but I was running out of things to do. I've already hit up the bookshop. It's got a good selection."

I have to stop myself from shouting "BOOKS ARE MY FAVORITE PEOPLE!" at him and instead I'm trying to compose myself enough to answer the question in a normal way. But he keeps brushing his dark hair out of his eyes as the wavy dark strands fall and he's smiling at me with his little dimples. I cannot . . .

"I like to read" is all I manage to say.

"What do you like reading?" he asks me, and suddenly I can't remember names of books, not a single author springs to mind. It's as if my brain is screaming "WHAT IS BOOK?" over and over again into a void.

My palms are sweating. He likes reading, and the bands I like, and he has dimples; it's too much for me to cope with. I feel like I might choke on my tongue whenever I imagine saying more words to this guy. My vagina is on fire. Is this what they mean when they say "burning loins"? Am I dying? Have I met someone that is so hot and perfect that I am now deceased?

I imagine my tombstone: She met a hottie and alas it killed her.

"Fiction," I exclaim as if proud that I've reminded myself of words. "And crime," I add for good measure, almost patting myself on the back that I managed to remember two whole genres.

"Oh, me too. I loved *The Shining*. It was just so poetic, you know," he says as I stare deeply into his eyes and nod at him trying to search for something to say back, probably looking like a creep, and yet completely unable to stop myself.

"Oh, same," I say, wondering why I said it because I've actually only read half of *The Shining*. My parents took it away from me after I started screaming in my sleep, so I never finished. But it's probably for the best I don't tell him that. He thinks I'm cool right now.

I look desperately around to see where Annie is. I feel like if she was with me, I'd be more relaxed and confident.

"Oh, wow, your friend's really going for it," Scott says, following my eyes as I find Annie on the kitchen counter, a circle of people surrounding her while she dances to Salt-N-Pepa's "Push It." She's taken someone's cardigan, and she's holding both sleeves miming some kind of push-it/pull-it-style dance.

I feel something die inside me, and I think it might be my last slither of self-respect. She's doing some grade A dad dancing. I start to wonder if the two of us will have to seek some kind of witness protection after tonight. We can start again, a new village, a new school, lessons will have been learned. Maybe it's for the best?

To my absolute astonishment, though, Colin jumps up on the counter with her and takes the cardigan. He starts wrapping her in it, swirling her around, and pulling each arm. He's dancing WITH her. I don't think he's even making fun of her. People are joining in from the floor, and while I don't fully understand what's going on, I feel amazed.

"She's . . . an enigma!" I say, laughing nervously as she mimes spanking Colin in time to the music, and I wish just for a second that I could be more like my friend. Have fewer inhibitions. Kiss this hot guy standing next to me, rather than standing here feeling that I might have a heart attack and die at any minute.

"Hey, I saw something earlier you might like!" he says. "Wanna see?"

55

I blink at him. He wants me to go somewhere on my own with him? I decide for once to ignore all the questions and possible scenarios in my head and instead nod and follow him. I don't know where we're going, but in the infamous words of the *Gilmore Girls* theme song, "where you lead, I will follow," and I don't care where it is.

I hear the opening of another retro song my mum loves, called "China in Your Hand," and glance back at Annie to see her grabbing crockery from the shelves, so she can have literal china in her hand as a prop. The last thing I see before the two of us head down a quieter corridor just off the kitchen is her pushing her plates at Audrey, who's also joined in the dancing.

I follow Scott for a bit before we're completely alone. The kitchen has become a distant rumble, and I doubt Annie's even noticed I'm gone. The corridor gets darker, but I don't hate it. Scott stops in front of a closed door, turns, and points at the wall opposite. Hanging there, to my horror, is a huge, almost life-size poster for *The Shining*. It brings back terrible memories, but it's not his fault I lied and said I liked it.

"Isn't it cool?!" he says, before turning to look at me.

"So cool," I say. When I look up, though, I only remember the terror I felt trying to read it. I'd certainly never want to WATCH it. I gulp and turn around, facing him instead of the poster.

"It's so cool to meet someone who likes Sonic Youth *and* books. Two of my favorite things," he says to me, my eyes meeting his, shining green through the darkness.

I feel as if I'm moving closer to him, getting bolder in the dark, and it feels like he's moving closer to me, too. He's staring so intensely; I know if I carry on with eye contact I'm going to ruin this moment by laughing. I need to be more like Annie; seize the moment! Take the crockery by the horns. I close my eyes and purse my lips.

I'm going to kiss him. I'm going to kiss him, and it's going to be amazing.

I lean forward; all I have to do is keep leaning forward until my lips meet his, and shut my eyes so I don't seem creepy, and then there will be fireworks, lights, bangs in the sky . . .

There's a bang as my face hits the study door, which was behind Scott. I've somehow managed to miss him and land against the door instead. I open my eyes as the door springs open against my weight; to my horror, I'm still falling forward with absolutely no way of stopping myself, while Scott stands next to me, confused.

Eventually, after what feels like years, my body and face make full contact with the floor of what I presume is the study. Instead of kissing Scott, I'm kissing carpet.

"Shit! Are you okay?" Scott crouches next to me.

"Totally fine!" I scrabble myself together and offer him a huge nothing-to-see-here-style grin. But when I look at him, he's not smiling. There's light coming from somewhere in the room, illuminating his pale face. As I turn and follow his gaze into the study, I hear a high-pitched scream, before I realize it's coming from my own mouth.

There, sitting at a grand oak desk, as if she's about to chair a meeting, is Selena Munroe, dead. A menstrual cup stuffed in her mouth, and her blank eyes staring straight ahead at nothing.

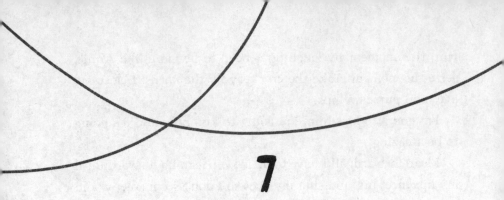

7

As a fight-or-flight person, I've always considered myself to be flight. But for some reason, even at the sight of a dead body I'm just standing here screaming and completely unable to move.

Annie's the first person by my side, and I hear other people start to gather, their gasps filling the dead air. I realize the screaming's stopped; *I* must have stopped screaming. But I've got no idea *when* I stopped. I need to look away, but I feel completely unable to take my eyes off Selena, sitting at the desk, lit up by a desk lamp that almost looks like it was crudely positioned to light up her face.

Annie looks between me and Scott for answers, but neither of us are able to say anything, so she heads over to the body. Leaning delicately over Selena so as not to disturb the crime scene, she takes her pulse.

"She's dead," she confirms, as if this is CBS reruns on a Saturday afternoon.

There's complete silence with only Lady Gaga's "Poker Face" still playing in the background.

How can she be dead? Can someone die at a party in Barbourough on a Friday night with a menstrual cup dangling out of her mouth? When did this happen? She was fine just a little while ago—well enough to throw coffee and insults all day.

I try to comprehend the scene in front of me, staring at the menstrual cup, trying to work out if that's definitely what it is or if I'm just so focused on my upcoming period that I'm seeing them everywhere. But that's definitely what it is. Just sitting in her open mouth.

"SELENA?" Heather flies through the door to the study—Audrey and Colin behind her—and for a little while, I can't work out if she's annoyed at her, or heartbroken. Then her face crumples.

She flings herself onto her friend, seemingly unbothered by the chance of disturbing any DNA.

"Someone needs to call the police and an ambulance, before the crime scene gets completely contaminated," Annie says. She grabs her phone, and I'm so pleased she's here because for the first time ever Annie's the calmest person in the room.

I'm aware of Scott behind me, his face still deathly pale. I want to reach out for his hand, for some kind of reassurance, but the embarrassment of what happened between us before we found Selena still hangs in the air. I can't bring myself to meet his eye.

Audrey and Colin manage to separate Heather from Selena while Annie paces behind them on the phone. She's pointing at something on the desk, trying to get me to see it, but my vision's too blurry to take it in. I wish someone would shut Selena's eyes. With them still staring at me, I feel like I might pass out. I wonder if I might need to take "Good in a crisis" off my résumé.

As more people gather, Adam vaults through the door. Ever the dutiful boyfriend, he immediately pulls Heather away from Selena. Everyone's attention turns to the pair of them. None of us sure if he knows that Heather knows yet. He barely gives Selena a second glance. Watching the two of them feels better than watching Selena, so I carry on staring, intrigued. Maybe he'll plead innocence now that Selena's dead. Claim it was all a made-up story, and Annie and I don't know what we're talking about.

I'm searching his face for any kind of emotion about the fact that Selena, the girl he was hooking up with just hours ago, is dead right in front of him—but he's blank. Maybe it's shock, maybe it's not registering, or maybe he really is the biggest asshole in the world.

He tries to hug Heather, but she wriggles free from his grasp straightaway and starts punching his chest harder and harder.

"YOU DICK!" she's shouting, and hitting him over and over again while Colin and Audrey tearfully try to separate the two of them. "YOU WERE FUCKING HER. YOU WERE FUCKING MY *BEST FRIEND*. YOU ASSHOLE!"

The people crowded in the doorway freeze, watching in shock and horror as she repeatedly smacks him. His face changes as he realizes she knows.

"What are you talking about?" He widens his eyes, giving her a lost-puppy expression. "I could never cheat on you, my love. . . ."

No matter what he says, it sounds fake, there's no way he can get out of this one. No matter what he does now, he's been outed, and everyone knows it.

60

More and more people gather to see what's happened, shocked chatter filling the air, as Selena Munroe, the cause of so much drama, sits quietly, dead in the middle of it all, menstrual cup quirkily protruding from her mouth. I feel the walls start to close in, the chatter and shock around me mixing with Heather's shouting to create one huge wall of noise in my brain, and I need to get out. It feels like I'm gasping, trying to get the air into my lungs, the noise blurring into one mass in my head, stealing each breath. But before I can make it to the door, the crowd surges forward.

"What the hell is happening here?" A man's voice breaks through the drama, and we all turn to see a guy in a black rain slicker and suit standing in the hallway flanked by uniformed police officers.

Paramedics appear behind them and rush to Selena. They're moving so fast that for a minute I think they believe they can save her. But almost the moment they get to her body, they slow down, and I think know they can't.

The man in the suit looks like the sort of guy that would be the old and wise detective dude about to be retired back to desk duty in a crime drama. He's got a red nose, and raggedy stubble across his ruddy cheeks. Through tufts of gray hair I can see bald patches that he's tried to cover up with wayward, unkempt strands. A younger man joins him, dressed the same but clearly fresher, newer, his face pale but more open and approachable, his eyes wide, with more of a sparkle. He doesn't seem that much older than us and definitely can't be more than late twenties. He'd be the new impressionable upstart, with good intentions but a lack of experience.

"Let's clear the scene, please, people!" one of the paramedics shouts, pushing through the gathered crowd as more police follow her in.

I half expect Selena to jump up from the desk and laugh at us all, like it was all a big joke and she was just screwing with us. But she doesn't. The only thing that we all know for sure right now is that Selena Munroe is dead, and Heather Stevens was furious with her when she died.

I look over to Annie and see she's already staring at me, her face looking scarily like she's had an idea, and unfortunately I think I know what it is.

We've been given strict instructions not to leave the house, but the detectives have moved us out of the study and away from the body. So here we are, slumped against the living room wall with our legs straight out in front of us. I've got Annie to my right and Scott to my left, and I feel awkward as hell.

As Scott and I found Selena, we've been told we have to stay together, and someone will take our statement. I still haven't been able to bring myself to look at him. Embarrassment courses through my veins as I constantly relive the moment I thought he was going to kiss me and instead I fell into a room and discovered a dead person. Thankfully at least Annie's breaking up the tension slightly, by muttering to herself trying to Sherlock the mystery of what happened to Selena in real time.

Adding to the awkwardness, the rest of the party are packed in here with us and every single one of them knows that it was us that found the body. That's a lot of people staring at two nobodies, one of whom has only just arrived in this town, the other of whom just fell flat on her face in a failed make-out attempt.

Unlike Scott and me, though, Annie seems to be thriving on being the center of attention. She's beaming from ear to ear, reveling in it, in a completely inappropriate way considering the circumstances.

Somewhat tastelessly, and because I'm a terrible person, I keep wondering if Scott wanted to kiss me or if I read it wrong. And if he *did* want to kiss me, does he *still* want to kiss me? Or has the whole dead-body thing put him off? Ever the optimist, I think he probably doesn't want to kiss me. Especially not now.

To distract myself from my own terrible love life, I glance as subtly as possible at the romantic catastrophe to my left. Heather, Colin, and Audrey are sitting next to us while Adam—having been separated from Heather—is across from her with the football team. He's staring at her like a lost puppy. Most of the room is looking from us to them as if at any point one of us is going to provide some kind of entertainment.

"Do you think she did it?" Annie whispers on my right. "She was furious."

"Annie, we don't know what happened. This is Barbourough. No one gets murdered in Barbourough," I whisper back, hoping that Scott hasn't heard.

"Oh yeah, so how do you explain the dead body, then?" she whispers back. She's like a dog with a bone. I know her well enough to know she won't give this up until Selena Munroe herself comes back from the dead and explains what's happened, or something nearly as dramatic. "And why was there one of the V-Lyte menstrual cups in her mouth? I mean, there are plenty of them around; they seem to be in every room. But what was it doing in her mouth?" She rests her fingers on her chin in a thinking pose. "Heather was furious with Selena, so she killed her. Everyone thinks it—just listen to people's conversations. Do you think she did it with the menstrual cup? And if she did, WHY?"

She's right that a lot of people are whispering about how furious Heather was with Selena before she died, but the rest of Annie's ramblings just sound ridiculous. There has to be another reason why Selena died, something medical or something.

"There are hundreds of menstrual cups all over this house, and pads and tampons. It's where the owners of V-Lyte live, and where they have their office," I explain. I'm willing her to stop this because Scott must be catching on now. "Also, why would the menstrual cup have anything to do with her death?"

"Do you often put your menstrual products in your mouth?" Annie asks, and I know she's right; it's really weird but makes no sense. "You mark my words, one of them did it with the menstrual cup, in the study. And my money's on hotheaded Heather." It's as if she's playing a real-life game of Clue. I watch as she tightens her mouth into a thin line. "Well, she's not getting away with it scot-free on my watch."

"Did you say my name?" Scott leans in and joins the whisper.

"No?" Annie says completely innocently while I stare across the room to Adam, who looks sad, but I dunno . . . not quite as sad as you'd expect. There are certainly no tears.

"Oh, and Adam's another thing," she says, leaning back in to whisper in my ear. "You know, I find him considerably less attractive now that he's a cheater. Also, those noises he was making when they were having sex? It's a no from me."

She's right—he's much less attractive now. I wouldn't even sniff him. I look across at him and follow his gaze to see Heather crying and shaking. If Annie's right and she murdered Selena, then her performance is BAFTA if not Oscar worthy. Oh my god, I can't believe I'm even thinking about it. Get out of my brain, Annie. I raise my head to see her giving me a small cheeky smile and wonder if she's finally, actually worked out a way to get into my mind telepathically. If she has, I'll never know peace again.

But this is Barbourough village, not a Hollywood movie. Nobody gets murdered in Barbourough. There's hundreds of ways Selena could have died: heart attack, brain hemorrhage, too much to drink. There are so many possible explanations in fact that it almost makes me certain that I could drop dead any second.

The tension is finally broken by Heather's mum rushing in and racing straight over to her.

"Mrs. Stevens, I presume?" The older detective intercepts her while Heather falls into her mum's arms crying.

"Yes?" Mrs. Stevens gives him a harassed look over her daughter's sobbing head.

"Detective Inspector Wallace." He grabs a badge and flashes it at her. "I'm in charge of the investigation."

"The investigation is in my house, so I think you'll find I'm actually in charge of it," Mary Stevens snaps, not missing a beat. "I'm taking my daughter and her friends upstairs so that they can grieve in private."

"We actually need everyone to stay in this room while we

secure the scene and gather evidence. We also need to move the body."

Heather's mum doesn't even flinch at the mention of a body and instead gets right into the detective's face, looking furious.

"I'm taking my daughter upstairs and away from this circus. Then I'll come back down, and you can explain to me exactly what the hell is going on here," she snaps as Heather, Colin, and Audrey follow her out of the room.

DI Wallace looks like he's been smacked in the face, a puce color rising up his cheeks as they all traipse up the stairs, flouting his authority. I see him take a deep breath before marching out of the room, trying to regain his dignity.

A wave of whispers starts in the room the moment they all leave. I can make out little snippets of people muttering their own theories about what happened between Selena Munroe and Heather Stevens, and most of them have to do with Heather's temper.

How would she have done it without us seeing her going in or out, though? And wouldn't that make us responsible? After all, we're the ones that told her about Selena and Adam in the first place. The guilt begins swirling around my stomach, and I feel sick, which is silly because at this point we don't know anything. Maybe no one's murdered anyone.

"What were you two doing down there anyway?" Annie asks, raising an eyebrow to me. If I could simply bury my head in my hands and leave it there for the rest of time, I would.

"I was showing Kerry the original poster for *The Shining* that I saw down by the study, seeing as we both loved the book," Scott says so normally as Annie smirks.

"I see, yes, she loves *The Shining*. Can't get enough of it. Some days it's all she talks about," Annie says pointedly. Either Scott doesn't notice her sarcasm or doesn't address it. Instead, he sort of leans forward and looks around.

"This place is kind of weird. How long have they lived here?" Scott asks.

"All Heather's life. Her dad owned a company called V-Lyte. They make period products. He died in a speedboat accident—the perils of being rich—so now Heather's mum runs it and she's actually gotten rid of some of the period-shamey taglines they had when Mr. Stevens was in charge, like 'No one has to know you're with Aunt Flo,'" Annie says.

"Not a huge fan of Mr. Stevens, then?" Scott asks, looking amused. The period chat doesn't seem to have fazed him at all. "When did he die?"

"Almost a year ago now," I say. "And don't get her started on her feelings about Mr. Stevens."

"I just don't think we should have to hide our periods, and it gives me the rage when someone tries to make out like we should be being discreet about them," Annie says.

"So, Heather's an only child? No other siblings? And they just all lived in this massive house?" Scott asks, ignoring the way he's stoked her rage.

"Yeah, pretty big, huh?" I say, grateful that he's at least distracting Annie from her thoughts about murder.

Scott gives me a thin smile and I feel my stomach flip-flop, but he just asks another question about the house. "Does everyone around here live in places like this?"

"God no, Kerry's house is MUCH smaller, just two bedrooms

rather than ten, and mine's about a sixth of the size of this place, if I'm being scientific about it. We're poor," Annie explains. "Where do you live?"

"The Moores?" He phrases it like a question, and I feel immediately embarrassed at how Kerry described us as poor.

The Moores is an apartment building on the outskirts of the village. It's in really bad condition, and I'm surprised because I thought they were talking about knocking it down last year to build what they called "affordable housing," which my dad says everyone knows is code for "unaffordable housing."

"How come you live there?" Annie asks, and I want to smack her.

"It's just me and Mum, and she's been sick, so hasn't been able to work much." He says it like he's used to these questions, but I feel the embarrassment rising to my cheeks again that Annie's been so rude about it.

We sit for a minute staring ahead, listening to everyone chattering around us, discussing their theories, many of them pointing to us. Scott shuffles next to me, and I feel his hand brushing against mine, making the flutters in my stomach start up again. The butterflies aren't just flapping—they're positively whooshing and dancing at the merest whisper of physical contact.

"So you like music? Do you play in a band or something?" Annie asks, trying to break through the awkward tension in her usual way, while I sit feeling it all intensely, paralyzed by that and a new and inappropriate horny lust. What if he *does* play in a band? Then he'd definitely be way too cool to ever actually like me.

"Yeah, I was in a band in Manchester. I play guitar," he says casually, like he doesn't know that the butterflies in my stomach are ramping up their assault at the same time as I realize I've got no hope with him.

"Oh, cool, what kind of music did you play?" I ask, at least grateful that Annie's opened up this conversation for us.

"I guess we're a bit like Sonic Youth—I think you'd like it. It's kind of experimental, alternative. We had quite a big fan base in Manchester, but I had to leave the band when I left Manchester. It's too hard to do long distance."

"Oh. Those guys over there are in a band, but you probably already know that." Annie points over to the guys that Scott was hanging with earlier when I walked into him outside the toilet, raging about my period.

"Yeah, they're pretty cool. They played me their stuff. I'm going to jam with them next week."

He's been in school one (1) day and already he's in a band. While Annie's been chatting with him like a normal person I've just been sitting here, mouth open, finding him sexier by the sentence.

Suddenly more police officers head through the house in the direction of the study. They've got white plastic coveralls over their uniforms, which I know from TV is to stop them contaminating the scene. Usually a crime scene. What if Annie's right?

"What do you think they're all doing?" I ask, watching them go through.

"Dusting for fingerprints, trying to determine a cause of death, searching for any evidence of foul play," Annie says.

"Jeez, are you a police officer?" Scott asks. He shoots a shocked look at Annie.

"She reads a lot of murder mysteries and watches a lot of crime drama," I explain.

"Right," he says, smiling slightly at me and resting his hand on his thigh, so it slightly touches mine.

I have trouble concentrating on the conversation because a lot of my headspace is spent wondering if he knows that his hand is touching mine and if he's doing it on purpose. I worry it's extremely disrespectful to the dead that every time he moves and his skin brushes more against mine, I feel a tingle in my pant area.

Although speaking of disrespecting the dead, I notice that Adam appears to have started flirting with one of the sophomores. I'm baffled as to how he's getting away with it and she's actually flirting back, but he's always been very charming, I guess. If Heather could see him now, there'd be two dead bodies for the police to deal with. Oh god, why am I thinking like this?

"Does he have no shame?" Annie asks as the three of us watch him attempting to hook up.

"Poor Selena. I mean, she sounds like she wasn't the nicest, but that's pretty douchey," Scott says.

"She was as bad as him," Annie says, showing no mercy for poor dead Selena.

The sophomore twists her hair around her finger, her cheeks flushing as Adam playfully touches her arm. This is the worst display of shameless flirting I've ever seen.

Police officers walk back into the living room with evidence bags, and I see Annie's face light up as she pulls out her phone.

Over her shoulder, I can see her texting the troll account. She looks up swiftly after sending a message saying **Who are you?** just in time to see one of the evidence bags light up. The evidence bag that is unmistakably containing Selena's phone.

"But why, though?" Annie mumbles under her breath.

"Why what?" Scott asks.

"Oh, just a general why," Annie says.

"I think Annie's a bit sad," I say to him.

"She was a monster, but I still have feelings," Annie agrees, trying to hide what we both know. For some reason, despite everything that's happened, I still feel like we should keep Heather's confidence. After all, we don't want her to make our lives hell if she did kill Selena.

Get out of my head, Annie.

When I turn around, she's squinting at me, a slightly constipated look on her face, probably from accessing my actual mind.

"Are you okay?" Scott asks, and I realize I'm shaking with some kind of delayed adrenaline rush.

"Yeah, just, shocked, I guess?" I say rubbing my goosebumped arms.

As if in slow motion, he takes off the hoodie he's been wearing and drapes it over my shoulders, and I think I might be about to join Selena Munroe in death. He takes my hand in his, rubbing my shaking fingers, and I feel like I'm having an out-of-body experience.

I'm relieved that he still wants to make physical contact after . . . everything—death, and me almost falling onto his face. Oh god, what if he gets off on finding the dead body, though? I look sideways at him. He seems to look completely normal, although I guess you can never tell.

71

I'm staring dreamily down at our linked hands when DI Wallace's gruff voice breaks me out of my trance.

"You two, the ones that found the body. We need to interview you now. Come on. Quick sticks," he barks at us as we stand up, Annie following suit. "*Just* the two that found the body!" DI Wallace stares Annie down.

"Oh, no, I was with them *just* before, plus we have something *pretty* interesting that I think you're going to want to hear," Annie says, and frankly I know from the tone in her voice that DI Wallace is getting her in this interview as well, whether he likes it or not.

As Scott lets go of my hand and it drops to my side, I realize that I'm going to have to recount how my failed attempt at a kiss led us to discovering a dead body. The embarrassment is palpable.

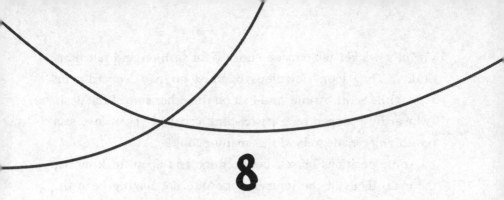

8

I hadn't expected to be retelling my first attempt at the vaguest notion of sexual activity to police detectives about five seconds after it didn't take place, but I guess I also hadn't expected to find Selena Munroe dead with a menstrual cup in her mouth the first time I tried to ravish someone. Surprises at every turn.

The police lead us through the house to a room that I'm presuming must be Heather's mum's office. It's different from the rest of the house, mostly wicker and white with hints of leopard print and pastel. An Instagrammer's wet dream. But still filled with the telltale sickly pink product labels of V-Lyte. It's a mystery to me why people think we need to make periods more palatable for society.

There's a huge clock over the desk, and I'm shocked to discover that it's half past midnight. I've definitely missed my retainer deadline. I wonder if I should email my orthodontist and just confess tomorrow before the guilt eats me up inside.

DI Wallace is stern-faced and tired-looking, but his younger-looking partner smiles broadly and offers a welcome from one side of a wicker table made entirely for fashion and not prac-ticality. They look ridiculous perched on two leopard-print seats while Scott, Annie, and I sit on the other side of the desk, awkwardly propped on a pastel-pink crushed-velvet love seat possibly not made to hold this many people.

Annie positions herself between me and Scott, making her the main focus of the interview despite not having been the one to find the body, but I'm relieved.

The younger man clears his throat delicately. "Hi, I'm DI Collins, and this is DI Wallace. We're so sorry about everything you've been through tonight. If it's not too much for you, we just wanted to hear a little more about how you came to dis-cover your classmate Selena." DI Collins keeps his voice light and careful, almost sensitive; he's the antithesis of DI Wallace and his stern face staring us down.

"So, Scott and Kerry, I believe that's you two." DI Wallace dives straight in, with considerably less warmth. He points at Scott and me with two fingers, deliberately trying to ignore Annie—not a mistake I would attempt to make if I were him. "I need you to explain to me how you came across the body."

"Well, Officer, they were—" Annie starts.

"JUST Kerry and Scott," DI Wallace cuts Annie off, and I can see already that she's plotting revenge.

"Well, er . . ." Scott starts, and I stare at the ring light above the desk, with visions of DI Wallace leaning across and aggressively shining it in my eyes until I confess to a murder I definitely didn't commit. Meanwhile, Scott stutters out, "We went down the corridor toward the study to get away from all the . . . noise. And then we were sort of talking . . . and . . ." I

74

realize Scott has no idea how I actually fell through the door, not really, so I'm going to have to finish the story here.

"I just sort of lost my balance, fell through the door, and then she was there," I say, but I can feel my palms sweating. Was that a lie? Did I just lie to the police officers? Or did I just say what happened without the mortifyingly embarrassing bit?

I stare down, not knowing what else to do, and thoroughly inspect my cuticles. I've never paid much attention to them before, but they really are quite wild. Although not as wild as Annie's eyes. I can feel them BORING into me.

"And was the door open then or shut?" DI Wallace presses while DI Collins smiles at me encouragingly.

"Kind of ajar," I say, my head still bent so far over my fingernails that I'm surprised I can still breathe.

"Kind of ajar . . ." DI Wallace repeats as if these three words are something that need analyzing to further draw out my agony.

"Look, yeah, that isn't even the bit that you need to know! There are SO MANY MOTIVES at this party right now!" Annie bursts out, getting bored of holding in all the knowledge she has. "SELENA WAS TROLLING HEATHER ON INSTAGRAM *AND* WE SAW SELENA AND ADAM—HEATHER'S BOY-FRIEND—*TOGETHER* BEFORE SHE DIED."

Annie's moved straight into detective mode for a crime that we don't even know has actually been committed. I for one, find it really hard to believe that a murder's actually been committed in Barbourough. I look up because I feel like we're in a safer zone now, where I won't have to talk about my sexual exploits (or lack thereof), and we can comfortably move on to someone else's.

75

Both detectives are staring at the three of us blankly, and we're staring back.

"Sorry, together?" DI Collins blinks. "Just to clarify, Annie, how were they together?"

Annie pauses for dramatic effect, even though she doesn't need to. I feel like a death is dramatic enough on its own.

"You know . . . *tooooo-gether,*" she says, and I think for a mortifying minute that she's about to do the international finger gesture for sex with her hands, passing a finger through a hole made by her thumb and first finger on the opposite hand.

And then she actually does it.

DI Wallace and DI Collins stare at her for a few seconds before DI Collins starts copying her action, eyebrow raised inquisitively.

"What is . . . ?" DI Wallace joins in, so now we have three people doing the international finger gesture for sex while Scott and I sit completely perplexed.

"FUCKING!" Annie finally says, exasperated, as the two detectives immediately put their hands down and look like they want the floor to swallow them up. DI Wallace's cheeks flush so red I think he might need some ice, and DI Collins looks less embarrassed but certainly like he might burst into hysterics at any point.

"Thanks, Annie, that's really useful," DI Collins says over DI Wallace's coughing and spluttering as he tries to regain his composure. He looks down at his notebook intently, clearly trying to be anywhere but here.

"Anyway, we don't think that we need a motive at this stage. It's too early to tell, but it looks to us like an accident. A tragic one, but an accident nonetheless," DI Wallace finally says dismissively, clasping his hands together to demonstrate that he's closed and solved the case and that's that.

"Sorry, an accident how?" Annie asks, leaning so far forward I start to wonder if she's about to turn the ring light on him.

"Misadventure. Clearly she was messing around in the study, she was fooling around with one of these stemmed shot glasses." DI Wallace picks up one of the menstrual cups on Mrs. Stevens's desk between thumb and forefinger to demonstrate. "Maybe she'd taken a shot and then put it stem side in her mouth for some reason. Either way, she couldn't get it out."

"Um, what?" Annie's looking at him in disbelief while I try and work out how any of that's even possible. "What shot glass? It's a menstrual cup."

"A what?" DI Wallace looks pissed off that anyone would question his authority, and he's ready to dismiss it right off the bat, still holding the menstrual cup like a shot glass.

The three of us stare at the detectives in shock.

"Just to clarify for us again, sorry," DI Collins says, offering far more interest in Annie's information. "What is a menstrual cup?"

"So, this"—Annie grabs one of the menstrual cups from the V-Lyte box—"is used to collect the blood from a period. It gets inserted into the vagina and collects the blood, and you just clean it out every day. It's an eco-friendlier way for us to stem our monthly flows."

I watch as DI Wallace lowers the cup from his face and places it hastily onto the desk in front of him, his face a paler shade than before.

"They're manufactured by V-Lyte, the company founded

by Heather's dad, before he died," Annie continues. "And now taken over by Heather's mum, Mary, since he passed away last year." Annie's now looking at them as if they're silly for not knowing the history of everyone in the village.

I note that Scott doesn't even flinch during this explanation. DI Wallace on the other hand is rendered speechless by Annie's biology lesson, while DI Collins gathers himself together, still coughing his throat clear.

"Right, thank you for that, Annie; that's good to know," DI Collins says. "Gosh, you're very knowledgeable, aren't you?"

Annie's basking in DI Collins's flattery of her only lasts so long before she remembers what her original point was.

"Why would she have that in her mouth voluntarily?" Annie asks as DI Wallace rallies himself. His face gets redder and redder.

"As I've said, it's really too soon to be speculating, but I will say this"—Annie opens her mouth to butt in, but DI Wallace continues, his voice getting louder—"in all my forty years of service on the force, there has never been foul play in Barbourough, and I'll eat my hat if I see it. It's most likely to me that she simply accidentally choked. But as I have said, numerous times, there is nothing to be gained from guessing or 'playing' detective."

At the words "playing detective," I almost feel Annie's rage bubble up next to me. She's radiating heat like a campfire. DI Wallace is so red now that I can also feel the embarrassment coming off him. The two of them are boiling pots ready to explode. I'm trying to work out which one of them's going to pop first. Scott and I both silently look between the two of them.

"How is that the only possible explanation?" Annie brings

her hand to her chin as if contemplating calmly when I know she's really just holding in the anger. "How is that *even* an explanation? No one just chokes on a menstrual cup; someone has to hold it in place. She would have just taken it out of her mouth. It was already sticking out!"

DI Wallace's face wrinkles in an impressive frown. "I don't know what you're insinuating, but at this stage, there's no other way of looking at it. She was alone, she found one of the MANY . . . erm . . . products in this house, she was experimenting with it or whatever you young folk do these days, and it was an experiment that went wrong. It's far too early to be speculating and causing hysteria."

Annie's raging next to me—the word "hysteria" when aimed at a woman will never fail to provoke anger—and I'm just in complete disbelief that this is their solution. Scott shuffles awkwardly in the seat while I sit completely still, paralyzed with fear at what Annie might do to DI Wallace after his mention of hysteria.

"Anyway, we'll go back, report the findings, there'll be an inquest eventually and then we can release the body and that's that. All done and dusted." DI Wallace wipes off his hands.

"But people had motive! Selena was trolling Heather. She'd set up an account pretending to be Heather's dead dad. She was sleeping with Heather's boyfriend. This is no accident! Are you not even going to ask people where they were at the time of death?" Annie's voice is getting more and more high-pitched the more she talks, and I rest my hand on her knee to stop her. I know she's got her suspicions, but she could really get Heather arrested if she carries on like this, not to mention herself if she keeps arguing with the actual police.

"People always try and do this; they always want things to be more exciting than they are. I'm sorry to break it to you, but this is an open-and-shut case. We've reviewed the evidence already," DI Wallace says while DI Collins sits awkwardly next to him, unable to get a word in over his superior.

"Absolute nonsense," Annie says, clambering over Scott, using him like a jungle gym to get out of the love seat swiftly and dramatically before marching out of the room to the dismay of the two officers.

The four of us are left sitting in complete silence, awkwardly staring at each other across the table.

"You can go," DI Wallace eventually says.

"We'll be in touch if we have any further questions. Thank you for all your help, we really appreciate it," DI Collins says kindly, clearly trying to make up for the rage caused by his colleague.

"Oh, right, yeah, thanks, sorry about . . . yes, thanks, bye," I say as if I've anything to thank them for.

Scott and I stand up quietly, and for some involuntary reason, I do a small bob to the officers before we head out in the direction Annie went. The two of us have to run to catch up with her because she's walking so fast; it's like the angry pissing all over again.

"Annie, they might be right. We don't know. It's like he said, it's just too early to tell. They'll do all the tests and stuff and there'll be an inquest, they'll find something if it's there, but they just don't think it is. This is, after all, Barbourough," I try and reason, not entirely sure that I believe it myself at this point, when she stops abruptly and turns to me.

"Why would she put a menstrual cup in her mouth?!" Annie fumes.

"She has a point," Scott says.

I feel my vagina flutter slightly at the knowledge that this sexy man understands. Frankly there is nothing sexier to me than a cis man who knows about periods and has at least tried to understand what's going on.

"Okay, fine," I give in, and wave goodbye to the vague notion of innocence and simplicity I was trying to trick myself into. "You might be right."

"You KNOW I'm right," Annie concludes as she marches toward the door and out of this hell house. "Something shady's happened there, whether those guys can be bothered to investigate it or not."

The three of us step out of the front door and into the dark. There's a late-summer breeze, and it's definitely fresher out here but still not cold, even at this time of night/early morning. It's weird to see the ambulance and police cars outside the house, illuminating the farm blue and red with their fruitless flashing lights. Proof that what's happened isn't just inside the house; it's spilled into the outside world.

"It wasn't an accident," Annie whispers in my ear. "And we need to find out who did it before they kill again."

She's being a bit overdramatic with the whole "kill again" bit there. It's not like Heather could realistically cross off every girl that Adam has ever flirted with. If I actually believe she did it. But I agree now, this was no accident—and we have to find out who did it, because Selena Munroe is never leaving the party, and someone knows why.

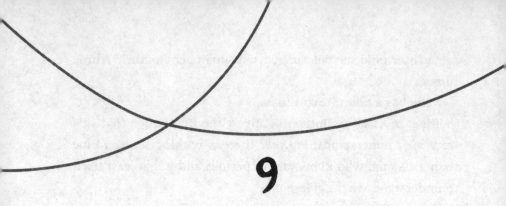

9

When I wake up, the sun's already streaming through the blinds in my bedroom, the birds are singing, it's the perfect late-summer Saturday, except for one thing: Selena Monroe is dead, and I discovered her body in the most embarrassing attempt at a sexual encounter ever.

I roll over to see that Annie's already sitting up and on her phone. We often have sleepovers on the weekends; my parents are used to us staying over at each other's houses. What they're not used to is us coming home after a party where I found our classmate dead.

The mums' army went into overdrive after they'd exchanged phone calls and WhatsApps shortly before we got in, spreading the word about what had happened. By the time we arrived home, it was chaos. Dad pacing, Mum hysterically WhatsApping. Trying to calm her down enough to even let us go to bed took ages.

"Oh, thank god, you're awake. Your mum's already popped her head in three times to drop off tea and ask if we need to see a therapist," Annie says, turning her phone to me. "And Selena is all over the news. A tragic 'accident' apparently."

I look at the headlines reporting on the tragic accident and feel like I'm in a parallel universe.

"Darling! You're awake! Good!" Mum comes sweeping into the room in a silk kimono with a tray of fruit and toast. "Here, you've got to keep your strength up. You've both had a terrible shock."

She sits on the edge of the bed staring at me in an analytical way. I think she's expecting me to start wailing or do something mildly interesting, but instead I pick up my phone. Her attention on us is intense, something Annie's far better at dealing with than I am.

I see there's a message on my phone, but when I see who it's from, I wonder if it's a prank or something.

> **Scott:** Hey, Kerry, it's Scott. Last night was
> pretty wild. Glad you were there to give me the
> lowdown on everyone. Wondered if you felt
> like carrying on your Barbourough induction
> by giving me the grand tour of the village?

In my head, I run through all the rules. You're supposed to leave it a bit before you reply, not seem too excited, be nonchalant, seem busy. I ignore everything that I've ever been told to do, my heart racing as I type.

> **Kerry:** Hey Scott, I'd love that. Meet in an
> hour at the church?

I've broken all the laws of dating, but I just have to get out of the house and away from my mother's constant watchful eye, not to mention Annie's conspiracy theories.

The village is a ghost town this early, and there's a feeling of mourning that stretches from the leaves on the trees to the grass underfoot. A somber cloud seems to cover everything, even with the bright sun. Despite it all, when I see him leaning against the church doors, I feel a lurch in my chest. There's a moment before he sees me where I can take in the sun hitting his brown hair, the battered creases of his leather jacket, a David Bowie T-shirt, and black jeans with worn Converse. To me he looks so perfect he's almost holy. He smiles and waves, heading over, and for a moment, I have to stop myself looking behind me.

He's definitely here for me.

"Hey," he says when he reaches me.

"Hey," I say back.

I don't know whether we should hug, and there's an awkward moment where I wonder if I've imagined him slightly inclining toward me, but after last night, I'm not risking leaning in to fall over again. Instead, the two of us fall into step beside each other.

"There's a café just across the grass there, next to the bookshop." I point over to the small village green.

In the summer, it plays host to the occasional soccer or Frisbee game. Its main purpose is for things like the fairs and music competitions, and in winter, caroling takes place there next to a huge Christmas tree.

"Mrs. Thomas at the café will make an egg-and-cheese, an English breakfast tea, instant hot chocolate, or your average coffee. You can have it black or with milk, but she'll throw you out if you ask for anything more complex than that. She's very much of the you'll-get-what-you're-given school of thought," I warn him, and he nods.

"Good to know. I was about to ask for an oat milk latte, made to exactly ninety-five degrees," he says, and it takes me a moment to realize he's joking—it's only when I see the dimples appear that I feel in on the joke.

We walk across the green, watching the bees pollinate flowers. It's hard for me to process that nature and life carry on despite the death of Selena Munroe.

"Last night was pretty wild, huh?" Scott says. "I can't imagine how weird it must be for you just to have lost someone like that."

"It's definitely weird," I say. "But we weren't exactly close to Selena. She didn't really like Annie and me, to be honest. I guess you could say we don't exactly fit in with Heather and Les Populaires."

"Le what?" Scott asks.

"That's what Heather and all her friends call themselves, Les Populaires," I say, and Scott starts giggling.

"I don't even think that's a correct French translation. So ridiculous." He laughs, and when I start laughing, too, he takes my hand, stopping my heart. "To be honest, none of them seem that interesting to me. I knew I wanted to talk to you the moment you were explaining what you did over the summer in homeroom."

I feel my hand become clammy, doing a double take at his

words. He WANTED to talk to me. Me specifically? And now that he's talking to me I don't seem to be capable of words. I feel his hand in mine, our fingers laced together, and I run over his words in my head. All I keep thinking is "Don't fuck this up, Kerry." But I'm going to have to make a confession.

"I have something I need to tell you," I say, savoring the feeling of his fingers between mine, nervous that any minute now that could all be over.

"Sounds serious," Scott says, and turns to look at me, still holding my hand. I don't know why I feel like I have to unburden myself of this secret, maybe because I don't want him liking a fake version of me.

"*The Shining.*" I gulp. "I couldn't finish it. I had to stop reading it. It was too scary, too dark. It made me anxious and stressed and scared. I'm sorry I lied. I couldn't even watch the trailer for the film, let alone the actual film. I'm really more of an Agatha Christie kind of person. I'm sorry. I bet you don't find me quite so interesting anymore."

And then Scott starts laughing. He looks at me, his eyes crinkled, dimple dents accenting his chuckles. He grabs my other hand, holding both of them while a rogue wave of hair flops over his forehead.

"Actually, if anything, it makes me like you more," he says, smiling at me, his eyes connecting with mine. He lets go of my right hand, and I feel bereft until he reaches up, rubbing the soft pad of his right thumb against my cheek. I reach up, boldly brushing the lock of hair from his eyes, and he takes my hand in his, kissing my palm. Shivers shoot up my spine and down my arms and legs. I'd normally want to run from this situation, the attention, and the vulnerability, and in daylight no less. He leans down and kisses my cheek so gently it's as if his lips barely graze it, his fingers lightly rubbing my bottom lip for a second before he reaches down again. Our lips connect, and I forget everything. How scary it is to open myself up to him, how embarrassed I was last night, everything. If this were Regency times, my loins would be alight with lust right now.

We pull away and I expect to feel embarrassed, but I don't. Instead, I'm staring into his eyes, the two of us smiling at each other. He wraps his arms around me, and I rest my head on the shoulder of his leather jacket. Inhaling the smell of him. It's definitely better than Adam Devers.

"Maybe it's time for that bad coffee and sandwich you promised me," Scott says, pulling away and pointing toward the coffee hut.

"We've got some important sights to show you today, I guess," I say.

My phone beeps in my pocket. When I look down, I see it's Annie.

> **Annie:** It's Heather, it has to have been.
> And we're going to prove it.

> **Annie:** Hellooo? Earth to Kerry? How long
> are you going to be with Scott? I can't
> believe you've left me when there's an
> actual crime to investigate, finally!

"Isn't that one of Heather's friends?" Scott asks. He points down the green, distracting me from Annie's constant questions with one of his own.

"Yeah, that's Audrey," I say, looking over to where Audrey, in sunglasses and a baseball cap, waits outside Selena's house looking decidedly on edge. "I wonder what she's doing at Selena's place."

"Paying her respects, I guess?" Scott offers.

But why would she be on her own? And where's Colin?

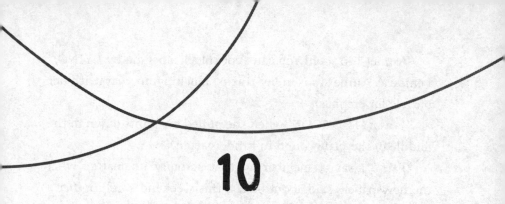

10

I can't believe it's Monday already and two whole days have passed since Selena Munroe died. But knowing that she won't be there when we get to school this morning is even weirder.

"I guess at least I won't get coffee thrown at my tits today," Annie says, as the two of us cycle toward school.

If it weren't for the fact that she was so insistent about trying to get the police to see it as a murder rather than an accident, and that *everyone* thinks Heather did it, I would think that Annie was actually the one that murdered Selena.

"I can't believe you're getting it on with the hottest guy in school," Annie squeals, getting off her bike when we reach the gates. She's just about forgiven me for being completely MIA on Saturday when I was with Scott, especially since I told her all about it in excruciating detail. I join her in getting off my bike, and the two of us wheel our bikes along next to us, walking through the gates.

"It's good to know Selena Munroe didn't completely cock-block you."

"Annie! Too soon! You can't cockblock a person by DYING," I chide as Annie stops in her tracks, blocking my way with her bicycle for emphasis.

"Was it 'TOO SOON' when she pulled my pants down in the middle of the playground in kindergarten?"

"Fair," I say, remembering that actually no matter what the newspapers said about Selena this weekend—calling her a loved student, classmate, friend, and daughter—she spent most of her sixteen years finding ways to make other people miserable. Which I guess would make the suspect list pretty long, if it weren't for the fact that the person she wronged the most was her best friend.

"Anyway, I thought you said Adam Devers was the hottest guy in school?" I ask.

"Adam Devers is a cheating scumbag. He's kind of become less sexy to me now, you know?"

"Annie! Have your morals finally made a dent in your horniness?"

"Maybe, I mean Adam's just so obviously hot, whereas Scott's more interesting. A mysterious stranger, leather jacket, bad-boy vibes . . . Oh my god, hottie dead ahead." Annie nods toward the band guys all dressed in black leather jackets leaning by the bike racks. I almost don't notice Scott because he fits in so well with them.

"Hey," he calls. Despite knowing he's there, his voice kind of startles me, and I wheel my bike slightly into the path of Annie's tiny Paw Patroller.

"Hey," I try to say, but it seems to come out as mostly air, the only bit of it audible is the "ey" and I appear to have done a jolly little wave with that, too.

"Hey, Scott!" Annie shouts over to him, loud enough to make the entire school turn around, as if she doesn't quite stand out enough with the bike situation.

My vagina's doing acrobatics, remembering our kiss on Saturday. It's amazing how quickly that kiss has eclipsed everything bad that happened on Friday for me. Amazing and bad. Someone died, and all I'm thinking about is kissing boys. I'm an awful person. Terrible.

As much as Annie tried to distract me with her chats of DNA and crime scenes, and articles on asphyxiation, I spent the whole weekend with an underlying feeling of deep shame. At least today we're on the same page. And that page is all about Scott.

"HOT," Annie mouths to me as we reach the racks, and she leans down to chain her bike. There's no way that he won't have seen that. Immediately my faux sense of pride and decorum take a nosedive into a kiddie pool of shame, and in my fluster, I drop my bike lock on the ground. I go to pick it up, but Scott's already there, bending down to get it. My knight in shining Jeff Buckley hoodie. Our noses meet, and we have a prolonged moment of eye contact, before Annie interrupts with a pointed cough.

"Oh god, thanks, sorry," I say, not sure why everything I say has to be punctuated by an apology.

As I take my bike lock from him and he helps me chain it, our hands brush past each other, and I feel a buzzing in my skin where it makes contact. It feels like just the two of us for a moment, our eyes meeting, the soft fabric of his hoodie touching my arm.

"Uh-oh." Annie breaks the spell again as Heather's car

comes around the corner going much slower than usual. A quiet descends over the parking lot.

There's no Lizzo playing, no screaming and laughing out of the windows, and no Selena throwing coffee over us. The whole school stops what they're doing and watches the car as it rolls slowly into the parking lot.

As the Jeep grinds to a sensible halt, the Elton John song "Candle in the Wind" starts streaming out of the windows, and the doors open slowly under the watchful eye of all of Barbourough High. Colin emerges first, wearing black pants, a black turtleneck, and black Ray-Bans. He has his head down as he helps Audrey come out next to him. She slips down from the Jeep, slowly and with purpose. Her hair is loose; she's wearing a black dress that stops at the knee, with black suede boots.

Colin opens the front passenger door, and the last member of the party joins them. At first, we can only see Heather's foot in some kind of lacy black heeled shoe, red-nail-polished toes poking out of the tips. Then comes the rest of her, a netty mid-length black dress with something white written on the front, too screwed up for anyone to read, long red nails, hair down the same as Audrey, and huge black Chanel sunglasses covering her face.

As Heather brushes her dress down, the white letters printed on the front become legible, and the words "SHE'S DEAD" scream from her front in block capitals. Gasps pepper the parking lot as everyone reads it at the same moment.

They're in mourning, and they've made it very Prada.

"I was going to say I didn't think she'd be in today, but now I see *why* she's in," Annie says.

"NEVER miss an opportunity to make an entrance," I say, but I feel like it's more than that. She's making a point. She knows everyone thinks she did it, so she's gone OTT to try and prove she didn't.

"I . . . This is a lot," I hear Scott mutter from where he's standing next to me.

"Buckle up. They love drama," Annie says.

Audrey and Colin form a kind of protective barrier around Heather, the whole school silently staring, as the three of them walk up the steps. Heather puts her hand around her face, cupping it slightly, as if shielding herself from a braying mob of journalists and paparazzi. There are, however, absolutely no journalists or paparazzi in the school parking lot.

"I wonder how long it took them to plan those outfits," Annie says.

"I don't think mourning chic is something you plan; I think it just comes naturally," I say, staring down at our own jeans-and-brightly-colored-T-shirt combos.

"Sure, sure." Annie nods.

As they walk up the steps to school with everyone staring at them, I do start to feel a pang of sympathy for Heather again. Just a small one, but a pang nonetheless. She *has* lost her best friend and sort of her boyfriend also, after all.

"Heather's gone for sunglasses that cover her face so we can't see if it's tearstained or not. All look very sad, but we can't know for sure what's *really* going on in their heads—" Who on earth is Annie talking to?

I turn to see Annie speaking into a small plastic box, and I'm thankful that Scott's been distracted by some guy arriving with his new guitar.

93

"Um, I know I'm going to regret asking, but what exactly is that that you're commentating into?" I ask quietly.

"A Dictaphone," she says, like I should know what one of those is.

"I'm sorry, a what?" All I heard was dick.

"Look, okay, I don't want to have everything on my phone in case someone gets wind of the investigation and hacks it, so I've started recording my thoughts on here. It records voice notes like a phone, but it can't be hacked."

"Okay, having a totally normal one this morning, then," I say.

"NOTHING about this week is going to be normal," Annie says. "For one thing, I can wear a skirt again without fear of my panties being pulled down, and I thought I'd have to leave the village before I could do that."

"Annie, seriously, someone *died*," I whisper hurriedly.

"I know, and now I'm going to find out who did it." Annie's eyes light up, making her look so intense it verges on rabid. "A first murder in Barbourough. And I'm going to uncover the murderer!"

"To have them face the consequences or to shake their hand?" I ask, my stomach flip-flopping as I realize that Scott's coming back over to us.

"So you think Heather did it?" he asks, and I feel like begging him not to encourage her.

"You mean the woman who—just moments before Selena was found dead—found out that she was hooking up with her boyfriend and trolling her pretending to be her dead dad? Yeah, shockingly she is still my main suspect," Annie says. A smile spreads across Scott's face, his little dimples popping like he's amused by her detective skills. It almost makes me jealous. Like, should I start detecting?

"Not to mention," Annie plows onward, "the way she rushed over to Selena's body, covering it in DNA!"

"I don't think she knew what she was doing; she was in shock," I reason.

"She looks pretty dark today, though. That outfit?" he says.

"Oh, puhllleaase." Annie throws her hands up as if Scott's a fool. "When she was six, she pretended to be sad about her parakeet dying so that she could get an addition on her already-life-size Barbie Dreamhouse. She *knows* how to fake and manipulate."

She has a point about that, actually. I remember it well, a true early indication of manipulative, serial-killer behavior.

"What, so you think she's just pretending to grieve her best friend?" Scott asks, as we all walk toward school.

"SHHH!" Annie silences him, looking around her shiftily. And then, in a stage whisper, Annie continues, "Bingo, she didn't like Selena playing with her dolls . . . so she . . ." She makes a slicing gesture across her neck.

"Oh, wow! And calling Adam a 'doll,' too? I think equality just got set back a few thousand years. It works both ways, you know," I say, but this is exactly what I've been thinking all weekend, that and that we're seriously underqualified to be even thinking about investigating this. No matter how little those detectives knew about periods.

"Okay, well . . . you might have a point, but I'm STILL RIGHT. And Adam's a slut," Annie shouts back at me and Scott as we enter the deadly silence of the school corridor, and everyone turns to look at us with disapproval. Which is what Annie deserves for calling anyone a slut, I guess.

It's still early, but somehow the whole corridor's become a kind of chapel already. There are fake plastic candles on the floor leading up to a sea of flowers, messages, and teddy bears surrounding Selena's locker. Everyone's still and silent. People that have never even spoken to Selena before clutch tissues and weep performatively into them while Heather, Audrey, and Colin kneel on the ground in front of the shrine, their heads bowed.

"Oh, great, how am I supposed to get my biology textbook now?" Annie whispers to me.

Principal Styles stands behind the big formal lectern in the auditorium, her voice booming around the deadly silent room. "As teachers, we strive to do everything we can to protect our students, and what happened this weekend was a tragic accident that has shaken this school to its very core."

People are still clutching tissues to their faces, sniffing along with everything she's saying. As I look around the room, I can just see the people that Selena bullied or mocked. These people that she made feel so small are now mourning her passing. I just don't get it. Unless they did it and they're covering up with some fake grief? Maybe she's upset so many people that it was more than just Heather who snapped? After all, everyone was at that party. Oh god, it's happened; Annie's fully sucked me into this whole thing. I'm beginning to think like her.

I look at Annie and see that she's already jotting in a

notebook who's crying an extra amount and the things that Selena did to them.

TERI: Crying with snot—Selena tripped them over and they lost three teeth freshman year. Location at time of murder: in the kitchen drinking something unidentifiable. Probably crying because their stomach will never be the same again after whatever they drank.

PAULA: Delicate weeps—Selena put chewing gum in her hair in middle school. Location at time of murder: frenching Simon the school pyromaniac. Interestingly they're sitting together now. Wonder if she'll buy him kindling for Valentine's Day.

TOM: Attempt at a distraught look but just looks strained. Note: Watch his fiber intake later; he may in fact just be constipated. Rumor is that Selena gave him a hand job last year and told everyone he had a small dick. I believe what actually happened was that Selena asked him out and he declined, so she spread the rumor. I saw it happen with my own eyes. Location at time of murder: in the garden staring broodily into the middle distance, probably thinking about the meaning of life.

Even the teachers are doing a good job of looking sad despite the fact that she threatened to get some of them fired on more than one occasion. They're all lined up behind Principal Styles as she speaks. Some of them are staring ahead looking sad and serious; some of them have their heads bowed. Even Mr. C's wiped his usually cocky grin off his smug face.

"A crime of passion over Adam Devers wouldn't be the most unimaginable thing to happen," Annie whispers in my ear. "After all, up until Friday when we learned what a gross douche he is, *I* would have probably committed a crime of passion for him. Amazing how quickly someone becomes unattractive when you realize what a gigantic dick they are."

I nod in agreement.

We're cut off by Heather turning and staring at us from under a black wedding-style veil that has been added to her mourning-chic repertoire. I'm no mind reader, but I think she might have heard our conversation, and with Heather as Annie's top suspect, it's really not her attention that I want right now.

The two of us look down at our feet and try to tune back in to what Principal Styles is saying. I hope Scott didn't hear, but to be fair, he's way at the other end of the row with some of the guys from his band. Apparently I can legit call it his band now because he did a tryout yesterday and he's in. Here less than a week and already in the coolest band in the county.

Mrs. Joy, the school counselor, gets up to join Principal Styles behind the lectern.

"As we don't know when the family might be able to hold a funeral due to the ongoing investigation, there will be a memorial service tomorrow afternoon at St. Barnabas, to honor Selena's memory. All juniors will be given the afternoon off to attend. It will be a chance for you to express your feelings and memories about Selena. An important part of the grieving process," Mrs. Joy says.

"All the memories of the coffees she threw over us and the time she pushed me in the pond at preschool," Annie whispers, rolling her eyes.

This combined with the shrine that already stretches halfway along the corridor makes it feel like the school's setting up some kind of hero worship for Selena, when she wasn't even kind to her best friend.

"Your homeroom teachers and Mrs. Joy are also here to help. We're always available to talk through any issues or feelings that you might be experiencing. We're here for all of you during this terrible time, and we'll get through it together," Principal Styles finishes, nodding at Mrs. Joy next to her.

Usually everyone would be standing up to leave before Principal Styles had even got the last word out, but today everyone moves slower. There's less eagerness in the air of a school in mourning.

Except Annie. She springs out of her seat, scanning the crowd and furiously making more notes. And for once, I'm almost glad to be roped into her investigation. Something weird is happening here.

11

Chatter about Heather and her possible role in
Selena's death sweeps across the common room in delicate whispers. Even the sound of Gayle blaring across the room can't hide
the stares and whispers as she sits in the corner with Audrey
and Colin, holding a tissue up to her face. She's stopped crying
quite some time ago by the looks of things. Now she's just hiding
behind the tissue, and who could blame her. Everyone thinks
she did it. Even me if I'm really being honest with myself.

At first, I think I'm imagining it when I see Heather waving
in our direction, but then Annie clutches my arm in a way that
lets me know it's really happening. The two of us look at each
other and then back at Heather, crooking her finger at us like
the old woman in *Snow White*, beckoning us to come and eat
her poisoned apple.

"Is she asking us to go over there?" Annie asks out of
the corner of her mouth while making full eye contact with
Heather.

"I think so, yeah, probably because you've been staring at
her like she's a tiger in a zoo all morning?" I suggest.

"What do we do?" Annie gulps. "What if she IS the murderer?"

"I think we have to go over there. I don't think she's going to murder us in the common room. Also, isn't this what you wanted? To be part of the popular crew?" I ask while the two of us gather our stuff and Annie smooths down her jeans delicately, as if she's about to ask someone to dance.

"Oh my god, shut up, no," she says, looking ready to sprint over there.

I try not to be offended (am I not enough for her?) at her eagerness to join the popular crew despite the fact that from what we know about them so far, they are at least adulterers and maybe murderers. We head across the room, and I'm not feeling any of this. I look over at Scott with his band, all of them sitting talking about lovely wholesome music, and not about to make BFFs with a possible killer.

"Come, sit," Heather says, patting the seat next to her, smiling weakly. Annie races for it immediately, seeming to have forgotten that Heather is apparently her main suspect.

Both of us sit down, although one of us is more cautious than the other (me—because I still have my senses). I worry this might be some kind of Last Supper situation. Annie's finally getting the popularity she craves, only for us to be led to our deaths. Not an unreasonable fear considering what's happened lately.

"I just wanted to say thank you for everything on Friday. For finding out about Adam and Selena, and the messages, and for telling me right away. I knew I could depend on the two of you," Heather says, and I wonder what gives because she honestly didn't seem that grateful on Friday.

"That's okay. It's girl code!" Annie says.

She's so excited she's seconds away from sticking two fingers up and shouting "Girl power" and probably getting us kicked out of the common room and junior class forever for being total dweebs.

"No worries," I whisper, because Heather looks at me like I have to say something.

"We've never really hung out before, have we? Why is that, do you think?" Heather asks.

I nearly choke on my own indignation.

Oh, I don't know, Heather, maybe because your best friend kept throwing coffee on us? Or because you've been permanently attached to Adam's face for the last five to six years? *Or* because you even said yourself that you didn't want us at your party unless we'd solved your troll issue?

"I don't know," Annie says, feigning an ignorance that we both know simply does not exist.

"Well, you're cool," Heather says, and it's like she's knighting us. "You had my back, and you were honest with me. You told me what was going on. So many people are scared of me; they'd never dare tell me something like you did." I can't help but feel like this is a weird warning. "You can sit with us now." She finishes with a smile, and Annie's face immediately lights up in gratitude and joy.

I, however, have two thoughts:

What does she want?

Why is she being nice to us?

"Audrey, why don't you and Colin get our new friends some water," Heather announces suddenly, as if the two of them weren't already shocked at her inviting us to join them. I'm about to tell Heather I'm not even thirsty, seeing the furious expressions of Audrey and Colin, but Heather raises her eyebrow, with a warning look. "Now."

I don't understand what's going on, how they've both been dismissed but we've been invited over, and I can see Annie's as puzzled as they are.

Once they're gone, Heather folds her hands in her lap, shooting her eyes downward like the very picture of propriety.

"I wasn't born yesterday; I can hear what everyone's saying about me. Everyone thinks I killed Selena after my little outburst on Friday." She pauses for dramatic effect, and I can almost hear Annie's panicked thoughts as she shuffles next to me.

"Oh, no, I'm sure no one thinks that," Annie lies quickly, having literally said she thought that mere minutes ago.

"Like I said, I wasn't born yesterday." Heather stares pointedly at me, and I wonder if she can actually hear thoughts. "Anyway, you both worked out Selena was the troll on Friday so easily. I need you to figure out what happened to her for me. Clear my name. The police may know I didn't do it, but no one else seems to believe it."

It's not a question for Heather about whether or not we'll do this. She's assumed we will, and she probably hasn't even imagined an alternative universe where we dare to say no.

"Of course," Annie says, beaming inappropriately. I can see the excitement of getting what she's always wanted and a legitimate reason to investigate positively boiling over in her head.

"Great, don't tell anyone I asked, obviously," she whispers hurriedly as Colin and Audrey come stalking back across the common room looking furious, two glasses of water in their hands. "Trust no one."

I'm less thrilled about all this than Annie. Private investigators usually get paid actual money, and yet Heather's somehow treating us like her personal private investigators and the only thing we're getting in return is . . . being allowed to hang out with her?

I think again how sad it is that Heather doesn't even trust her friends, and that this is their version of friendship. I could trust Annie with any- and everything, and these guys can't seem to trust each other with their lives.

Before Colin and Audrey reach us, Heather's got her hankie back over her face and she's crying tears that don't seem visible to the naked eye. They immediately rush to rub her shoulders and offer words of consolation, but it all feels performative, as seconds before I saw Colin holding a middle finger up in Heather's direction. She ramps up the emotion as people start to turn and stare. She's getting the attention of everyone in here, making her point to those that doubt her. It's a good performance, and we can see people's faces changing; she's starting to get more sympathy. Annie's already taking her new role very seriously, eyeing everyone's reactions with suspicion, but I'm shuffling awkwardly in my seat.

I see Scott join the rest of the room in looking over at us. His eyebrow lifts in surprise to see we're sitting with Heather in the first place. He's known us four days, and he can probably already tell this is down to Annie's scheming. I give him a small wave, and he gives me one back, sending the butterflies wild again.

"Poor thing, she was like this all weekend," Audrey whispers, grabbing my attention back from Scott. She's stroking

Heather's hair, and I catch Annie's eye because I've told her about seeing Audrey on Saturday and how shifty she looked, so she can't have been with her *all* weekend.

"I just wish that Heather and I had been there and been able to save Selena. Instead, I was just sitting outside the bathroom, while Heather locked herself in there and cried her eyes out," Audrey says.

"It's a real double-edged sword," Colin says wisely. "If it wasn't for what she did to Heather, then they would have all been together. No doubt about it. I guess actions have consequences, and in Selena's case, it was the ultimate consequence." The thing is, they didn't even know the whole story. They only know about the cheating, not the trolling as well.

I think back to Annie dancing on the kitchen counter with just Colin, no Audrey in sight. I guess that's where she was, with Heather. She has an alibi. Albeit a very convenient one, for both of them.

I look at Annie, shuffling in her pockets and see the corner of the Dictaphone poking out. Of course. She's recording all of this because she's Annie.

"Absolutely none of it is helped by that dickhead trying to send flowers every five seconds, though," Colin chimes, nodding over at Adam, who certainly doesn't look like he spent the weekend begging for forgiveness as he stares at the captain of the volleyball team's ass.

"He sent flowers?" Annie asks.

Colin nods soberly. "Three times on Saturday and twice on Sunday. Both days Heather rejected the deliveries."

I watch as Adam heads off after the volleyball captain he

was recently perving on and follows her into the study area. There I see them, flirting as she twirls her hair around her finger and he touches her arm.

I check to see that Annie's noticed it, too, but of course she's already looking over. It doesn't look as if Heather's noticed because she's still concerned with weeping loudly into her tissue.

"None of it makes sense," Colin says sadly as Audrey shakes her head alongside him. "That Selena can be here one minute and then gone. It doesn't seem fair that a person can just have an accident and then be dead like that."

So, they believe it's an accident? Literally no one else in this room does, but her best friends do. Fishy. I can see Annie itching to talk to me about it all. Wanting to discuss the huge amount of information that we've learned in the last five minutes.

"Such a terrible accident." Annie shakes her head while somehow simultaneously giving me a side-eye. It's a miracle it doesn't make her dizzy.

"And look at him over there." Audrey points her finger to where Adam's emerging from his little chat in the study room with the volleyball captain. "Behaving as if nothing's happening now, when Selena's dead. Doesn't he even care?"

"Urgh, gross. He doesn't deserve her," Colin says, shooting a filthy look over to Adam and rubbing Heather's back.

Heather doesn't look up, but Colin looks so protective over her right now, when two minutes ago he was giving her the finger behind her back. Adam cheats on her and they immediately band together against him. But they can talk behind each other's backs all the time? What are the rules in their weird little friendship group? I wonder if Selena had survived whether they would have taken sides in the cheating scandal.

"I have to go." Heather stands up, moving the tissue from her dry face. "I'm supposed to be going to see Mrs. Joy. She told my parents I need to go in and see her so they know I'm coping okay or something."

She rolls her eyes as she stands up, smoothing down her dress, the words "She's Dead" unraveling, bold and unflinching, in case anyone could forget what happened over the weekend.

"So sad," Audrey and Colin say in unison to each other as she leaves.

For a moment, we watch her go, tottering in her heels.

But once she's rounded the corner, Colin leans toward his sister conspiratorially.

"We've tried our best this weekend, but how do you recover from that? How does someone get over what she's been through? I've just never seen anything like it, not even on TV," Colin says mournfully to Audrey as Annie and I sit next to them like spare parts. "I just wish Selena were still here so she could see what she's done to her."

"At least she's wearing Prada shoes, though. If you're going to cry, cry in Prada, right?" Annie says. Audrey and Colin turn to her, shocked, as if they'd completely forgotten we were here. Their shock turns to disgust as they assess us, but I'm just impressed that Annie could even tell what brand they were.

"They were Dior," Audrey says, collecting her things as the bell goes. Her and Colin stand up and walk to class without even so much as a look back to Annie and me.

We watch them go. This has to be the first time that Annie hasn't jumped up as soon as the bell rings and run straight to homeroom. She waits until they're out of earshot before slinking over onto the seat next to me.

"What do you think?" Annie whispers. "It CANNOT be Heather now, right? Or else why would she have got us to investigate?"

"To cover her tracks?" I suggest because surely it's obvious. "Make it look like she's trying to find the killer to distract from the fact that *she's* the killer? But she does have an alibi now, I guess. We didn't know that before."

I take a second to think about what I've just said, to really listen to myself, and I'm disappointed. Somehow Annie's managed to get me into this investigation with her.

"Interesting," Annie says, cocking her head and raising an eyebrow at me. She knows she's cracked me. I'm fully invested in this investigation.

"Don't look at me like that..." I say, my voice stern.

"And so the student appears to have become the master. . . . Anyway, if we add the fact that Heather was in the bathroom crying when Selena died to her engaging us to investigate, that leads us to suspect number two—Adam. Has to have been," Annie says, ignoring my pleas. "Also, I should have seen it before, everyone knows the first suspect's the red herring."

The two of us get up and head to homeroom. I look ahead at Adam, walking down the corridor, a man who previously I would have paid money to sniff, who now just falls incredibly flat to me. He walks past Selena's memorial without even so much as a second glance.

"Fishy behavior if ever I saw it," Annie whispers in my ear. "He was having an affair with her; he wanted to keep quiet. You mark my words: He's suspect numero duo."

I follow her, assuming that we're still going to homeroom like everyone else, but instead she walks straight past homeroom, following Adam as he keeps going down the corridor.

"Annie, where are you going? This is the wrong way!" I say urgently, but I'm too late; Annie follows Adam into the boys' locker room. "What are you doing?" I hiss, following her in.

"SHH!! He'll hear you!" Annie hisses back at me, squashing her back against the lockers as if she's trying to camouflage herself in them and peering around them to get a better look at Adam. "Get back!" she demands when I try to join her.

"What are we doing?" I whisper again.

"Observing him!" she replies as if I'm a complete fool.

"Okay, but like, we can't do this all afternoon because I have biology and you have math," I say, but Annie hushes me. Don't get me wrong: in the before times, I would have loved nothing more than an entire afternoon observing Adam. But not so much now.

We silently watch Adam slapping the back of a football teammate and commenting on the size of someone's boobs and how he'd love to shove his face in them, and I consider once more what a total douchebag he is. The two of us remain, squashed as tightly as possible behind the block of lockers, our backs jammed against locks, as we try to stay as still as possible so as not to be seen by Adam walking across the other side of the locker room.

My phone beeps and vibrates in my hand, and I almost gasp with joy when I see it's from Scott.

Scott: What u up to later? Wanna hang?

"Oh my GOD, do you want us to get caught?" Annie whispers as if I should have known that (A) we were going to have a stakeout in plain sight in the BOYS' locker room, and (B) Scott was going to text me. She leans over my shoulder to read. "Also, while I obvs *adore* this new love interest for you, we're investigating tonight. Murder investigations before make-outs."

I stare at her while reluctantly writing my reply to Scott because apparently I can't have anything nice. Ahead, Adam's just stopped at another bank of lockers and opened one, which I presume is his, a completely normal act.

"Get down!" Annie hisses as Adam closes his locker, a gym bag in hand. He turns to come back this way. The two of us crouch on the floor for absolutely no reason. If anything, this movement is going to draw more attention to us than already being in the locker room in the first place.

"Could I get to my locker, please?" A boy in uniform with two friends, presumably the owner of the locker with its lock currently digging into my shoulder blade, is looking strangely at us.

"Of course, sorry, just warming it up for you. You're welcome," Annie says, not missing a beat as we stand up and walk away, and out of the boys' locker room.

Outside in the hallway, we shuffle away quickly, both looking over our shoulders, convinced that Adam will have realized that we were watching him and come chasing after us.

"Are you coming to homeroom or just being weird?" Mr. C's voice makes us both jump.

I close my eyes and spin around to face him, right in front of us.

"Coming," Annie says, and I can hear the strain from sounding polite in her voice.

"Would it kill you to add a 'sir' on the end of that?" Mr. C says sweetly. His little smirk coupled with that condescending comment makes me nauseous.

The two of us just stare at him.

"See you in there, then," he says, spotting Adam walking past and falling into step next to him, slapping his back. "Devers, heard you've been a busy boy."

"Guess dicks are drawn to each other," I whisper.

Both our phones beep, and Annie makes the loudest and most high-pitched noise I've ever heard, so intense they could hear it in space. I'm about to ask if she's okay, but when I look at my phone, I can see exactly what's up. It's a WhatsApp notification telling us that we've been added to a new group. It's the group chat for Les Populaires.

"Is it real?" She turns to me and clutches my arm. "Am I really in?"

"It's real," I say.

"And look," Annie says, raising her phone as more notifications immediately appear stating that Adam and Selena have been removed from the group. "They're out, and we're in!"

"Great," I say as my phone starts vibrating itself out of my hand.

If it wasn't helpful for the investigation, I'd have that group muted faster than a rat up a drainpipe in a hurricane. At least if I switch my phone to silent I might not feel quite so bombarded.

12

"Where's he going now?" I ask. The two of us followed Adam out of school as soon as the final bell rang. Now we're watching him from afar walking through the village graveyard, trying to make sure he can't see us.

It's small; only about a hundred people are buried here, and many of the graves are so old that the stones have crumbled and cracked, or as Annie likes to believe, the dead rose and smashed them. A theory that used to scare the shit out of me as a kid, but now I can see it for what it is—someone who got into *Buffy the Vampire Slayer* way too young. The old trees that hang over the graves are still covered in their summer leaves, not yet shedding them for autumn, offering us a little extra protection from being seen, but also unhelpfully occasionally eclipsing Adam and making it harder for us to shadow him.

Annie raided the theater closet during last period, so the disguises that she has insisted on us wearing—a deerstalker hat for her and a cheesy-smelling blond wig for me—probably aren't the most stealth of things, but apparently they're working.

"Oh my god, get down!" she whispers, grabbing my arm and pulling me down behind some gravestones.

"What?" I ask, huddled behind the worn old gravestone among empty beer cans, its inhabitant's name barely visible.

"He's stopped!" Annie hisses, and points above the grave, but when I try and bob up to look, she pushes me back down again despite her head still poking over the stone. "He's typing something on his phone and looking around him. He's got to be meeting someone."

"Another conquest?" I ask.

"Maybe, and if it is, what if they're also in danger?" Annie asks.

"I dunno," I say, trying to add some reality to the situation from my blond-wigged squat position. "If he killed Selena because he was worried the two of them were going to be found out and it would ruin his relationship with Heather, then why would he need to kill anyone now? His relationship with Heather's over."

"What if it was a crime of passion?" Annie asks. "He loved Selena and she wanted to end things and so he killed her because he couldn't bear it?"

"One, she didn't sound like she wanted to end it from where I was sitting in that closet, and two, if that was the case, why wouldn't he just break up with Heather and be with Selena?"

I see Annie's eyes roll back. "Because then BOTH of their popularity would be threatened. Heather would ruin the pair of them," she hisses.

"So, what's he doing now, then?" I ask, having run out of arguments against Adam being a killer.

"He's just standing in the doorway to the church, staring at his phone," Annie says, looking annoyed at the lack of progress. "Hey, I was thinking, do you reckon we should bring back our secret language, for investigative purposes?"

We had a secret language that we invented in middle school. We haven't done it since the summer before freshman year.

"Haey ll'taht yletinifed peek uoy ni htiw s'rehtaeH werc," I whisper back in said secret language, which translates to: "Yeah, that'll definitely keep you in with Heather's crew."

"Okay, rude, Ker. How else am I supposed to tell you what I'm thinking without people knowing? Plus, we're going to keep hanging with Heather and everyone so we know what they're up to at all times. We don't want them to overhear us, obviously. Since they're all suspects."

"Just make notes or something and share them with me later?"

"This is a serious, fast-paced murder investigation," Annie whispers back aggressively, the ears of her deerstalker hat wobbling as she talks. "Where's the urgency in taking notes and sharing them with you later? If we were on the police force, you'd have access to all my important investigative thoughts at all times."

"But we're not on the police force, we're . . ." I say, gesturing around us and spotting Annie's hand in her pocket. "You're recording this on your Dictaphone, aren't you?"

I see Annie's hand rummage in her pocket before hearing my voice played back to me, muffled and quiet. The sound of my own voice promotes a shame spiral because I hate it so much, so I distract myself by stretching out my legs, one after the other. I have always had the flexibility of a ninety-year-old. It's a point of pride for me that I will NEVER be a yoga person, no matter how much my mother tries to convert me.

"Oh shit!" Annie scrambles to turn the Dictaphone off and hunches up really small behind the stone.

"What?" I whisper, watching her eyes shift from side to side.

"He's there!" she mouths, eyes wide, pointing behind her.

"Where are you, man?" The sound of Adam's voice makes me tense all over. Stiff as boards, the two of us stay hunched behind the stones as we hear his footsteps slowly moving away.

I sniff the air. I think the smell of what I initially thought was fox piss may actually be human piss when I see that there's a big damp patch behind this gravestone, alongside all the empty cans of lager. I may very well be squatting in someone's toilet right now, but for the good of the investigation, Annie flutters her hands angrily to make it clear that I cannot move despite the fact I can hear Adam getting farther away. This wig's starting to get super itchy as well, but every time I scratch under it, a plume of dust comes from my head like dandruff.

Eventually I can't take the heat and itching anymore and reach under it to have a good scratch. The dust flies around my face, and before I know it, I'm breaking the relative quiet of the graveyard with a small squeak of a sneeze that sends my wig flying off into the pool of piss. Annie's fuming with me as she peers behind the gravestone to see Adam's location.

"STOP IT!" she hisses at me, despite Adam being far enough away now not to hear. "We're going to get spotted at this rate."

"It's not like he's looking anywhere other than his phone anyway." I gesture to where he's leaning against the church door. "He won't spot us! And I can't help having allergies." I glare at her and rescue my wig from its gross predicament on the floor. Holding it between thumb and forefinger.

"HOLD THEM IN!" she hisses just as Adam starts to move again. "Oh my god, look!"

Annie gasps, pointing toward the direction that Adam's headed. I see someone emerging through the trees and squint to try and get a better look.

"It's Audrey!" Annie whispers, using the same tone as if she'd just discovered a precious ring. "They're heading around the side of the church—come on!"

Annie rises up behind the graves and does an odd little squat run between the stones in hot pursuit. I follow her, feeling utterly ridiculous.

"Watch it! For goodness' sake!" Mrs. R's voice trills over the graveyard, and the two of us turn around, paralyzed with fear. She looks just as angry as she does when she's shaking her fist at Annie in the mornings. "You're standing on all the bloody flowers!"

She gestures to the grass where some bluebells have sprung up, although no one knows quite how. One of them now squashed into the ground with the imprint of Annie's Converse.

"Mrs. R," Annie says in a welcoming voice as the two of us straighten up, as if this is completely normal and we weren't just running between graves like weirdos.

"What on earth are you wearing that getup for?" Mrs. R asks, pointing to Annie's hat.

Crap. I guess these disguises aren't quite as great as we thought they were. I whip the glasses off, and Annie does the same with her hat just in time to see Audrey and Adam disappear completely around the side of the church.

"Listen here," Mrs. R says, leaning into us. "You best not be

116

up to anything foolish. I know all about that girl in your year. Accidental death, my ass. I've seen many things in this town in my time, but your generation has just about come up with the worst. I blame that bloody ClockTok or whatever it is."

I feel Annie's stress levels rise knowing that the longer we're here the less chance we have of catching up with Audrey and Adam, but then she registers what Mrs. R has just said.

Neither of us say anything, but I think by our expressions Mrs. R can tell that we think the same thing.

"There's a lot that goes on in this village that doesn't get seen, you know. A lot happening under the surface that people wouldn't expect. I see things, but will anyone listen to me? When the truck crash happened in 2005, I had suspicions, but no one would pay attention to me. And that's before I've even got to what happened at the village fair in 1998 or the bake sale in 1985. I've investigated all these things, but would anyone listen to me? You mark my words, dark deeds have happened in Barbourough."

Sometimes if I squint, I can see Annie morphing into Mrs. R in her old age. Especially right now as she talks about her theories of dark deeds in the village. Oh god, we're just like her with her conspiracy theories now, aren't we?

"Thanks, Mrs. R. Gotta be off now, though," Annie says, rushing to try and get rid of her so that we can see what Audrey and Adam are up to. Although I can't help but assume it's probably sex.

"Yeah, thanks, Mrs. R," I chime in.

Mrs. R shakes her head at us like we've let her down again, and she and Herbert the dog slowly start to amble away.

"Quick," Annie whispers as soon as Mrs. R gets to the next

gravestone. "They might still be behind the church."

I don't know why, but the two of us continue to do our kind of squat run over to the side of the church, and despite knowing what little impact they had before, we both put our disguises back on. I'll just have to have a thorough wash when I get home.

We get to the corner of the church, and Annie squashes herself flat against the wall, her deerstalker hat making her look even more unhinged than this movement would usually make a person look. I follow suit in my blond wig, shoulders up around my ears, a look of alarm probably plastered firmly on my face.

There's barely anyone in the churchyard now, but old Mr. Harris walks past with his dog, and nods at Annie and me. Not sure what he thinks we're doing, but he doesn't seem to be surprised by our disguises or our weird stance. So that's cool.

"Okay." Annie peeks around the corner. "Negative, they're not there. Maybe they're around the back."

The two of us creep around the corner, where the light and the rest of the village becomes blocked out by big overgrown bushes. I don't know why, but I'm tiptoeing my way around to the next corner. At this point, it's not clear whether I'm trying to be a detective or a cat burglar.

At the corner, Annie peers around again. This time I stick my head a little lower than hers as we both take a look, but there's no one there, either.

"I can't believe we lost them," Annie says, stamping her foot against the ground. But the moment of annoyance passes quickly, and I see the light bulb go on over her head. "I've got a plan."

Annie takes out her phone and starts to text. I don't need to look to know that Annie's sent a message to Les Populaires WhatsApp group. She turns her phone to me so I can see.

Annie: Hey, Wild day. What's everyone up to tonight?

"Dammit, I was hoping I'd be able to hear Audrey's phone beep," Annie says, cupping her hand around her ear. But all she's met with is silence. "Oh my god, look, Heather's typing!"

I stare at Annie's phone, disappointed that Heather has so much of my attention.

Heather: Drama homework. I took drama because I thought I wouldn't have to do this shit.

Audrey: At my piano lesson.

Colin: Me too.

"They're *both* lying," Annie says. "Colin wasn't with Audrey, and she certainly wasn't at a piano lesson."

"Interesting, but what do we do now?" I ask as the two of us start traipsing back around the church to where we came from.

"I don't know," Annie wails. "It's sus that she's lying about where she's been when she's been meeting Adam, but we both know he doesn't have sex *that* quickly. . . ."

"Please, don't remind me. Maybe they were going to perform a séance?" I suggest.

"It's still daylight. I don't think you can perform a séance in daylight. It's most likely he was hooking up with her, really. I guess when you're screwing as many people as he is, it's just one after the other, isn't it? Wham, bam, thank you, ma'am," Annie says, looking proud of herself.

"Wham, bam, thank you, ma'am?" I ask disgusted. "What have you become?"

"WAIT!" Annie stops abruptly just as we get around to the front of the church again and peers around the corner. "Look!"

My eyes follow the direction of her hushed whisper. Coming out of the big wooden church doors is Mr. C. He's completely alone, so I'm not sure what she thinks Mr. C being at a church proves, if anything.

"Weird outfits, girls," Mr. C says, walking past us and the two of us slink against the wall.

"Do you think he knew it was us?" Annie whispers as he walks off into the village.

"Nah," I say, rolling my eyes. I grab my phone out of my pocket, ready to clear a load of notifications from Les Populaires WhatsApp group.

I'm shocked by how many messages there are when I look though—and most of them don't actually seem to be from the WhatsApp group. It's been on silent and "do not disturb" while we were following Adam. I didn't want to face Annie's wrath again if it went off and drew his attention to us. I'd secretly hoped that Scott would have messaged, so seeing all the notifications makes me excited. Until I realize that they're all from the same person, and it definitely isn't Scott.

Mum: Where are you?

Mum: Please respond, it's understandable I'm worried after what happened on Friday.

Mum: Kerry?

Mum: Are you dead?

Mum: You've been kidnapped haven't you?

Mum: Please just let mummy know you're ok?

Mum: I've launched an appeal on Instagram I will find you and I will hold whoever has you accountable.

Mum: Mrs. Robbins says she saw you in the church yard. I will phone the police, get the search dogs out.

Mum: At your funeral I will get BTS to perform and Taylor Swift. Taylor Swift and Harry Styles will reunite for me because it is such a sad and special occasion.

Mum: Don't worry my darling, I'll make sure no one ever forgets you.

                    Me: I'm with Annie.

Mum has the capacity to be extremely overdramatic, but this feels like too much even for her. Especially when I look at Instagram and she's actually tried to get #KatchKerry trending with her follower base of middle-aged women looking for lube and HRT advice. I decide it's best to take my phone off "do not disturb," to avoid further frenzies from her.

"Hmm," Annie says, taking her phone out of her pocket. "Let's just head back to my house and look at the evidence."

She's behaving as if she's got a murder board with bits of red string at home.

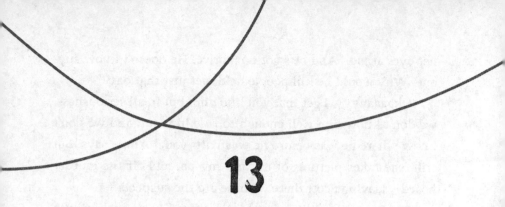

13

She's got a murder board with bits of red string connecting the clues on her bedroom wall.

It's concealed by the world's largest Billie Eilish poster, and when she unveils it to me, I'm shocked at the scale and creepiness. The latter especially helped by the grainy nature of pictures—or as she calls them "mug shots"—printed from the internet. And then I notice something that truly crosses a line.

"Annie, take my parents off your murder board this instant!" I shout. "More to the point, take ME off your murder board! You even know where I was!"

"DO I? Or did you and Scott murder her and come up with the whole cockblocked-by-a-dead-body story to cover it up?" She beams at me proudly, knowing full well that she's being annoying.

If she wasn't wearing jean overalls, I'd wedgie her. I maintain steely eye contact with her until she relents.

"Fine, but I'm leaving Scott on there. New boy arrives the week of a murder? Helloooo, serious red flags."

"Except he was with me," I say again, and she simply rolls

her eyes at me. "And he's got no motive. He doesn't know anyone. Why would he kill people he'd met just that day?"

"Okaaaayyyy, I get that you like him, but in all seriousness, we don't know him well enough to rule him out, and we don't know where he was before he was with you," Annie says. But still, she takes pictures of me and my parents off the murder board—leaving Scott there. "These are the suspects."

"So, we're left with quite the selection," I say, looking at a wall that includes everyone we have pictures of and know the names of from the party, all the teachers despite them not being at the party, and, of course, Selena's nearest and dearest: Les Populaires.

"Yep, we know it's always someone close to the victim," Annie says authoritatively, gesturing at the pictures of Les Populaires right at the top of the board.

"Based on TV dramas?" I ask, but she ignores me. I see her shift the dreaded Dictaphone out of her pocket and hold it up under her mouth.

"We've got Adam." Annie moves the picture of Adam, topless, taken from our sophomore-year yearbook to the top of the board. We used to drool over this picture before he became the chief suspect and mega creep in our murder investigation.

"The adulterer," I say to the picture.

"He was cheating with the deceased, which he may have wanted to cover up. Also seemingly has no morals. He was flirting with that volleyball player like a total sleazebag, so we should watch in case she's next."

"Why didn't he kill her when they were in the bedroom together, though?" I ask.

"Hmm, I get your point, but if she'd have screamed for

124

help from there, someone would have heard. Whereas if she screamed for help from the study, which was down that long, isolated corridor, no one could hear. So he might have realized it's far easier to kill her there than in the bedroom."

"Well reasoned," I agree. "So, he's still the top suspect?"

"He is. No one knows where he was. He wasn't seen around the party after we last saw him in the bedroom. Until he came running in after Selena was found. Definitely top suspect. Then we have Heather." She moves Heather's yearbook picture from slightly under Adam.

"The scorned friend and lover," I say, my voice low, like a commentator, as Annie holds the Dictaphone out to me.

"But now in fact she has an alibi as she was locked in the bathroom crying *and* she also showed me earlier that she'd recorded a voice note to Adam from the toilet, telling him what a shit he was." She moves Heather's picture to the fringes of the board.

"When did she show you this?" I ask, feeling a bit jealous. Were they hanging out without me?

"Biology this afternoon. Moving on to: Audrey." Annie sticks a picture of Audrey dressed as Rudolph for our winter talent show just next to Heather. "Was supposedly outside the bathroom while Heather cried although we don't have any proof. Also, she came and danced with me at some point, so she wasn't there the whole time. What kind of bad friend leaves you when you're crying?"

"Good point. Also, an adulterer, maybe, we think, because what else do you meet a boy in the graveyard for?" I commentate further.

"Maybe she was killing off her main competition?" Annie suggests.

"Hmm, possible. What about Colin?" I ask. "Do we think he's a suspect? Would he have motive? Anger about Selena hurting Heather, maybe? But that would have meant he took sides very early on."

"Colin was dancing with me," Annie says.

"Not the whole time. He came and joined you, but he wasn't there at the start," I say. "And Audrey could have come a little later because she was finishing off the job?"

Annie stares thoughtfully at the pictures of Colin and Audrey.

"And where was Colin before he was dancing with you? Maybe they took turns? Covering for each other while they did it?"

"Absolutely not. They put too much emotion into the dancing. No one could push and pull it with that much vigor after committing murder."

"Unless they'd already been 'pushing it' right into Selena's mouth? And they were dancing with you to cover their tracks."

Annie glares at me like I've just pissed on her popularity bonfire and moves Audrey's and Colin's pictures to the bottom of the board, all while maintaining eye contact. She also pulls a ball of red wool out from her desk drawer and starts unraveling it. I watch her try to pin it between pictures, demonstrating relationships and links between people, all the time still keeping her eyes fixed on me, like a murderous game of pin the tail on the donkey.

"You're going to pin your fingers to it if you carry on like that. You've made your point. You're very popular, well done," I say to her, and she lets out a massive sigh.

"Fine, anyway, what we've figured out is that Adam is our

top suspect now. We just need to link the board a bit. When we find a clue, we add it to a Post-it Note and add a bit of string to it connecting it to the people that it applies to. See," she says, popping a note about Audrey and Adam in the graveyard on there and yet still maintaining Audrey's position at the bottom of the board due to the very professional reasoning of "vigorous dancing."

"Don't forget to put Mr. C in the church on there," I say.

"Of course, and I want to add in a list of Adam's motives on here, as we think he's our top suspect." She points at his picture at the very top of the board, king suspect, adding a list of motives under him:

To cover up the affair

To silence Selena and protect his reputation

A crime of passion because she was going to end it

A crime of passion because he wanted to end it and she was making it hard for him

"It just makes the most sense, doesn't it?" Annie asks, and I know better than to disagree.

"So, what now? What do we do?" I ask instead as the two of us stare blankly at the currently completely meaningless board. Without any concrete proof, it's a whole lot of string and not much substance.

"We find evidence," she says, squinting at all the clues.

Both our phones beep as she adds a line of red string connecting Heather with Audrey and Colin. They beep again as a string of texts come into the WhatsApp group from Les Populaires. I feel like I've been caught doing something I shouldn't by them, suddenly worried that they can see what we're up to.

"What are they talking about?" I ask, staring at reams of messages I don't understand at all.

"I think it's some kind of reality TV thing. Something about couples meeting on an island and falling in love?" Annie says, looking as puzzled as I am. "Oh, this is interesting though. Audrey and Colin are going to have people over for Selena after the memorial, to celebrate her life apparently."

"Oh god, another party," I say, feeling dizzy already.

"We have to go." Annie's eyes light up just as mine dim and my phone vibrates with another text.

> **Audrey:** We've sent our nanny to Costco
> to bulk buy booze.

"Oh my god!" Annie squeals after reading the text.

"Hardly responsible nannying, right? Aren't they also like twelve years too old for a nanny?"

"Oh yeah, not that though. She's said she's at a piano lesson but she's also talking to Nanny? Holes in the plot there, Audrey. I've had an idea, I know how to catch her out for earlier."

Annie starts typing into the WhatsApp group, replying to Audrey's message earlier where she claimed to be in a piano lesson.

> **Annie:** I've been looking for a piano teacher
> is yours any good? Hook a bitch up?

It says that Audrey's typing, and then she stops and then starts again. This happens a few times before it disappears entirely, still no message from Audrey.

"Maybe she knows we're onto her," Annie says.

"Or you went too far?" I suggest, specifically thinking of the "Hook a bitch up" portion of the text.

"Oh wait, Colin's typing!"

We both sit and watch the screen waiting to see if a message actually appears.

> **Colin:** He's so bad. We go together.
> Literally the worst teacher. I wouldn't
> recommend.

> **Heather:** Ew nerds, all of you! 😭

"Colin's in on it!" Annie shrieks. "*Neither* of them were at a piano lesson or he'd just say who the teacher was, and they most definitely weren't together. He's covering up. They're both lying to Heather. If she was with Adam, I wonder where he was."

Something's happened that I never ever thought would be possible, but I've started to feel really bad for Heather. Does she have a single friend she can trust?

"We need to find out what they were doing together." Annie moves Audrey's picture back up next to Adam's. As if she could be in on it somehow. "If only Mrs. R hadn't inter-rupted," Annie muses, and scratches her chin, like she's totally pensive. But she's reminded me of something Mrs. R said, so I head over to her computer and open Google.

"What are you doing?" Annie asks.

"Looking up some of the things Mrs. R was talking about earlier. Maybe something she said might turn into a lead." I type "Village fair 1998" into the search bar.

The only article that comes up is one saying that the fair was canceled due to a wasp's nest that had been found where it was being held.

"That's not a mystery; that's just nature and basic health and safety," Annie says, leaning over and typing "Bake Sale 1985" into the search.

"Was the internet even invented back then?" I ask.

"I don't think so," Annie says, sighing, but an article from the archives of the *Barbourough Bizarre* still shows up. The article proclaims that the winner of that year's bake sale is the vicar's wife. It notes that the usual winner—Mrs. R— abnormally came last in the competition due to a mix-up with salt and sugar. "No prizes for guessing why she has a bee (or wasp, haha) in her bonnet about it, but it's not exactly a mystery."

"Imagine still holding on to that anger over thirty years later," I sigh, and type in the last search about the truck crash, wondering if this one is just another imagined slight that Mrs. R has held on to all these years.

The headline "Truck Crash Disaster" and huge images of period products littering the streets of Barbourough fill the screen.

"Now we're talking," Annie says, settling in to read it with me.

"It says that the driver disappeared after the crash?" I say.

"But there's a correction at the end that says that the driver was an employee of Mr. Stevens at V-Lyte and he'd just gone to find Mr. Stevens after the accident and tell him what happened. So, it *was* a mystery, but one that was solved very quickly. We could have double-checked with Mr. Stevens, but what with him being dead and all we'll just have to accept this as fact." Annie sighs. "I swear to god nothing interesting EVER happens here."

"Your classmate has literally just been murdered?" I narrow my eyes at her.

"So you agree it's murder now?" she asks, and I pretend not to hear.

Instead, I scan the article, feeling rage at the way they call the period products "feminine hygiene products," when women aren't the only people that menstruate.

My phone beeps, and I'm almost tempted to ignore it— considering it's probably either Mum or Les Populaires—but there's still a small part of me that wonders if it might be Scott and if it is that's WAY more exciting. I slightly wonder if I've imagined it when I see it is actually a message from him.

> **Scott:** Saw this and thought of you *GIF of a squirrel reading*

> **Me:** Are you calling me a squirrel?

> **Scott:** Oh man, I thought it'd be cute. Now I worry I've made you think I think you're a rodent.

> **Me:**

Scott: Do you think we might get time to hang out tomorrow? Maybe after the memorial?

"KERRY! EARTH TO KERRY!" Annie's waving at me. "We're trying to solve a murder. Do you think you could put your phone down for five seconds and stop texting Scott pictures of animals?"

"Sorry," I say. "Just not sure what else there is to add to the evidence?"

Just then her phone beeps, and I notice she's not going to tell herself off for getting distracted by *her* phone.

"OH MY GOD OH MY GOD! LOOK!" She thrusts her phone in my face, displaying three new follower notifications on Instagram from Heather, Audrey, and Colin.

"Are they following you, too?!" she shouts. I can't decide if this is more or less dramatic than when they added us to that bloody WhatsApp group. I open Instagram and see that they are indeed following me, too.

"Yep," I say.

"We're in!!" she says. "We're fully in!!! WhatsApp AND Instagram! This is great news! . . . For the investigation obviously." She regains some kind of composure.

"YAY! Three possible murder suspects follow us on Instagram!" I cheer sarcastically. "Could they be following us because they want to keep tabs on us just the way that we're keeping tabs on them?"

"I honestly don't believe they're that smart," Annie says, which I worry may be her first mistake.

What if they really are that smart—smart enough to get away with murder?

14

"Can you actually believe that today we get to go into the common room and just immediately sit with Les Populaires? *And* this morning they were texting us about last night's *Love Island*?" Annie's eyes are shining so brightly on the day of Selena's memorial that it's almost disrespectful to the dead.

The fact that she didn't even know what *Love Island* was until an hour ago doesn't matter to her.

"You said you thought reality TV sat in a morally gray area and you'd never watch it." I roll my eyes at her as we bike to school, feeling superior both morally and physically due to the bike situation.

"Yes, but that's not the point," Annie says, moving on quickly so I can't ask exactly what the point is. "Anyway, we need to focus on the investigation. Heather needs to know that we're seriously investigating, but we also need to make sure that Colin and Audrey don't catch us. Especially as we now know that Audrey's been meeting Adam in secret, and we need to know what for. We need to work out what he's up to."

"Right," I say, cycling super slowly so that Annie and the tiny bike can keep up.

"We keep watching Adam like hawks. Especially if he talks to Audrey or interacts with her in any way. If he's getting her to meet him alone, she could be in danger."

"I wonder if he'll come to the memorial later?" I ask, thinking about what I would do if I were having an affair with the deceased.

The journalist I went to see talk over the summer said she always tries to put herself in the place of the person she's investigating. Get under their skin and know their thoughts. I've wanted to get under Adam's skin for years, just in a very different way.

"If he does, I think it'll be to try and stop people suspecting him. To play the grieving . . . what do you call a guy that's cheating? A woman gets 'mistress'—why isn't there a word for the cheating guy?"

"Dick?" I suggest.

"Fair. He needs to play the grieving dick. But we also can't let him hear us calling him that. We need him to trust us. We need them all to trust us." Annie somehow still manages to look superior from her tiny bike, and I have a strong suspicion that a teaching is about to come out of her mouth.

"I don't feel like people *don't* trust us, though," I say. "We're not exactly shady characters at school, are we?"

"I was watching *CSI* last night, and they said if you can get people to trust you then they'll get relaxed, and things will slip out. We're already trusted by Heather; I reckon Audrey and Colin won't be far behind, and then we just need to ask the right questions without making anyone suspicious! Being undercover's actually pretty easy," Annie finishes triumphantly.

"Okay, great," I say, feeling a bit cautious. I'm worried that she's getting far too excited about this now and that every single news outlet and other person on the planet seems to have accepted that this was definitely an accident, except for us, and possibly Mrs. R if what she was saying yesterday's anything to go by. Speaking of, when we cycled past her earlier, it was concerning to me that she simply waved at us and said good morning. No fist shaking, no rage, nothing normal.

"What's going on?" Annie asks, stopping her bike so abruptly on the corner before school that I nearly crash into her.

There's a huge crowd buzzing with excitement just outside the gates, but there's one noise cutting through the chatter: the noise of Heather shouting and screaming at what I can only assume is Adam.

"FUCK YOU, EXCEPT NOT FUCK YOU BECAUSE EVERYONE ELSE HAS FUCKING FUCKED YOU ANYWAY, SO YOU WOULDN'T EVEN FUCKING NOTICE WHO WAS FUCKING FUCKING YOU!" she's screaming.

The two of us start weaving through the crowd and toward the noise just in time for a jockstrap to come flying out and land on Annie's head. We can hear Heather's voice clearly as Annie peels the offending, sweaty item off of her.

"Take your smelly, STD-ridden jockstrap and shove it up your ass!" Heather's screaming.

"Uh-oh," says Annie. "I guess the divorce is final, then."

"TAKE ALL YOUR SHIT BACK! ALL OF IT!" she's screaming

135

across the parking lot while lobbing various things from a box at him.

There's a wild look in Heather's eyes that suggests to me that this isn't just about what we found out on Friday, but there's been a fresh development. Meanwhile, Adam looks petrified for the first time in his life. I'm looking around the parking lot to see where Colin and Audrey might be so we can find out more. Unsurprisingly, they're right at the front; if this were a boxing ring, they'd be in Heather's corner, quite literally. We head over to join them right at the front of the crowd, near enough to feel the heat of the rage coming off Heather.

"What happened?" Annie asks.

For a moment, I wonder if Heather's found out about Audrey and her secret meeting with Adam last night. But then I don't expect Audrey would be safe standing this close to her, and I imagine she'd get kicked out of the WhatsApp group. I remember the savageness with which she kicked Adam and Selena out of the group yesterday. For Selena, I'm not sure whether it was because she's dead, because she betrayed her, or both. But it was savage nonetheless.

"Urgh, who even knows anymore," Audrey says, but I get the impression she just doesn't want to tell us, and I can see so does Annie.

"She looks pretty angry," Annie probes.

"Yeah, well, I guess you would be too if you'd found out your boyfriend was hooking up with your best friend and then your best friend died, so you only had one person to take it out on," Colin says, which makes sense, but I still get the impression there's more going on here that we don't know about.

Annie grabs my arm and leads me slightly away from them.

"They've closed ranks," she whispers. "They're letting us in but still keeping the big stuff from us."

I see Scott across the crowd, and the two of us wave at each other. Last night, I fell asleep cradling my phone as we sent each other good night–style cat GIFs. It was probably the most romantic night of my life.

Just as Scott reaches us, a pair of red lacy panties comes flying through the air, only to be intercepted by Adam's face. They land with the crotch covering his eyes and nose.

"Please, Heather, let's talk about this properly," he says, peeling them off.

"Those aren't Selena's panties," Annie whispers into my ear excitedly.

"What makes you say that?" I whisper back slowly because I'm almost dreading the answer.

"Selena only ever wore silk ones, all pink silk with *SM* embroidered on the hip. It was her thing," Annie says.

"I'm going to regret asking this, but how do you know that?" I ask.

"She did a whole Instagram post on it last year. She only ever wore that underwear," Annie says.

"She was posting underwear shots online?" I ask.

"She did an unboxing of them," Annie says.

"Okay, but could she have had an off day? Like, when all your underwear are in the wash and you have to wear the Disney Princesses ones?" I ask.

"Oh please, Selena Munroe never had an off day." Annie's right, of course. "So, whose are they?"

The two of us stare at Audrey for a while too long, trying to see any hint of panty over her waistband.

"Hey," Scott says, surprising and embarrassing me all at once. I hope he didn't catch me staring at Audrey's butt. He blushes slightly as he says hey. I told him about the party last night, and he seems pretty down with going. I'm hoping we can sneak off at some point.

We turn our attention back over to Adam and Heather just as a bong comes flying out of Heather's box and is caught by one of the stoner crew.

I see Annie writing "BONG = DRUGS" in her Notes app, attempting to be discreet about it. At least she doesn't have her Dictaphone out this time.

"Do you think one of us should intervene? Before she gets arrested for assault or something?" Annie asks, as more things come flying out of the box aimed at his head.

"And why would we do that? The little dirtbag's getting everything he deserves." Colin lowers his Ray-Bans to give Annie a look that suggests if she does anything to interfere with his entertainment he will kill her.

"I know better than to interrupt her mid-flow," Audrey says, sunglasses in place, bright red lips shining in the sun. She looks like she couldn't care less if she tried. If she was sleeping with him and those are her panties, she's doing a very good job of feigning nonchalance while they get flung around the parking lot.

I'm starting to wonder if being popular is actually all that. It doesn't seem like you get much loyalty from your so-called friends.

"IT WAS ONE TIME!" Adam's shouting at her while dodging a football trophy, which instead hits a poor freshman square in the eye.

"Oh sure . . ." Colin looks to Audrey and rolls his eyes.

"As if," Audrey joins in, and I study her face to work out whether she's saying this because she knows there's more because she's one of them, or if those underwear are hers, *or* if she just actually hates him.

"ONE TIME WITH HOW MANY GIRLS?" Heather screams, and I see Annie beaming with excitement to be right in the middle of the action for once. "YOU'VE FUCKED HALF THE FUCKING COUNTY, ADAM!"

Annie gasps and turns to me, eyes wide. If Adam's our number one suspect and he was also sleeping with other people, does that mean that those other people are now also in danger? I look to Audrey again, but she doesn't seem fazed. Maybe we've got it wrong?

"Honestly, who would sleep with him? He's probably riddled with STDs." Audrey looks disgusted. Definitely not sleeping with Adam, then.

"The cheating little, micropenised ass," Colin tuts as I see Annie rummaging in her pocket, no doubt trying to use her Dictaphone in secret.

I watch Annie trying to write discreetly in her Notes app—clearly realizing that the notebook is just too conspicuous:

Audrey disgusted by Adam—definitely not hooking up.
Does Adam actually have a micro-penis? And if so how
does Colin know?

139

Has he really fucked half the county?

*Why was Audrey meeting Adam if not for secret grave-
yard sex??*

"Please, you're upset. I get that, but don't throw away what
we have. We've been together for five years!" Adam pleads.

Heather opens her mouth to say something, but instead,
without warning, she pulls her fist back and punches him
square in the face. Knocking him down with her swing.

Adam's lying on the ground nursing his jaw while the whole
school stands open-mouthed in shock. There are only a few
seconds of Heather shaking out her fist before she continues
launching his stuff at him from the box. Including a pair of
boxers that I see Annie eyeing up as a souvenir for later.

"Seriously, how much stuff did he leave at her house?" I
think aloud.

"Five years' worth," Audrey answers reasonably as the
crowd silences slightly at the appearance of Principal Styles
and some of the other teachers.

"WHAT THE HELL IS GOING ON HERE?!" Principal Styles
breaks through the crowd toward Heather and her box.

"Nothing, Principal Styles." Heather pouts.

"I want this mess cleaned up. On the day of Selena's memorial, I expected a bit more respect," Principal Styles scolds,
seemingly not noticing the massive shiner appearing around
Adam's eye. "Everyone to their homerooms, NOW!"

She walks off, tutting and shaking her head, while other
teachers come to usher us all away from the scene. It's no

surprise to me that Mr. C runs straight to Adam and checks he's okay. Meanwhile I wave goodbye to Scott and any chance of spending today with the fruits of my lustiness, as Annie pulls me along with her in hot pursuit of Heather, Audrey, and Colin.

15

Audrey, Colin, and Heather are already sitting in their usual place in the common room by the time we get there at break time. At least Adam's taken the hint and is nowhere to be seen, although he could just be having sex with one of the many women that it turns out he's been diddling all over town.

Annie's in her element when they all look up and say hey, but it feels weird to me to be coming and sitting with them. And I don't know if I like sitting in the center of the common room like this. It feels somehow safer on the fringes watching everyone getting on with things rather than being a part of it. It's like how I prefer reading books to feeling like I'm living one.

"What do you think?" Heather asks. She turns her phone around to face us, displaying an Instagram post she's yet to publish. It's a picture of Adam looking sweet and innocent, hugging Heather at homecoming sophomore year. Heather obviously looks fantastic. Underneath the picture are the words "Do not trust this man, he is a slut and a skank."

"Love it," Annie says, shocking me because usually the word "slut" would send her flying off into a rage. We might need to discuss her double standards at some point.

"It's the least he deserves," Heather says bitterly as Colin and Audrey rub her back like they're burping a baby.

"How did you find out? About all the other women?" Annie asks. She's already asked in the WhatsApp group this morning but been ignored. Colin simply moved on to talking about someone in the year above with a fake Prada bag and how sad it was. It seems to me that being in their WhatsApp group isn't helping us much. It's mostly just them gossiping about people. It's kind of exhausting to watch all the ways in which they hate people. It's possible that they really need more hobbies.

"I did my own digging. Set up a web page for women wronged by Adam Devers last night. Within the hour, I'd had over fifty girls sharing their experiences."

I can see Annie's impressed with this. Maybe Heather's somewhat smarter than we gave her credit for?

My phone vibrates despite me barely seeing Annie text. She's become a texting ventriloquist.

> **Annie:** Dammit, why didn't I think of that. We need to see the page. I still say it was someone known to Selena but what if one of those girls got wind of what was going on with her and Adam and they wanted her out of their way.

> **Me:** Wouldn't they have got rid of Heather first? Surely she's the biggest obstacle? The PUBLIC girlfriend?

I see Annie read my text and shake her head as if I'm clearly missing some kind of magic logic that she's got on this one. But she'd never confess that I was right and she was wrong anyway.

"Then I wanted to make sure he was as embarrassed as I've been. I wanted everyone to see and to know what a loser he is," Heather says.

"Yas, queen!" Colin and Audrey say in unison.

"But now, today's about Selena, as much as she was a little skank and she totally screwed me over, she was my best friend," Heather says, and I feel incredibly sad for her, what a trash best friend to have.

Scott catches my eye across the common room. He's with the band, and when he gives me a smile, I feel my entire body fizz with excitement.

"Oh my god, are you doing the new guy?" Heather's voice snaps me out of my trance.

"Oh, erm, yes, no, sort of," I mumble, hating this attention.

"Oh, he's so mysterious!" Audrey claps her hands. "Totally not my type, but good for you."

Such a backhanded compliment.

"Oh yes, Audrey only likes college guys who are complete dicks to her," Colin chastises.

"As opposed to you?" Audrey sulks back at him. "Name me one guy you've dated who wasn't a dick."

The two of them are in a stalemate staring at each other. I wonder if what they say about twins being able to communicate without words is true. I can feel the hate vibes between the two of them.

"Oh my god, anyway, less about our disastrous love lives,

tell me everything," Audrey says, clapping her hands together and patting a seat next to her.

"And leave nothing out!" Colin says on the edge of his seat.

"Spill!" Heather says, eyes lighting up while Annie flings herself down onto a seat in joy.

"Yes, Kerry, tell us all," Annie adds to the group of eyes staring at me.

"Um, there's not too much to tell, really," I say, feeling uncomfortable, but Annie's ecstatic.

She thought that Scott was a distraction yesterday, but today he's securing our place with Audrey, Colin, and Heather. I feel red-faced and exposed being the center of their attention like this, but I guess I'm going to have to suck it up, for the investigation.

16

The sun's so bright outside the church as we all stream in through an arch of pink balloons in our black outfits and sunglasses. The entire junior class is here, having been allowed to go home and change at lunch. Selena's parents are at the front of the church, but thankfully everyone's calmed down since this morning's drama. Although I note that Heather, Colin, and Audrey aren't actually here yet. They told us they'd meet us here because they were going ahead with Selena's parents, but now they're nowhere to be seen.

Annie, Scott, and I slink into the third row. I was pretty excited when Scott came to sit with us, which is probably not how you should be feeling about a memorial service for a dead classmate. It's not like the decorations will let me forget why we're here. There are pink balloons dotted around the church and a larger-than-life portrait of Selena's face complete with a pink glow about it. I'm slightly surprised they didn't ask us all to wear pink, if I'm being honest.

"Where's Heather and everyone? I'd have thought she'd be up front lapping up the attention by now, no?" I ask.

146

"Good point," Annie says. The three of us start looking around.

"It must be good for Heather to find out that Adam wasn't just hooking up with her best friend, but was hooking up with everyone, right? Must have taken the edge off a bit?" Scott asks in what he must think is a reasonable way.

"You don't know much about women, do you?" Annie asks. She nods toward the door. "Speaking of."

I spin around to where Annie's looking and see that Adam's slid into the back row, slunk down in his seat, his hoodie pulled up tightly around his face and sunglasses obscuring his fresh black eye from this morning.

"Well, look what the cat dragged in," I say.

"I wouldn't have come if I were him," Scott says.

"Absolutely not. Facing all of Selena's family and friends when everyone knows what an absolute dirtbag he's been, and how he's used her?" Annie chimes in. "But I guess he might have looked guilty if he didn't come."

"Yeah, except that he was miles away when Selena died," Scott says, and the two of us turn around to him, silently openmouthed.

"Exqueeze me?" Annie gasps.

"Yeah, him and Heather had some kind of argument before she even found out about Selena. It must have been after you guys saw him and Selena, they had a fight about something, and he stormed out. Everyone saw him speed off in a rage, scratched his car on one of the bushes and everything. Apparently he only came back because one of his friends texted him and told him what happened?"

"Hmmmmm. Why didn't we know this?" Annie asks. I

147

can see the cogs turning in her brain. And her murder board shuffling. Adam, suspect number one, isn't looking so suspect anymore.

"I only know because Dave in the band saw it." Scott shrugs unaware that this is totally unhinging Annie's entire murder board. "He told me he looked pretty pissed off about something."

"But he could have come back earlier or . . ." Annie's looking less convinced by her own words by the second.

"Not without everyone seeing his car come back earlier," I say.

"Yeah, Dave said he was in the driveway until Kerry screamed and Adam never came back," Scott says.

Annie looks furious to have had her second suspect in as many days wiped out, and even more furious not to have known about this sooner. I can tell she's wondering how Scott's been here like two minutes and already knows more that goes on than us.

"This feels like the inside of a vagina," Annie whispers petulantly, changing the subject and referring to the pink balloons that are floating around everywhere.

I feel bad for snorting with laughter, and several people turn to give me a look of disapproval. Being disrespectful at a memorial, in the house of God, I imagine I'm going directly to hell and not passing go.

"I wonder if he loved Selena, then?" Annie continues staring back at Adam, who, despite trying to detract attention from himself, has only succeeded in making everyone look at him. "I mean, I guess they were star-crossed lovers when you think about it. Like Romeo and Juliet."

148

"Except Romeo had about a hundred other Juliets," Scott quips.

"And there's no way he'd drink poison," I mutter.

My thoughts are interrupted by the noise of the church's heavy wooden door being thrown open and crashing against the wall. The whole congregation falls completely silent and turns to see what's going on.

Standing in the doorway is Heather, dressed all in black, a black lacy mantilla draped over her head and shoulders, black sunglasses perched on her nose, red lipstick offering a dramatic accent to her face, like a slick of murder. She just poses there for ages, making her silhouette, with Audrey and Colin behind her, and I wonder if she'll ever move or if she'll just stay like that forever.

It feels like hours before the group of them start slowly walking down the aisle. Heather's treating it as if this is her wedding march, not her best friend's death march.

The whole room's turned to watch and are totally focused on her. Of course, this memorial had to be about her. Heather's ensuring that no matter what Selena took from her in life (Adam), she's going to make sure she's taking back more in death.

It wouldn't surprise me if Heather was late because she'd just offered to do a tell-all interview to one of the two journalists outside covering the memorial of Barbourough's most tragic teen.

"Christ, we get it," mutters Annie after the ten thousandth hour of Heather solemnly walking down the aisle. Behind her Colin and Audrey give us an inappropriately cheery wave as they pass, with Audrey winking at me and nodding toward Scott.

Eventually, after what feels like the length of an entire season of *Game of Thrones*, everyone's seated and the only noise that can be heard is sniffing.

The vicar stands, looking nervous and solemn, and takes to the lectern.

"We're here to celebrate the life of Selena Munroe, taken from us far too soon," he begins. "Selena was born . . ."

I start to zone out because there's not a person in here who doesn't know Selena's life story; we've all been in it the whole time.

I look over and see Mr. C and Principal Styles sitting together. With them are a few more teachers, as many as could make it and were teaching junior classes this afternoon. The rest of this room is packed with upperclassmen.

"And next, the family has requested that her best friend, Heather, read from what I believe is a favorite poem of Selena's."

Heather stands up, straightening her skirt in a way that would suggest she's far demurer than we all know she is. She takes her time walking to the lectern, the room tense and shrouded in complete silence. I worry that people can hear me holding my breath.

Finally, she stands at the lectern, surveying us all. It strikes me as a terrifying glimpse into a future where she's in charge of something, and I can't think of anything worse. Eventually, after a period of time staring into the room, making sure there are no distractions and everyone's attention is firmly focused on her, Heather begins.

She starts reading lines about sunshine and always being a friend, something about an oath. She speaks slowly and purposefully, like a poet. There's something familiar about it, that makes me wonder if Heather has somehow discovered one of my favorite bits of poetry. Until—

"Is that 'Umbrella' by Rihanna?" Annie whispers, and it takes me a minute, but I realize she's right, it is.

As she reads the last line, Heather stands behind the lectern dabbing at the corner of her eyes, assessing us as she says the last "eh," wobbling either in an impression of Rihanna's vocals or in a manifestation of her grief, with handkerchief dabs but no actual tears. She's certainly putting on a good show; you wouldn't have thought that this was the same Heather who just hours ago was screaming at Adam across the parking lot and throwing panties at his head. It's as if she's got two personalities at the moment, the grieving friend and then the betrayed BFF and lover.

I think she's about to come down from the lectern, and I've relaxed so much I'm starting to slump in my seat, when she booms forth again, much louder than before.

"UMBRELLA, ELLA . . . ELLA . . . EH . . . EH . . ."

She's paused for so long that I'm worried she's forgotten to do the third "eh."

"EH," she sighs, dabbing her eyes, her voice cracking as Audrey stands in the congregation and joins her with the final "eh."

"I am deceased," Annie whispers in my ear.

I turn to look at her, my mouth falling open. "Annie! Bad choice of words," I say.

I hear a couple of girls sniffing behind us and look to see them passing a tissue between each other, extremely moved by Heather's utterly emotionless performance of Rhianna's "Umbrella" and I can't help but feel I might laugh. As the vicar carries on talking about Selena's extraordinary life, I search the church for something to distract me.

I turn back for a second and see Adam slumped in his seat. He's wiping his cheek, and as I stare harder, I see that he's crying. Real tears. They're coming down his face fast, and I tap Annie on the shoulder to draw her attention to it.

"Oh my god," Annie breathes next to me.

"Maybe he really did love her," Scott whispers, flummoxed by what we're looking at.

"To play us out, we're going to have one of Selena's favorite songs," the vicar says, and I'm so relieved that it's over. I need to get outside, to feel the air on my face and to escape from a place where Rihanna's "Umbrella" was just used as an expression of grief.

I mean, what next, Girls Aloud's "Sound of the Underground" at her burial? It's bordering on disrespectful.

The opening bars of Harry Styles's "Watermelon Sugar" start pounding through the church, and eventually everyone begins trailing out.

Just like that, it's over. Someone's life condensed into half an hour, a Rihanna song, a bit of Harry Styles, and then that's that. I know there'll be a proper funeral when the police release her body, but I very much doubt we'll all be invited to that.

As we all file out into the bright sun, we're greeted by a photographer and journalist from the local paper, taking pictures and trying to get quotes from people about the girl who choked to death on a menstrual cup, accidentally, apparently. I know it's not us that they're interested in—we're nobodies—but I still have an intense desire to get away from them.

Scott slinks off with the band to see if they're all coming to the party, while Annie and I stand on the steps of the church.

She's using her hand to shield her eyes from the sun, when she must see what she's looking for: Adam getting into his car. Just like Scott said, there're scratches all over the side that I know for a fact weren't there before the party. I remember that side of his car all too well from when we were having beer shot at us on the way there.

"Audrey and Colin," Annie says, turning to me. "They were with Heather, they knew he was cheating, they knew Selena's scent. What if they'd figured it out and they were worried their friendship group, their whole world, was about to come crashing down around them?"

"So you're moving from Adam as a suspect to them now?" I ask.

"Well, we already know they're hiding something, don't we?" Annie asks.

"Thought you said they were out on the grounds of . . . dancing and being with Heather?" I ask, and Annie rolls her eyes, heading down the steps to join the twins, who are currently putting all their energy into consoling Heather as she poses tearfully for the one solitary photographer.

"They weren't always together, were they? They were in different places at different times," Annie finally repeats what I've been suggesting to her the whole time, but I choose to stay quiet on this, for my own sanity. "I think it's time we get to this party at their place, maybe rummage through some underwear drawers, don't you?" I look at Annie with trepidation because I really hope we're not actually rummaging through anyone's underwear drawer. That sounds gross.

17

It's so weird entering a party where you're actually there as a "friend" of the host, and guaranteed entry.

"Does it feel a little bit odd to be having a rager of a party to celebrate a dead person, though? Aren't these things normally a bit more sedate?" Scott asks as we watch someone trying to speed eat twenty hot dogs in one minute.

"Is this an afterparty?" Annie says, her eyes shining with glee that she's finally made it to the holy grail.

The three of us stand in the kitchen of what I think should be described as more of an estate and less of a house. There's a huge yard that apparently stretches for miles and contains a croquet lawn and tennis courts, a pool, and one kitchen that appears to just be for show and another which is for actual cooking, a game room, and several TV rooms. There's even a bar in the game room, which Audrey told us has been restocked with cheap booze by Nanny so that no one drinks her father's fifteen-thousand-dollar whiskey.

"I would have sold that to pay for college," Annie joked

when she told us, and yet I know she's not fully joking.

This may be how these people live, but it's certainly not how we live. The neighborhood these guys live in is close to Heather's farm and so incredibly far away from the reality of where Annie and I live, just a few roads away, where the houses are much, much smaller and the yards are barely able to house a pond for tadpoles, let alone a pool and a bocce court.

Everyone may have just been at a memorial, but the mood is so far from somber, and the nanny appears to be mixing Pimm's for everyone like this is Wimbledon.

"To Selena!" Colin shouts across the kitchen, raising his glass of fruit and booze. "May she rest in peace."

Absolutely no one pays attention.

"Your house is so nice, Audrey!" Annie says as Audrey props herself on the kitchen counter.

"It's okay." She shrugs.

Heather's wandered off into the yard, enjoying her time as center of attention. She now appears to be flirting with members of the football team in front of Adam in a very pointed fashion. But Annie and I are using it as a chance to get to know Audrey and Colin even better now that my relationship with Scott has given us "cool points" with them. I'm not sure it's cool of me to say "cool points," but I'm going with it anyway. Especially if we're using said cool points to maybe investigate them as murder suspects.

"Is Heather rubbing Kieran's thigh?" Colin asks. He pulls down his sunglasses and leans against Audrey as we all watch.

"Urgh, yeah," Audrey sighs, a hint of disappointment on her face.

"But she knows you like him," Colin says.

"Why would she be flirting with someone you like?" Annie asks.

"She doesn't really understand those kinds of boundaries. They're for other people," Colin says.

"Does Kieran know you like him?" I ask as I sneak a peek at Scott chatting with Dave the drummer.

"Yeah, we had a small thing at Heather's party," Audrey says, getting looser with her fourth Pimm's. "But Heather always gets her way, you know, and if she wants him, better for me to step aside."

Audrey shakes her head and takes another sip of her drink. She's clearly trying to mask her sadness and anger at what Heather is doing, but the more she drinks, the less likely she's going to be to hold any of it in.

"To always coming second to our dear friend." Colin clinks glasses with Audrey, and the two of them take a resigned sip.

"She's done this before?" Annie asks. "But she was with Adam for years?"

"Yes, on paper," Audrey says. "In practice they've broken up a few times."

"I don't think we should—" Colin goes to interrupt, but Audrey holds her hand up to silence him.

"Heather's invited them in, and do you know what—maybe we've kept her secrets long enough. After all, she has plenty of them. She can't always have it her way." The two of them stare at each other again, as if figuring something out silently before Audrey sighs and takes another drink. I can't see them spilling their own secrets this easily, unfortunately.

"I heard Kieran has crabs anyway," Colin says. "And terrible halitosis."

"Can attest to the halitosis but not the crabs, fortunately. I hope she has a terrible time making out with him," Audrey says.

Annie chuckles at their conversation and I try to join in, but I feel so awkward. She's propped up on the counter, sitting next to them while Colin and her laugh at crabs and Audrey swats them both away, and I'm just standing here watching. Physically I'm standing close to them, so why do I feel so detached? I worry that Annie's just slipping in with them and I'm always going to be on the outside.

Colin and Audrey decide to start a game of beer pong with some of the football team, and Annie starts cheering them on, jumping up off the counter in the process and heading over to me. I'm surprised that she's remembered I'm here.

"We need to get a better look around the house," she whispers out of the corner of her mouth. "Follow my lead."

I'm so relieved that we're getting out of this situation, into a more normal one where it's just me and her. I'm fine one on one—it's groups that I don't work well in. There're too many things going on at once, too much to be nervous about.

"Just going to the restroom," Annie says to Colin and Audrey as they cheer a beer pong victory, turning to give me a very obvious, not very sober wink. So it's a ruse, then.

"Oh, hey, use the one in my room. Second door on the right up the stairs. You don't want to use the one that all these ferals have been using." Audrey wrinkles her nose as she says it. Referring to the people she willingly invited as friends to her house as feral? Is it any wonder I find myself anxious?

"Oh, wow, thanks." Annie grabs my hand and skips off toward the stairs, dragging me behind her while I try and keep up. "That was a bit of luck."

The two of us go past Scott, who is looking dreamy as he talks about what I can only assume are very sexy, very mysterious things with his bandmates. I give him a small wave as I'm whooshed past.

"Okay, right, we leave no stone unturned," Annie whispers to me as we fly up the stairs and to the second door on the right. "We need to see if there's anything we've missed, anything that suggests why she was meeting up with Adam, what the two of them are hiding."

"Okay, but what exactly are you expecting to find? A burn book and nunchucks? Considering the murder weapon was a menstrual cup, I don't know that if we find one of those in a teenage girl's bedroom it's that wild of a find."

"Don't do that," Annie says, turning to me as we stand outside the bedroom door. "Don't ruin this investigation for me by talking rationally."

"Sorry, Annie, yes, let's ransack the place," I say.

"Attagirl!" Annie turns the doorknob, and an overwhelming sickly sweet vanilla scent hits my nasal passages, so strong it almost makes my eyes water.

"Clean and tidy. Impressive." Annie pivots to take in the entire picture-perfect bedroom with its pastel-pink bedsheets and matching curtains. Across from the bed is a sofa, and next to that a desk. Above the desk there's a pinboard with pictures of Les Populaires and next to her bed sits a picture of Selena in a heart-shaped frame. Probably a new addition, given recent events, I guess.

"So, what do we think? You start in the drawers by the bed, and I'll start in the en suite?" I gesture at the bedside cabinet, where the picture of Selena rests.

"Perfect," she says, immediately opening the drawer next to the bed. "Well, she doesn't own a vibrator."

"How can you tell that from the first drawer you open?"

"Top drawer next to the bed is vibrator drawer—everyone knows that. It's like fact."

I head through into the bathroom and hope to god that this isn't where I might find said vibrator. I'm really not a prude, honest. I'm trying really hard not to be, anyway.

I'm so *not* here to find vibrators that I put my hand over my eyes before I open the bathroom cabinet and peek through the gaps in my fingers. It doesn't look like there's anything sexy in there, but I take my hands away to have a closer look.

Pimple cream, moisturizer, toothpaste, diarrhea medicine—I do a double take because this is such a normal thing, a normal bodily function, and I'd always assumed Les Populaires were above those. It's almost a relief—exfoliator and a face mask that looks like a unicorn when you put it on, complete with "moisturizing horn."

"Anything?" Annie calls through to me.

"Nothing, just diarrhea medicine and a moisturizing horn," I report back. I'm expecting an immediate witty response, so when one isn't forthcoming, I pop my head around the bathroom door. "You okay?"

Annie's sitting on the bed, and with her are Baggies containing brown-y green mush.

"DRUGS!!" She looks up at me, cradling one in her hands, doing an excellent impression of Gollum with the ring.

"Oregano? Could it be oregano?" I ask, and narrow my eyes at her because the last thing I need now is for Annie to decide she needs to experience her best party montage scene again and become a stoner.

I rush over to her before she has time to roll up or whatever it is the cool kids do these days and take the Baggie right out of her hand. I open it up and the immediate disgusting smell hits me. I close it again quickly to save my nostrils and turn it over in my hands. Definitely not oregano. There's a symbol on the bag, a leaf with a *T* inside it.

"Urgh, why would anyone smoke something that smells like ass?" I ask. "People like people when they smoke this? This is a thing that is considered cool to do? Now I know why her bedroom smells so strongly of vanilla—to mask this vile smell. Where did you find these?"

"In the second drawer down, there was a copy of *Pride and Prejudice* with a weird cover I'd never seen before, so I opened it up and it wasn't a book at all, it was a box, containing THE DRUGS," she almost hisses the last bit, eyes wide.

"Okay, but we knew she smoked weed, they all do, right? The bong this morning? Not exactly a shock, is it?" I say.

"No, but I think there's other stuff in here. We've clearly found where she hides all the stuff she wants to keep secret," Annie says. She digs into the book box further, but all she pulls out are lighters and papers, all the things you'd expect in a box with weed.

She's stopped, her hand hovering in the box, and then she knocks the bottom of it. I think she was expecting a secret compartment, but when one isn't forthcoming, she gets annoyed.

"What about the laptop?" I ask, trying to distract her from her disappointment.

"Oooh! Great call!" Annie says as the two of us walk over to the MacBook on Audrey's desk. "We just have to remember what we learned in CSI Coders, and we can crack into it."

"Annie, we didn't actually learn anything in CSI Coders apart from that hacking is hard and takes ages." I don't mean it to come out as defeatist as it does, so when Annie gives me a disappointed stare, I know I deserve it.

"Well, it's Face ID, for a start, so." Annie grabs one of the photos of Audrey from the wall and starts waving it in front of the camera, but it's not opening.

"What if you made it more face shaped?" I suggest, curving the photo to make it more face shaped, but it still won't budge. "I guess Face ID wouldn't be very secure if you could actually do that."

"Hmmmm," Annie says. "That's okay. We just have to work out what her password is."

We look around, but I don't even know where to start looking for a clue; it could be anything.

The two of us stare at the laptop, foiled by a security I'd normally be grateful for as Annie starts leafing through things on the desk.

"Oh my god, what's this?" She picks up a copy of a book called *The Queen's Gambit*. "I loved this book. Is it grossly unfair of me that I'm shocked to find this in her room?"

"Yep," I say as she waves the book around and something comes fluttering out of the back of it.

I watch Annie's eyes light up as she scrambles to the floor to pick up the bit of paper.

"What does it say?" I ask, taking in her excitement.

"It says six-thirty, Wearvington, and then tomorrow's date." She looks like she's won the jackpot. "Whatever's going on there, you know we're going to follow her, don't you?"

"Yep," I say, reluctantly accepting that I won't be hanging out with Scott for yet another night of my life.

"Anyway, what else is going on here?" Annie says, peering under the bed. "A shoebox?"

"It probably has shoes in it," I say. "I just don't think people are as devious as you think they are."

We've been in here awhile and I'm starting to feel pretty shifty, so anytime she wants to get out of here would be fine by me. Really.

"There are shoes in it, but there's also this," Annie says, holding up a notebook triumphantly.

"What is it?" I ask, starting to feel a bit triumphant too despite myself.

"I don't know—maybe a diary? Maybe this is *Selena's* diary? Maybe that's what Audrey was doing on Saturday going to Selena's place. . . . She was grabbing the diary that contains all the secrets and information that they have on each other, and she was going to save herself by collecting it fro—"

Annie looks inside the notebook, and it's just lots of grids. Grids with crosses and dots in it.

"Or it's just an elaborate notebook where her and Colin played tic-tac-toe?" I say, only half joking.

"It must be some kind of code," she says, biting her lip.

Annie's face is super perplexed, and I feel bad for her because I've no idea what this notebook is, but I don't think it's the big clue we were looking for.

162

We don't have time to dwell for too long, because there's footsteps outside the door and Annie immediately pops into action, throwing the notebook back in the box and kicking it under the bed. The two of us jump up just as Colin enters the room.

"Oh, hey, forgot you guys were up here. Just had to get something from up here for Aud," he says, and heads straight for the drawer by Audrey's bedside, pulling out the *Pride and Prejudice* box.

"Wanna come down for a drink? Aud made margaritas— well, at least I think she tried. It tastes terrible." Colin casually grabs the Baggies and papers from the not-so-secret box we just hid away.

"Oh, yes, please!" Annie says, excitedly following him out of the room. In the threshold, she swivels to mouth "ohmygosh" at me, and then prances after Colin to take her spot with Les Populaires.

"God, she didn't waste any time." Annie points over through the window to where Heather and Kieran are making out in the pool. Heather certainly doesn't look as upset now as she did at the church.

The two of us are standing in the kitchen with Audrey and Colin as everyone cheers on someone from the football team drinking something fluorescent.

Annie's joining in the cheers with her whole self while I'm limply making vague noises of encouragement because the whole thing seems utterly ridiculous to me. Drink something gross or don't drink something gross; I'm not going to give you a medal for messing up your insides, dude.

"When do you think they're going to smoke *the weed*?" Annie whispers at me as we watch Colin and Audrey.

"I don't know," I say.

"Maybe we should join in, for the investigation," Annie says.

"You should NOT smoke weed for an investigation," I say. "Also, you get paranoid enough when you've eaten too much sugar. I don't think we're drug people."

"I'm paranoid just thinking about the weed," Annie says. "I touched it. What if I'm high from touching it?"

"I think you're okay, hon," I say, rubbing Annie's back soothingly. As I'm patting her, I spot Scott laughing with his band, his face shining in the moonlight, and find myself being less consoling and more wondering if I might finally get a moment with him.

"You're right, and we've got work to do," Annie says. My shoulders sag—no alone time, then. "We need to keep a close eye on the twins."

The twins are literally two feet away from us, so I'm not sure how much closer she wants us to get.

"And stop getting distracted by your bit of fluff," she says.

"There are so many things wrong with that sentence," I say.

"No time; we've got too much surveillance to do," Annie says.

"Where do you think Adam's got to now? While his ex-girlfriend's getting it on with someone else, he's not exactly with his old friendship group?" I ask.

"Dunno, I can't see him anywhere, though. Look," she whispers, pointing to a discarded phone on the kitchen counter. "It's Colin's. And he's all the way over there distracted by feeling that guy's muscles while he drinks." She points to where

Colin is indeed, stroking a football player's arm while he chugs a beer, as if he's trying to impress Colin, like an old man at a harvest festival.

"Right . . ." I take a minute because whatever she's about to do next is clearly going to send my stress levels through the roof.

She saunters over to the counter, looking around her shiftily, and in a flash, she's grabbed the phone and attempted to put it in her bra. Unfortunately for her, the phone is bigger than her boobs, so she now has a single rectangular-shaped bosom.

She assesses the room and then heads for the kitchen table, ducking expertly under the tablecloth and settling herself underneath. I lean against it, trying to look as relaxed and chill as I possibly can, which isn't really my forte. But from under the table a noise of glee emanates, and I know she must have gotten into the phone. I'm going to be patient and ask her how she did it later despite my urge to whoosh in there and ask right away.

I'm so distracted with trying to look like everything's completely normal that I don't notice Scott coming. Usually, I have time to deal with all the butterflies swirling around in my tummy before he reaches me.

He's standing in front of me, a big smile on his face before I have the chance to work out what's going on. I'm unprepared, and I just stare at him, in awe of how hot he looks. I bitterly resent this party every time I remember what I wanted to do, which was make out in the graveyard on the way home from the memorial, and absolutely none of this partying that I hate.

"Hey! I think Dave found the croquet lawn. Wanna game?

It'll be ironic." Scott gestures to the other guys from the band that are standing by waiting for us, as if what he's just said isn't completely baffling.

"What?" I ask, wondering if I'm so bored of this party that I've started hearing things.

"Croquet?" he says.

"That's a sport. . . ." I eye him suspiciously.

"Come! It'll be fun—I promise!" Scott says. "Also, there's something I want to show you on the way." He's gone slightly red, and my hands have gone slightly clammy. I'm about to tell him I'm one hundred percent IN when there's a stirring under the table and Annie's little face appears, squeezing from under the tablecloth like a turtle emerging from its shell.

"You'll never guess what I— Oh, hey, Scott." She stands and puts Colin's phone on the kitchen table behind her back so he can't see.

"Hey, Annie." Scott looks completely perplexed.

"Just got a bit, you know . . . needed some alone time. All quite emotional, isn't it?" Annie says.

"We're just going to play croquet with the guys from the band," I say. "Wanna come?"

"Errr, I think I should . . ."

I watch Annie looking around for Colin and Audrey and realize they've disappeared. I worry she's going to start laying into me for losing focus and getting distracted by my "bit of fluff" again. "Sure, I mean I'm a croquet demon though and Kerry gets super competitive, so . . . good luck to the rest of you," she says chirpily.

She's found something, and she's itching to tell me. I know it.

"Cool. Let's go!" Scott heads to his bandmates as Annie grabs my arm.

"I found something," she says, her eyes huge and bright. "Pictures."

She turns her phone around to face me and zooms in on grainy pictures she's taken of Colin's phone screen. There are pictures of Selena, Audrey, and Colin dressed in Heather's clothes, making duck-face pouts, holding signs saying #PRProduct #Ad #Fake.

"They're copying the pictures from Heather's Instagram posts, see?" Annie scrolls through to Heather's Instagram. "Except Heather's taken the hashtags off all of the posts on her Instagram . . . ALL OF THEM."

"What do you think it means?" I ask.

"I'm not sure yet. But it looks like they're calling her a fake and the hashtags have been removed from all Heather's old posts, so . . ." Annie shrugs.

"They're saying she's a fake?" I ask. "Could this be what Selena was blackmailing her about? Fake posts?"

"I think so," Annie says, biting her lip. "Oh, and Colin's got a secret lover. There are texts on there between him and someone called D, and they're *quite* steamy!"

"Still no proof they're killers though?" I suggest.

"Not yet . . . but they've got secrets!" Annie says.

"Annie?" I ask, slightly spooked by her detecting abilities at this point. "How did you even get into his phone?"

"Oh, I just looked at where the grubby thumbprints were on the phone and punched them in in order. People always do it in order, you know. . . . It's silly, really."

"What if they weren't in order?" I ask.

"There are really only so many other combinations it could have been," Annie says. "But I got there quick because I'm smart."

With that she angelically flounces off to catch up with Scott and the band while I follow.

"This is another world," Scott says as we all walk past people in the yard in varying degrees of inebriation. Apparently they're celebrating the life of Selena Munroe, but very few of them seem to be in actual mourning.

Annie's chattering away happily with the guys from Scott's band, and I'm starting to wonder if all this time she's actually been this great at socializing and it's me that's holding us back. Holding *her* back. I brush the thought out of my mind almost immediately; that's one of those unhelpful thoughts my old therapist told me about.

"It stretches out for miles," I say. "Where's the croquet lawn?"

"It's up that way," he says, pointing into the distance. "But I figured we could get away for a minute. There's somewhere I want to show you."

"Are you just leading me into the darkness?" I joke.

"You trust me?" Scott asks, stretching out his hand to reach for mine.

I stare at his hand. I've only known him a few days, and the last time I went somewhere with him, we found a dead body. But I feel like reminding him of that might ruin the romance, and maybe I should just take his hand. After all, despite the dead body, everything about him feels safe, and relaxed, the opposite of the inside of my brain on a regular day. I nod and take his hand, feeling his fingers clasp tightly around mine and smiling.

"Let's go," he says, and suddenly he starts to run across the grass. I try to keep up, our linked hands tugging me onward.

It doesn't take long for me to be out of breath. I'm not exactly sporty, and I doubt somehow that Scott is, either. But the two of us reach a bench under a fairy-light-covered canopy, and he stops running, grabbing me by the arm and pulling me in close to him while I try not to wheeze in his face, getting my breath back. Finally, we're alone. Kind of.

"I've wanted to do this all day," he says, staring into my eyes.

"Me too," I say. My eyes drink him in as he leans closer to me, his lips brushing mine before I lean forward, my arms around his neck shivering at the feel of his hands on my face as he strokes my cheek.

"How did you know this place was here?" I ask, pulling away. "It's beautiful."

"I was exploring with the guys earlier, trying to get away from all the losers doing shots," he says, but his eyes are unfocused, fingers playing with a lock of my hair. "So you're a killer on the croquet pitch, huh?"

"Very little to do in this village as a kid," I say. I can't help but feel my cheeks warm at the way he's smiling at me. "So I learned all the important life skills."

"Croquet and crochet?" he says as I look surprised. "I remember from when you and Annie were talking about what you did over the summer."

I can't believe he remembered that. I put my head in my hands at the embarrassment of the memory of just last week.

"Mr. C's kinda a douche, hey?" he says.

"Big douche energy," I agree as my phone beeps with a message from Annie asking what we're doing and telling us to hurry up and stop being losers.

Scott and I sit for a bit, though, and I try to ignore the beeps and just enjoy this, sitting with a boy, holding his hand in the darkness. I see the silver bracelet glinting on his arm and rub it with my thumb.

"My mum gave me that," he says gently.

"It's nice," I say. "How's she doing? Your mum? Any better now that she's in the countryside?"

"Oh yeah." He looks down at the floor. "She's good, thanks."

Guess bringing up his sick mum wasn't the most romantic thing to do. My phone beeps again with another message from Annie, this time in all caps.

Annie: COME NOW OR I WILL DECLARE
YOU BOTH CROQUET LOSERS X

"We better go, before Annie comes after us with a croquet mallet, I guess," Scott says. He takes my hand and leans in. "Just one more kiss . . ."

I've never disliked croquet more than now when it's coming between us. We stand up and head hand in hand to find the croquet lawn.

It doesn't take us long to find it despite the light fading the farther away we are from the house, the sun now well and truly down for the day. Through the darkness, we can hear them all shouting with each other. Annie joking about hard balls and making everyone laugh warms my overwhelmed heart.

When we get there, she hands me a mallet, her face lit up by her phone.

"Finally," she says, as if I've been gone years rather than just the minutes of horniness it was. "It's your turn."

I stand with the mallet, adopting the traditional croquet stance, Scott and I both giggling at the seriousness.

"I think there's a hoop just over there toward the right?" Scott says as I aim my mallet toward what I think is the ball, but it's honestly so dark out here, I can barely see where I'm supposed to connect ball with mallet.

"NO HELPING!" Annie shouts. "This is a SERIOUS game."

The two of us stifle more giggles while I take aim and swing. Despite being unable to see, I give it a good go, anyway, and feel the mallet connecting with the ball before the ball hits something less than a meter ahead of me with a solid clunk. I head to where I think it may have landed, but I can't see a thing. I'm going to need some help.

"Lights," I request as if I'm a surgeon in an operating room. All of the band, Scott, and Annie get their phones out to help. I also reach into my bag and find my own phone, putting the flashlight on. Thank god. At least now I won't trip over anything in front of Scott, and finally I can see where I'm aiming the balls.

I turn to Annie and Scott, putting the light under my chin like the dork I am, the standard horror-stories-around-a-campfire action. I know this isn't a cool thing to be doing as soon as I do it, but I've done it now and I'm standing here pretending to be spooky.

It's obviously working because everyone looks a bit freaked. The two of them even look slightly pale, and the three guys from the band have completely stopped moving. One of them drops his phone as I move my free hand around my face making spooky noises and start laughing to myself. I lose my balance slightly, distracted by my own hilarity, and step back, almost tripping over something behind me. In a flash, her expression unchanged, Annie races toward me, grabs my arm, and pulls me forward.

"Uh, Kerry, don't freak out. But maybe just come away from there." Her voice is shaking, which instantly makes me afraid, and Scott's reaching his hand out to me.

It's not until I turn around that Annie starts screaming, but as soon as I realize what I'm looking at, I scream, too.

On the ground, right by my foot and in the middle of the croquet lawn with my ball next to it, is a body.

It takes me a little while for my eyes to adjust to the light, but eventually I see it. There in the darkness, tethered down by croquet hoops, is Adam Devers, his face completely blue, a huge bump protruding from his head, and a period pad stuck over his eyes.

"I told you he didn't do it," Annie whispers into the night.

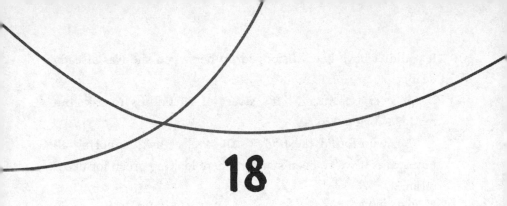

18

The police arrive within what feels like minutes, but I don't move the whole time. None of us do. Even the Goths who said Selena's dead body was "nothing to be afraid of" are struggling. The rest of the party gathered around us some time ago, but there's no whisper of Audrey, Colin, or Heather.

"There's no way that the police can call this an accident," Annie whispers. I nod, unable to take my eyes off the body.

"Are we sure he's dead though?" Scott says, his arm around my waist, holding me up. "This could all be an elaborate joke."

"He's dead," I say, watching as the paramedics stop taking his pulse and vital signs. They slide him into a body bag.

"Oh god, here comes, the DI, Dickhead In Charge," Annie mutters as DI Wallace heads over to us, shortly followed by DI Collins, not even having the courtesy to look sheepish about the fact that there's been a second murder and it's probably because they said the first one wasn't a murder.

There were so many clues—for starters, if she choked on a menstrual cup, why was it already hanging out of her mouth?

It couldn't have been dislodged by her when she was already dead.

"Is everyone okay?" It's sweet of DI Collins to ask, but really? No, not okay.

"So, who found the body?" DI Wallace asks, ignoring all niceties, as if we've been standing here looking green for decoration.

"We did," Scott says, gripping my hand tightly.

"Right, of course you did," he mutters. "And what were you doing when you found the body?"

All of us stare at him because what did he think we were doing?

"We were playing croquet." Annie sweeps an arm over the mallets and hoops.

"Okay, but what were you really doing? Drugs?" he asks.

"No, we were playing croquet. It's vintage," Scott says, completely deadpan and uninterested in DI Wallace's sneering tone.

As if he knows what's cool and what's not.

"Right, so if I'm going to believe that, then you just came up here, during a party, to play croquet and you found a dead body?" DI Wallace presses.

"Yes, that's correct," Annie says.

"Right." DI Wallace stares at the space where Adam Devers's body used to be and scratches his head, looking like a bear that can't find home.

"Shouldn't you guys have taken pictures of the crime scene before you put him in the body bag?" Annie asks correctly.

"Please don't question my investigation," DI Wallace cuts her off, looking furious.

"But you've disrupted evidence?" Annie says. "Do you

know NOTHING about conducting a murder investigation?"

"I don't need some schoolgirl who's read too many murder mysteries questioning *my* investigation!" DI Wallace starts shouting, but I can see that other people think we're right, too. The tension between him and Annie, because she knows she's right, is unbearable.

"Where is he? WHERE IS HE?" Heather's screaming her way through the crowd with Audrey and Colin trailing behind.

"Where were those guys?" Annie asks.

"Getting high? Hooking up with Kieran?" I offer out of the corner of my mouth.

I notice that it's Heather making the most noise, but her face is completely dry. Colin and Audrey look pale.

"Please stand back. We'll get to you when we've spoken to these guys." DI Wallace reaches an arm out to stop Heather from going near the body, but she barges through it and heads straight over to the stretcher with the body bag on it.

Once she reaches the bag, she unzips it and barely takes a moment to look but just falls to the floor dramatically screaming and wailing. I feel like I'm watching a really bad play.

"Her face is still dry," Annie mutters to me.

"Like her soul," I mutter back . . . then feel a bit guilty.

Maybe she can't cry? Maybe she's so emotional about it that she's reached a deeper level of grief where she just can't make tears? What if that's it and all this time we're being mean about her, judging her for it?

"Oh my god, what happened?" Colin asks, his voice shaking, and for a second, I'm mortified that he might have heard what I just said, but from everything we've found out this week, I'm starting to wonder if Heather has any real friends at all.

I'd feel sorry for her, but the way she behaves toward every-one makes me wonder if she doesn't deserve it. Just a tiny bit?

"We just got here, and he was dead," I say. I figure I'll leave out the gruesome bits like me thwacking him in the head with a ball and the pad over his eyes—after all, they were his friends.

"On the croquet lawn?!" Audrey gasps as if that's the most disconcerting thing about this.

I look at Colin and Audrey, trying to work out what's going on inside their heads, but they're both completely still. Emo-tionless.

"WHYYYYYYYYYYYYYYYYYYYYYYY?" Heather screams up at the sky, kneeling on the ground.

She continues staring up at it as if expecting a heavy rain to start falling on her face, sending tracks of black mascara run-ning down her cheeks.

When that doesn't happen, she reaches into the bag, which she'd thrown on the floor in front of her and pulls out the black lacy mantilla from Selena's memorial service. She places the mantilla back over her head and shakes her fists to the sky.

It's been three hours since we stumbled upon Adam's body and two hours since we came to the police station. As Scott, Annie, and I found the body, and because this is now an official mur-der investigation, DI Wallace and DI Collins wanted us to come to the station to give official statements.

Scott and Annie have already done theirs and now it's my turn. I know that I'm not in any trouble so why do I feel so shifty? Often it's when I haven't done anything wrong that I can look most guilty and I've no idea why I do it.

"Sorry about the long wait. I know you're probably itching to get home now," DI Collins says to me kindly, and I notice that the clock on the wall says midnight. It doesn't feel like that much time has passed. Another night without my retainer, I guess.

"We just need you to clear up for us what it was that you were doing at the time that you found the body," DI Wallace says.

"Playing croquet," I say, unsure why I'm having to tell them this again, when I've already made it quite clear once.

"Yes, that's what your friends said. You see, we're just finding it hard to believe that kids these days would be playing croquet, in the dark, at a party. Especially when the rest of your peers were in the pool or hanging out in the house? Why did you choose to do this?" DI Wallace asks as DI Collins smiles at me. I wonder if the investigation would be different if it was run by him, if he understands people our age a bit more.

"It was ironic," I say, and DI Collins nods as if for him this is an acceptable answer, but DI Wallace still looks unconvinced.

"Again, that's what your friends said. The fact that all of you have said the same thing seems a little fishy to me." DI Wallace glares at me, but I say nothing. I'm too afraid, despite the fact that in my head I'm screaming, "It's because it's the truth, you giant dickhead."

"Okay, and just to move on," says DI Collins, breaking the tension between DI Wallace and me, "you found him when you hit the ball, and it hit the body?"

"Correct," I say, my hands shaking under the table while

I try and keep my face straight. I'm too anxious to be questioned by the police, and I'm also too anxious to be finding dead bodies but it seems like life has other plans for me this week. "I shone my phone light to see where the ball was, and that's when we discovered him." My voice is shaking despite my attempts to stay calm.

"Don't worry, Kerry, you're not in any trouble. We just need to make sure we've got an account of everything that happened. And did you touch him?" DI Collins seems perfectly satisfied while DI Wallace makes a series of faces at me that I'm sure are supposed to depict uncertainty but make him look constipated.

"No, absolutely not," I say.

"Not even to put a sanitary towel over his eyes?" DI Wallace asks, his brow furrowed.

"No," I say, restraining myself from correcting his language and telling him they're period pads.

"Right, if you say so," DI Wallace says, as if I might be lying about putting a period pad over a dead boy's eyes.

"I don't think we have any further questions. This all matches up with what your friends have told us," DI Collins says. He briefly glances up from his notes to smile at me. "It's been a long night. Let us show you and your friends out of the station."

I stand up, my legs still wobbling, and head out of the interview room into the waiting area. Scott and Annie stand up as soon as I appear, Scott putting his arm around me.

"We'll be in touch if we need anything more from you," DI Collins says calmly.

"At this stage, we think it likely that the two deaths are linked, especially with the use of, err, sanitary items in both,"

DI Wallace says. I hear Annie take a sharp inhale as she feels vindicated. Everything she said was right.

It feels like a hollow victory, though. How can any of us feel safe now? How do we know that the murderer's not going to kill anyone else? Not to sound like Annie, but they *have* already killed twice.

I'm definitely not going to say any of this out loud.

"So I was—" Annie starts, but DI Wallace cuts her off as she's about to claim glory.

"Due to this, it's most likely that we're looking for a female suspect," DI Wallace says. "Probably one on her period."

"I beg your pardon?" Annie narrows her eyes at the detectives while my head spins, trying to work out if this is a joke or not. "Why?"

"The items used in the murder. The motive seems to be rage, and, well, we all know not to cross a woman on their period." DI Wallace chuckles, as if this is all one big sexist joke to him, and I think I can actually hear my own blood boiling.

"Well, firstly, it's not just women that menstruate, and not all women menstruate, either. Secondly, anyone can access period products—I mean, hello, V-Lyte was run by a cis man until his death. Thirdly, are you serious?" Annie's eyes meet DI Wallace's, and I think we're going to have to tear her away from him.

"Okay, Annie, come on, let's go," I say gently because I don't want to spend the night in a cell when Annie gets booked for attempted murder of a police officer.

19

I blink, my exhausted eyes stunned by the morning light, and grab my phone from the pillow next to me. I fell asleep texting Scott and Annie alternately last night at around three a.m. Before then, I honestly didn't think I would get any sleep at all.

Annie's clearly already been awake awhile this morning because she's sent me a stream of links to articles. The headlines blare out at me from my screen, "Menstrual Murders Take Village by Storm!" "Who Is the Menstrual Murderer?"

I don't know if I can bring myself to open any of them. The last one that she's sent me is "The Period Empire at the Heart of the Menstrual Murders," with an old picture of Heather's mum and dad next to the first small V-Lyte factory that they had on the farm before they had to move it to much bigger premises when the company grew.

> **Annie:** Mum said we don't have to go to
> school today but we're definitely going
> to school today right? We NEED to go to

school today. Those detectives might be
FINALLY investigating the murder, but I'm
damned if they're going to find out who it
is before me.

Me: They might though Annie,
they are after all, THE POLICE.

Annie: This is a matter of pride, and I will
not let my pride be dented. Also, if they'd
have investigated the first murder properly
and actually called it a murder rather than
an accident then there wouldn't have even
been a second murder in the first place.
They are not getting any of the glory for
this one.

Me: Is there really glory
involved when two people
have already DIED?

Annie: Yes, and that glory is MINE.

The next text she sends is a picture of her murder wall.
There are so many bits of red string on there that it burns my
retinas to look at it. I wonder if she slept at all or if she just
stayed up all night frantically pinning wool.

Annie: So, Audrey and Colin are still my
number one suspects after Adam's murder.

Me: Explain your workings?

Annie: I'm facetiming you. I can't type it all out. This is wayyy too long and someone might hack us.

Me: No one knows how to hack in Barbourough

Annie voice note: Yeah well you thought no one knew how to murder in Barbourough but guess what? Anyway. I'm calling you now.

My phone rings as soon as I've listened to the voice note. I rub my face and answer after precisely one ring.

"What took you so long to answer?" Annie questions breathlessly. She's definitely not slept and is fully wired, holding a massive cup of coffee in one hand that she keeps swigging from. Still wearing last night's clothes, her eyes and hair have taken a wild turn. She's in front of the board, which makes my vision go slightly fuzzy with all the red lines.

"Are you okay? Your hair is kind of . . ." I feel I have to ask, because physically she does not look good, but spiritually I reckon she's in her element.

"I'm great. Do you want to hear my theory, or do you want to trade hair tips?" She looks annoyed.

"Theory, obviously," I say, gathering my duvet around myself and sitting up, propped with my pillows, ready for her Miss Marple moment.

"Okay, so!" She picks up a big, long pointing stick, which I think she may have purchased on Amazon specifically for this and uses it to point at Adam's picture, which I see now has a giant red cross through it. Bit harsh. "Adam's dead, which means that although in my eyes he was no longer a suspect anyway, he is now definitely out of the running."

"Agree." I nod to show willingness and participation.

"Audrey and Colin were both absent at party number one for a short while before Selena's death, at different times. They were absent together at party number two because we lost them when you were flirting with your boyfriend." She gives me a stern look while circling the pictures of Audrey and Colin with her pointy stick, and I feel I have to defend myself here.

"I object. We haven't defined the relationship yet, and also you were more than happy to come and play croquet with us rather than look for Audrey and Colin, weren't you?" I see her shrug this off and take another long sip from her coffee, because she'll not hear a bad word against her own detecting methods.

"Annnnyyywayyyyyy, *I* found those photos where they were mocking Heather's Instagram account, and now all the hashtags have been removed, which we believe proves that this was why Selena was trolling Heather." Annie points from Selena's brutally crossed-out image to Heather's picture with the stick while still staring at me intensely.

"What does that have to do with them killing Adam or Selena?" I ask.

"Nothing, but I'd like to note that we've basically solved the trolling thing. It'd be great to sign off on at least one mystery today, you know?" She looks superior as she paces in front of

183

the phone screen, jabbing her pointing stick in the direction of the phone for emphasis. She really needs to chill out on the coffee.

"Fine, okay. Although I'd like more concrete evidence on that than just a theory." The moment I say it, I see Annie look like she's going to tell me off. "But very well done," I add hastily before she bursts through the screen and hits me with the stick.

"Right, well." She eyes me suspiciously over the rim of her coffee cup. "They have secrets. The D on Colin's phone— could that have been for Devers? Could Colin ALSO have been hooking up with Adam? Could it have been a crime of passion?! Bumping off his competition at first and then bumping off Adam when he found out exactly how many others there were? But even with that theory, we still don't have the answer as to why Audrey was meeting Adam in the graveyard? And what does that piece of paper we found mean?" She's now swirling the stick around the board so much I feel a bit dizzy. "I'm sure we'll find the answer to that one when we follow them later."

Crap, I'd actually forgotten about that in all of last night's drama. I'm a terrible detective.

"Or . . . could it have been"—Annie stops pacing and stares at the screen intensely with her hand on her chin—"COULD IT HAVE BEEN . . . that Adam was breaking up their friendship group with his fuckboi ways and they needed to stop him? They wanted Selena to stop also, so would killing both the perps prevent their friendship group from losing status?"

"I feel like we're in unfounded theory territory now, but I'm here for it. Although we'd have to assume that Adam and Colin weren't hooking up for this to be the case."

The fact that Annie's theories aren't sounding that far-fetched to me makes me think I probably need to get some more sleep.

"Agreed." Annie's cut off by both of our phones vibrating, and I jump when I see Audrey's name appearing at the top of my screen.

It's only a WhatsApp message, and yet I feel like I should hide in case she can see or hear us.

> **Audrey:** Yo, so Heather's too distressed to text. But everyone's gathering on the football field at the end of school for Adam. There's going to be press there and stuff so bring your best look.

"Did she KNOW we were like talking about her?" Annie's eyes are wide with fear and too much coffee as she tips her mug right up to get the final dregs of liquid hype.

"Creepy but just a coincidence, I think. Don't worry." I'm going to spend the whole day calming Annie down from her sleep-deprived and paranoid state. "Message is a bit odd, though, isn't it?"

"Adam and Selena are *dead*, and we're supposed to be worried about our best look? Very weird," Annie agrees. "I'm suspicious of her and Colin. I guess whatever this is after school will give us a chance to observe them more. What's my best look, by the way?"

"I was about to ask you the same thing," I say, staring at the T-shirts and jeans I have on rotation and wondering if any of them would be considered by Heather as my best look, really.

"Gotta go and find my vibe or best look or whatever, but remember we need to watch Colin like a hawk. Work out if he was hooking up with Adam or if there's someone else in the picture. TOODLES!"

Annie hangs up before I have a chance to even reply, and I toss my phone aside to start digging through my closet. I still think people are having MUCH less sex in this village than Annie thinks they are, and that's not just because my best look is apparently the same jeans I wear every day and a T-shirt that says "Books Are My Bae."

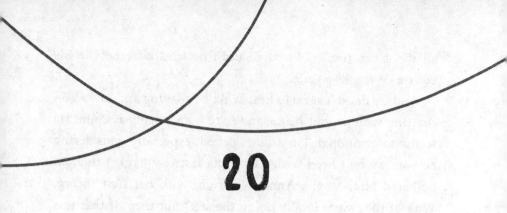

20

There are so many people crammed on the football stands when we get there that I instantly want to leave. Scott and Annie both notice Audrey and Colin waving at us from their seats before I have a chance to run, and so we head over to them instead of going to hide in the bathroom like I want to.

I am brave and intrepid. I wish I was at home in bed living as a hermit.

"Heya," Audrey says quite perkily, *too* perkily.

"Heya," Annie says back, a suspicious look on her face. "How are you both doing?"

"We're okay," Audrey says.

Colin's completely silent next to her, Ray-Bans covering his eyes. He's wearing black pants and a black turtleneck like it's become like his uniform these days.

"Where's Heather?" Annie asks. She looks around as Scott goes to say hey to some of the guys from the band.

"She said she'd be here in a bit," Audrey says.

"No doubt she's planning on a grand entrance to make this

all about her, too," Colin says, and I notice a bitterness in his voice as it cracks a little.

Audrey doesn't seem to hear what he's saying and carries on chatting with us, but Annie and I are both staring at Colin. He seems so emotional. I'm a bit shocked, especially considering how angry he's been with Adam the last few days. I thought he hated him. Maybe Annie was right with her first theory. What if they were totally doing the sex? But then, if that was the case, he definitely doesn't look like the murderer. Despite Annie's crime-of-passion theory.

"I just can't believe he's gone, you know," Audrey says. "It's amazing how many people are here."

For the first time, I look at exactly *who* is here and realize that there're loads of girls I've never seen before. Girls who don't go to our school. Some of them are wearing uniforms for schools in other counties. Exactly how far and wide had he spread his "seed"?

I can practically hear Annie thinking the same thing next to me as we scootch up on the benches and Scott comes back over to sit with us. Before we have a chance to say anything else, the school brass band silences the entire field with the opening bars of Whitney Houston's "I Will Always Love You." Almost every girl here is silently nodding their head and sniffing along, possibly all of them thinking about how they'll always love Adam.

Next to me, I hear sniffs and assume it's Audrey, but when I look over, it's Colin, nose red, tears running out from under his Ray-Bans. He tries to wipe them away and stay composed before anyone sees him, but it's too late.

I pass him over a tissue from my bag, and he looks at me

gratefully. He takes his glasses off, and his eyes are so puffy that it looks as if he's been crying for hours.

"Thank you," he whispers.

I look at Audrey, who's just staring straight ahead, her sunglasses stoically in place, and I wonder whether she's hiding something similar under them. Where's Heather? Why isn't she here with her friends?

A sudden silence descends and the crowds gasp as the football team appears, holding Heather aloft. They march onto the football field with her lying horizontally above their heads like some kind of Hollywood starlet. She's wearing a dramatic bloodred dress, with matching lips and nails, and she definitely doesn't look like she's been up all night crying like Colin does. She's staged, perfected, and purposeful. Her hair looks like it's been blow-dried freshly into red waves, her makeup professionally done, and her dress crisp, not a wrinkle in sight. She radiates an air of composure only slightly tinged with the appropriate amount of grief—a wounded but dry expression and clean, unblemished tissue in her hand.

When they put her down next to the lectern, I swear she winks at one of the football players.

She manages to walk herself to stand behind the podium just as the final notes of "I Will Always Love You" ring out. A deathly silence bounces around the field, punctuated only by the occasional sniff, as Heather stands completely still, staring out into the crowd.

"Adam Devers," she finally booms, making everyone jump, "was a cheat, a liar, and a bastard."

There are gasps around the bleachers giving her exactly what she wanted: drama.

"But he was my boyfriend for five years, and I loved him." It's as if she's telling every single person here who may have had a dalliance with Adam. She's staking her claim on a dead boy who we all know wasn't faithful. And all this, while she was making out with Kieran in the pool when he died anyway. Not that she'll let anyone else know that, having sworn Kieran to secrecy.

I hear Colin tut next to me and wonder if he's on the verge of some kind of explosion. If he might stand up soon and start shouting at everyone. It's becoming more and more obvious to me that clearly he *was* having an affair with Adam. After all he seems to be more upset than anyone else. His reaction's pretty on par with some of the girls from other schools who are shaking their heads and delicately wiping their eyes.

My phone vibrates in my pocket, and when I pull it out, I see a text from Annie.

Annie: The Scarlet Woman. Miss Scarlet. I do wonder if Heather's going a bit far.

When I look up, she winks at me.

"Adam was kind, he was talented, he was handsome, he was an exceptional lover," Heather projects at top volume, her voice rolling through the stadium seating. I nearly choke.

"She doesn't need to tell these guys that," Annie quips through gritted teeth.

"If he were here today, I'd tell him how much he meant to me, how special he was. I'd tell him I forgave him for all of his little indiscretions, the things that didn't really matter to him or me, because what we had was so much more important."

"Jesus. Blame the other women but not the man? Excellent bit of feminism there," Annie mutters under her breath.

"This morning, I've been talking with DI Wallace and DI Collins to assist them in their inquiries," Heather continues.

"What was she doing talking to them? What did they need to talk to her about? I bet they're way off the mark in their investigations," Annie whispers excitedly.

"And," Heather says with a regal nod, "I have every faith that they will find out who was responsible for these terrible crimes, and that they will punish the person or persons responsible."

Everyone else seems to think it was her still, and it would be quite a classic move, calling for the persons responsible to be caught when you did it yourself, I think. Except we both know that it can't have been her and that she has alibis for both murders. Doesn't she?

"I know that everyone here wants to find the vile, despicable human that did this, just like I do. And so, I ask you, please"—she gets down on her knees next to the lectern, with her hands clasped in prayer—"please, if you know something, come forward. Let's catch the person responsible and get justice for Adam and Selena, my boyfriend and best friend."

"They weren't even still together," Colin whispers. I look over and see Audrey clasping his hand.

"It is our duty now to be diligent, to look out for each other, and to make sure that this never happens to anyone else," Heather continues. "And so Principal Styles and I have invited DI Wallace and DI Collins to talk to us all about how we can stay safe and prevent any more murders."

DI Wallace and DI Collins come ambling up to the podium,

and I can already feel Annie go rigid with hatred. Heather's still on her knees in front of them hands clasped in prayer, and I can tell that they've got no idea what they're supposed to do about that. DI Collins goes to help her up, and she stands elegantly and with grace before walking off the field. I worry that she might be about to join us.

"With the events of the past week in mind, we know that parents and students are keen to hear ways of staying safe. Our advice would be for you all to be vigilant. If someone's behaving strangely, let us know. Don't go anywhere on your own, and ladies, don't go out after dark," DI Wallace says.

"What? Why just ladies?" Annie whispers in my ear.

"MMMM-hmmmm," I murmur. "Always the patriarchy. Leave the murderers to be free, but the women must stay home in case someone slips and does an 'accidental' rape or murder. Also, one of the victims was a boy. So how does just keeping the ladies home help here?"

Before I know what's happening and have time to regret agreeing with her, Annie's hand shoots up into the air, powered by rage and feminism.

"Excuse me, but why just the women? Why are we being gender specific about this?" Annie shouts across the field as Principal Styles looks approvingly at her and turns to look at DI Wallace expectantly.

"Well, er, we know that a young woman was one of the victims and that statistically it's more likely to happen to a woman, we think, maybe." DI Wallace is flailing because he doesn't even know if what he's saying here is true—he just wants to try and cover up the fact that he's a big sexist pig.

"Always the women who are told to watch out and be careful

and not do things though in case the men attack us. Have you noticed that?" Annie continues, and I hear a couple of guys groan. I make a mental note never to go near their penises, not that I would have, anyway. "And in this case a young *man* has now also been murdered. Maybe it's better to be addressing the murderers and telling them not to murder." Annie mirrors DI Wallace's tone demonstrating what a nonsense she thinks it all is.

"Erm, well." DI Wallace looks like he's actually sweating, and Principal Styles has crossed her arms and arched an eyebrow at him.

"So maybe just try to stay safe, everyone, I think is what we're saying," DI Collins quickly adds in, rescuing archaic DI Wallace from his own misogyny.

These guys . . . I massage my temples, barely able to believe what I'm hearing from them.

"Anyway, thank you for that, Detectives." Principal Styles looks about ready to chuck them both out of her school. She looks thoroughly fuming with them. "I'm going to suggest we all take a minute's silence to sit and contemplate what Adam meant to us. I really want you to try and connect with your emotions here. It's a difficult time for all of us, so I wanted to give this time for silent reflection."

There are a few seconds of silence before Annie taps my arm and jerks her head to make me look over. Colin's brushing another tear from his face.

"Are you okay?" Annie whispers over me to Colin disrespectfully.

Colin nods, but we can tell he isn't.

"He's just upset because he and Adam didn't patch things

up before he died," Audrey says. "He was so angry with him about what happened with Selena, and the two of them never talked it out. They had a very . . . special friendship. One without secrets. Or so we thought."

"I'm sorry, Colin," Annie says, rubbing his arm. She has to reach over me to do this, so she ends up partially elbowing me in the boob.

"Sorry, Colin," I say because I feel like I need to add something to the conversation other than just rubbing my injured boob.

"It's just so awful, and now our supplier's gone as well," Audrey fills in desperately.

"Supplier?" Annie asks.

Suddenly everything fits into place.

"Adam. He was the only place you could get weed around here now. There used to be other options, but everyone's so unreliable. Adam was really the only one left that we could depend on," Audrey says, confirming my suspicions.

The drugs we found yesterday in the drawer flash into my head. That's what she was doing in the graveyard on Monday: she was buying drugs from Adam. And Colin was covering for his sister while she was getting the weed from him?

My phone vibrates in my hand.

Annie: Audrey buying drugs? Mr. C too?

I think Annie's right. I look over at Mr. C, and it's clear to see with his dark glasses and red nose that he's grieving Adam far more than he ever grieved Selena. I'd put this down to his

194

straight-up sexism previously, but now I know what else he's got to be sad about. After all, when someone's that much of a prick, it's only when something directly affects them they get upset, isn't it?

Suddenly Colin whips his sunglasses off. "This is the WORST thing that has EVER happened in this shitty little village!" he wails. Audrey goes to comfort him, but he brushes her away dramatically.

I've never seen Colin so upset, and I can't help but think that this puts a dent in Annie's theory that it was him and Audrey. If it's so important to them, why would they cut off their own supply? But then, there's also more going on with these two than we know about, and maybe we'll find out when we follow them later.

"Where was he getting weed from so reliably?" Annie asks in a low voice.

"We had rules," Audrey says. "We didn't ask because he said he could never tell. It's something he only started doing recently, like in the last couple of months or so."

"Who else was he dealing to?" Annie presses, and I worry that she might need to dial it back a bit. They're going to start wondering why she's asking all these questions, and they won't be so forthcoming if they think we suspect them of something.

"At first it was just us, and then he started getting more over the summer. I think he was dealing to pretty much everyone in our class by the time he died. I guess except for you two. Oh, and Heather," Audrey says.

"He said she could never know. He knew she'd be furious, so he never told her what he was up to. He used to make us all keep the secret. But then, he used to keep a lot of secrets from Heather. So that was nothing new, really," Colin finishes.

I wonder for a second if this could be the secret that Selena was trolling Heather over rather than the fake posts? What if Selena was threatening to tell Heather? Or she thought Heather already knew? But what would Selena gain from that? Apart from Heather breaking up with Adam so she could have him all to herself?

"Why do you think he didn't want her to know?" Annie asks. "Seems weird when so many other people knew. And it's not as if Heather's some kind of majorly pure being who would be shocked by drugs? I don't understand," Annie says. She glances down at Heather, who's gently sobbing without tears—as is her trademark now—and peeking her eyes open to flash a smile at the captain of the football team.

"Oh, there's quite a difference between doing drugs and dealing them," Colin says over the rim of his glasses. "Jail time for one."

"SHHHHH!" An angry-looking girl turns around in front of us, tears streaming down her face. Yet another outsider, someone I've never seen before, from what looks like another school.

As the moment of silence comes to an end, people look around them, tearstained faces everywhere, and I wonder if anyone else is thinking the same thing we are.

That the murderer must be among us.

21

The six of us emerge from the football stands after far too long spent that close to sports.

"I have to go home," Heather says. "Mum's got some crystal healer coming to see me."

"We have to go, too," Audrey says. "Piano lesson."

"Shame your piano teacher's so bad; I'd still love some help with those high notes." Annie tilts her head, and I nearly choke on my own saliva.

"Nerds," Heather says, and marches off in a different direction from the twins.

"I have to head as well. I've got some stuff I need to sort out for Mum," Scott says, leaning over and kissing me on the head casually like he's my actual boyfriend, which I still do not know. Maybe when I've finished detecting murders, I'll detect my relationship status.

"Okay," I say. Actually I'm a bit relieved because that'll make it easier for us to follow Audrey and Colin to wherever that piece of paper was about, which is definitely not a piano lesson. Annie's already getting the bikes to make sure she doesn't lose sight of them.

"I'll call you later," he says before I watch his cute ass walking off into the distance.

Is this objectification?

My hormones care not.

Annie appears next to me as soon as he's gone, with our bikes.

"They're a bit ahead, but if we bike fast, we can catch up," she says, jumping on the tiny bike, weaving through confused people, pedaling with all her might.

Audrey and Colin peel away from the crowds, with Heather heading off to her waiting driver alone.

"Okay, so whatever they're up to, Heather doesn't know about it," Annie says from behind me, and when I turn around, I see she's wearing a page-boy hat and some sunglasses.

"Strong look . . ." I say. "Bit hot for the hat, but sure, sure." I nod to her as she thrusts some oversize sunglasses at me.

"This is no time for fashion; we have to make ourselves incognito," she says from her cartoon-dog-covered bicycle.

We hang back slightly as they cross the road and head over to the bus stop. They must be waiting for the bus, which comes approximately every hour. This in itself is a shock because I didn't even realize they knew buses existed. Annie and I huddle behind one of the large oak trees in the churchyard opposite the bus stop, watching.

"What are we going to do now? It's not like we can get on the bus without them seeing us." I say.

"Just follow the bus, duh?" Annie says.

"Oh yeah? All the way to Wearvington? How are we going to keep up with that?" I ask.

"It'll be fine. It stops every five seconds . . . and Wearvington's only really two villages away. Shouldn't take longer than half an hour." Annie looks uncertain, but I want to have faith in the dream, for her sake.

Just as I'm getting my breath back and preparing myself for what might be my greatest athletic challenge to date, the bus arrives, and Audrey and Colin get on it.

"Go, go, go!" Annie shouts at me, steaming forward, her knees smacking her elbows, while I overtake her in seconds. "GO AHEAD WITHOUT ME! I'LL CATCH UP!" she's shouting as I speed ahead trying to keep track of the bus, worrying that there'll be another dead body by the end of this physical exertion—me.

It's ten bus stops and two villages later when they eventually get off the bus in Wearvington. I'm so happy and exhausted that I almost cry. I keep an eye on them while I wait for Annie to catch up. The last thing I want is to lose them now, not after everything I've done. It's not hard, though. When they emerge from the bus, they go behind a tree.

"What are they doing?" I mutter to myself as Annie catches up to me, red-faced and sweating, with her hat askew. The pair of us hover behind the bus stop, peering around its wooden side.

"Someone's coming out from behind the tree," Annie gasps.

Two figures emerge from behind the tree, wearing headscarves and sunglasses.

"It's obviously them," Annie says.

By the looks of them, they learned about disguises from the same place as Annie.

We get off our bikes and wheel them beside us, following behind at a distance, making sure not to get clocked. It's quite hard, considering the cobbled streets are busy with kids and their parents on their way home for the evening, and we don't know this village as well. But eventually the two of them come to a stop outside a church hall. We nearly get seen and have to duck behind a car when they turn to look around shiftily, then disappear inside.

The two of us shuffle to the door and inspect a sign stuck to it.

"Huh, what?" Annie asks.

"That's . . ."

The two of us stare at the sign proclaiming a chess tournament is taking place inside right now.

"What are they doing here?" I ask.

"*The Queen's Gambit*," Annie whispers to me, dropping her bike and heading to the door. What is she on about?

I watch her peer through it, lowering her cap before turning around and beaming at me. She hurries back to me, running low to the ground, still in stealth mode.

"What is it?" I ask.

"It's exactly what I thought it was," she says smugly. "Go and take a look."

I adjust my sunglasses and peer through the door. At a table in the center of the hall, sitting opposite an old man in glasses and tweed with his bony fingers on a black pawn, is Audrey. A silk scarf's draped over her head and sunglasses cover half her face, but it's unmistakably her.

I look back at the notice on the board.

CHESS TOURNAMENT FINAL
Grand Master Chess vs. the Chess Kween

Oh my god. Audrey's a secret chess champion.

22

"I can't believe that Audrey's ashamed of being a chess champion and feels like she has to hide it," Annie says. "That's, like, such a cool thing. Why wouldn't she be screaming it from the rooftops?"

"I guess their world's different than ours, and maybe Heather wouldn't appreciate it as much as it should be appreciated," I say. "How much do you love that Colin goes with her and cheers her on, though?"

Colin was standing at the sidelines like a proud soccer mum when I stuck my head through. He looked tense on her behalf, like her winning meant as much to him as it did to her.

"Being a chess pro doesn't mean she didn't do it, though," Annie says. "She has motive and means—they both do. And now we just know that one of them can't have a secret without the other one. They'd be in on it together for sure."

"You don't buy them being sad at the memorial this afternoon?" I ask.

"About missing their dealer? No way! You saw how angry Colin was with Adam the other day, about Adam cheating on

Heather with Selena. You heard Colin; they properly fell out over it. And as for him being their dealer? I mean, come on . . . how hard is it to just find another weed dealer?" Annie asks.

"I didn't realize finding a weed dealer was something you knew so much about," I say.

"Not me personally, but people have been getting weed since long before Adam Devers was born." She makes a good point.

"So we're still going to follow them?" I ask. "Even though that chess game could last hours?"

"Of course," Annie says. "Sometimes a stakeout is boring, but you have to put in the work to get the results. Also if she's smart enough to be a chess champion, who knows what else she's smart enough to be doing."

She props her bike down and sits on the ground, resting her back against the trunk of a tree.

"Dorito?" she asks, pulling a pack of chips out of her bag. "Juice? Gummy Bear?"

Well, at least someone came prepared.

It's dark by the time they come out, and judging by their expressions and high excitement, it sounds like Audrey won. She beat an old man who calls himself Grand Master Chess and she's not posting this all over the gram? This is the kind of achievement that's worth shouting about, surely?

Annie hits my arm as if I'm not already alert enough and poises herself on her bike. I know what's coming. We're going to have to follow the bus again. Fortunately, it's already at the stop when Colin and Audrey run for it, so the two of us get straight back on our bikes.

The ride back behind the bus feels even longer than on the way there. We're still two stops away when my legs feel like they're going to give out, not to mention the fear associated with having to cycle in the dark without lights on because Annie thinks we'll get seen if we apply the tiniest bit of health and safety. As the bus grinds to a halt at another stop, I take my feet off the pedals and try to stretch my legs out. Annie appears next to me just as I'm starting to work out a cramp, hissing in my ear, something about nearly being home, but it's started raining and there's a stormy wind kicking in, so I barely hear her.

I start biking again as soon as the bus starts, these dark country lanes are creepy enough without the wind and the rain. I just want to get home now. The rain gets harder, assaulting me from the sky, and I keep having to wipe my face to stop it obscuring my vision. The wind whistling in my ears is making me lose my sense of space, and I have to focus really hard to keep riding into it. I'll be home soon. I keep repeating this to myself, but it's just getting dangerous now.

I wobble precariously along the road, trying to make sure I don't leave Annie behind, cursing her tiny tires for extending this journey and making this feel like we're rolling through Jell-O. We're starting to lose the bus, our only source of light.

All my senses feel blurry while I try to make it through the storm. I jump as a shadow moves to my left, something comes out of the bushes. I try to veer away from it, but whatever it is gets stuck on a bush. A noise like fabric tearing rips through the wind, and I realize that the shadow's human and coming toward me. I panic, and my feet slip off the wet pedals; I've lost complete control. The figure bounds toward me, having freed themselves from the bush. They race into my side, shouting as my bike slips from under me and I hit the rough pavement. It seems to take years for me to stop falling, fear paralyzing me on the ground. I manage to look up and see their feet racing away in the darkness. As my vision comes to, I make out a tall figure sprinting away in a jacket, the sleeve of it torn and flapping in the night.

"KEERRRRRRYYYYY! OH MY GOD, KERRY!!!" Annie rolls up next to me, throws her tiny bike on the ground, and squats down as I sit up slowly. "Are you okay?!"

"I'm okay." I sit up and check myself over, trying to work out if any part of me is hurt. I can feel grazes on my knees, but apart from that, I think I'm okay. I scrabble up from the floor, picking up my bike, which also seems to be okay, thankfully.

"Who was that?" I ask while Annie helps me to my feet.

"I don't know." Annie squints into the distance, but the figure's completely gone.

I feel a coldness settle over my whole body, chilling deep within my bones. As I try to stand up, my legs are jellylike.

"Where did they come from?" Annie stares into the bushes, scratching her head and turning on the flashlight on her phone.

"In there somewhere," I say, picking up my bike.

"There's a hole in the fence here," Annie says, rolling her bike over to the bushes.

"Annie, I want to go home," I protest, feeling a panic rise. I've reached my limit now. I just want to feel safe.

"Yeah, just one sec." Annie heads deeper into the bushes toward the hole, and I've got no choice but to follow her, despite my entire body tingling in protest. "Oh my god."

Annie turns to face me, shining her flashlight through the

gap in the fence to display a sign. I try to read it, but my vision's still blurry and I can't focus, the rain lashing down on my face.

"I can't see what it says," I admit, almost shouting to her, trying to be heard over the rain and wind.

"It's the old V-Lyte factory!" she exclaims as the letters come into focus for me. "A dark figure at the old period product factory the night after a murder with period products . . ." She trails off, and I feel my whole-body shiver.

"Please, Annie," I say urgently, the wind stealing my breath. "I just want to go home. Whoever that was, they might come back."

Annie turns to me, her flashlight and eyes shining. "And they might be the killer."

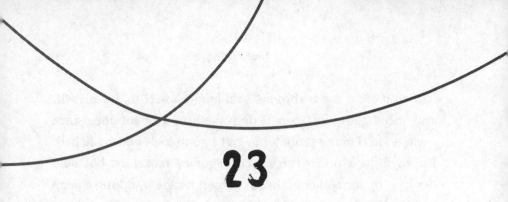

23

I was hoping Mum and Dad would be in, but instead when I get home, the house is dark and still. Great, more dark spaces, exactly what I don't want. I'm soaking wet and I can feel a tightening in my chest. I know there's only one thing for it: hot chocolate and my favorite book under the covers.

I make sure that all the doors and windows are locked and start turning on lights. I turn on all the lights down here and put the kettle on, but the noise fills the air instantly and I'm worried there are other noises I'm not hearing because the kettle noise is covering them up. I turn it off, grabbing a glass of water instead. On the way up to my room, I switch on every single light I pass. I'm getting rid of this darkness, and I'm going to be safe. All of the lights in the kitchen, all of the lights in the hallway, all the way up to my room—I keep turning on lights.

My hands start shaking with some kind of residual adrenaline from earlier. I take out my phone to text Annie. Let her know that I made it the two streets from where I left her at her place and I'm safe, because I *am* safe.

Me: I'm home.

I stop off at the bathroom, grabbing a towel to dry myself, and once I get to my room, I do something I've not done since I was a kid. I'm not proud of it, but I go to look under the bed. I used to look under there for imaginary monsters, but now I'm looking for real ones. I squat down beside it, taking a deep breath. If I close my eyes, all I hear is the noise of the bushes rustling before the mystery figure ran. I can almost feel the impact of them knocking me off my bike. I take a deep breath, filling my lungs with air, count to three, and look under the bed, my head spinning.

There's nothing under there except some old socks. I stand up, shaking my head at myself. What a ridiculous thing to do. I'm being silly. I'm being silly. I'm being . . . What was that noise? The pipes rumble into action in the floorboards under my feet. It's just the hot water kicking in, which happens every night at the same time. I press a hand to my collarbone, like I can still my thundering heart.

I need to get changed and get into bed. I want a shower, but the shower scene from *Psycho* fills my head and I decide against it. Instead, I hop into shorts and a T-shirt as fast as possible, feeling a tug in the air, as if I can't move fast enough to beat whatever or whoever's coming for me. I jump straight into bed, my grazed knees tanging as I hastily pull the covers up around my ears and pick up one of my favorite books, *Miss Marple: At Bertram's Hotel*. I think about the fact that whoever that was in the bushes, they could have been the murderer. I could have been there in the dark with the murderer. Just us and them. It's less of a shiver down my spine and more of a prickle, stabbing at me as I try to lose myself in the book. Miss Marple goes to her favorite hotel from when she was a kid. It's glitzy and glamorous and she's with the murderer for loads of it, but she doesn't get murdered. And somehow this is a comfort to me right now. If Miss Marple can do it, so can I.

I pull the duvet up closer around my ears and wonder if there's a flashlight that I can read this under the covers with, like I used to with Goosebumps books as a kid. I'm totally calm and composed, I am Miss Marple, fearless and wise. I am— Oh god.

There's a tapping noise at the window, and I instantly feel all the blood rush to my head. What if whoever it was followed me home? What if they've already paid Annie a visit? I grab my phone to check if she's still alive, hopefully in a casual and not panicky way that will alert Annie to my current status under the covers using a stuffed bear as a weapon.

Me: What you up to?

Annie: Just staring at the board.

Okay, Annie's fine. She's fine, and it's probably just the wind knocking a branch or something against the window. I exhale and feel my pulse start to settle.

Then there's another tap at the window. Soon I'm hearing the thump of my own heart, beating through my head. It's becoming so loud that I almost don't hear the next tap.

I slink down farther into my duvet. They can't get me if I don't open the window. I'm safe here, I'm in bed, all the doors are locked, everything's safe. I'm home and secure and no one can get in.

Tap

Tap

TAP

TAP

TAP TAP TAP

My hands start to shake so that reading the book becomes impossible.

TAPTAPTAPTAPTAP.

I throw the book in the air and sit up.

Someone is definitely out there, and I can't keep pretending that's the wind. I need to be brave. I need to be bold. What would Annie do? She'd face it head-on and defend herself. What if the figure from earlier has followed me home?

Christ, I really am going to die before I turn seventeen, aren't I? Before I lose my virginity or drive a car. Before I even have a legal drink.

All I keep thinking as I creep out of bed is that this old T-shirt-and-jersey-shorts combo is so *not* the outfit I want them to find my dead corpse in. I tentatively walk toward the window. If Miss Marple can be brave, then so can I, especially as I'm a quarter of her age and I'm in my own bedroom. I look around for something to protect myself with, and in the end, all I can find is my descant recorder from elementary school. If nothing else, I'll make the most hideous noise and scare them off with that.

I stand a bit away from the window and peer cautiously over the frame into the street. Outside it's still raining, but despite the poor visibility, underneath my window, bathed in street-lights, I can see a hooded figure. For a second, I think I might pass out, fear making the room spin. I grip the windowsill with one hand and my recorder with the other and take a better look. Is it . . . ? It looks like . . .

My phone beeps.

Scott: Hey

And the figure waves at me before looking back down at their phone.

Scott: May I shinny up your drainpipe?

I clutch my chest in relief and breathe out hard: it's Scott. Thank god, now I don't have to be scared anymore. I take some deep breaths, not wanting him to see how freaked out I was. I'm so relieved.

Me: You may.

Oh my god, oh my god, oh my god. This is a different sort of panic. A boy is about to climb into my room. My *bed*room.

I didn't think people actually shinnied up things in real life, but here he comes. He must have amazing upper body strength to be doing this. I'd definitely never make it up there.

I push the sash window up to let him in and throw the recorder onto the bed as he tumbles in, pushing his hair back. I shut the window and put a finger to my lips. I can't quite believe he's here. Because in all the places I've seen him, here is where I dream about him, not where his physical person actually is.

"Parents?" he whispers.

211

"Out. You could have come in the front door," I whisper back, giggling at him.

"This feels more romantic," he says, beaming with pride. "Besides, I wanted to check you were okay and to bring you this." He reaches into his pocket and brings out a rose, somewhat squashed from the trip up the drainpipe and definitely taken from Mrs. R's bush on the way here.

Rainwater drips from his hair onto the rose as he hands it to me, his leather jacket and hoodie soaked.

"Dammit, I thought that'd be romantic, but it's kind of mangled. Sorry," he says as I look up and lock eyes with him.

"You're all wet," I say, and I don't know what boldness it is but I'm wiping rainwater from his cheek.

"Hey, what happened to your knees?" he asks, staring at my scratched legs.

"Fell off my bike." I shrug. I don't know why I don't tell him what really happened. Maybe because I don't want him to think I'm a scaredy-cat? Or I don't want to ruin the magic. Either way I don't.

"Are you okay?" he asks, looking concerned. "Are they sore?"

"Nah, I'm fine," I say bravely, forgetting that two minutes ago I was freaking out under the covers, wincing at the pain of bedsheets against the grazes.

He moves his face closer to mine, and I can smell his hair. I push a rogue strand of it off his face and reach up to kiss him softly on the lips. He kisses me back, his fingers gently brushing my cheek. He traces my jawline, lightly stroking with his fingertips, moving down my neck, so I feel a tingle the whole way down my spine. But this time it's a good tingle, not a tingle telling me to run away.

I always thought I'd be shy when it came to being alone with a guy or that I wouldn't know what to do, but my hands seem to have a sexy mind of their own. He starts tugging at his leather jacket and hoodie, shrugging them off. He looks down at me, his hands cupped around my face, and he kisses me so intensely that I think my knees might buckle. I grab at the edges of his T-shirt, running my fingers along his stomach and touching his chest.

We fall onto the bed, and he starts kissing down my neck, and along my collarbone, his hands moving down my shoulders. It feels so out of body that I have to remind myself that we're on my bed. My hugely unsexy single bed that I've had since I was five. With its doily-esque bedsheets and the posters of Harry Styles on the wall above it.

I look down at him underneath me, and a look of pain crosses his face. I worry for a minute that I've hurt him somehow, and then he reaches behind and grabs the recorder from under his back.

"Um, what?" He holds it up.

"I was looking for something to defend myself with. I thought you were going to be the murderer."

"What were you going to do? 'Three Blind Mice' me to death?" he says, putting it respectfully on my bedside table. "You're pretty badass, you know."

I have a small freak-out when I realize his hand's right next to my anxiety meds, and for a minute, I think about hiding them, but then I realize it doesn't matter if he sees them. So what?

He reaches up and brings my face closer to his again, laughing and rubbing my cheek before he starts kissing me. He tastes like beer and smells kind of sweet, and his hands on my waist make me impatient for more, my hormones are about to absolutely slay me. Just as I feel his hand on my ACTUAL BOOB, there's a noise in the hallway, and the two of us freeze.

I hear the front door clicking shut and the sound of my parents chattering downstairs. Neither of us move as Mum's footsteps clank on the steps. I silently wish she'd go away. It sounds like she's going into the toilet, and I hear the bathroom door lock. We're inches away from each other's faces, stuck like that, unable to carry on in case we make any noise and Mum hears. He realizes his hand's on my boob and tries to move it off. Gentleman. Instead, he starts gently stroking my arm, the two of us making eye contact while I pray that Mum's doing a pee and not a poo and that she'll hurry up about it. *And* that she won't just burst in here to say hi.

His fingers against my skin are making me even hornier, and I'm not sure how much longer I can hold off from absolutely ravishing him (why, yes, I AM Jane Austen). I hold my hand against his chest, feeling his heart beat so hard that it could leave bruises.

The noise of Mum flushing the toilet comes as a sweet relief and adds a sexy backing track all in one. I find myself playing with the buttons on his jeans. Teasing them with my fingers. I've become some kind of bold, seductive person around him now it's just the two of us. Am I actually going to touch his actual penis?

I can hear Mum on the landing about to walk down the stairs, and I find myself boldly unbuttoning his jeans. Who is this horny beast I've become?

214

Knock, knock!

Oh crap! Mum wasn't walking down the stairs; she was walking toward my room.

"You okay, love? Can I come in?" she asks on the other side of the door, my hand frozen over Scott's penis area.

"Crap," I mutter as the two of us scramble off the bed. "ONE SEX, ER, SEC! JUST GETTING CHANGED!" I shout as Scott and I head over to the window.

He scrambles his jacket back on along the way and heads out toward the ledge. As he's about to go, he pops his head back up through the window and kisses me.

"To be continued," he whispers, a small smile on his face, his cheeks slightly pink, before popping out and back down the drainpipe.

I feel like I'm entirely made from jelly as I straighten my T-shirt and shorts, brush out my hair, and pull the duvet across, lest there's suddenly some kind of penis-was-here sign on the bedsheets, before opening the door to Mum.

"Sorry, just getting into my pj's," I say.

"Annie?" Mum asks, pointing at my beeping phone.

"Annie!" I lie as I look down.

Scott: You're so hot xx

24

I'm on Thursday of the longest week ever. It's been nearly a week since Selena died, two days since Adam got croquet-ed, and about half a second since Annie texted me her latest picture of the murder board. With so much red wool, it's starting to resemble one of the crochet hats I made over the summer.

I'm heading down the stairs into our kitchen, when I have to stop on the final step. I thought I'd been through all the trauma I was going to go through this week, but clearly my parents had other ideas. The first thing I see upon entering the kitchen, a place where food is made, where we *eat*, is my parents bathed in the golden morning light, "at it."

They're sprawled across the table over a whole bunch of open tabloids while the news blares in the background about the murders. It's possibly the most disrespectful amorous activity the world has ever seen.

"MY EYES!" I grab the nearest thing to me—a cutting board—and cover my eyes with it while Dad grabs a mixing bowl—which is unfortunately see-through—to cover his bits. It has hideously only served to magnify them.

I question whether this interaction is actually more traumatic than finding two dead bodies in less than a week and decide that either way I'm going to need to start saving up for the hard-core therapy I'll be needing for the rest of my life.

"KEZ! Sorry!" Dad's saying.

"Darling, don't be so dramatic; you know how you were made, right?" Mum says while fixing her kimono.

"Yes, and knowing is enough; that is the peak of information I need. I don't need to SEE it," I say, grabbing some coffee and an apple as I fly out the door to meet Annie on the curb.

It's super annoying that she's not already out here—I really wanted to make a quick exit. I feel like I did when I was five and told them I was running away from home because they wouldn't let me have a kitten (then I realized I was scared of going any farther than the front yard). I slump down on the curb with my coffee and apple, feeling a bit too sick to consume either of them.

How the hell did this become my life? I just want to go back to normal. I don't think I ever fully appreciated how great it was to have spent the summer crocheting hats for babies in need while having absolutely no excitement in my life. But then I remember Scott coming through my window last night. Maybe *some* excitement is good.

"Hey, dude, what's up!" Annie rolls up to the curb, still on the Paw Patrol bike. I'm starting to wonder if she'll ever get her own bike fixed now.

"Let's go, Annie!" I say, grabbing my bike as the two of us cycle off down the street.

"Good VULVA, Mrs. Robbins!" Annie shouts across the road as we get to Mrs. R's house and see her and Herbert putting out her bins.

"Here! You two!" Mrs. R says, raising her hand. For a minute, I wonder if she's about to chase Annie down the street in response to the vulva comment, but it seems she's got something else on her mind. "I need to talk with you!"

Annie and I stop cycling, and Mrs. R comes out of her gate looking pure business. She doesn't even have her hair net on this morning; it's as if she was awake and waiting for us before we showed up.

"What's up, Mrs. R?" Annie asks.

"I've got something for the two of you. I tried to talk to those young police detectives about it again yesterday, but they seem to think I'm just some old codger and they won't take me seriously. Pair of fools."

Mrs. R looks kind of sad and small as she's telling us this.

"We don't exactly think they're geniuses, either," Annie says, and I'm taken aback to witness Annie and Mrs. R agreeing with each other for the first time ever.

"Have you got time for a chat?" she asks. Mrs. R not shooing us out of her vicinity is weird enough, but this is starting to get creepy. Annie's at pearl-clutching levels of shocked.

"We're a bit late for school, Mrs. R," I say, because I know that Annie wants to get there before Heather, Audrey, and Colin to see if they all arrive together this morning. She wondered if them leaving separately last night might have signified them growing apart.

But Mrs. R looks pretty down at this; it makes me feel guilt deep in my bones, and Annie must feel it, too.

"We can come back after school?" Annie offers.

"Thank you, dear," Mrs. R says, looking around her shiftily. "Come back, but tell no one. There are eyes and ears everywhere."

When she says it, I feel a tingle shoot down my spine. I find myself glancing around as well, not even sure who or what I would be looking out for, because it seems to me that on both occasions when a murder's happened I've been right by it. So maybe spotting danger isn't my strong point.

We head off on our bikes, and I can see that Mrs. R doesn't quite know how to wave us off if she's not shaking her fist and screaming at Annie in disapproval. She sort of raises her hand awkwardly and then gives up.

"Oh god, that's going to be a waste of time, isn't it?" Annie whispers, looking up at me from her bike.

"I dunno," I say. "Something about the way she was talking and behaving makes me think she might actually have something for us, you know."

I look back over my shoulder at Mrs. R as her and her dog, Herbert, head back into her little cottage. The two of them definitely look a bit burdened by something.

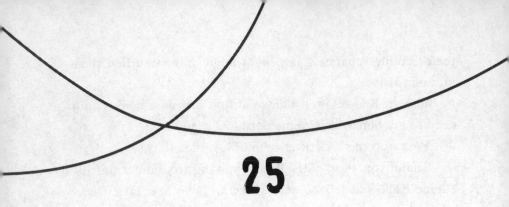

25

There seem to be police everywhere at school. It's as if they've just realized that there might be tons of evidence here, which of course me and Annie have known all along. There are officers looking into lockers and classrooms and talking to teachers.

"Amazing that it took a boy to die before they took things seriously," Annie says loudly as we walk down the hallway to the common room.

I'm so busy paying attention to her that I forget to be on alert for Mr. C and he catches me completely off guard.

"Great job letting all the serial killers out, Kerry," Mr. C says sulkily at me so that I have to turn around and do a double take.

"Huh?" I ask.

"Your little friend over the summer. The psychologist lady, letting all the serial killers out because she thinks they're reformed? GREAT JOB. Maybe Adam'd still be alive if it wasn't for people like her."

I'm standing with my mouth open as he swaggers off down

the corridor. Surely there's some kind of rule that stops him talking to me like that or something. Surely? No?

"Christ," Annie says as the two of us continue along the corridor. "It's going to be another spicy day in hell."

The first thing I see when we walk through the common room doors is Scott hanging with the band. Dave's drumming a chair with some sticks in a way that would be seriously annoying if I wasn't too busy making eye contact with Scott and feeling my vagina flip-flop.

He smiles shyly, and I remember him last night in my room, his hands all over me. OH MY GOD, he's coming over.

Annie's been talking to me for the last few minutes, and I've honestly no idea what she's been rabbiting on about. I can hear her getting irate with my lack of response until she sees Scott and she twigs.

"Oh, okay, I'll try talking sense to you again once he's not around," she huffs, and immediately goes to sit with Audrey, Colin, and Heather. We never used to separate, so something about how quickly and naturally she goes to sit next to Heather feels jarring.

"Hey," he says with his actual mouth, which was on my actual mouth and in my actual bed last night.

"Hey," I say back, feeling like I'm wading through glue even getting that one word out.

"You okay?" he asks.

"Yeah," I say in the most thrilling of conversations ever.

"Wanna hang out later? After school?" he asks.

"Yeah," I say, again using my words well.

"Cool," he says, brushing his hair off his face as I feel something hit my leg.

I look down to see a tampon on the floor next to my foot, and when I look up, Annie's gesturing at me wildly.

"Oh crap, I'm sorry, I forgot, I'm supposed to hang with Annie right after school, but maybe later? Like tonight? Maybe we could hang?"

"I'd like that," he whispers, his dimples showing as he smiles at me shyly.

He walks away from me, and I'm left staring at him dreamily, my eyes glazing over.

"KERRY!" Not content with just throwing period products at me, Annie is now shouting at me across the common room while Audrey, Colin, and Heather stare at us. I know we've got investigating to do, but can't I just have five seconds with a guy who FINALLY likes me and who I like, too?

I love how she feels like she's just got tampons to fling about the place as well, like they're not precious things that we actually NEED, which cost a FORTUNE. It must be great for Heather, though, living in her house, with all her period products just there whenever she needs them. I guess Audrey and Colin spend so much time in her house that they always know where to find them. Ample opportunity to stock up, and an easy way to frame their friend, using the products made by her family . . .

"Hey," I say, joining Colin, Audrey, and Heather, trying not to look as afraid of Colin and Audrey as I feel.

A week ago, I wouldn't have dreamed of coming over here and sitting with them. Now it would be weird if I didn't. Annie looks like she's always been sitting with them, laughing with Colin and Audrey like we don't suspect them of double murder.

I don't know how she looks so comfortable with them when I still feel like an outsider.

"Audrey was just saying that DI Wallace and DI Collins are in Mrs. Joy's office. They have some people they need to talk to apparently," Annie says pointedly.

"It'll be a cold day in hell before anyone gets me in that office again." Audrey shakes her head.

"It's where textiles go to die," Colin explains.

As if people didn't already find that office triggering enough, Mrs. Joy's got cross-stitched cats covering almost every surface in there. Most of them have little speech bubbles coming out of their mouths saying platitudes like "Live, laugh, love." It truly is a nightmare. Right on cue, DI Wallace and DI Collins appear in front of us with Principal Styles.

"Heather? Can we have a word?" Principal Styles looks like she's just about tolerating the detectives after their speech yesterday. She's kind of zero tolerance with sexism.

Heather grabs her bag silently while Colin and Audrey give her reassuring arm pats, and follows them out of the common room. She looks cool as a cucumber, and when I turn around, Colin and Audrey also look completely calm. It does make me wonder; how do they manage to stay so together even when everything's completely fallen apart?

The whole common room gradually starts talking again after the silence that descended when the detectives arrived.

"I don't know how they're ever going to find someone that knew all of Adam's secrets," Colin says.

"I mean, no one really did, even those who knew him . . . intimately," Audrey says.

The two of them go back to what they were doing before the police came—Audrey filing her nails, Colin flicking through a magazine.

"So, what you were saying yesterday about Adam," Annie says, before mouthing "THE DRUGS," in an exaggerated fashion, like someone who has never been near drugs before, "did Heather really not know about that?"

"God no, she would have dumped him. She can't have anything getting in the way of her college applications and having a drug dealer boyfriend might very well do that, you know." Colin skims over his copy of *Hello!* magazine, reading the latest on Posh and Becks's house renovations.

"And you have no idea where he got the drugs from?" Annie asks.

"Nah, he had secrets," Audrey says. "A LOT of secrets, so it could have been anyone, really."

"Don't you feel bad keeping things from Heather?" I ask.

"Oh, hell no, that bitch has her own secrets," Colin says.

"Such as?" Annie prods. "That dress she was wearing today. Was that a gifted thing?"

Colin snorts.

"Col!" Audrey chastises. "I don't know what you mean."

"Yeah . . ." Colin says sarcastically. "No idea."

"Does she get them often? I'm wondering if she might be able to help me with a project for, err, Instagram influencing in economics class."

Annie doesn't even take economics, but Audrey and Colin don't know that.

"Oh, I doubt she can help you," Audrey says with a smirk.

"Aud." Colin blinks warningly at her.

"What?! I didn't say a word, did I? Maybe just look at her Instagram. You can see who she's tagged. That's really all there is to it," Audrey says.

Neither of us need to look at the posts to know that the hashtags have been removed, so Audrey's just confirming what Annie had already figured out.

"None of them were ads, were they?" Annie whispers to them. "She lies to get followers, doesn't she? She doesn't get sent these things by big labels, does she?"

"I always knew you were smart, Annie." Colin gives Annie the sort of grin you'd get from a proud father, and I feel a weird jealousy creeping into my veins. Annie opens Instagram and clicks on to Heather's followers list.

"And a lot of these followers look kind of spammy." Annie rests on several that have very bot-y names, like "Simon1290473628."

"Almost as if . . ." Audrey starts.

"They've been bought?!" Annie says triumphantly, but still in hushed tones.

"Precisely, my little brain box," Colin says, giving Annie a patronizing little pat on the head that she seems to positively eat up, forgetting that he's got motive and opportunity to be a murderer.

"How did you find out?" Annie asks. "Does she know you know?"

"Oh, she doesn't know we know. Selena found out over the summer. It was her proudest moment. Heather had pissed her off one too many times, probably because she'd dumped Adam and then got back together with him again," Colin says.

"And then Selena started trolling her with an account that was set up pretending to be her dead dad?" Annie asks.

"What?" Colin asks too loudly. Both of them startle, and a few people glance our way curiously.

"I thought . . ." Annie trails off. "No nothing. Don't worry."

The bell rings. Annie's brows knit firmly together. So how is it that the two of them didn't know about the account? And if Selena had already told them, why was she even bothering to blackmail Heather?

"Merde!" Annie whispers in my ear, throwing her hands up to the sky as we grab our bags and follow the crowd to first period. "I thought they were all in on the Instagram account together. I'm going to have to take that bit off the board."

"Unless they were trying to prevent Heather's secret getting out?" I suggest, feeling smart.

"They literally just told us the secret," Annie says.

The investigation giveth and then taketh away. And apparently, the investigation now taketh us to first period.

26

At the end of last period, right when I was getting excited about my date with Scott, Annie messaged me to say that she has something to tell me and not to freak out, but it might upset me. I agreed to meet her by her locker and then once she's shown me whatever it is we can head to Mrs. R's. But I've been standing here waiting for her for ten minutes, and when I see her approach, she's laughing and joking with Colin, Audrey, and Heather.

"See you later." She waves them off with a cheery smile as I stand, my brow furrowed, scowling at her for leaving me waiting here worrying about what on earth she could need to tell me.

"What's later?" I ask.

"Oh, we're just going to hang out; I figured you'll be with Scott, so I'll hang with them at Heather's?"

I can't actually believe what I'm hearing. Now she's hanging out with them on her own? Making plans with them without me? I'm trying not to be jealous, but what happened to her thinking they were murderers? Now she wants to *hang* with them?

"So, don't hate me," Annie says, clearly not realizing that I'm still crushed from her first confession. "But there's something I need to show you, something I found in class that's a bit weird."

"Oh god," I say because the last time she said "Don't hate me" to me was when she'd spilled cherry soda down my supercool *Animal Crossing* T-shirt. She looks slightly more afraid this time, so it must be something really bad.

She bites her lip and pulls out her phone, her eyes wide.

"What is it, Annie?" I'm starting to get a bit worried now.

"It's . . . I found this." Annie turns her phone around to show me a picture on Selena's Instagram profile.

The main part of the picture is Selena. It already looks like it's aged. That's what happens when people die, though, isn't it? Pictures of them always look like they're stuck way in the past. I'm not sure exactly what it is that she's nervous about showing me. It's Selena putting cans into a box. I look at the tag and see it's listed as a food bank in Manchester.

"What would I be ticked off about?" I ask, reading the caption where she's said that she's helping at a food bank with her BBC colleagues as part of a piece they're doing reporting on the rise in food bank usage. I feel completely puzzled by what on earth there is for me to be concerned about.

Annie pinches the screen with her fingers and zooms in on the picture. I have to squint a little, but I finally see it. It's Scott. In the background of the picture.

"Taken in the summer, like way before he would have met her," Annie says.

"Well, they're quite far away in that picture?" I say, trying to stay calm, because they aren't actually standing next to each other or anything.

"True," Annie reasons. "But if they were both volunteering, don't you think they'd have recognized each other when they saw each other again?"

I feel a bit weird because isn't this the kind of thing that he would have mentioned? And why is Annie trying to make this a thing? I've got a bit of a sinking feeling as I try and picture any point at the party where he was talking to her or even near her, and I remember them walking through the living room chatting together.

"There's actually more," Annie says.

"Oh god, go on," I say, expecting another picture of Selena draped over him or something.

"The word on the street is that Scott was seen coming out of the police station last night. Apparently, after the memorial, he went in and spent hours in there with the detectives."

Since when did Annie start hearing "the word on the street"? Why do I feel so annoyed by this? I'm sure it's rubbish because he was with me last night.

"What time did 'the street' say that he left the police station?" I ask, knowing that I can save this, it's got to be wrong, and I'm sure I can prove it.

"About seven-thirty," Annie says.

He showed up at my place at eight. He came to my place from the police station. I feel my head start to spin, and I become hot and nauseous.

Before he came to my house, to my bed, he was being questioned by the police. But he never mentioned it. Not once.

Although I guess it's not exactly sexy talk, it feels like the sort of thing you would tell someone who you saw right after it happened. Unless you were hiding something.

I stare at the picture trying to work out what to do next, but everything's gone blurry and it's hard for me to even focus on the picture. A million thoughts are crowding for space in my head at once.

"I think I need to talk to him," I say, unsure how I'm actually going to do that when everything's blurring around me.

"Yeah, I think we probably should." His voice appears behind me.

I jump back and turn, struggling to read his expression. It's more serious than I've ever seen it before. He looks kind of sad. I can't believe he's been lying to me, and I hate that I might be about to find out something that'll end us before we've even really begun.

"I can explain," he says, and I guess he's been standing by, listening for a while, too.

"I'll leave you guys to it," Annie says, and heads back toward the common room, probably to find her new friends. They're probably the ones that showed her the picture in the first place. Anything to avoid suspicion falling on them.

"Come outside?" Scott asks. "Somewhere we can have a bit of privacy?"

I nod and follow him out of the school and into the sunshine.

"This is kind of embarrassing," Scott says. He jiggles his foot as we sit on the bench opposite the lanes, a small, wooded, overgrown footpath that used to be a train line.

"Go on," I say, because I can't bear this long drawn-out reveal of whatever it is he has to tell me. If he's about to tell me that he was actually hooking up with Selena, or he's a bigger player than Adam Devers was, I just need him to get on with it because last night's still too fresh in my mind and my hormones are far too in charge right now.

"I told you my mum's sick, and that's why we moved here?" He stares at the ground and kicks the dust up with his sneaker.

"Yeah?" I realize I've revved myself for shock, all my instincts protecting myself, my legs crossed away from him, arms hugging my body.

"She hasn't been able to work because she's been having treatment," he says. "We've not really had any money. There are benefits but they don't stretch far and it's been really difficult. I'm in that picture because we've been relying on food banks for a while now. I recognized Selena when I came here because we had a chat when she was helping out. But when I went to say hey, she said she didn't remember me. She was, as you know, charming."

My anger instantly lifts. That explains me seeing them talking at the party. But how could he think that it was embarrassing to use a food bank? How could he worry about telling me that?

"Why would that be embarrassing?" I ask, putting my arm around him instantly. "That's so far from embarrassing. You have nothing to be ashamed of!"

"I know that deep down, it just feels . . . the whole thing feels so dehumanizing. It feels shameful, and yet we can't do anything about it," he says. "Also, you're so normal I just wanted you to think I was normal, too."

231

"How is using a food bank not normal?? And I'm not normal!" I practically shout. "I'm the weirdest person I know!"

"You're more normal than you think you are, Kerry," he says, pulling me in and kissing me softly on the lips. "You're extraordinary, but that's a good thing."

I feel myself relaxing, but there's still the matter of his visit to the police last night and why he didn't tell me about that.

"What about the police last night?" I ask, and immediately I feel his shoulders tense up.

"I should have told you about that, too. I should have said as soon as I got to your place, but when I got there and I saw you, I just wasn't thinking. I got kind of distracted." His eyes drift over me, and I feel my cheeks go red. "They wanted to ask me some questions about why I came to town and where I was before. I guess they felt like me arriving in the village and then immediately finding two dead bodies was kind of odd."

"But you were with me both times?" I ask, feeling nervous.

"Yeah, but you've always lived here. I'm an outsider," he says, and I think how ridiculous it is that they even thought that. If they knew him, they wouldn't even question it. Like I don't, either.

"They're fools," I say, leaning into his shoulder while he puts his arm around me.

"Yeah, you can say that again," Scott says.

I put my hand over his, and we sit for a while in silence. I can't imagine what it must be like for his mum to be so sick.

"Is she okay? Your mum? I can help, you know?" I suggest. "I can like bring food over or help with house stuff or . . ." I trail off because I realize that I've just invited myself to his house and our relationship might not be ready for that.

"Oh, um, it's okay; we've got it covered. The two of us are used to it now," he says, but the rejection feels like a slap in the face. "Thank you, though." He gives me an encouraging smile, which helps to bat down the humiliation slightly, and then we sit in silence again.

"Is that Annie?" Scott asks, pointing over at the lanes. I can't see what he's talking about at first, but then one of the bushes starts moving and I realize that Annie's taped a bit of bush to her head and she's trying to become one with the hedgerow.

"Um . . . not sure . . ." I say, trying to distract him. "Could be, but I want to hear about you. Let's not talk about Annie right now."

I try to focus in on what Scott's saying and not think at all about the fact that Annie is doing something super strange over by the entrance to the lanes.

"That's all there is to tell, really," he says.

"What about your dad? Can't he help?" I ask, and see Scott's face change.

"Oh, no, he's not been around for years." He says it so quickly, like he's brushing it off. It seems super weird to me.

I don't want to push him because his mum's sick and he's had so much to deal with. I know he doesn't want me questioning him on stuff, but surely his dad should be helping them? At least sending money or something?

"Do you know where he lives?" I ask innocently.

"He's no use to us. I'd rather not talk about him," he says, looking a bit annoyed with me. I feel like I've pushed it too far. But I still don't understand.

"Doesn't he legally have to help with money, though?"

233

His face says I've definitely gone too far.

"He's dead," Scott says it so quietly, I know I've screwed up.

"Oh god, I'm sorry, I'm such a douche," I say. "I shouldn't have pushed—I'm so sorry."

I don't think there are enough apologies in the world to convey how awful I feel right now.

"It's cool; honestly, I should have told you, and it's not your fault, is it?" He says it like he just wants to move on, but I can't help thinking that I should be apologizing more. I should have kept my mouth shut.

The two of us sit in silence.

"Do you still want to hang later?" he asks, staring straight ahead.

"Of course I do! We're just popping around to see Mrs. R first; she's got something she wants to tell me and Annie about apparently. Something to do with Selena!"

"Really?" Scott looks as surprised as we were.

"Yeah, I doubt it's anything. She's mostly just a rage-filled old lady, though, so best to do what she says. Shouldn't take too long."

"Cool, so, like, maybe seven p.m.? Meet me outside the bookshop in the village? I'll think of something we can do that'll be super fun?" His expression changes and he looks so sexy and excited about tonight, how could I not go now?

"Sounds good," I say.

"Look, I gotta run, but I'll catch you later." He kisses my forehead, and I breathe in his smell, trying to do it subtly so he doesn't notice me inhaling him like a big creeper.

Something's pinging in the back of my mind, though.

234

Something doesn't quite add up, but I don't want to ruin things now, not after everything he's just trusted me with.

At that moment, Annie comes running out of the bush screaming.

"WASPP WASSSSPPPPP!" she's shouting, with branches stuck to her head and pinging out of her hair at wild angles.

There's always something going on. Scott takes this as a cue to duck out, and I follow her down the lane.

I finally catch up to Annie, bent over and out of breath just a little farther down the lanes, pulling bits of twig and nettle out of her hair.

"What the hell?" I ask, as if I think I'm about to get a rational explanation for this behavior.

"Colin," she breathes at me. "He went down the lanes. And I followed him down there. I know who it is! His secret lover, you will not BELIEVE who I saw him with! But then I got worried they'd see me and I felt kinda pervy just sitting in the bush with them there and I had to come back and I got stung by so many nettles and then the wasp came. . . ."

"Annie, slow down," I say, taking her shoulders in my hands. "You saw Colin? You worked out who his secret lover is?"

"It's—" Annie's broken off by the sight of Trey, one of the CSI Coders, coming down the lanes toward us. She starts to mouth his name, but I've already figured it out myself.

Trey's really nice and really smart and really nerdy. I get the same feeling I had when we learned that Audrey was a chess champion. They shouldn't have to hide these things. Trey shouldn't be hidden; he's a great guy.

"I know," Annie says as he walks on past us. "He shouldn't be anyone's secret—he's such a dude."

"But why's he in his phone as D—" I'm interrupted mid-question.

"Hey! What are you two doing?" Heather's voice comes booming at us from the entrance to the lanes, where she's standing with Audrey.

"Hey, Heather, nothing!" Annie says. She takes a deep breath as I signal to her that she's got a bit of bush in her hair, and she tries to brush it out. "Just hanging." She pulls at the twig dangling out of her hair.

"Have you seen Colin?" Heather asks. "I could have sworn I saw him go down here."

"I still don't think you did," Audrey says calmly, but it's easy to see that this is another secret between her and her twin brother, and I know we think they're probably the murderers, but to be honest, I'm in danger of starting to like them.

"Did you see him?" Heather asks.

"NO!" Annie says it so quickly that Audrey notices and gives her a look, and Annie regains some composure. "No one came past."

"Maybe I'll just go and take a look for him down that way," Audrey says, pointing in the direction that Trey's just come from.

"Thought you said he wasn't down here?" Heather asks.

"No harm in double-checking, though, right?" Audrey says before heading off down the lane.

"I've been meaning to catch up with you two anyway," Heather says. "What have you got so far?"

"Nothing concrete yet," Annie says. "But we've been tailing

a suspect—I just can't tell you who until I'm one hundred per-cent."

"I knew you'd figure it out." Heather beams at Annie.

It's like I'm in the twilight zone. When did she and Annie become so chummy?

"Thank god for you two, because there's no way the police are going to solve this, you know," Heather says as she and Annie exchange a small smile.

I wonder if she knows we know her secrets and she's trying to keep us in line?

"Don't worry, we have some leads. We'll keep you in the loop," Annie says. But I'm pretty sure the only leads we have right now are Mrs. R and Heather's two best friends.

"I'll try not to. I guess I'm just scared. Those two are gone—it makes sense I'm next, right?" Heather's face is showing genuine emotion, and I wonder if losing her best friend and her boyfriend to murder in the same week really *has* changed her. Brought down her barriers. It's a shock to see her more human, more vulnerable.

I hadn't thought of her as "next," and I can tell Annie hadn't, either. I'd kind of hoped there would be no "next." It just makes me realize how much more urgent it is we find out who did this.

"We will find them," Annie says, rubbing Heather's arm, a gesture that a week ago would have resulted in Heather scream-ing at her. "There'll be no 'next.'"

"Christ, FINALLY," Heather says, regaining her composure. I watch her walls go back up as Colin and Audrey come down the lane toward us, Colin stealthily pulling twigs out of his hair. "Come ON; we've got important stuff to do tonight."

"We do?" Colin asks.

"I've got no weekend mourning outfits, Colin. We talked about this. You need to help me dress for mourning at all times."

"Right, yes, of course," he says, turning to Annie and me. "Are you two coming?"

"I'll be there a bit later. Kerry's got a hot date," Annie says. Colin and Audrey grin at the mention of my love life.

"Cool, well, laters," Heather says, turning on her heel.

"Have fun!" Audrey and Colin both wink at me.

The second they're out of earshot, Annie grabs my arm and tugs me down the lane.

"Quick, let's go and see Mrs. R!"

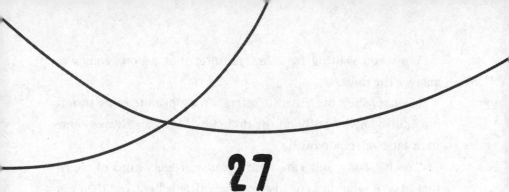

27

"I don't want to alarm you, but you do kinda look a bit sore," I say, pointing to Annie's bright red, nettle-stung legs.

"A SCRATCH!" she shouts at me dramatically. "This investigation won't solve itself, and no matter what EXTREME PHYSICAL PAIN AND DISCOMFORT I am currently experiencing, I must persist! I cannot let some nettles hold me back!"

I think things really got bleak about ten minutes ago, when Annie thought she'd found a dock leaf to ease the stings and sadly, it turned out to be an average leaf with possibly what we think may have been some dog piss on it. Now every time I look at her legs, I wince.

"ONWARD!" Annie charges, ignoring my concern and marching her bright red legs to Mrs. R's front door, a shining beacon of misfortune.

"Maybe Mrs. R will have something for the stings, too," I say encouragingly.

I press the bell, and some quaint kind of tinkly music plays out much louder and longer than I think should be legal for a doorbell.

We stand waiting for a few minutes, but no one comes to answer the door.

"I guess she's out," Annie offers after a minute of us standing waiting awkwardly on the doorstep. "We can always come back later or tomorrow?"

"Yeah," I say, but I hesitate because it feels kind of weird that Mrs. R would tell us to come over after school and then not be here after school when we arrived. But it *is* also perfectly normal for her to go out, though.

"Let's just head back to my house. I feel like we've got a lot to talk about, especially after everything we found out today," she says it with a mischievous glint in her eye.

I sigh, too tired to fight her on this.

"Wait, what's that?" Annie asks suddenly, putting her head to the door. "Can you hear that? It sounds like Herbert barking. Why would she go out without Herbie?"

"People go out without their dogs all the time if they're going somewhere where dogs aren't allowed," I reason, shrugging.

"Not Mrs. R," Annie persists. I see her face change, and detective mode is officially activated. "Something weird's going on."

She jiggles the handle, and the door opens a crack before she turns around, her eyebrow arched at me.

"Annie, no," I say. "We can't just walk into people's houses. I'm tired, and I want to go home and get ready for my date with Scott later. MY FIRST EVER PROPER DATE, ANNIE. Just let me go. I've found two dead bodies this week; don't I deserve something NICE?"

But Annie's not listening to me. The moment she opens the door, Herbie's on us, barking and running at us, then running back the other way, down the hallway, stopping to bark some more and check we're coming.

"He wants us to follow him," Annie says as we both stand in the doorway. We haven't technically trespassed on someone else's property yet. But I have a funny feeling that's about to change.

Annie follows him in with no regard for my thoughts and wishes, and I know there's no going back now. Something's off, and Herbie's pretty insistent that we go with him, and if Annie's going, I guess I'm going, too.

It's as if I can smell the danger at this point, but I'm so numb to it after everything that's already happened this week that I keep going. If something's up with Mrs. R, we need to find out. I am brave and strong, and I've got Annie, the fiercest person I know.

The three of us head slowly down the hallway, Herbie jumping around barking, Annie and I looking at each other, holding hands for safety. The old bare floorboards of the hallway creak underfoot, and it feels like the people in the pictures that cover the walls are all watching us. There's a sinister feel to the whole place, but that could be because Mrs. R's made the bold choice to paint her hallway bright red.

"Mrs. R?" Annie shouts down the long hallway. But there's no reply.

We pass the open doorway into what looks like the living room. Crochet blankets cover the sofas and doilies are scattered over the tables. The net curtains Mrs. R usually peeks around flutter in the breeze of an open window.

"Mrs. R?" I ask fruitlessly as Herbert rushes ahead of us, down the hall and into the kitchen at the end. He's standing in the doorway, beckoning us through, his bark persistent.

"Maybe she accidentally left the door unlocked and she's totally fine?" Annie suggests, creeping farther down the hallway past an open door that leads to a cupboard under the stairs.

There's a pair of walking boots that look like they were halfway through being put away, one shoe in the cupboard and one out. And her walking stick's propped against the wall. She doesn't go anywhere without that stick—it's her tool to gesture at people with when she's mad, and she's also been known to trip people up with it and take them out in the middle of the village when they've got on her nerves.

"I'm starting to get a bad feeling about this, Annie." I stare at the discarded stick.

"Yeah, now that you mention it, I am starting to get the heebie-jeebies, too," Annie says.

I just keep thinking about how many horror movies start like this. Or at least with this exact feeling in the pit of my stomach, except this time the whole thing is very real, and I can't press pause and watch something else.

This is it. The dog has led us to some kind of evil, and that will be the end of us. We are going to die. I won't even be able to haunt Annie for leading me to my death because she'll be dead, too. And yet, here we are, still walking toward danger.

We keep walking, past Herbie and into the kitchen, and that's when my heart stops.

From behind the kitchen island, I can see a pair of feet poking out. A pair of what are unmistakably Mrs. R's feet.

"She's had a fall!" Annie cries, heading toward the kitchen island. "MRS. R! Mrs.—"

And then she makes a noise I've never heard before. A

gagging. Herbie's run around the kitchen island with her, and I can hear him making a whining noise. I'm scared that I already know what I'm going to find, but it's far too late to turn back now.

The moment I round the corner of the kitchen island, I wish I hadn't. There's blood coming from Mrs. R's head, her eyes are closed, and she's got string coming out of her ears. It takes me a minute, but I can see what they are . . . tampons. Annie checks for a pulse, but all my hope fades when she shakes her head sadly. Mrs. R is dead, and it's not rocket science to work out that she probably didn't put tampons in her ears herself.

Annie leans over Mrs. R, fat, wet tears landing on the body. Even though I feel totally numb, somehow I find myself kneeling and putting my arm around her, hugging her while she cries on my shoulder.

I dial the police and try to get Annie and Herbie away from Mrs. R. I'm amazed by how calm, rational, and together I'm being when I realize that I'm crying, not just a little bit, but a lot. Huge, wet, snotty tears. I only notice this when the officer on the end of the line asks me to repeat myself several times. Once I hang up, I don't know what to do or how to deal with this, and I've found myself texting Scott without even really thinking about it.

> **Me:** Mrs. R's dead. We just
> found her.

I'm so angry. This shouldn't have happened. The police should have found the killer after they killed once. They shouldn't have even been able to kill a second time, never mind

243

a third. Mrs. R was an old woman. She may have hated everyone, but she didn't deserve this. I can't stand by and watch as the police bumble about anymore.

Things have been happening in double speed since the police arrived. There's tape up, and we've all been moved away from the body to the living room, where the police questioned us. Since then, Annie and I have been sitting with Herb, clinging to him and crying into his fur. I assumed Scott would have been here by now. When I sent that text, I knew he'd come and comfort me like he did before. But there's no sign of him yet, and it doesn't look like he's seen the text, either.

"It's interesting, don't you think, Kerry, that in the case of every single one of these murders, you've been the first on the scene?" DI Wallace asks.

"I would say it's more bad luck than interesting . . ." I start.

"But do you see where I'm coming from? That you seem to be finding a lot of dead bodies lately?"

I blink at him, seething as I look from him to Annie and back again. What a prick.

"Interesting that she's always been with others when the murders took place though and never for any second been without an alibi, too." Annie glares at him, ready to take him out at any second.

That seems to do the job, and he skulks away, back to DI Collins in the hallway. They're still able to keep their watchful eye on us from there, but they're not close enough to hear what we're saying.

I'd never been in Mrs. R's house before; it seems wrong that the only time I saw it was when we found her body. There are things a person's house can tell you about them, things that you don't get even from spending a lot of time with them. Annie knows this, and she tries to snoop around without getting caught, probably hoping to collect as much evidence as she can without the police spotting her.

Her house is nice. I look at the mantelpiece covered in pictures of people I've never seen before, some of them the same people that were on the walls in the hall. I wonder if they were her family and if any of them are still alive, if there'll be someone here to grieve her now she's gone. She deserves people to grieve her.

I look down at Herbie next to me, his little chin tucked on the sofa, resigned to his owner no longer being with us. He's grieving, too.

"What will happen to Herb?" I ask, scratching behind his ears as DI Collins approaches us.

"We can take him and sort out him being rehomed," DI Collins says.

"Can he come with us? I don't like to think of him all alone after losing Mrs. R. He's so upset," I say.

"I think that should be fine," DI Collins says kindly, confirming to me that he's definitely the good cop to DI Wallace's bad cop.

I hold the two of them responsible for Mrs. R's and Adam's deaths but definitely more DI Wallace than DI Collins because of his attitude with us. Surely no one else would have died if they'd just taken Selena's death seriously in the first place. How foolish do you have to be to believe that Selena's death was an accident?

And what about the fact that all of these people have had some kind of period product left at the scene? What's that about? Why would they do that? What does it mean?

"Annie," I whisper, seeing her turn to me, clearly having the same realization. "The period products."

"I know," she says, her eyes wide.

"The menstrual cup in Selena's mouth, the pad over Adam's eyes, and the tampons in Mrs. R's ears."

"Speak no evil, see no evil, hear no evil . . ." Annie lists them in order first before repeating the saying. "See no evil, hear no evil, speak no evil."

"They're trying to send a message. I think they're trying to shut someone up. They're scaring someone into being quiet about something," I say, looking around to check the police can't hear us. The last thing we need is them telling us we're being hysterical again.

"But what about?" Annie whispers back just as DI Wallace and DI Collins edge closer to us.

We're onto something—I know we are. I'm going to make sure Mrs. R's honored correctly, and I'm going to make sure that Annie and I find the killer. It's what she would have wanted.

"Don't worry, Herb," I whisper as he licks my hand gratefully. "We'll find out who did this."

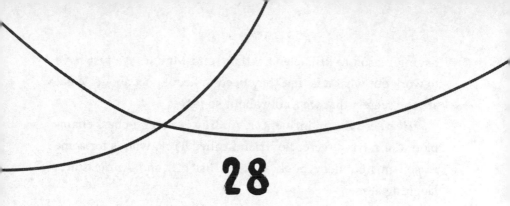

28

The three of us sit on Annie's bed, me, Annie, and Herb, staring at the murder board. It feels like the first time I'm really seeing it because it's the first time I think the two of us can actually crack this. We *need* to solve it, and I feel bad for ever thinking Annie was being overdramatic.

I write "see no evil," "hear no evil," and "speak no evil" on three Post-it Notes, before sticking them up on the board matching them to each of the victims.

"Okay, so if that was the message, they wanted Selena to stop speaking, Adam to stop seeing, and Mrs. R to stop hearing?" Annie suggests, but I can see she knows as soon as it comes out of her mouth that that doesn't quite make sense. Once someone's dead, they can't see, hear, or speak. So that wouldn't work.

"If they've done all three—see, hear, and speak—maybe it means that there'll be no more murders after this?" I suggest hopefully, but I don't believe that, either.

"It's definitely what we said earlier: whoever it is, is sending a message to someone to keep quiet about something , as well as having reason to kill Selena, Adam, and Mrs. R. We just have to work out what it is that they need to keep quiet about. What are the secrets that we know about so far?"

"Heather's not an influencer. Audrey is a secret chess champion. Colin has a secret boyfriend called Trey, who is for some reason in his phone book as D," I list off, and Annie starts laughing at me.

"Sorry, but D? Don't you get it? The D?" Annie's about to roll off her bed with delight as I shrug my shoulders. "DICK!"

"Oh!" I gasp. There are times that I feel like I might be one hundred years old and completely unaware of any of the culture of my peers. Now is one of them.

Normally, we would have cackled about that for hours, but all events of the day considered we just sort of half-heartedly chuckle once or twice. Then the two of us sit staring at the board as Annie adds the secrets next to people's pictures.

"Are any of these really reasons to murder?" I ask. "Combined with the fact that Heather was with us and Audrey and Colin were both in the lanes somewhere, which is nowhere near Mrs. R's place, when she was killed. I think we have to assume that all three of them are innocent now."

"Agreed," Annie says, but I think she actually looks happy about this. She's pleased her new friends aren't murderers.

We can tell Herbie's in mourning because of the way that he's sitting, head slumped over the bed, just staring at us blankly, and to be honest, I know exactly how he feels as the two of us slump down, too. Audrey and Colin were our last obvious suspects, and now it can't be them, either. I just wish he could talk—after all, he must have seen everything. It seems silly that he knows exactly who did this, and he can't tell us.

I look at my phone and realize I've been so distracted by all of this that I'd almost forgotten about my date with Scott. I'm supposed to be there in an hour. It's weird because I was at least expecting to see a message back from him on my phone; after all, I'd messaged about Mrs. R, hadn't I? But there's nothing on there. Not a single message even to check I'm okay.

"Do you have to head for your date?" Annie says, noticing me checking my phone.

"Maybe," I say. "I mean, should I even still be going on a date?"

"Why not?"

"Mrs. R? I can't leave you on your own now, can I?"

"I've got Herbie, and my parents are just downstairs should I need more fussing than I can cope with," Annie reasons.

"Okay," I say. "I'd have to leave, like, NOW, though."

"GOD JUST GO! You'd only sit there sadly like a lovesick puppy missing your date anyway. I've only got patience to deal with one of those at a time, and I'm afraid my sympathies lie with Herbie right now."

"Okay, fine," I say, wondering though if I should really be going out into the world just before nightfall when three people have already been murdered.

But Scott will protect me, won't he?

Although I obviously don't need a man to protect me. I can protect myself. Thanks. God, I hope Annie couldn't tell I was thinking that.

Outside the bookshop, the village's still pretty busy. The blue and red lights flashing by Mrs. R's house have attracted an audience, and around the village everyone's chatting about the latest tragedy while glaring at me like I'm a curse. Everywhere I go, I can feel people's eyes on me. But the only people who actually speak to me are Betsy and Carol, who own the bookshop. They ask if I'm okay while they're closing the shop, which is a relief because I'm starting to feel like I might get stared out of town or something.

After they leave, I stay propped outside the bookshop with my bike, waiting for Scott and trying to avoid the glares and whispers of passersby. I look at my phone, but there's still nothing from him and he's already five minutes later than he said he would be. I keep perched against the wall, trying not to look at anything on the news app that might potentially upset me, but I'm failing miserably.

I feel so on edge, I don't know what to do with my hands. I keep tucking my hair behind my ears and then taking it out again, crossing and uncrossing my arms, my legs. Trying to look casual, but then realizing I look weird instead. I wish he'd hurry up because I feel like I'm being constantly watched by the whole village. I'm also scared that he can see me, and I don't know why. If he could see me, he'd just be over here with me by now. Brains are weird sometimes.

Why am I holding my hands clasped in front of me, like a child posing in a formal class photo? He'll get here and think I'm standing at attention. Great, I've unclasped them, but now what do I do with them? It would be super weird if he finally arrived, and I just had my fingers, like, in my ears or something.

What if he doesn't arrive? What if he's not coming? Why

wouldn't he be coming? This is not helpful, brain.

It's coming up to ten minutes past. Maybe I was right the first time and he's not coming. I open my phone and stare at the last message I sent him. He never replied. Why wouldn't you reply to that? He said he'd meet me, though, so he will, won't he? Just because he didn't reply doesn't mean he's not coming, does it?

Almost as if I'm doing it as part of an out-of-body experience, I click on his name, and the phone does two short rings before going straight to voice mail. He's hung up on me. He's stood me up, *and* he's hung up on me.

I'm just texting Annie to tell her what's happened so she can help me calm down, when I see a message appear at the top of my screen.

> **Scott:** I'm sorry, this is all too much. I can't do this anymore, it's not working out.

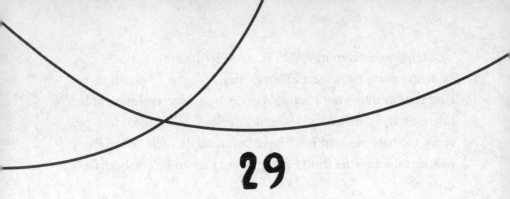

29

It's ten p.m., and I'm lying in bed with Annie next to me
and Herb in between us, staring at the ceiling. We're in the bed
where last night I thought I was going to have the hottest sex in
the world with the hottest boy in the world. But now that boy
has ended it with me via text and didn't even have the courtesy
to text back after I'd found my *third* dead body this week.

Annie came over as soon as I told her what had happened. I
think she struggled to understand me through the tears at first,
but she and Herb quickly showed up on her Paw Patrol bike
with him riding up front in the basket. No one could have fore-
seen quite how appropriate that bike was going to be for her.

"It's because of all the death, isn't it?" I say into some
tissues—although I'm telling myself not all these tears are for
a man, I'd like to point out that I'm still very upset about Mrs.
R—overall it's just been a very emotional day—while Herbie
nuzzles into my arm.

"I mean, if a few dead bodies scare him off, was he really the
one for you?" Annie asks, handing me a strawberry lace, my
favorite red licorice.

"But I just don't understand it. He was fine earlier. It's the only thing I can think of," I sniff.

"You make a good point," Annie says. "Maybe him and his mum decided to leave the village? After all, they did move here for peace and quiet, didn't they? Murders hardly give that. I guess we don't know. But you know what, if he couldn't just stay in this murderous little village for you, then screw him; he wasn't worth it."

I hate the thought that I might have to see him tomorrow at school if he hasn't left. That he'd stay in this "murderous little village" but not want to be with me.

Annie and I are sitting in bed scrolling through Netflix, trying to find anything to watch that stops us from thinking about murders or romance, because unsurprisingly we just want a small break.

"Look, tomorrow, we'll get up, we'll be rested, and we'll investigate. Like you said, we'll find out who did it, for Mrs. R. And to show those bastard detectives. The period products are a huge clue, and we need to work out why they're using them. Are they trying to get to Heather? They're linked to V-Lyte in some way, surely? How does Mrs. R link to Adam and Selena? And what are they trying to communicate? We need to get into the mind of a killer," Annie says dramatically, remote in hand as she passes on the *Scream* movies. "It would seem that without sex or death, there is no film."

Annie sighs deeply as she heads to the comedy section, which unfortunately appears to consist of pictures of couples laughing cheesily.

"The Bechdel Test! Remember, that test where the film only passes it if it contains conversations between two women without mentioning a man. Maybe that'll help?" I say, googling to see which films I might possibly be able to stomach tonight.

"*Booksmart!*" Annie shouts just as a news alert pings in the corner of my screen.

"Oh," the two of us mouth, looking at the strip that's popped up in the corner of the screen.

I want to click on it because my human urge to know more is screaming at me, but the other urge that tells me NOT to look because it will make my stomach feel even sicker than it already does is also sending a siren straight to my brain that's screaming, "DON'T CLICK ON IT!"

BARBOUROUGH SCHOOL CLOSED
FOLLOWING THIRD DEATH IN A WEEK—
MENSTRUAL MURDERS LATEST

"Huh?" Annie asks as I click in, and the two of us read on. "Why would they close the school? Mrs. R wasn't a student."

MENSTRUAL MURDERS LATEST—
BARBOUROUGH'S THIRD MURDER IN A WEEK

The village of Barbourough has tonight been witness to its third menstrual murder in a week. Elderly resident Mrs. Robbins was discovered by teens from the area with tampons in her ears and a blunt force trauma to the head. The death comes just forty-eight hours after local teen Adam Devers was discovered dead at the house of a friend and nearly a week after student Selena Munroe was found deceased in similar circumstances.

The police have this evening suggested a twenty-four-hour closure for the school attended by two of the victims as they gather evidence and protect residents, following this third murder. The police suggestion is that students should stay largely at home in safety and be prepared to cooperate with police investigations to prevent any further murders taking place. Police are appealing for any witnesses to come forward and talk to them as a matter of urgency.

Our phones beep before we've even finished reading it and I know exactly who it'll be, one of our new BFFs. The Les Populaires WhatsApp group fires into action right away.

> **Audrey:** Did you guys see about Mrs. R?
> I can't believe it.

> **Annie:** We found her.

> **Heather:** OMG! Are you guys like, ok? Have the police like confiscated your phones?

> **Colin:** I cannot believe that sweet old lady died.

> **Heather:** Tell me everything that happened immediately.

> **Audrey:** What did the police say to you guys?

"It happened, it finally happened—we're the full focus of their attention!" Annie shrieks, then takes a moment to think. "Now that we know they're not the murderers though, we have to focus on who actually IS the murderer before they're in danger themselves. I'll get back to them in a bit."

"Did you ever think there would come a time when you were ignoring messages from Heather where she's basically begging you to be her friend?" I ask Annie.

"No, and yet here I am, ignoring those messages to save actual lives," she says. "I just feel like we must be missing something obvious, and I can't work out what."

"Maybe you're tired?" I suggest. "We should get some sleep, or at least try?"

"You're right," Annie says.

I'm tired, too, but mostly I desperately want Annie to go to sleep so that she doesn't see how much more I'm about to cry over Scott. I didn't reply to his text. I don't feel like I can. I don't even think he deserves a response right now.

Herbie puts his head on Annie's leg and lets out a long sigh.

"Tomorrow morning, first thing. We go back to the murder board. If we can't go to school, that just means we've got more time to figure it out," I promise Herbie, and maybe also myself.

30

I open my eyes. The bed feels damp and sticky around my legs and butt, and I shuffle around trying to work out whether or not I'm imagining it, but it definitely feels kind of off. I was expecting my pillow to be damp—after all, I cried for three solid hours before I eventually fell asleep last night. I want to say it was over Mrs. R, but the main focus of my grief was Scott. I kept looking at the pictures I have of him, and then I went looking for other pictures. I even looked at the one of him in the food bank with Selena.

Something feels very wrong in the bed where it's wet. It's jarring, and I feel the kind of fear you have when you worry you've made contact with a spider in the dark. I peek under the duvet and feel a tingle shoot up my spine, sending me flying out of the bed. My head's spinning, my breath catching in the back of my throat as I feel the tightening of panic in my chest and gullet. Under the duvet, there's blood, loads of blood. Like at Mrs. Robbins's house. It's the crime scene all over again.

Annie and Herbie sleep soundly as I stand, assessing the blood on my legs, the pain in my stomach. It's just my period.

I head over to the box of tampons, ready and waiting on my dresser. I feel my body temperature start to lower and my breath start to even out.

Not that a period's "just" a thing. To be honest, we normalize a whole lot of blood loss and pain as "just" something that happens to us every month until our bodies stop being used as baby factories, or potential baby factories, at least.

"What's going on?" Annie asks, sleepily rubbing her eyes before clocking the blood in the bed and jumping out. "WHO DIED?"

She screams so loud that poor Herb at the bottom of the bed wakes up.

"My uterus," I reply, sighing. "And these sheets. Sorry. Back in a minute."

I grab a tampon and head into the bathroom. So far being a junior has been a positive bloodbath, and I'd really like it to stop. After yesterday, I'm really not sure that I can face tampons right now. But I can't let whoever this killer is put me off of my favorite method of period stemming.

I wash my hands in the sink and have a small sulk at another nightgown and another bedsheet ruined.

I guess in all that's been going on over the last couple of days I completely forgot my period was due. Not that it's exactly regular anyway. I swear regular periods are a myth.

I get back into my room, and Annie's already up and stripping the sheets.

"It's not too much on the bed, really," she says. "Hasn't soaked through, so it can't have started long ago."

I look down at my bloodstained sheets and think about the blood that Mrs. R had on her. I try to remember how dry it was. Maybe then I can work out exactly what time the murder was committed and that might make it easier for us to pinpoint where every single person was at the time of her death. If I really strain, I think I can picture that the blood was still wet, still reasonably fresh. But I don't know if I can trust it. The whole thing feels like a blur.

"The blood wasn't dry," I say, and Annie gives me a weird look but I blunder onward. "If the blood was still fresh, then the murder must have been committed within the hour before we got there. We've already ruled out Heather, Audrey, and Colin because they were down the lane with us in that time-frame and wouldn't have had time to get there and back out before we got there. Did we cross paths with anyone else on our way there? Or in the lanes? Do you remember seeing any-one?" Annie has caught on and leaps into action. "Trey?" I ask, screwing my face up because it's so unlikely.

"Still wasn't enough time. He'd have had to have left when we got there. We would have seen him surely? Also—" Annie pulls out her phone and goes to Trey's Instagram stories. "Yeah, he was on Twitch right after he saw Colin, see."

Annie puts her phone back away, and the two of us sit on the bed stroking Herb, thinking. Trying to remember if we saw anyone else on the way there at all.

"The period products are linked in some way, but they're not placed by Heather," Annie says.

"Was there anyone that we bumped into going the other way on our way there?" I suggest.

"No one I can think of, but I was distracted with the stings," Annie confesses. "What we really need to know is who that person was that came rushing out of the bushes toward us on

Wednesday night, because I bet you now that we've ruled out Colin and Audrey, it's got to be something to do with them."

"We've got no way of knowing who they are, though," I say, feeling frustrated.

"So, we don't know who that person was, and we don't know why someone would kill Mrs. R." Annie chews on her fingernail.

"I guess at least we know Mrs. R wasn't sleeping with Adam, right?" I ask, narrowing my eyes and gagging slightly.

"Oh yeah, definitely not." Annie shakes her head furiously.

"But Mrs. R said yesterday morning she knew something she needed to tell us, what if it was that she knew who the murderer is and now she's dead? And we didn't think it could have been anything that important." I feel awful. "We ignored her, and we were late, and now she's dead."

"But how could the murderer have known that she'd asked to see us? How could anyone have known that? Neither of us really said anything to anyone about it . . . did we?"

"Nope," I say. Except I said something to Scott, but we already ruled him out for the other murders, didn't we? There's no point telling Annie because I doubt he even knew Mrs. R, let alone where she lived.

Just because he broke up with me by text and stood me up after I'd found another dead body doesn't make him a murderer. Just a bad person. Right?

"What are we going to do, then?" Annie asks, distracting me from my own annoyance at myself. "We aren't actually going to stay here all day, are we?"

"God no," I say. The thought of just sitting here thinking about Mrs. R and Scott all day is too terrible to contemplate.

Also, Mum's about to come flying back through the door to ask if we're okay again any minute, and I'm going to lose my patience if I have to have another cup of tea with her while she tries to psychoanalyze me. "It's a shame we can't get back into Mrs. R's house, investigate a bit more. There must be a link between Selena, Adam, and Mrs. R. We just need to work out what it is."

Our phones beep in synchronization, and Annie's face lights up with another missive from Les Populaires. Despite murders, infidelities, secrets, and lies, for some reason she still wants to be part of their group. Which just makes me feel like a totally stellar best friend.

> **Heather:** Mum's organized a vigil for
> tonight with the police. Everyone needs to
> be there at seven pm to pay their respects
> to Mrs. R.

> **Heather:** Annie, Kerry, we're here for you.
> We'll support you through this.

> **Colin:** 🖤

> **Audrey:** I'm so sorry guys let us know if
> there's anything we can do. X

> **Colin:** Guys, are brogues a good mourning
> shoe? I've lost track now. Because when
> I wore them for Selena's memorial I saw
> Mr. C wearing some.

Heather: Instant boner killer, especially if
Mr. C wore them.

Colin: What about a boat shoe? My new
Sperrys?

Audrey: What? Are we giving Mrs. R a
watery grave? She's not a goldfish Colin.

Heather: Guys RESPECT! Annie and Kerry
actually *liked* Mrs R you know?

Did we? I mean, we mostly just got shouted at by her. Why do they presume we liked her? Is it just because we're nerds?

"Well, at least that's something. We can get a good measure of who's there to mourn Mrs. R tonight?" Annie offers as I have a thought.

The idea of sitting around with my mum hovering and maybe Annie also asking me about Scott scares me more than stalking a murderer.

"If there's no one at school today, maybe we should make the most of that opportunity?" I suggest. "What if we just pop into school and accidentally take a look in Selena's and Adam's lockers."

"KERRY! Breaking into lockers! What kind of bad girl have you become?!" Annie mock-gasps at me.

"Someone has to figure out what's going on, especially with what happened to Mrs. R. It just doesn't fit," I say.

"Serial killers follow a pattern usually, don't they?" Annie says, using wisdom gained from watching *Luther*. "Where's the pattern between the victims here?"

"It's time to dig deeper," I say, realizing there's no turning back now. I'm in this investigation until the end. Whenever that may be. "Besides, I need to forget about Scott, and maybe the best way to do that is to finally go completely off the rails and have my teenage rebellion phase via breaking into school, looking through lockers, and solving a murder case?"

"OH!!" Annie says, hand up to her mouth. "I love it. LOVE IT."

No less than twenty minutes later, Annie and I are skulking around the empty corridors of our school, wearing black jeans and turtlenecks, a cross between a mime act and chic tortured poets.

Really, I thought getting in here would be harder. What kind of police investigation leaves the school unmanned? I thought we'd at least have to sweet-talk a young rookie officer or slide on our bellies army style around something. Annie even came prepared with the deerstalker hat and blond wig despite me having thus far refused to wear them. But she could change my mind if I hear so much as a single footstep.

Instead of any of this drama, we've just walked through the front door of school, and besides the fact that it's deathly quiet in here, it's so far been pretty smooth sailing.

"How are we going to actually get into their lockers, though?" I ask.

"Duh, don't you remember how we got into Adam's locker

263

that time? After we accidentally wrote him love notes in seventh grade and then *someone accidentally* got cold feet and needed to *accidentally* get it out again?" Annie looks at me as if I'm being annoying, but really, I think I've blocked the memory out for self-preservation.

Hormones are a dangerous drug when you're twelve years old and your crush looks really hot, so you decide to write him a note telling him that you love him, and you maybe also write a poem about the texture of his hair and then you post it into his locker and need to retrieve it when you realize it's the most embarrassing thing that you could ever have done.

We ended up making a device out of paper clips that slid through the slits in the locker door and worked as a winch to wiggle the lock open. I'm amazed when Annie produces the very same little paper clip invention from her backpack along with two pairs of gloves—not rubber ones, just H&M's finest—hands me one pair and heads stealthily to Selena's locker.

As she's pulling out the gloves though, Herbie's little head pops out with a gleeful bark, threatening to blow our cover.

"Herbie! NO! Stealth mode!" Annie hisses at him.

"You brought the dog? On the stealth mission?" I ask.

"He's just a dog, sitting in front of two feminist detectives, asking never to be left behind," Annie whispers as Herb puts his paws over the edge of her backpack, looking pretty happy with his adventure. I roll my eyes at her.

I still can't believe that there's no one around, and I'm half expecting Mr. C to pop out of one of the empty classrooms or come flying out of one of the lockers like a jack-in-the-box, so much so that I actually feel slightly breathless.

Annie puts the paper clip in the slit slowly, like a safecracker.

She's moving it really carefully, trying not to make a sound, but the school's so quiet that even the ting of paper clip against metal sounds like an orchestra. The putt as the lock clicks is so loud I imagine it being heard at the police station and them all jumping up, rushing to arrest us. I even jump as she slightly opens the door.

Both of us take a deep breath, and I swallow what feels like a hundred liters of excess saliva in my mouth.

"Okay," Annie whispers, probably more to reassure herself that the murderer isn't about to come out of a fifty-centimeter-by-fifty-centimeter cupboard.

The door lets out a sharp creak as it opens wide, and when we see inside, it's quickly clear that it hasn't been worth it. Of course! I'm such a fool. The police would have already taken everything from these lockers surely. That's the first thing they would have done. Maybe we're more amateur than I thought we were, and maybe they're not as silly as we thought *they* were. I can literally hear my confidence leaving the building.

"I mean, we may as well check the other one just in case, though, right?" Annie says, looking around her.

I nod, but I'm starting to feel like the consequences of getting caught would outweigh the gains at the moment.

She wiggles the clip with slightly less care now that we know that there's likely to be nothing there. I can't help but feel like this is an entirely pointless exercise, but we've come this far. We've even dressed for the occasion. Then Annie abruptly stops wiggling the paper clips through the slit.

"There's something in there," Annie says, her eyes huge. "I've just hit whatever it is with the mega clip."

"Oh crap," I say, my eyes now as huge as hers.

"Okay, I'm going to open it, and it's probably just going to be nothing, right?" Annie asks. It's like she wants a braver response from me.

"I think I just peed in my pants a little bit," I say, because I have indeed felt a small trickle, which isn't uncommon when I'm really scared or laughing too much.

She turns the lock and opens the door, and I'm surprised I don't pee a bit more if I'm being honest.

Inside the locker are two dolls, hanging down via tampon strings tied around their wrists, their eyes scratched off, red marker on their heads. It takes me a while, but after the initial shock, I see it. One of the dolls is wearing a deerstalker hat, the other one has badly cut, long blond hair.

They're us.

31

"What the . . . ?" Annie asks. I see a bit of paper on the bottom of the locker and try to look at it without touching anything.

It's easy to see what it says, though, because it's written in bright red lipstick.

Stop playing detective or you'll end up like this.

"Well, that is some straight-up *Pretty Little Liars* shit right there," Annie says flippantly, but I can see her hands shaking. "How did they get them in there? Do the police *know* they're there? No, surely they would have taken them and probably told us, so HOW did they get them in there? How did they know we'd look there?!"

"They're a serial killer," I say by way of explanation, my voice quivering. As soon as I get the words out, as if I've summoned them, I hear the thudding sound of feet coming toward us.

Annie gathers her bag, slinging it on her back with Herbie safely tucked inside.

Whoever it is that left those dolls there is coming for us. They're watching us, they were clearly watching us in the graveyard, and now they're coming to finish us off, just like the dolls. Annie and I stare at each other, and for a moment, I hesitate, feeling stuck to the spot again, before my legs finally jerk forward and the two of us make a run for it, moving faster than we ever have in our lives. All the while, barely behind us, I can hear the footsteps growing louder and louder.

This feels like one of those dreams where you can keep running and running but you'll never outrun the thing that's coming for you.

"Annie! I think I'm going to pee myself," I whisper as we charge down the corridor.

"That's okay; you can pee all you want as long as you keep running!" she whispers back.

We keep going until we get out of the school. It's only when we reach the lanes outside that I see three police cars pull up, officers jumping out en masse and heading in through the main doors.

I want to keep running. I really do. But Annie yanks me over into a bush at the opening to the lanes. We hide there in silent surveillance mode so we can see what's going on but stay hidden from the police. Now's not the time to be answering questions about what we're doing here rather than staying in our homes like we've been advised to do.

We peer around the bush at the scene in front of the school.

"Do you think whoever was running after us is still in there?" Annie asks.

"I didn't see anyone coming out—did you?" I pant, looking around me.

"No," Annie whispers.

"We should tell the police about the dolls," I say, panic making my voice wobble.

"We can't!" Annie almost yells. "Then they'll know we were poking around where we shouldn't be."

"So how are we going to stay safe?!" I ask. Desperation claws at my chest and stomach, making me feel like I'm about to puke. I never wanted to be part of this. I wanted to stay home and watch nineties rom-coms. How did I get here?

"We look out for each other," Annie says, her face fierce. "I'd never let anyone doll you."

"I'd never let anyone doll you, either," I say more uncertainly as she puts her arm around me and Herb licks us both affectionately.

Still somewhat hugging, the three of us stare straight ahead, waiting to see if someone else does emerge from the school. The officers eventually appear with boxes of things, but I can't see what. Even Herb's on full alert, paws resting on the outside of the backpack in case he needs to use them.

We're so tense that when Herb barks, we all jump, making him bark more. Annie has to clutch him closer to her chest to get him to calm down, but I see what he's barking at. DI Wallace and DI Collins are coming right this way.

"Quick," Annie says, digging through the bushes to create a hole the three of us can slide into. It's a lot like sitting inside a pincushion but hopefully they won't see us. Once we dive into her pit of brambles, we're completely covered.

And then Annie's phone wolf-whistles at her.

Herb and I give her a disappointed stare.

"What the hell was that?" I whisper.

"Look, you've had some sexy time with a real-life man, even if he did turn out to be a prize prick. What have I got? No one will come near me. The least I can do for myself is to make it feel like my phone has the hots for me," she mutters back.

"You should have said. I'd have wolf-whistled at you if you'd have asked," I reassure her.

Instead of laughing at me like I thought she was going to, Annie's mouth just hangs open as she reads whatever she's been sent, and she turns her phone around to face me.

Audrey: Mr. C's been ARRESTED

Colin: They found texts between him and
Adam on his phone!

Audrey: They had secret meet ups!

Heather: Oh, FFS another one?! ANOTHER
ONE?

Heather: Was there anyone in this village
that my ex-boyfriend wasn't sleeping with?

"Oh my god, what? Do you think that's what those boxes are? Mr. C's things?" I ask. On my phone, I'm googling and a stream of articles appear all along the lines of "Teacher in Tampon Trouble."

"Look," I say, pointing at the image of Mr. C being arrested outside his house. Something looks familiar. I zoom in on his arm. "That jacket, the tear, doesn't it remind you of—"

270

"Wednesday night outside the old V-Lyte factory! The one that ran out of the bushes! It was dark, but it looks the same, and the tear from when they got caught on the bushes would have been about there."

"Wow," I say, remembering how he shoved me off my bike. I've always hated him.

"It was him. It was Mr. C," Annie whispers, and I swear I can hear footsteps. I crouch down smaller in the bush. "And it doesn't take a genius to work out what he was meeting Adam for on Monday at the church, does it?"

"It doesn't?" I gulp.

"The same reason everyone else was meeting Adam . . . drugs," Annie whispers, eyes wide. "It has to have been! He was buying drugs from him. OR even weirder, he was the supplier! WHAT IF IT WAS MR C SUPPLYING THE DRUGS TO ADAM?"

"Ohhhh!" I say. It feels like a puzzle piece clicking in my brain—things are starting to make sense to me now. "But then, do the police think he was the murderer?"

"I don't know," Annie says just as I hear those footsteps coming even closer. Why is so much of my life spent frozen in fear these days? I shoot Annie a panicked look, eyes wide, and that shuts her up.

The only noise apart from the footsteps approaching louder and louder is the cracking of branches underfoot and the sound of my breathing. Somehow every inhale is as noisy as a dragon. I can see the tip of a black shoe under the bush, and I hold my breath until it walks on. I think we're in the clear, exhaling as four black shoes carry on past, but Annie's phone wolf-whistles again.

271

"Hello," the booming voice of DI Wallace comes from outside the bush. "I think you'd better come out of there, don't you, girls?"

Annie and I emerge. I'm slightly sheepish and covered in dirt. But she's somehow approaching this whole encounter with the confidence of a leading lady on the opening night of a school play.

"Oh, hi, DI Wallace," Annie greets him, unabashed.

"Hi," I mumble, doing a little wave, which DI Collins reciprocates.

"Kerry! Annie! Everything all right?" DI Wallace says with the sort of grin a teacher would give the troublemaker in class before sending them to the principal.

"Absolutely fine!" Annie says, flashing them a similar grin.

"Completely normal for you to be in a bush, is it?" DI Wallace asks. "You wouldn't be attempting to do your own detective work in there, would you? Because that would be *very* ill-advised."

"Oh, no, Herb here lost his ball, didn't you, buddy?" Annie tickles behind his ears. "Can we help you with something?"

"Yes, actually, now you're here, we were just wondering when you last heard from Scott, Kerry? I'm right in thinking that the two of you are somewhat of an item, aren't I?" DI Wallace's light tone lands like hail.

I feel my stomach physically drop as he's talking.

"Erm, yesterday evening," I say, remembering the text and the hours after that I spent crying myself to sleep.

"What time was this, and what was the nature of his message?" DI Wallace persists.

I take a deep breath because I'm really going to have to tell this smug old bastard that Scott broke up with me via text message.

"About quarter past seven. He was breaking it off. He was supposed to meet me at seven outside the bookshop, and instead he sent a text breaking up with me," I say, wondering why police officers always have to get me to recount the most embarrassing moments of my life.

"I'm sorry to hear that," DI Collins says, displaying a kind of empathy that DI Wallace isn't capable of.

"What *exactly* did it say?" DI Wallace asks, because he doesn't seem to think my embarrassment has been prolonged enough, clearly.

I can't face recounting every word, despite the fact that I know it so well because I've read and reread the text so many times, so instead I get my phone out of the front pocket of my jeans and show them the text.

They take their time, nodding and writing down every single detail as if they're in class, copying carefully from a whiteboard, a whiteboard of my trauma.

"And you didn't notice anything when you got to Mrs. Robbins's place that might have led you to believe that Scott had been there that day?" DI Wallace finally asks, breaking the silence and moving on from my hell.

"No," I say firmly because that's a weird thing to ask. "Scott didn't even know Mrs. R. They'd never even met, I don't think."

"We found some things belonging to him at the scene," DI Wallace says as DI Collins reaches into a file. "Do you recognize this?"

DI Collins holds up pictures of Scott's bracelet, the one that he wore every day and never took off. The one from his mother.

"Yes," I say, too shocked to measure my response. I can see Annie's eyes lock onto me as I gasp out the rest: "That's Scott's."

The moment the words come out of my mouth, I want to take them back. Have I just dropped him in it? Should I even care though after the way he broke things off? I shouldn't care. I shouldn't, but I do.

Annie and I are looking at each other trying to communicate telepathically, and she looks as suspicious as I am. What was it doing there? And why didn't I spot it before? What does this mean?

"Excuse me, but if you've arrested Mr. C, why are you asking questions about Scott?" Annie asks.

"Mr. C's been arrested on a separate matter," DI Collins starts.

"We really don't have to answer to teenagers, and that is privileged information. How do you even know that?" DI Wallace snaps.

"It's literally all over the news?" Annie turns her phone to show him. "I'd say someone on your team isn't as great at keeping their mouth shut as you think."

Annie carries on gloating, but I can't join in. Why was Scott's bracelet there? Where's Scott?

"At this stage, we've put out a warrant for Scott's arrest. We found his DNA on the body, and around Mrs. Robbins's house. We've been unable to locate him so far. It would appear that no one's seen him since the murder and he's bolted," DI Wallace says. "Do you have any idea where he might be?"

"No. Like I said, I haven't heard from him. Have you asked

his mum? He lives with her after all." I marvel slightly at my own sass, but to be honest, I'm cagey now.

I hate that they know things we don't know, and I hate what they're insinuating. That my longest and sexiest ever relationship has been with a menstrual murderer. But if the menstrual murderer's putting dead dolls of me in lockers, it can't be him, can it? He wouldn't do that, would he?

But the way the detectives are looking at me now suggests there's something else I don't know.

"His mother's dead," DI Collins says to me gently as I feel the world shake under my feet.

"Scott moved here alone," DI Wallace says. He's so smug. It doesn't matter to him that Scott's mum's dead; he's just proud to know something that I don't.

"What?" I regret the word as soon as it's out of my mouth, as if it's showing weakness or something. I just can't get my head around it. The way that Scott talked about his mum, how much he loved her, it's as if I can feel my heart breaking for him in real time.

But why wouldn't he tell me?

"From what we've learned, he's here to track down his father; did he mention anything about that to you at all?" DI Collins asks kindly.

"Yes." It's a lie. I've just lied to the police to save face. Scott told me his dad was dead. He told me his dad was dead and he lived with his sick mum. Why would he lie? There must have been a reason for it, and I feel like I need to protect him.

The first guy I've ever been in a relationship with has lied to me; *why* do I still feel like I need to protect him?

"He actually found his dad here." DI Wallace's smugness is

palpable. "A neighbor DI Collins interviewed told us that much at least."

I feel a bit of vomit come up into my mouth. Why would he have told this neighbor a different story from the one he told me? How do I know what the truth is, and who *is* this neighbor? How do they know more than me? I feel like I can't ask questions because I don't want to give them the satisfaction of knowing that I didn't know any of this, and that he lied to me. So instead, I've probably just committed a crime.

"Who is he?" Annie asks, as if she thinks they'll crack at her first questioning, but DI Wallace just stares at her.

"Look, all we're saying is that maybe you didn't know Scott as well as you think you did. And if you're hiding anything for him, perhaps now's the time to tell us before he drags you any further into the mess that he's made for himself," DI Wallace says. "Let us know if he gets in touch with you. We just want to talk to him, but at the moment, we have to treat him like a missing person *and* a suspect."

"Okay," I say, taking his card and feeling totally ambushed, not for the first time this week. I'm hoping my face doesn't give away the fact that I feel like a fool.

"Thank you for your time, girls," DI Collins says, and this time I'm too freaked out and confused to even bother being pissed off about the use of "girls."

They walk away from us heading back the way that they came, while Annie, Herb, and I watch them go in silence. His words keep running round my head. Scott's mum's dead, and maybe his dad, too, depending on whether what he said to me was true or not. But he's told me so many lies. How do I know what's true, and what's not? What if I *really* didn't know Scott as well as I thought I did?

"OH MY GOD, that is so shady. What if it's him? What if he did it? WHAT IF YOU NEARLY TOUCHED A SERIAL KILLER'S DICK?!" Annie's practically screaming, but I'm not taking in a word she says, because at this point, she doesn't even know the half of it.

I can't have nearly touched a serial killer's penis. I refuse. There has to be another explanation, for the bracelet at Mrs. R's place after her murder, the lies about his mum and dad, and the fact that all of this only started happening when he came to town. There *has* to be an explanation for *all* of this. But I'd told him we were going to see Mrs. R and that she had something to tell us. He could have had time to get to Mrs. R's before us. . . . That can't be what happened. It just can't be. I didn't think he even knew where she lived. My head feels like a tangled mess of all the half-truths he told me.

"First thing's first. We need to find out what the 'other matter' was that Mr. C was arrested over," Annie says with glee, her words muffled by all the chaos in my head. "And whether or not it's enough to get him banned from teaching for life."

I can't focus on that right now, because what if the police are right and what if Mrs. R's death's my fault because I told Scott she knew something? I feel like Annie saying this, but surely serial killers don't kiss like that?

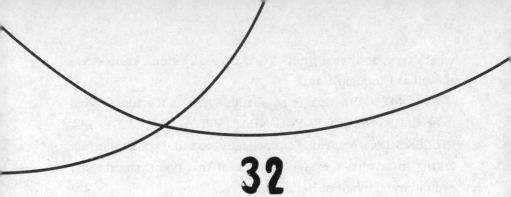

32

We're sitting in my room while I shove pillows over my head to try and stop my brain from exploding. I've just confessed to Annie that I told Scott we were going to see Mrs. R, and despite the pillows, I can unfortunately still hear her talking me through how much time he had to get to Mrs. R's before us.

"Okay, so what do we have now I know this VITAL piece of information?" Annie asks, as if I'd have some kind of case file hanging around my room. We really should have gone to her house for access to the murder wall, but I was too freaked out and stressed and needed to be around my things, my nice, comforting things.

"Errr . . . well, Scott's gone missing. He was here to track down his dad, who he found, despite telling me he was dead, and he lives alone rather than with his sick mum like he told me because his sick mum is actually dead." I emerge from my pillows so that I can speak, only to see Annie riffling through my drawers to find something to write it all on.

"Dude, you must have Post-it Notes in here, right?" Annie

asks, emptying out the contents of my drawers like she's hunting for gold in there.

"Next drawer down," I say. "Highlighters and marker pens are in that drawer, too."

She doesn't even try to replace the stuff in the drawer that she's turned over already, so I find myself reluctantly leaving my cocoon to tidy up after her.

"He arrived just days before the murders actually started, and there hasn't been one in the last two hours or however long it's been since they say he's disappeared. They found his bracelet there with . . . Mrs. R . . . and he had ample time to get there before us while we were talking to Heather," Annie fills in, scribbling frantically on Post-its.

"So now, hey, presto, I think I nearly slept with a serial killer!" I say, throwing glue sticks and paper clips back into the drawer with force. "And not *only* that, but the serial killer broke up with me. *He* broke up with *me!* By text no less!" I head straight back over to the bed and slump down on it with a thump.

"At least he didn't *murder* you," Annie reasons unhelpfully while writing "knew about Mrs. R" on a Post-it.

"URGHHHHHHHHH." I throw the pillows back over my head, but despite saying all of this, I can't align the boy that shinnied up my drainpipe with a rose with my image of a serial killer. "I know you're going to think I'm a fool, but it still doesn't feel right? Why would he have taken the bracelet off?"

"Maybe it fell off and he didn't notice?" Annie suggests, still scribbling all of the evidence that my ex-boyfriend's a serial killer down onto Post-its.

"He would have noticed." I shake my head. "He loved that

279

bracelet. And I'm sure I would have noticed it there? Do you really think we'd have missed evidence?" I know I've got Annie right in her sweet spot because she stops scribbling briefly; she'd never admit to missing evidence.

"A good point, but then what are the options?" Annie asks, writing on more Post-its. "One, it was left by Scott when he killed Mrs. R. Like, it got ripped off in the struggle. Two, it wasn't there when we got there; therefore it was placed by someone. Three, the person who placed it there was the killer during the murder. But this would mean that the killer has Scott. . . ."

"NOT HELPING, ANNIE!" I wail, making Herbie howl sympathetically. I pat him, which probably consoles me more to be honest. "So, Scott's either my ex and a serial killer or dead?"

"Except he texted you to dump you, so he was probably alive when he sent that?"

I turn to Annie really slowly, a smile spreading across my face, hope flooding my brain, because she's right. He texted me AFTER we found Mrs. R. He's been in touch since the murder!

"MAYBE HE DIDN'T SEND ME THAT TEXT!" I practically scream it across the room, having a small moment of hope, but Annie just stares back at me and even Herbie does a little head tilt at me. "MAYBE SOMEONE ELSE DID! MAYBE HE DIDN'T WANT TO BREAK UP WITH ME AFTER ALL!"

Annie mirrors Herbie and tilts her head to one side like she thinks I've completely lost the plot and she feels sorry for me.

"I mean, maybe . . . but that would mean he was probably dead if someone else was texting for him. . . . Unless he was kidnapped, but I don't know why they would kidnap him when they've already just straight-up killed everyone else." Annie

280

very ungently kills all my hope. "Don't worry, best friends are more important than guys anyway, especially if they're murderers."

I know she thinks I'm naive, but I don't believe her. I start googling "What kind of texts do serial killers send?" I can hear Herbie trot out, his little claws on the floor; he's clearly had enough of my naivety.

"The other option is that he was still in the house when we were there, so the bracelet came off or was dropped after we left?" Annie suggests, but I don't buy it; surely I would have sensed if he was there? Right? "Oh, stop looking like that; you would NOT have SENSED if he was there. You didn't even SENSE that he was going to break up with you via text."

How does Annie have the power to both tell what I'm thinking and destroy me? The best friend link is strong, and devastating.

"I'm sorry, but tough love," she continues. "You knew him a week, and we found out he was lying to you for most of it. What would Miss Marple do?" Annie puts a hand on my shoulder lovingly despite her words being razor-sharp.

"She'd just make sure she found out the truth, I guess," I say sulkily, because I also know she wouldn't have been taken in in the first place.

At least I can be sure of one thing: If he did send that text, he might have done it right after murdering an old lady, so I didn't really want him anyway. No one's *that* sexy. Are they?

"Why couldn't it have been Mr. C? He's actually been arrested?!" I suggest, but Annie screws up her face.

"I don't respect him enough to think he could pull it off." She squints.

As much as I want to believe in Scott, I hate Mr. C more, so I can't help but agree.

I have used approximately one hundred Post-it Notes, mostly trying to prove that Mr. C could be the killer. The more reasons I give the less likely it looks. Annie and I have been staring at them on my wall for the last half an hour in silence. Occasionally one of us will jump up and shout "OH! I KNOW!" but then make a kind of "hmmmmm" noise and sit back down again.

I'm trying my best to think that the boy I was dating for almost six days wasn't a serial killer, but it's starting to look dramatically like he might be *and* like DI Wallace and DI Collins might have figured it out before us. Which is possibly actually the worst bit, at least as far as Annie's concerned.

"We've got an hour until the vigil," Annie says, rubbing her chin. "What's the latest on Mr. C?" She grabs her phone to check on the news and answer her own question. "He's been released without charge, nothing to do with the murders, and there'll be a separate investigation with the school board. He's been suspended from teaching," she says as I read over her shoulder.

"'Released without charge, rumor has it he was accused of buying marijuana from Adam, will probably lose his job if they can prove anything.' That's pretty huge news! Who would be our homeroom teacher if Mr. C lost his job?"

"Hopefully someone who's less of a dickhead." Annie raises an eyebrow, googling on her phone. "It says here that he's had alibis for when all three of the murders took place, which is why they weren't investigating him for murder."

"Convenient, don't you think?" I arch my eyebrow.

"Or just fact," Annie says sympathetically. "I'm sorry, it doesn't sound like it was him. It's not like he was at Heather's party, or Audrey and Colin's."

I sigh and start removing all the Post-it Notes from the wall. The theories were loose and flaky, but I had some hope. Now we're back where we started. Well, almost; I leave one Post-it Note up that says "Mr. C—old V-Lyte factory," because we still haven't worked out what he was doing there and I'm willing to bet the police know nothing about it.

"What did Heather have to say about Adam dealing weed? Isn't this the first she's heard of him doing it?" I ask, staring sadly at the last Post-it Note on the wall that simply says "Scott."

"She says he was a 'shady jackass' and she 'wouldn't put anything past him.' And Colin and Audrey have agreed with her that he was indeed a 'shady jackass.' Thing is, though, half the school was buying weed from Adam by the sound of things. The real question, and the thing the police *really* need to investigate, is where was *Adam* getting the weed?" Annie says, sticking a leg up on her chair and lunging into a power pose that I've seen on many a crime drama, while she puts a finger to her lips deep in thought.

I write the question on a Post-it Note and stick it to the wall, eager to start a new thread of thinking away from Scott.

"What about your suggestion earlier that Mr. C was actually the dealer, and he was selling it to Adam rather than the other way around?" I suggest hopefully, still clinging to the hope that somehow Mr. C can answer some of the questions.

"No, the police arrested him because they read texts on

Adam's phone; it sounds like they were quite clear," Annie answers, showing me a newspaper's reconstruction of what they believe the text messages to have said.

"But he could have been buying it from someone who had some beef with him? But then what would the dealer have to do with Selena or Mrs. R for that matter?" I ask, adding the word "beef" with a question mark to another Post-it.

"And I know we worked out *why* Selena was trolling Heather." Annie starts pacing the room as she speaks. "But why didn't she let the others in on it if they all knew the secret? Something just isn't adding up there. She could have been trolling her about her boyfriend selling weed, but Heather had no idea about that anyway. And finally, why would whoever did this leave dolls of US in the lockers?"

I add "Instagram trolling" to one Post-it and "dolls" to another and stick them both on the board. If we can join all these things together somehow, we might crack it. I feel like there's something so simple connecting things that we must have missed.

"Because we were getting too close to the truth?" I suggest. "They want to scare us off, and to be honest, they've spooked me." I shiver involuntarily. "What if they can see us now and know what we're doing?"

"You still don't think it's Scott, do you?" Annie asks.

"I just can't see him making dolls of us," I say, thinking about how we were completely alone here. If he was the killer and he thought I was onto him, he could have easily killed me then. "Whoever made them really wants us to drop it. I wonder if we *should* stop investigating?"

"Would Miss Marple be scared off? Would Vera be scared off? Would Eve from *Killing Eve* be *scared off*?"

"No, and it's led to a lot of near-death experiences for them. I just wonder if we should try to avoid that? Maybe?" I ask hopefully. I'm scared and I'm upset about Scott, and I just don't think I have it in me to carry on anymore. "I know this is important to you, to us, but is it really worth dying over?" I ask, feeling stress rising in my voice. "Surely now's the time to just let the police take over?"

Every time I think about the dolls, my hands start shaking. I don't want to be the next menstrual murder victim—and I don't want Annie to be, either. We're supposed to make it to our old age together and embrace the spoils of the menopause and all its period-free-ness. I know how important it is to her that we solve this, but it's also important to me that I make it to my seventeenth birthday.

Annie's started rooting around in her bag and I don't know what she's looking for, but she looks super pissed off about it and about me suggesting that we go to the police.

"What, and never ever solve it?" she asks, her head now fully inside her backpack. "Let the detectives take over and pretend feminism never existed? Let them talk over us, and say things like 'Yeah, she probably just choked on the menstrual cup because she was shoving it in her mouth for . . . reasons . . . and it was all an accident? LOL, those silly menstruators and their period products.'" Annie perfectly replicates DI Wallace's condescending tone, making me feel even more triggered than I already was. "Jesus, Kerry, it's like you want the murderer never to be found and everyone to die."

She throws the bag down on the floor, clearly not finding whatever it was she was looking for.

"I'M JUST TRYING TO SURVIVE WITHOUT BEING MURDERED WITH MENSTRUAL PRODUCTS!" I feel my voice catch in my throat, and tears start to fall down my cheeks.

"Dude, I would NEVER let anyone get you, NEVER. I would kill them first, you hear me? I would poke them in the eye with the stem of a menstrual cup if they came anywhere near you," Annie says. She kneels down and sticks her face right in mine.

"Same," I sniff, snuggling into her hug. "What were you looking for?"

"My Dictaphone," Annie says as we separate. "Must have left it at home, though, I guess." She shrugs. "It's not like anyone's going to steal a Dictaphone. . . ."

"No one else under the age of fifty knows what one is." I chuckle.

"Hey!" She pushes me off the bed.

As if he's heard that someone needs distraction, Herbie comes rushing into my room, jumping on my bed absolutely caked in mud.

"Where have you been?" I ask him, heading over to the window, a fresh sense of impending doom starting to gather pace.

From the window, I see exactly what I feared might have happened. Herbert has dug up my dad's flower beds.

"Oh crap, Herbert!" I say to him. "You're gonna need a wash, buddy, so that no one ever finds out what you did."

"Come on, dirty dog!" Annie says, carrying him through to the bathroom, paws directed away from her. Maybe we can try and blame this on the sassy cat next door.

In the bathroom, we lock the door and run a bath.

"What do you think you can use on dogs? Do you think TRESemmé would do it?" Annie asks. She digs through the cabinet and then abruptly closes it. "Dear god, your parents' medicine cabinet."

"Why, what did you find?" I ask, despite not really wanting to know.

"Oh, sweetie, you're too young," Annie says, caressing my face with her hand.

"It was the lube, wasn't it?" I ask.

"Yep," Annie says.

"Mum says it's an essential part of sex and female pleasure and that we shouldn't be ashamed," I say. "She calls lube a life-saver. Of course, she said it in a limerick on her Instagram grid, next to her poem 'An Ode to the Clit,' about the root of a lot of female pleasure."

"Right on," Annie says, letting out a small giggle as I contemplate the fact that I may never need lube ever now that my only love interest has sailed off into the sunset via text message. And everyone thinks he may have killed. Multiple times.

"Herbert," I say sternly to him. "You're not going to like this, and I think I'm not going to like it, either, but we're all going to get through it together."

And with that, I place him in the two inches of warm water that sit in the bottom of the bath, and he yelps as if it's the worst thing anyone has ever done to him, betrayal etched on his tiny face.

"Oh god, he's so muddy. How did he get this filthy?" Annie asks, grabbing the showerhead and trying to rinse him while he does a big shake, spreading water everywhere, and the two of us try to get a grip on him before he destroys the bathroom as well as the flower beds.

"Oh, buddy, we should have taken your collar off. It's getting all wet." I reach around for the clasp and take it off as he spreads more mud and water everywhere. "This collar's heavy, mate; how does it not weigh you down?"

I look at the collar for a minute because it does seem extraordinarily bulky, and then I notice that there's something IN there.

"Annie, there's something in this collar," I say, pressing down on the inside of the collar to see the outline of a key in the fabric.

"Huh?" Annie turns and looks at the collar with me, giving Herb the perfect opportunity to start shaking again.

"There's a key sewn between the bits of fabric. Why would anyone do that?"

"So the dog can let himself in after a night out on the town?" Annie looks pleased with herself.

"Be serious, Annie," I say, unsure why she's not more interested in this. I grab for the nail scissors while Annie continues rinsing down Herb before he covers the whole bathroom in swamp water.

I carefully cut between the seams because if I'm neat about it I can sew it back up and Herb can have his collar back when I'm done. The seams come apart, and I pry out a small silver key with a note attached.

The Bureau of Village Secrets

"Annie," I say, showing her. My fingers shake.

"I think we need to get into Mrs. R's place tonight and find out what this is." Her eyes light up. "And we have the best cover story."

"Do you not think we could just hand the key to the police and let them do their job?" I ask, feeling nervous.

"NO!" Annie shouts, scaring both Herbie and me. "They'll fluff it up like they have with everything else. Look, I know you're scared since the dolls, and I'm scared, too. But we can do this. We're smart and we're the CSI CODERS! And CSI Coders never let other CSI Coders get murdered. I got you and you got me. We're going to be fine. I promise. What would M—"

"I beg of you." I hold up my hand. "Please don't ask what Miss Marple—a fictional character—would do again."

"What would Nancy Drew do?" She looks so pleased with herself for rhyming.

If she wasn't my best friend, I'd hate her.

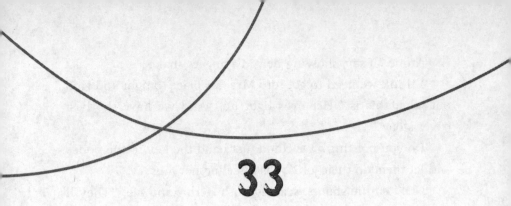

33

"Why did we decide that during a vigil, when there would be ten thousand million people on the street outside Mrs. R's place, was the right time to try and sneak in?" I ask.

"Because there's so many people around and so much going on that it'll be easier to distract the police officers," Annie says as Herbert rests his paws on the edge of her bike basket looking at us both.

It's certainly busy. The police cordon's still in place outside Mrs. R's house, and the street's swarming with police cars as people gather in the street outside it. The front yard's already filled with Heather's mum and her entourage. After Heather's mum advertised it on V-Lyte's Instagram and her own personal one, it was picked up by all the news channels, local and national. So, a lot of these people aren't even really from around here, and I'm struggling to find faces I recognize.

"Why would you come to a vigil for a woman that you've never met, though?" I ask Annie while we try to weave our way around the Glastonbury of Barbourough.

"I guess people connect to the murder of an old lady. She's

sweet and vulnerable, and someone killed her. People want to see justice," Annie reasons. "And they want to see the village where the menstrual murders are taking place, I guess."

I push a rather tall man aside and wiggle between two unfamiliar teens. "At least with this many people here, it'll be easy to fly under the radar. We need to keep a low profile until we've gotten into the house and managed to get whatever it is that Mrs. R's left in there," I say, still looking around me in case whoever planted the dolls is watching us.

I immediately see Heather across the lawn waving at us—I don't know how she can spot us from so far off. It's as if she's got an Annie and Kerry detector that goes off when we're near. I worry that Annie's getting her hopes up that they might have a real friendship, rather than just one based on Heather needing something from us, and I'm scared that when this is over, their friendship will be, too.

I find I'm eyeing her with suspicion as we head over there, and I have to remind myself that she, Audrey, and Colin are all way out of the question as suspects now. They have alibis. The most likely killer is the person I've been alone with at night, in my own bedroom. As much as I want to deny it.

I look around the fringes of the crowd, wondering if he'd be here, hiding, trying to clear his name somehow. Despite all my hopes to see a hooded or shadowy figure, he doesn't appear, though.

Heather's mum's not far from us, looking incredibly glamorous. It was as if when Heather's dad died she had a glow-up. People talk about how Heather's mum knew for years that her husband was cheating on her. That he was a tyrant who ran the company with an iron fist, and when he passed away and

Heather's mum took over, V-Lyte started performing better and staff were happier. I look at her now, smiling and chatting with everyone who comes to talk to her. I feel bad for Mum, who is lurking nearby. Every time a middle-aged woman walks past and doesn't recognize her, it's another dagger to the heart.

"Don't forget we need to get back in that house and find Mrs. R's secrets. Find out why someone would want to kill her in the first place," I say, but my words get lost in the wind as Annie runs toward Heather and Les Populaires.

I amble over at a more sedate pace, noting that Heather's far enough away from her mum not to look like a dork but close enough to the drama to be the center of everything. I wonder how she does that. Maybe there's some training school for being popular that teaches you all this, but I never went because I wasn't cool enough to even know about it.

"So have you like heard from Scott or anything?" Audrey asks as soon as I'm within earshot, ever subtle.

"Did you KNOW he was a serial killer? Like, did you ever get vibes?" Colin chimes in before I can even attempt to answer.

"Okay, so, the bad boys always break your heart, but it's like, 'We should treat hearts like they're made of glass because when you fall you break,' you know?" Audrey says.

At this point, I'm not even trying to answer.

"OMG, Shakespeare?" Colin asks.

"Cally from *Love Island* last night," Audrey says

"How do people know he's missing?" I ask, somehow getting a word in. Claustrophobia starts to take root as they all stare at me.

"I mean, have you not been online in the last two minutes? It's ALL OVER the news." Heather puts her phone in front of our faces, and I realize that Scott's face is indeed LITERALLY all over the news, as of five minutes ago.

I look at my mother calmly chatting and schmoozing with Heather's mum, and I'm relieved I never told her about Scott because if she'd have known she would have locked me up and never allowed me out again.

Whether or not I think he did it, the whole world's going to think he's the murderer now. The police have even set up a reward for anyone who can give information leading to his whereabouts and eventual arrest.

I feel myself slightly spin out of control and want to puke.

"Yeah, sure, she knew he was a serial killer, and she just kept hooking up with him," Heather snaps at them both. "Leave her alone, ok?"

I'm taken aback by Heather being so nice to me. It's all just adding to the general weirdness going on. If I'm being honest, I'd have given anything to be back to normal. I miss when we were just the losers that Selena threw coffee at every day. I miss being of no interest to anyone.

"Sorry, Heather, sorry, Kerry," Audrey mutters.

"Yeah, sorry." Colin gives me a sideways "eek" face.

I guess part of the reason Heather's been so much happier is that Annie's been telling everyone that Heather was with us when Mrs. R died. Rumors about Heather killing Selena have really simmered down. Now we just need to stop any more murders. We need to get into Mrs. R's house and find out what she knew that got her killed.

Heather's mum climbs up onto a podium, complete with a microphone and ring light set up behind it. Mrs. R would have hated every single second of this and probably found the ring light disrespectful. She would have been out of her house shaking her fist at everyone and telling them to get off her property and stop being so obsessed with fame and the gram.

Annie's looking at me and making weird nodding gestures toward Mrs. R's place. I think she's going to throw her neck out if she carries on, but finally I give in and lean in toward Les Populaires.

"Just gotta grab something from my parents," I say, slinking away, but honestly they're all so enraptured by Heather's glamorous mother that I doubt they'd even notice if someone did a loud fart right now.

Annie follows me, an arm around my shoulders like she's consoling and must go with me, shooting a smile back at them.

"Sometimes I still pinch myself that we're actually IN the inner circle, you know," Annie whispers hurriedly. "I spent years trying to work out how to get in there, and it turns out all it took was a couple of murders. Imagine how much simpler life would have been if this happened years ago!"

"I'm sorry, are you wishing Selena, Adam, and Mrs. R had died years ago?" I whisper back, appalled.

"NO! Not that, I didn't mean that. I'm just . . . really happy to be included now. . . . I wonder if Heather will share clothes?" she says dreamily.

"Aaaannnnyway, we need to work out how we're going to get in there?" I whisper, pointing toward the house, where a police officer stands, his cap over his face, guarding the front door.

"Look, I'll distract him, and you can maybe get in through the side or something?" Annie offers. "Don't the yards all link together? No one's going to be in those houses because everyone's out here. You can climb over the fences and through to the back. There must be a way to get in around there."

"I don't think the police are going to just be leaving back doors unlocked, Annie." I sigh. "Also, how come it's me that has to climb over fences and stuff while you just get to have a chat with a police officer?"

"Because I've got to hold Herbie." She cradles him, like an infant, in an old baby sling that she found for him. "Also, you're faster and nimbler than me, and I have the upper arm strength of a turtle."

"Do turtles even have arms? What kind of an example is that? You don't know, turtles might actually be freakishly strong?"

"Just get over the fence, Doctor Dolittle." Annie smiles at me.

"Okay, fine," I say, but I will remember this if we work out who the murderer is and there's some kind of prize. My share of whatever it is should definitely be bigger for climbing fences.

Why would you send in the most anxious person?? Why, why, WHY??

Annie heads off toward the officer guarding Mrs. R's front door with a purposeful stride. I'm almost convinced that she's got the confidence to persuade that officer to let her in anyway. I head down the road and around the block, trying to find a way into the yards. I get ten houses down when I see that there's an open gate next to one of the front doors. There's no one around, and I know that anyone who lives at these houses is at Mrs. R's place. After briefly looking around, I head through it.

I can't believe that I'm doing this, attempting to break and enter for the second time today.

I peer around the side of the gate. Adrenaline rushes straight to my head as I think about the dolls in the locker earlier and what would happen to me if whoever made them caught me now. I have to push the thought away, my head starting to spin. Taking a deep shaky breath, I try to assess the situation.

The coast looks clear. From here it's only three houses away, so I've just got to jump three fences. Just three. That's all. Simple. I've never jumped one before, but I'm sure three will be absolutely fine. And when I get there, I probably won't be able to find a way in anyway, and I can just come back and tell Annie it wasn't possible and she'll have to think of another way to get in there.

I'm comforted by the noise of the crowd outside. If something goes wrong, everyone's just there. As long as I can still hear them, it's okay, right? I just have to get over these fences and try to find Mrs. R's village secrets.

As I approach fence number one, I start to realize how very short I am and how little upper body strength I have. I can actually feel my muscles withering away as I attempt to use them. When I reach it, I put my hands on top of the fence and try to push myself up. I'm halfway there, but I have to use my legs to help me. If someone comes and catches me like this now, it's fair to say I'm in a pretty vulnerable position.

Eventually, after some huffing and puffing, I reach the top of the fence and look over to the other gardens while I'm up here. It doesn't look like there's anyone in those, either, so I should be totally fine. I take the break in between fences as a moment to take stock again, but all I can think is that there's absolutely no way on earth that I'm going to be doing this on the way back. There has to be a simpler way.

The second fence seems easier than the first, and by the third one, I'm convinced that I could be an Olympic hurdler.

I stand in Mrs. R's backyard, where a small pond and water feature give the constant tinkling of running water, making me need to pee. The house looks completely empty, and because it's dark, I think I can roam around in there entirely undetected. I just need to work out a way to get in without breaking anything.

I push the back door with force because I'm convinced it won't open and go tumbling into the kitchen, falling flat on my face. Crap, I guess I'm in, then. Mrs. R must be smiling on me from wherever she is, but probably also laughing. I get a sense of déjà vu walking in through the kitchen, my heart beating so hard that I can hear it as a thump in my head.

It smells different in here from last time, clinical. I guess from all the swabbing and dusting for evidence that they've done around the house. I try to creep through without looking at the spot where we found her, but I still seem to turn my head in an almost-involuntary way. There's nothing there; everything's been cleaned up. As if it never existed. I don't know what I find creepier.

My nerves are properly jangled as I tiptoe around like a meerkat on high alert. I just need to find the bureau and get out of here—alive. I head straight to the living room and see an actual bureau right away in the corner, covered in one of the doilies that adorn every surface. It has to be that, but there are about a thousand compartments. I get to work gently opening and closing each bit. I open the top and see a small drawer with a keyhole. It's GOT to be that. Triumphant, I produce the key and slide it in, but it won't turn.

I try to think like Mrs. R. Where else would it possibly be? Maybe the bureau is a decoy? Maybe it's something near or on top of the bureau? I run my fingers along the edges of it, and the only thing I can see is a small ledge between the drawers and the top opening. If I was a secret compartment, is that where I'd be?

There's no keyhole, though. I slide the key along the tiny gap between the ledge and the top, its tip fitting perfectly and slipping between the two as the ledge starts to come away.

The key wasn't for a lock; the key was for sliding through the edge and opening that tiny gap. The ledge pops out, and it's a small, shallow tray, filled with papers, newspaper cuttings, bits of dated paper, and slim diaries. Mrs. R, you truly were a genius. Anyone would be looking for a lock like I was.

There must be years and years' worth of stuff here, and I start to panic about getting caught as I gather it all up in my hands, trying to shove it into the backpack. As I pile it in, I see all Mrs. R's observations of Barbourough. The thing that strikes me most is a newspaper clipping from the day the truck crashed out in the village. But this article is different from the one Annie and me found. It reads "World's Most Embarrassing Truck Crash."

"What was so embarrassing about it?" I whisper, reading through. "Oh, you have GOT to be kidding me."

I feel my rage boil.

It reads: "Private Products Littered the Streets as Barbourough's Most Embarrassing Incident Occurred."

Oh my god, there's so much wrong here.

They've censored the period pads as if they're hugely offensive just to look at. What's that about?!

Underneath the image, Mrs. R has written in scrolly writing, "This is how he does it."

How who does *what*?

I hear a noise above my head and grab what's left quickly from the drawer, shoving all of it fast into my backpack, and close the secret compartment. Just as I close the zip on my bag, I hear footsteps on the stairs. It's too late. I can't get out of here. I crouch down and make myself as small as possible. Hopefully if I stay here behind the bureau in the dark, they won't see me.

I'm trying to be invisible, but my heavy, ragged breath's in danger of getting me caught. Under the bureau, I watch a pair of black shoes crossing the floor. I can't see anything else, but with every step they make, my fear ramps up a notch. Whoever it is, I don't mind betting that the fact they haven't turned on a light probably means they're not supposed to be in here, either.

The footsteps stop in the doorway through to the kitchen. They're having a good look around, making me nervous that they can tell I'm here. I'm sure that they're going to start coming this way; they're going to uncover me. I screw up my eyes tight for what feels like an hour before I hear the feet move again. It's not until I register the tone of the footsteps changing, the noise of shoes on the kitchen tiles, that I open them again. I hear whoever it is opening the back door and heading outside, closing it again behind them.

I sit for a minute, breathing into the darkness, still frozen in fear and shock. Whoever they were, they weren't meant to be here, and that's why the door was open. Not left open by accident. Open very purposefully.

I start to unfold myself from my fetal position on the floor.

What if they're still out in the yard? I don't want them to see me, but it's also my only way out of here, and if I don't get out soon, I'm going to have an actual heart attack.

I creep out from behind the bureau and look around me, panicked as I secure everything in my backpack. My legs are shaking underneath me as I wobble toward the kitchen. In the darkness, I walk into a side table in the hallway, and something falls off.

"I need to talk to you two. . . ." Mrs. R's voice echoes around the hallway, ghostly and muffled, my heart almost coming to a complete standstill. And then I hear Annie's voice in reply, and I realize what it is that's fallen on the floor.

It's Annie's Dictaphone. But what was it doing here? On a random side table in Mrs. R's hallway? I pick it up, switching it off straightaway, the haunting noise of Mrs. R's voice still rattling in my ears, and put it in my backpack with everything else. I've got to get out of here.

I head into the kitchen, creeping around, peering into the darkness of the yard, to make sure the coast's clear. It looks clear, but the adrenaline coursing through my veins powers me into action. I fly out of the door, making sure to close it, and jump over the fences. Too afraid to even register the physical effort this time around.

That may have been my bravest moment, but it's definitely not one I'd like to repeat. When I reach the final yard, I head out of the gate swiftly, pulling my hoodie off before I reach the street again. I've made it, but I can't breathe. I'm boiling, and despite being outside, I feel like I need more air. I can hear my pulse in my head and my sweaty hands shake.

I walk as calmly as possible away from the houses and away from the crowds until I get to a safe space a couple of roads away where I can be by myself. I squat under a tree, resting against the trunk breathing deeply with my head between my legs until I feel the world stop spinning, and my lungs take in air.

I look up around me, moving my head, slowly realizing that even here I'm in danger. Because I might not be alone.

"If you're here, Scott, and you're not the killer, I could really use your help right now," I whisper out into the night.

Except if he's here and he is the killer, I'm screwed.

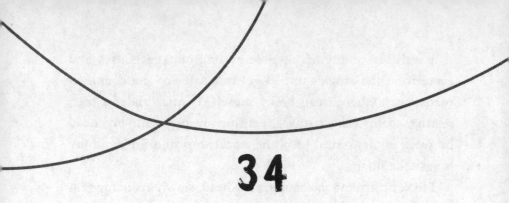

34

It feels like I've been gone for ages. When I look at my phone, I'm surprised that Annie hasn't messaged me. As I walk back into the street, I can see that she's not outside Mrs. R's house talking to the officers on duty anymore.

I scan the crowd for her. I'm guessing that she couldn't keep up the questions with the officer any longer and left. She's probably looking for me; I don't understand why she hasn't texted, though. She must be so worried by now.

There's a chill in the air that gets me now that I've calmed down, and I start to shiver. I feel shaken and tired. I need to find Annie and tell her what just happened, that I think I might have been in the same house as the actual killer. And then I need to get back home to safety, where we can be one hundred percent sure whoever made those dolls can't get us. I feel the weight of all the evidence in my backpack; at least now we can find out what Mrs. R knew that got her killed. Annie will definitely want to pore over everything right away, guaranteed; she's probably itching to already.

I see Heather with Audrey and Colin, all three of them

laughing, and I'm shocked when I realize what they're laughing at. It's Annie. After everything I've just been through, she's not even looking for me. She's just hanging out with them, pretending to make Herbie dance and messing around.

I try to shrug off the bitter feeling of anger rising in my stomach and head over there. I've got everything we need to solve this case in my backpack, and we're going to do it together.

As I walk over to her, it's not just the anger and jealousy I have to shake off, though. I feel uncomfortable, like I'm conscious of every step and arm movement I make. I feel like I'm being watched. The hairs on the back of my neck start to prick up again. What if the person in Mrs. R's place knew I was there? What if they're the murderer, the one that made the dolls? What if they're watching me now and they know I've got everything I need to prove what they've done in my backpack?

I shake off all my what-ifs and concentrate on what I have to do. Now isn't the time. Heather's mum still appears to be giving what must be the longest eulogy ever for Mrs. R, with people watching her fondly, tears in their eyes, despite most of them not even knowing her.

"We all knew and loved Lucinda Robbins; she was a staple around these parts. You could always depend upon her to know exactly what was going on and what had gone on, but you knew never to ask where she got her information from." Heather's mum pauses, and everyone starts laughing. "We loved her, and in her own way, I think she loved all of us, too. What happened to Lucinda Robbins, Selena Munroe, and Adam Devers is inhuman. To have their lives cut short in the way they were—is—something that none of us will stand for."

Heather's mum looks at the crowd, where people with their phones up are gathered, livestreaming her, her face solemn. "We will find out who's responsible for this, and we will make sure that they pay for taking away the lives of the innocent. The innocent and the loved. And that is why DI Collins and DI Wallace are asking us, please, that if ANYONE saw ANYTHING you must TELL THEM."

I wouldn't tell them ANYTHING after how rubbish they've been. It's their fault Mrs. R's dead.

"Please," Mrs. Stevens continues. "Especially regarding the missing person, Scott Woodley." My blood runs cold at the mention of his name. "They need to know whatever, even if it's small, because none of us know how important even the tiniest detail could be. Join me now while we listen to Mrs. Robbins's favorite piece of music: 'Lucy in the Sky with Diamonds' by the Beatles."

Heather's mum steps down from the podium to the opening bars of the song.

I take my place back with Annie, Audrey, Colin, and Heather, and it's as if none of them even noticed I was gone, least of all Annie. It looks like while I was having the scariest night of my life, she had the best night of hers.

"Here, I found this," I say to Annie, placing the Dictaphone in her hand while everyone's distracted.

"What? Where?" Annie asks, surprised.

"Mrs. R's place. You must have left it there after we . . . found her," I say, not even looking at her. I'm too annoyed. I could have been murdered, and all the while, she wasn't even worried about where I was.

"Is this song about getting high?" Colin asks, and all of us stop and squint, trying to listen to the words.

"Has to at least have been written by someone on acid," Audrey concludes reasonably.

"Imagine if Mrs. R liked getting high though," Colin mutters under his breath as Audrey giggles and Heather gives them both the look of an angry schoolteacher.

This whole week is making me feel like I've taken acid if I'm being honest, and I don't even really know what that's supposed to feel like.

35

"Okay, so I think what we've figured out is that Mrs. R was actually some kind of village oracle and that now we might never find out who did it because whoever did it killed the village oracle," Annie says as the two of us stare down at everything spread on her bedroom floor.

"She was killed because she knew too much," I agree.

"I can't believe there was someone in there with you. They could have been the murderer! What if they'd seen you?!" Annie went ballistic when I told her what happened earlier. Now she just keeps reminding me that I could be dead right now, and to be honest, I don't need it.

We came back here straight after the vigil so we could see what was in the files, and so far, there's a LOT, mostly diaries of Mrs. R's observations about the village. We sit in silence at first, in part because I don't particularly feel like talking to Annie since she's abandoned me for new friends, and also because there's just so much to read. It takes us a while, but we start looking at things from around the date of the truck crash because for starters the headline of that article incensed us, and secondly, it seems to us that there've been two huge incidents in the whole history of this tiny village: the truck crash, and the murders. And they're both connected to menstrual products.

"Why was it 'embarrassing'?!" Annie shouts, still fuming over the headline. "And why are they calling them 'female products'? it's not just women that menstruate. When did this happen—the Dark Ages?" She pauses, lowering her voice. "No, really, when actually was it, again?" Annie scans the article for a date. "2005, KERRY! How can this have only happened sixteen years ago. HOW? And they behave as if menstruation is offensive! They've blurred the picture so that you can't even see what they are?!"

"Wild," I say. "Did you know that they used to use blue liquid to demonstrate periods, too?"

"Oh, right? But they didn't use blue liquid to represent blood in *Psycho*? It's just blood for god's sake. Just because it's period blood, people get all weird about it! I am so mad!" she rages. She's so angry that I hold back on pointing out *Psycho* was filmed in black and white. "What do you think, Herbert? Who do you think she was saying was responsible for the period pads across the road?"

"How angry does it still make you that they called them 'sanitary products' as well?" I ask, starting to feel a little warmer toward her.

"The early noughties were ARCHAIC," Annie says. "I mean, seriously, it makes me realize how lucky we are not to live then. How hard is it to say 'period'?"

"All of these newspaper clippings and notes that she's written about things are mostly about Heather's dad, the great Terry Stevens, and his company, V-Lyte. Or, as it was called back then apparently, Sani-Terry," I say. "How arrogant can

307

one guy be? Can't imagine why they changed it . . ."

"So, what do we think this means?" Annie points to the "That's how he does it" written on the newspaper clipping about the truck crash. "How he does what?"

"I don't know. But we've got so much else to go through and that seems to be giving you rage . . . so I'm just going to remove it from your grasp here. . . ." I say, trying to pry the clipping from her angry fist. "And suggest we move on to some of the other, less-rage-inducing evidence."

"Okay, yes, good idea," Annie says, calming herself by picking up a list.

"What's that?" I ask. I've been trying to put things in chronological order as I find them.

"It's a list of women's names with dates and times next to them," Annie says. "She thinks that Terry—Mr. S to you and me—was having affairs. Which, of course, we know now he was. But this is a list of all his interactions with women in the town."

"She must have had a lot of free time back in the day," I say.

"Oh my god." Annie throws the bit of paper across the room and brings her hand to her mouth. "My mum's on there."

I go over and pick up the list.

"She's only on it once, though," I say.

"A one-night stand?" Annie has her head in her hands.

"It was at two forty-three in the afternoon." I cringe.

"GROTESQUE!" Annie rolls to the floor dramatically.

"Dude, they were probably just chatting on the street. Chill out. He can't have bedded all of these women. For one, Mrs. Joy would never cheat on Mr. Joy, and she's down here. Everyone knows she's far too straitlaced for that."

Annie composes herself as I carry on sifting through the papers.

"Oh, wow, says here she's convinced half the teenagers in this village were fathered by him." I giggle as Annie continues to roll about the floor feigning agony.

"HEATHER COULD BE MY SISTER!" Annie gasps. I try not to get too upset that she's thought of Heather being her sister before she's thought of me.

"OH, PISS OFF!" I say, half joking and half extremely hurt.

I need Annie. I've gained and lost Scott this week; I can't handle another loss.

"Kerry," Annie says. She waves Mrs. R's diary in the air. "I don't know if you're going to like this."

"What is it?" I ask, already concerned.

"It's the last diary entry from Mrs. R, she wrote it on Thursday before . . ."

Oh, I can't believe she wrote something the day she died.
"Can I see?"

"I think you'd better," Annie says.

> I saw Annie and Kerry this morning, and
> they're going to come over later. I'm now 100%
> sure that the boy is his son, so I need to tell them,
> especially as I've seen Kerry cavorting with him in
> the village. I haven't seen him for years, but he's
> definitely the one that I saw him with in Manches-
> ter that summer. His mother and Terry were very
> lovey-dovey; he'd have been furious if he saw me.

309

Probably would have tried to shut me up. I got a
good look at him the other day, so I can be quite
sure it's him. The boy. Arrived just as the mur-
ders started happening I believe. Scott's his name,
Terry's son. And if I'm right in thinking he's got
something to do with these murders, he's a chip off
the old block.

I realize my hand's shaking as I finish reading the note.

"He can't be," I say, but I see that Annie's already got a picture of him up and she's comparing it to pictures of Mr. S and
Heather. I can't believe I didn't see it before. They've got the
same nose, same color eyes, same jaw . . . "Just because he's his
son doesn't mean he's a murderer though. I mean, why would
he kill Selena? Or Adam?" I ask.

"She was trolling his sister. He might have known she was
onto some family secrets and wanted to protect them when he
saw her at the food bank?" Annie says, before taking a beat
and scrolling for some more pictures. "It always felt like too
much of a coincidence to me that they were in the same place
at the same time."

I shake my head at her because I can't quite believe it. This
is the sort of thing that happens in movies, not in Barbourough.

"What if they knew each other and kept it secret? Selena
knew about him, and she knew about Adam dealing drugs. She
knew everything. Maybe that's why she was trolling Heather?"
Annie suggests.

"But Heather didn't know about the drugs, and I doubt she
knew about Scott, either?" I say. "What would be the point in
that?"

"But what if they didn't know that she didn't know? What if they were in it together?" Annie's eyes have lit up now with the spark of her wild theories, but I'm still shaking my head.

"You checked by texting her phone when she died. You KNOW it was just her," I say. "And if they were in it together, then why would he kill her?"

But she's not listening to me. Annie's so absorbed in scribbling on her board. She thinks she's cracked it, and she won't hear any different from me.

"And then Mrs. R had worked out who he was, so she had to go," Annie continues, before noticing my face. "Think about it, Ker. He was with you when you discovered the bodies. Whose idea was it to play croquet? To go down to the study? He even pointed to where you should aim the croquet ball so that it hit Adam's body!"

"STOP IT! STOP!!! It wasn't him," I hiss, narrowing my eyes at Annie.

My head's swimming trying to think of an alternative. Annie always says I'm good at thinking up alternatives, but right now I can't think of any. It feels like every time I find a reason why it's not Scott, Annie thinks up ten reasons why it is. It's like she WANTS it to be him.

"She was onto him. WAKE UP, KERRY! He was using you to find the bodies with him, to give himself an alibi. He wanted you to trust him, to take advantage of you! And then when he knew he'd get found out, he bolted!" Annie throws her hands in the air, whispering hurriedly, and my blood starts to boil.

"Because it's so hard for you to believe that someone could like me like that? He can't just have been a normal guy that happens to have a shady father, a normal guy who actually LIKES ME?!"

"Well, if he likes you so much, then where is he now?" Annie raises her eyebrow at me, and she looks like one of them. Like a Heather clone.

I shiver. "Screw this. You're so obsessed with Heather and her crew that you've become just like her—a real bitch," I shout-whisper, grabbing my things. "And do you know what? She wouldn't even be your friend normally. She's just using you, too. You'll never be part of her crew, not really. Once they're finished with you, they'll chew you up and spit you out like they do with everyone else. Don't come crawling back to me when that happens."

I stagger toward the door, my anger making the room swim around me.

"Where are you going?" Annie's whispering furiously now, the two of us livid with each other and trying so hard not to wake her parents.

"HOME!" I hiss back, sending sheets of evidence from Mrs. R's house flying up into the air while I try and grab what I can.

"Don't throw the fucking clues, you dipshit," Annie whispers, narrowing her eyes at me. "You can't go out there. It's dark, and there's a murderer on the loose."

"I'd rather that than spend any more time in here with someone who thinks my only boyfriend ever was just using me to cover up his serial killings."

That should be enough, but something sour surges in me, and I bite out the words quietly: "Maybe he suggested croquet because he wanted *you* to be distracted so that *we* could finally have some alone time! Because you're always there; you'd never let us have any time to ourselves and now he's GONE."

After that, I can't stay, because I can't even look at her face, and my rage makes my hands positively vibrate. I fling my stuff together and launch myself out of Annie's window, onto the porch roof, and then swing down. It's a way I've let myself in and out of her house for years—she always leaves the window open for me at night just in case I need her. But right now, I need to get away from her.

I put my things into my bike basket and angrily fasten my helmet.

"Kerry, you're being silly," Annie hisses from the window. "Kerry! For god's sake! Fine, but if you bump into your boyfriend in the dark . . . call the police."

I try to think of a retort but I'm too tired, so instead I pedal out of her driveway, my head held high and my middle finger raised. I'm so filled with rage that I get nearly the whole way to my house before I think about the possibility that the menstrual murderer could be lying in wait. I don't even chain my bike up when I get in. I fling myself through the front door, hands shaking, tears streaming down my face, and creep up the stairs to my room.

I collapse onto my bed, staring at the last text that Scott sent me. My head's a mess. He told so many lies and so much of it doesn't add up, but everything Annie was saying did. I need to hear it from his mouth. I can't let her be right. Not about this. Not about any of it.

> **Me:** Please Scott, just let me
> know you're ok.

My phone buzzes in my fingers right after I send the text,

and for a second, I feel hope coursing through me like a sunbeam. And then I see the text.

Annie: I'm not talking to you but let me know you're home ok.

Me: Home

Annie: Fine

Me: Fine.

I look at my text to Scott. It hasn't even been delivered.

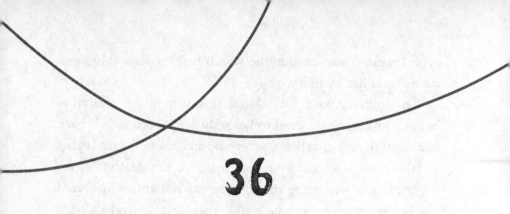

36

I don't feel like sleeping, so instead I go through everything that I've got from Mrs. R's place. I curse myself for not making sure that I had everything when I left in such a hurry. Anything that I've left behind will be used by Annie to try and prove Scott's guilt, and she'll be relentless. I've never felt like she's not on my team before, and I don't like it.

I'm looking through all the diary entries about Scott and about the affairs that Mr. Stevens was having, real ones and ones that Mrs. R might have just imagined. She seemed to think anyone who spoke to him was at it with him, including the postman.

I find a diary entry about Scott when he was a little boy. Mrs. R had seen them together in Manchester, and she followed them, speaking to his mum when Mr. S wasn't with them. She says she could be one hundred percent sure after that chat that he was definitely Mr. S's son. And she described Scott's mum as a lovely lady called Therese.

I go to Google. I'm presuming as Scott doesn't have the surname Stevens, his surname must be the same as his mum's. I type Therese Woodley into the search bar; the first thing that comes up is her obituary.

Her obituary loads; it's dated this summer. It describes her as a loving single mum to her only son, Scott. I click back and view the other articles, where he and his mum are trying to raise money for cancer research before her death. Despite everything he was going through, he worked and volunteered and helped in every way he could. They're described as loved throughout the community and the kind of people that would help and support anyone in need, including having opened their home to refugees in happier times for them. The more I read about him, the surer I am that he's a good guy. That there's no way he could have killed anyone.

But looking at the facts Annie knows, I can see it does look bad. Scott's mum isn't sick; she's dead, just like the cops said. And he actually came here to find his dad, rather than to get some peace and healing time for his mum, but his dad's dead, too. So he's found out he's an orphan. Now everyone thinks he's a killer. And I don't even know if the police actually definitely know who his dad was. They were being vague after all.

Poor Scott. He's already been through so much. Part of me wants to wallow in all that I've discovered, and that apparently the police know him better than I do. But I can't stop now. I can almost feel Annie, across Barbourough, stacking up the evidence against him. I'm going to stay here looking through all of this until I find out who did it and what happened to Scott. One thing's for sure: there's no way he would have taken that bracelet off willingly.

"Please," I whisper. "Please be okay wherever you are."

* * *

It's seven a.m. I've waded through almost everything, googling every single thing that Mrs. R talked about, and looked at things from every possible angle. The sun's come up, and I'm just left with the newspaper cutting from the truck crash, which I'd folded up at Annie's house. It seems like Mrs. R thought this was important, so I need to take another look. In the fresh light of a new day, I spread it out, and some loose pages fall that must have gotten caught in it when I scooped everything up in a hurry. I hadn't noticed these. They're diary entries that must have come loose. I stare at the article that made Annie so angry and the thin, raggedy pages that were in it. I miss her so much it hasn't really sunk in that we're not talking. Every time I figure something out, I want to go and tell her. We've never fought before, and it feels wrong to be without her.

There are two pages of furious writing. Some of it's hard to read, like it's been written in an excited hurry. But what I can read makes me gasp and then feel silly for not seeing it sooner.

This is how he does it. I woke up early to go for my walk, and everything I've always suspected about Terry Stevens was proven to me. One of his trucks had overturned in the high street. Not a soul to be seen around there, but period products everywhere.

I picked up a box with a strange sort of leaf mark on it, a T in the leaf—none of the others seemed to have it—and BINGO. Just as I've said all along, in the box with the sanitary towels was weed, skunk, wacky baccy. Whatever the kids call it these days. I smoked some just to be sure.

It was the only box there with that mark, the

leaf with the T inside, and when I checked some of
the others, they were just pads, no drugs. So, this is
how he does it. He uses period products to smuggle
the weed.

I reach for my phone ready to tell Annie about this and remember again that we're not speaking. I forgot for a second in the moment of excitement. But I can't *not* tell her. I type off the text furiously and wait. Watching as the ticks turn from delivered, to read, and hoping that she's going to type back. But she doesn't. I stare at the screen for a few minutes, but nothing happens. She's seen it, she's read it, and she's ignoring me. Maybe she's annoyed that I've figured out something without her.

I can't help thinking that if Annie were here, though, she'd know what to do with this information, but she seemed determined to pin it all on Scott, and now she's ignoring me, so I have to do this on my own.

I get out Post-it Notes, and I start to make my own murder board. If Adam was supplying drugs, were they from Heather's dad's stash? They had the same leaf with a *T* that Mrs. R describes, so I feel like they MUST have been. Was Mr. S still smuggling them when he died? And then did Adam take over when Mr. S passed away or, more likely—because I doubt Mr. S knew he was going to die—did he steal them and supply the school? He wasn't just cheating on Heather and dealing drugs behind her back; he was also stealing the drugs from her dead dad. But then how does it connect? I scratch my chin.

Could it have been that someone *was* left in charge of the drugs in the event of Heather's dad's death? Whoever they are,

I bet they weren't pleased Adam was selling them. That would give them motive, at least in that murder.

We know Mrs. R knew about it, too. That's her link. And Selena's? Maybe she stumbled upon something. Learned something—she was close with Heather and Adam after all and seemed to be good at squirreling out information. In which case, the thing linking it all would be the drugs.

There's another page of Mrs. R's scrawly writing still to decipher, so I lay it out in front of me.

They've found the boy that was driving the truck apparently. Well, so Terry Stevens says. I wouldn't be surprised if he's dead. Killed by Terry or some of his other international drug lord friends. The police have closed the case anyway, so he's convinced them. Whatever's happened there, these are scary men and I'm going to do my best to stay out of it. There's a difference between bravery and stupidity, and I think to confront him now would be stupidity.

I'm going to hide all this away, somewhere where no one can find it. But keep it just in case it's ever needed.

Oh, Mrs. R. It's really needed. But this doesn't help me with who could have been left in charge of the drugs when Mr. Stevens died. Unless it was whoever was driving the truck when it crashed? But if they crashed the truck, they weren't exactly trustworthy.

It has to be someone who was at the Stevens house the

night of Selena's murder, who had a stake in the drug business. Someone who wanted to keep Mrs. R quiet about Mr. S, and who didn't like Adam stealing from their drug farm.

What about . . . *Mrs*. Stevens?

Surely she would have known about the drugs? She took over his business, after all. She wouldn't have committed the murders herself, though? Not with a reputation like hers and that much money. I pick up my phone, having silenced it around midnight when the WhatsApp chat for Les Populaires was still in full flow. Heather's happily messaging about the Kardashians, unaware that she's got a brother who might currently be in serious trouble, a dad who was an international drug lord, and a mother who might now also be an international drug lord, as well as the one murdering people.

My phone beeps and I quickly open it as soon as I see Annie's name on the screen. She's finally responded to me.

Annie: I'm on my way to Heather's place
now anyway to tell her about her brother.

I sit bolt upright and realize how naive I've been obsessing about saving Scott when actually it's not just him who's in danger. If Heather's mum is the murderer, Annie's heading to her house with a bag full of evidence about her evildoing. She could be the next victim.

Me: Don't go. It's not safe

Annie: I'm already on the way.

320

Me: Stop, turn around!

Annie: Why?

> **Me:** It's too much to explain.
> Look, I'm coming. Don't go in
> there.

I throw on yesterday's clothes, take my anxiety meds, and head out the window (the last thing I need now is having to explain things to my parents). I don't have time to waste. There's no me without Annie. I can't let her put herself in danger. I have to keep her safe; I promised.

I shove a menstrual cup between my fingers, stem out, ready to poke anyone in the eye who comes near her.

I'm cycling so fast that I feel sick, all the while imagining Annie, innocently heading into the path of danger. It gets me moving quicker than ever before. The sound of sirens approaches behind me, and I start pushing my legs harder, trying to make the wheels go around quicker. I can't be too late, can I? Heather was *just* messaging in the group. Annie can't have got there already. If Heather's mum knows she's worked anything out, she's in danger. I need to save her.

The police car zooms behind me and then slows down, its siren and lights making my head swim. It doesn't seem to be overtaking, so I pull over to let it pass despite the fact that there's plenty of room on the road. Maybe they're just being super cautious. I need to catch up with Annie, though, so I wish they'd hurry up. But instead of carrying on, they stop, and my full-body panic really ramps up, including dizziness and sweaty palms. Whatever it is they want to talk to me about, I probably look pretty guilty right now.

I turn around and see DI Wallace and DI Collins through the windshield. Of course it has to be those guys. What if they saw me sneaking around Mrs. R's house last night through the window? Or saw me jumping fences? They turn the siren off but leave the blue and red lights flashing. Curtains are starting to twitch in the houses around me as DI Wallace and DI Collins get out of the car. Their siren may be turned off, but I can still hear it ringing, like there's one blaring away in my head.

I'll never save Annie at this rate.

"Can I help you?" I ask, shielding the sun from my eyes, trying to speed this up.

"We just need to ask you a couple of questions," DI Wallace says, and I feel irritated. Just get on with it before another person gets killed, you shitbag.

DI Collins stands next to him, his usual welcoming smile plastered on his face.

"Sure," I say, putting my bike down on the ground and stepping away from it. I leave my helmet on, because god knows I'll need full protection from these guys.

"Do you recognize this?" DI Wallace holds out a plastic evidence bag. In it the Sonic Youth T-shirt that Scott was wearing on the first day I met him lies in a crumpled heap.

I try not to shudder when I see it, but I want to reach out, stuff my face in it, and wail dramatically like they do in the movies.

322

Instead, I just nod. At least it doesn't seem like they're about to arrest me for trespassing.

"Scott's?" DI Collins asks.

I nod again. How do they have it? He wasn't even wearing it on Thursday.

"One of our team found it upstairs at Mrs. Robbins's house this morning," DI Wallace says. "I guess it was missed in the initial sweep."

Why would he have taken off his T-shirt and left it there? A T-shirt that he wasn't even wearing? Why do they think a murderer would leave their T-shirt at the scene? They just wouldn't. Unless it was put there by someone else . . . the someone else who was in there with me last night.

I look up to make eye contact with the detectives, feeling bold and full of bravery for the first time in my life.

"He wasn't even wearing that T-shirt on Thursday," I say, being sure to keep eye contact with DI Wallace; he seems like the worse of the two. I want him to know I'm not scared of him.

Whoever was there last night is framing Scott. That's why the bracelet was there. That's why the T-shirt he wasn't even wearing was there. Whoever it was knows where he is, too. It can't have been Mrs. S because she was doing her speech. She must have someone working with her. I was so close to them last night, I wish I was braver, that I could have followed them. But I might also be dead by now if I'd done that.

"Look, we all know how young love feels, and you might think you've got some Bonnie and Clyde situation going with Scott," DI Wallace starts. "But we just want you to know that wherever he is, he's not thinking of you. Not really,"

His words blend into the background because he's got no idea what he's talking about and all I can think is that the longer DI Wallace drones on, the less chance I have of saving Annie and Scott, wherever he is. I need to get Annie, and the two of us need to find Scott all without being caught by Mrs. S.

"Boys like Scott, they do this, they cause trouble, they get girls like you into trouble. Do you want to spend your whole life on the run with a murderer?" DI Wallace is still asking. I feel my phone beeping in my hand as DI Wallace speaks, and when I look down, I see Annie's name, multiple times.

> **Annie:** Audrey said that everyone's talking about how the police have pulled you over.

> **Annie:** ARE THEY ARRESTING YOU?

> **Annie:** I'm coming to get you.

> **Annie:** I HAVE BAIL MONEY

> **Annie:** #FreeKerry

I feel relieved because at least she's cycling away from Heather's house and toward me.

"And we just wanted you to know, we can get you out of this situation," DI Wallace says. "If you tell us where he's hiding, we can arrest him, and it'll be all over. You can carry on with your life as a promising young woman and go to college. Just tell us where he is."

I look up at him with my arms crossed, squinting in the low morning sunshine.

"I haven't got a clue where he is, but I do know that you've got it wrong and that he's in danger. He's not a killer. You should be looking for him to help him, not to arrest him. Is he just the easy option for you? A kid with no parents or money to fight your accusations. Either way, it's not him, and you should be putting your efforts into finding and saving him. Before you have a fourth person's blood on your hands."

DI Wallace is so wrapped up in his own embarrassment and rage at being spoken to like that by a teenage girl that I take my chance and start to walk away.

"Look," DI Collins retorts as his partner glares at me, "maybe he's got you confused or fooled, brainwashing can happen, especially with impressionable young girls. . . . We only want what's best for you."

I feel my rage bubble under the surface as DI Collins talks, my hands balling into angry fists. It's time to get out of here before I do something I'll regret.

I look between the two of them, my teeth set on edge trying to work out how they can't see it. How they can't understand that no murderer leaves their T-shirt at a crime scene. That he's clearly being framed. Despite my heart thumping, I don't look away. All of my adrenaline seems to shoot straight to my head, the edges of everything blurring. But out of the corner of my eye, I can see Annie approaching behind the detectives. Her gold cycling helmet visible first, followed by her sweet, rosy-cheeked face, sweating as she pedals away, the tiny bicycle working overtime.

Relief floods my veins as she pulls up next to the detectives.

Standing with the little bike between her legs, gold cycling helmet still in situ, she squints up at the two men, mirroring my expression.

"Should you be interviewing my friend without a lawyer present?" are the first words out of her mouth. I want to leap onto her and hug her, but there's no time for that. Scott's in danger wherever he is, and these two are going to be no help. We need to get to Heather's and find out where her mum is, and hopefully she can lead us to Scott, preferably without killing us as well.

"We're just asking some informal questions at this stage," DI Wallace says, and DI Collins finally takes his attention away from me to look at Annie.

"Yes, just some informal questions, although if we have further ones, we might need you to come down to the station." DI Collins looks to DI Wallace, who seems puzzled by this.

Oh, hell no. We need to get out of here before they decide to take me down the station for further questions. I can't save Scott from there. It doesn't seem like anyone can.

"Actually, we've got things to do, so we best be off." I can barely believe my own sass at this point, but I feel like I've got nothing to lose.

I watch DI Wallace's face turn beet red again, and DI Collins narrows his eyes at me. Annie and I get back on our bikes and start to ride off, slowly at first, in the direction of Heather's house.

"No worries, Kerry. Look, you have a nice day and be careful, now," DI Collins calls after us, and as I turn back, he's giving me the fakest smile I've ever seen.

"Thanks, you too," I say, narrowing my eyes back. Then I

lean in as close to Annie as I can on our mismatched bicycles. "We need to get to Heather's place," I whisper to her. "Someone's planted the evidence against Scott, and he didn't do it. Please just trust me."

"I do." Annie reaches across and puts her hand on mine, resting on my handlebar. "I believe you, and I'm sorry."

"I'm sorry, too," I whisper back. "I missed you, dude."

"Missed you, too," she says. The two of us wobble to a halt so we can hug, our bikes propped between our legs, ready for action. Annie wipes a small tear off my cheek.

"We need to get to the farm," I say, my feet back on the pedals. "We need to tell Heather about Scott, and we need to find him. I think Heather's mum knows where he is."

"Dude, do you think she, like, did it?" Annie says, eyes wide as we zoom past the calm houses of Barbourough, only just starting to wake up to another day in menstrual murder hell.

"Mr. S was smuggling drugs in his period products. Mrs. R had figured it out. And I mean, if Heather's mum took over the period business, then she has to have taken over the drug one, too, right? Or at the very least has to have found out about it." I pause to pant. All this biking is hard to do while explaining my solution to the mystery.

"What if she killed Heather's dad to get the businesses?" Annie asks, her eyes flashing with excitement.

"We need to get to Heather's and find out what she's done with Scott ASAP. And we need to get away from these losers," I say, pointing behind me to where the police car still seems to be tailing us.

"We'll get to him as fast as we can," Annie says. "We just need to lose these guys because they're really slowing us down." And with that, I crank my knees and pedal ahead.

I pause at the top of the hill for Annie, before we speed away as fast as Annie's Paw Patrol wheels will take us. Making our getaway from the cops, the feds, the—I am such a badass right now.

DI Wallace and DI Collins are still slowly rolling in their car behind us the whole way to Heather's house. Unfortunately, due to Annie's small wheel circumference, we just haven't been able to shake them. At one point, I thought we may lose them at the church, as old Mr. Harris was crossing the road with a bouquet of flowers, but DI Collins instead chose to nearly run over poor old Mr. H. He was left shaking his fist and swearing at the back of the police car, while they barely noticed that anything was happening.

You'd think that since we knew a doll-leaving serial killer was after us, having the police being constantly on our tail would be reassuring. The only problem is that the police seem to be falling for every single red herring the doll-leaving serial killer is throwing at them.

We brake suddenly, forcing them to brake behind us before the entrance of the lane leading up to the farm. We turn around and stare at them, and they look back at us as if they've been found out. DI Collins takes a beat before continuing to drive around us and then speeds off into the distance, like he's trying to make out that they weren't following in the first place.

"They are the least stealthy police I have ever seen in my entire life," Annie says.

"Yep," I say. "And not just that, they're really bad at their job, too." I try to swallow the nausea that rises in my throat as the two of us speed down the lane.

Every second counts right now if we're going to find out the truth about what happened before someone else dies.

There are two Jeeps outside the house, so I know Heather's in, I just hope her mum isn't also at home. After trading a look, we dump our bikes and head for the front door.

I pull the heavy metal knocker, and it lands with a booming echoey sound.

"Come in!" Heather's voice reaches us from inside.

I push the huge wooden front door, and it creaks open. As we walk through the hall, I can't help but be slightly creeped out. But then I see Heather alone, stood in the doorway looking pale, in jogging bottoms and a sweatshirt, no makeup on, her hair pulled back in a messy bun. It's the least put together I've ever seen her looking and yet she's still, as expected, utterly stunning.

"Come in," she says, gesturing to us to join her where she's standing.

"Where's your mum?" I ask.

"It all got too much for her, so she went to a spa day with my aunt," Heather says, and I relax, despite a voice in the back of my head saying, "But what if that's a lie?"

We follow Heather through to the kitchen and she hops up onto a stool at the counter.

"You can grab anything you like. Mum's got some samples from a brand partnership with KomBOOTYA at the moment, so there's loads of that if you want." She offers a bottle to us.

There's a picture of Mrs. S and the Dalai Lama above the fridge, and I stare at it, wondering if the woman in the picture here, shaking hands with the most peaceful and wise man in the world, could really be a drug-smuggling murderer.

"Thanks," I say, taking the drink. The ride has actually made me quite thirsty.

I take a gulp and wince. It's yeasty, very yeasty.

"Oh Christ!" Annie doesn't manage to be as polite as me.

"What? It's not that bad, is it?" Heather asks, taking a gulp of her own and gags before we can answer. "Fuck me, it tastes like thrush."

We start laughing, slightly taken aback by the fact that she's actually said something funny and that she's behaving reasonably calmly. But then we sit in silence at the bar. I need to work out the right way to broach the subject, to find out how much she knows. I'm finding it hard enough to get my head around any of this, so I can't imagine how hard it's going to be for her.

She doesn't even know about her dad's side business. Or her boyfriend robbing it after his death.

"We need to talk to you about Scott," Annie says bluntly. "We think he's your brother."

"I know," Heather says, startling us.

She doesn't look at all surprised, and I start to wonder how long she's known this for, and what else she knows. Maybe this'll be easier than I thought. Unless she already knows more about the murders than she's letting on? I shake off the suspicion because Heather's all we've got right now.

"Mum told me yesterday afternoon. She found some stuff in Dad's will right after he died. She said the moment she saw him the night Selena died she knew it was him. She's been keeping it from me this whole time, but when he disappeared and the police said he was wanted, she knew she was going to have to tell me."

I think back to Heather and her mum last night, hosting that whole vigil. I would have had no idea about any of it. Mrs. S knows how to Poker Face. I look over at Annie on her phone, checking Mrs. S's Instagram account to confirm that she is indeed at the spa, and not about to ambush us.

"I got kind of angry when she left today, because I know it's been a lot for her, but it's a lot for me, too," Heather continues, swinging her legs from her perch on the barstool. "She's known this whole time. I literally JUST found out, and she's left me." Heather looks furious. "I went into his study, and I busted open the drawer of his desk that we couldn't find a key for after he died. There's so much in there, it got a bit overwhelming. I can't believe he's my brother *and* he's killed my best friend, my boyfriend, and a sweet old lady."

"He's not the murderer," I say firmly, blinking at her.

"What do you mean?" Heather looks at me as if what I've said is incomprehensible.

"He didn't do it. We don't know who did, but we know it wasn't him," I repeat, deciding not to mention that I think it was actually her mum that did it. Best to start with the drug empire first and work from there, I think. "There's some other stuff that we've found out, if you're ready to hear it?"

Heather takes a deep breath. "Okay, I'm ready," she says. "But I think there's something you should know first. I did know why Selena was trolling me."

Annie tilts her head like she's trying to comprehend, when I know full well that both of us already know what's going on. Heather sinks down on her stool, her head resting on her hands.

"She knew my biggest secret. I bought my Instagram followers. Well, my dad did. And I don't get PR samples—I buy everything, Prada, Dior, Gucci, all of it. It's all a lie. Just so I can stay important. I worry that when we all go to college and move away I'll be irrelevant, and I never want that. I thought being irrelevant was the worst thing, but it turns out after this week, it's not." She shakes her head. "Sometimes I got in trouble for the posts I did. Dad used to manage my account and deal with the angry DMs; he paid some of them off. But now that he's dead, I've been trying my best to do it all myself. . . . I don't know how Selena found out, but she did. And that must be why she set up the account."

"We know that already," Annie says, beaming with pride in a totally inappropriate way.

"Of course you do." Heather smiles, surprised. "So what else did you have to tell me, and why don't you think Scott did it?"

"I think someone's trying to frame him. It's a long story, but the T-shirt they've just found at Mrs. R's house, Scott wasn't even wearing the day he died; and he'd never leave his bracelet behind. It was from his mum."

"Why would someone frame him?" Heather asks.

"I think the murderer's doing it to detract attention from themselves," I say.

"So how do we work out who it is?" Heather asks.

"Here's the tricky bit—" I start, but Annie cuts me off.

"We think your dad was an international drug lord," Annie blurts out.

"Annie! Subtlety," I chastise as Heather stares at us both open-mouthed. "There are ways of doing these things, you know?"

"What? Like there's etiquette for telling someone their dad's *Breaking Bad* and *Narcos* in one?" Annie asks as I sigh at her.

Heather's turned completely pale, and I'm just relieved Annie didn't drop in the bit about Mrs. S as well.

"Mrs. R discovered that your dad was smuggling drugs in with period products. And after he died, Adam started dealing drugs. We think he was stealing them from wherever your dad was growing them," I say. Her eyes flit from side to side as she tries to digest what I'm telling her. "And that's why he died. Mrs. R was killed because she'd figured it all out. We're not sure about Selena. Unless . . ."

"Unless she'd figured out about the drugs as well? She didn't say in the DMs what the secrets she knew were, did she?" Annie asks. "It could have been secrets about your dad's business?"

"I think you'd better come and see what I found in the study. Some of it might make more sense now." Heather stands up, a little wobbly, and the two of us follow her out of the kitchen and down the corridor to the right.

I get a feeling like someone's walking over my grave when I step into the study. Seeing the desk, I keep remembering the way Selena looked, sitting at it like she was ready for business.

Heather takes me around to the other side, to right where Selena was. I look down at the desk and see the front's been completely bashed in and there are papers spewing out. She wasn't joking about smashing it open—she must have been pretty angry.

"Look." Heather thrusts bits of paper and photographs at me and finally a clutch of passports. "I guess the drug thing explains why he's got five passports here with his image and different names on them."

333

I see Annie's eyes light up as we pass the fraudulent passports between us.

"All of the trips abroad he made, all the time . . . I know what those were for now." Heather tears through more papers on the desk and grabs some letters. "Here, these are letters from Scott's mum, pictures of her and Scott, and there're even ones with my dad in them. Look at this one."

She shows me a picture of a much younger Scott, her dad, and a woman who I recognize as Therese, Scott's mum.

"Scott must have been about six here? Which means I was also six. When I was six, he was going to visit his son, buying him gifts and spending time with him. I remember vaguely that he used to always be away on business when I was little." Her voice cracks slightly, and I see her lip wobble before she composes herself. "Every weekend it seemed like he'd have to go somewhere to negotiate or something. And this is what he was doing. He was hanging out with them or smuggling drugs. All of it instead of being with me."

I can see tears in her eyes, but I also can't help thinking about it from Scott's perspective; at some point, his dad stopped coming to visit him, and now he's caught up in all this. He deserves better than everything he's had. We need to find him.

"Wait." Heather looks up from the pictures, wiping away a tear. "So if Scott didn't do it, then where is he now? Is he okay?" A frantic look takes over while she realizes what I came to realize already. "You think the murderer has him?" I nod. "And who do you think the murderer is?"

I stare awkwardly at Heather before turning to Annie.

334

There's already been so much bad news for Heather I don't know if I can bring myself to tell her my latest thoughts. Annie's scrolling on her phone, before she sighs, staring at me urgently.

"We don't know," she says finally. "But I can tell you it definitely wasn't your mother!" She gives me a subtle look and turns her phone around. "Because she was away with her friends for every single one of the murders and all her friends have posted pictures at the same time. So that is some cast-iron alibi!"

I feel myself deflate. But if it wasn't her . . . who was it?

Heather's looking at us both, confused.

"I think the best thing to do is to find out where the drugs are kept; should help us work out who's in charge of the operation now, and maybe even help us find Scott," Annie finishes.

Suddenly everything slots into place, and I can't believe I've been so imperceptive.

"The drugs were in the period products. Mr. C was sniffing around the old V-Lyte factory . . ." I say.

"It's there! That's where the stash is!" Annie sighs, and I can tell she feels as foolish as I do.

"Mr. C? At the original factory?" Heather looks confused. "But Dad told us never to go up there. He said there was asbestos, and it was unsafe," Heather says, comprehending as she says the words and slapping her forehead. "Oh god, another lie."

"Quick, the sooner we get up there the sooner we can figure out who's in charge of the drugs now and find Scott," I say, feeling a foolish kind of hope.

"If he's still alive, then every second counts! How long would it take us to get up there?" Annie asks while I feel a helpless kind of impatience. "It's quite a way from here, isn't it? It's on the boundary with another town."

"This sounds extremely dangerous, if the killer's there . . ." Heather starts.

"What are you going to do? Call the police who are convinced that Scott did it and will probably just arrest him if they find him?" Annie tilts her head to the side. "At this point, people seem more likely to die when the police are helping than when they're not."

"Fair point," Heather sighs; I've never seen her vulnerable before. Without her usual bravado, she's actually kind of likeable.

"We'll all be together." I squeeze Heather's hand. "Protect each other."

"Quickest way's by car. I'll get the keys," Heather says. We follow her back out of the study, where all this began.

Annie looks so eager right now, which is coincidentally so the opposite of how I feel.

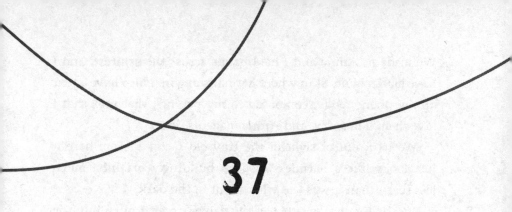

37

"Just checking!" I shout after Heather as she strides ahead, leading us to one of the big tanklike Jeeps in the driveway. "Have you got your license or . . . I mean, is your driver not about?"

"This is my property. I don't need a license!" Heather shouts back.

"But for us to not die . . ." I start. But Annie looks at me, and I know now's probably not the time.

"I'm a great driver," Heather says with a confidence I can't deny.

I pray to Taylor Swift that Heather is as good a driver as Heather is currently claiming to be.

Heather is not as good a driver as Heather has been claiming to be. If I don't die in this very car, it will be a miracle.

A holy fucking miracle.

✳ ✳ ✳

We made it; Annie and I held hands across the armrest, and I have marks in my skin where her nails dug in. I also have a text on my phone ready, composed to my parents, that says that I love them, I'm sorry, and Annie made us do it.

We park out of sight of the tiny old factory. From here it just looks like a harmless disused building. Certainly, much less scary than it was the other night in the dark.

Just as Heather gets out of the driver's seat, I pitch into the front seat and yank the hand brake up. No shade to her; it's an easy mistake to make and I'm not one to judge, because I'm too afraid to even get behind a wheel, but I do feel like her Jeep would make more of a mess rolling down a hill than the Nissan Micra that my parents drive would.

"It looks way less scary in the light, but it's massive," Annie says.

All three of us stand in a row staring up at the old factory. If this is it, I think it's fair to say that the "international drug lord" label that Mrs. R gave him was justified.

Heather pulls in a breath and heads up to a large steel security door.

"The door's got an electronic keypad entry system." Annie snorts, following her. "Subtle. Definitely nothing sketchy in this place."

"I feel like such a douche." Heather's eyes look glassy. "I can't believe I just bought the whole asbestos line and never came up here. Even Adam had figured it out. Well, I guess this is where I find out whether or not my dad really was an international drug lord. Christ, is anything real?"

"I am," Annie and I both say, at the same time raising our hands.

"Oh, gross, chill out, guys." Heather smiles. "I'm not, like, having emotions again or whatever."

She punches a code confidently into the door and then stares at it perplexed when it doesn't open.

"What did you try?" Annie asks.

"My birth date," Heather sulks.

"Oh . . ." The two of us stand quietly, and I want to suggest that she try Scott's date of birth, but I don't want to be insensitive.

"Try Scott's date of birth," Annie chirps.

Heather narrows her eyes at Annie, doing the most aggressive glare I've ever seen.

"What is it?" she asks me, eyes still narrowed at Annie, looking like she's ready for a fight.

"Oh, um . . . oh five, oh six, oh five," I say, about ready to run away from all the tension, when the door makes a happy beeping noise and clicks open.

"Don't say a word," I whisper to Annie as Heather walks ahead, putting on a front so no one knows she's upset her dad didn't pick her birth date for the secret drug hideout passcode.

When we get in, the lights are already on, which is either a really great sign or a really terrible one. UV strip lights hanging over rows and rows of plants give off a bluish, sterile, tinted light. There's a buzzing sound that echoes around the bare walls, concrete floors, and corrugated roof. Under the lights sit hundreds and hundreds of green plants, all set up neatly. I'd say there're approximately twenty rows stretching at least ten meters of the same plant. And I don't have to be a botanist to work out what they are. They all look happy and healthy and definitely cared for by someone very recently. It smells strongly of something a bit like pee that I can't quite put my finger on, but I feel like I've smelled before, and it's super creepy. If I'm going to get murdered, it's going to be here. Every surface is sterile, there's no natural light, and it feels like the bleakest and most likely place to die.

"Holy moly," Annie says, at the sheer scale of everything that's in here. "Well, that's conclusive on the drug lord thing, then. Look, before we go in any farther, we should be wearing gloves if we're going to touch anything!" Annie produces a pair of yellow dishwashing gloves out of her bag.

"Oh, great, tell me now that I've put my prints all over the keypad and the door, why don't you?" Heather rolls her eyes and hisses at Annie.

I don't need gloves. I don't plan on touching anything. In fact, I'd almost rather that I didn't see anything, either.

"What are we looking for?" Annie says thoughtfully, pulling the gloves on.

"What's that noise?" Heather shushes us both, walking farther into the warehouse.

"It's just the lights." Annie points upward to the buzzing UV lights that fill the room.

"No, not that!" Heather says, and stands completely still and silent for a moment before a clanging noise hits. She points upward as if indicating the bang. "That."

The noise is coming from somewhere deeper in the warehouse, and whatever it is, I have the creepy feeling that we're not alone in here, and not being alone in a warehouse full of drugs can never be a good thing.

I feel hope soaring through my veins that the noise might be Scott, but that feels like I'm being naive. What if we follow the noise and it's the murderer, tricking us to our death?

"Right, let me do the touching if you two haven't got gloves," Annie whispers dramatically, and with that, she forges ahead.

As we walk deeper into the warehouse, I become accustomed to the weird light, but my throat and chest grow tighter, and I can feel my heart flutter with panic. The clanging noise is getting louder, and I feel like we should have weapons or something to keep us safe in case it *is* the murderer. But when I look around, there's nothing but plants, and despite their sinister nature, they won't save my life.

"Shouldn't we have something to protect ourselves with?" I whisper.

"Pepper spray." Annie pulls a can out of her bag.

"Same," Heather says, grabbing some out of hers.

"Um, oh-kay, I did not get the pepper spray memo." I feel even more scared. I'm the smallest and most vulnerable of the group now. I don't even have fucking gloves.

The banging gets louder and louder, and I'm torn between fear of what it could be and the hope of finding out who's responsible. I'm not sure I can bear it.

"Guys," I finally declare in what I hope is a brave whisper, "I'm not going any farther; I'm staying here." My feet root to the spot.

"Oh, okay. Sure, you stay there for the murderer to find you alone," Annie says, and for a minute, I think about moving to follow but she's heading straight for the noise, and I can't work out which is the lesser of two evils.

The two of them stop and stare down an aisle of drugs to the right.

"Um, Kerry, I'd actually come here if I were you," Annie calls before she goes rushing into the aisle with Heather.

Okay, right, so they've both run in there willingly, maybe it's okay, then? It must be—they're not screaming. I can't hear them talking much at all actually; in fact, I can hear—

Is that?

I run down toward the aisle and stop at the end of it when I see them all together.

Under fluorescent lamps, among troughs of cannabis plants, is Scott. Tied to a pole, a period pad fixed over his eyes, and it looks like Annie and Heather have just taken another one off his mouth.

"Scott!" I breathe.

"Kerry?" he asks, sounding relieved, but he can't be as relieved as I am.

"He's been *Pretty Little Liars*–ed!" Annie screeches with way too much glee in her voice.

"It's me," I say, reaching to try and gently pull the period pad off his face, but those sticky tabs are really effective.

"Kerry!" He winces at the pain of me peeling.

"Yeah," I say, still trying to pry it away.

"Just yank it." He braces himself and I pull really hard, taking some eyebrow with me, but when he sees me, his face still lights up.

"Oh, gross, you guys." Heather says as we stare at each other, and I peel the rest of a sticky protective wing from his cheek.

I untie his hands, and he shakes them free.

"My knight in shining armor!" he says, wiggling his wrists and grabbing me in a hug. "I'm so pleased to see you that I'm starting to wonder if I have actually died."

342

His lips are really dry, and he definitely smells like he's been here since we found Mrs. R, but nothing can stop me reaching down and kissing him.

"So you didn't send a text breaking up with me, then?" I ask, even though I know there are probably bigger questions to ask.

"What? No!" Scott says. "Whoever kidnapped me has my phone."

"Didn't think it sounded like you," I say, a pang of guilt hitting me that for a short while I genuinely wondered if he was a killer. But now's not the time; we need to get him out of here and to safety in case whoever tied him up comes back.

"How did you end up here?" Annie asks as I help him stand up, our arms around each other.

"I went to see Mrs. R. She said she had something to tell me about my dad, and when I knocked on the door, it was already open. Someone smacked me over the head as soon as I got in there, and before I knew it, I was back here."

"This is a great reunion," Heather says. "But let's get back to my house; it's safer there. Whoever put you here could come back any moment. Can you walk?" Heather asks Scott.

"Yeah, I should be fine," Scott says as Heather offers him a hand. "Thanks."

"No worries, bro." Heather tries a tight smile.

"Hey! You know!" Scott says.

"Yeah, and you're all over the news, you know?" She helps him up, and the two of them walk out into the sunlight. I take deep gulps of fresh air before we get in the Jeep.

Scott and I settle in the back, and I don't know whether it's because I've got Scott here or not, but the drive back to the house is much quicker and much less frightening.

We reach the house, and I finally start to feel calm when I'm out of that Jeep and the four of us are walking to the house, and not just because of Heather's terrible driving. We're not out of the woods, but we've got Scott back. Together we can all figure out this mess, and in the meantime, I'm not letting anything else happen to him.

"STOP RIGHT THERE!!" The voice of DI Wallace booms out from a mouse-shaped topiary in Heather's front driveway.

Although all of us freeze, none of us can actually see DI Wallace or DI Collins anywhere, and it's only after a lot of rustling that the two of them emerge into the driveway, looking slightly worse for wear, bits of leaf springing out from their hair and suits.

"I KNEW IT!" DI Wallace says, as if he's about to do one of those big reveal scenes that they do on *Midsomer Murders* or *Death in Paradise* where they get everyone together to tell them who it was.

"Knew what?" Heather sighs, turning around to face them. "That Scott's my brother? And that someone kidnapped him and they're trying to frame him for murders he didn't commit?" She's making me really start to like her, if I'm being honest. "He wasn't even wearing that T-shirt you found, and do you really think he'd leave it behind as evidence anyway?"

"What on earth are you talking about?" DI Wallace looks appalled.

"Someone was in Mrs. R's place last night, and they must have been planting evidence," I say boldly. "Whoever they were, they planted Scott's bracelet and his T-shirt. Scott didn't do it." After everything Scott's been through, I'm not letting him get arrested now. I've got to stand up for him. "I was in the house last night; I saw someone."

"What?" DI Collins looks confused.

"I went to see Mrs. R and I was hit over the head and knocked out and then kidnapped by someone, but I don't know who because I never saw their face, and—" Scott's interrupted by Annie making a strangled gasping noise.

"AND HEATHER'S DEAD DAD IS THE MURDERER!" Annie practically screams over him, the color completely draining from her face as she stares over at the bush.

We all squint at her a bit confused for a second. I'm all for dramatic reveals, but how is that even possible?

That's when I realize the look on her face is more terror than excitement. Like she's just seen a ghost.

"Hello, princess." The gruff voice of Terry Stevens brings us all to a standstill as everyone turns, paling at the sight of him emerging from a topiary cat, very much alive and very much holding a gun.

38

"Dad." Heather's face turns green, and I watch her lips start to tremble.

"Got a hug for your dad?" He smiles at her, but Heather stays frozen. "Seems like your friend's got a bit of misinformation about me here unfortunately." He points his gun at Annie, and I flinch.

I immediately go to shield her, my fearless friend. Even standing half in front of her, my arms out, feels flimsy as she stands there shaking, her usually rosy cheeks now completely green.

"Hello, boss," DI Collins says cheerfully. He pulls a gun from his waistband and points it at DI Wallace, who takes a half step back in surprise. All of us gasp in shock.

"Daddy?" Heather looks like she's going to pass out.

"You were in on it?" Annie asks DI Collins.

"You could say we have an arrangement," DI Collins replies, and I can see Annie's brain working away, filling in the gaps. "Or at least we did, until Mr. Stevens here made plans to leave without me this afternoon, thinking I wouldn't find out. Despite owing me thousands of pounds."

"It's rude to talk business in front of people," Mr. S responds bluntly.

The four of us are frozen waiting for someone to do something. The color's drained from DI Wallace's face, and I watch as he clutches the bush next to him. It turns out no one's fearless when met by the mouth of a gun. He raises his hands to the sky as I feel all hope of being rescued by the police and getting out of here unscathed vanish into thin air. Mr. S barely loses focus as he waves his gun between Annie and me.

We're all frozen in fear while DI Collins heads over to Mr. S.

"What do you reckon, Terry?" DI Collins directs at Mr. S. "I think it's time we sorted some stuff out, don't you?"

"He's got a gun, he's got a gun, he's got a gun, he's got a gun," Annie starts muttering to herself.

"Stop saying that; it's not making the gun go away," I whisper.

"What the hell are you two whispering about now?" DI Collins shouts to us. He swings around with his gun so it's also pointing at us, and now there are two guns pointing at us and I'm quite sure I'm about to vomit. "We don't want any heroes, so everyone put your phones on the ground and we're going to go inside for a nice chat."

All of us drop our phones to the floor except for Scott, who just raises his hands.

"I've been kidnapped for three days. If I had a phone, don't you think I'd have used it by now?" he says.

"Oh, don't you worry; I've got that," Mr. S agrees, and I see

347

the glint in his eye. He was the one that kidnapped Scott, and the one that texted me.

"Great, my own dad kidnapped me," Scott whispers.

"Sorry, son, I had to keep you out of the way. I was going to take you back with me when I left," Mr. S says. "That's why we figured we frame you, then you'd just come with me. I can give you a nice life, finally the life with my son I always wanted without anyone getting in the way."

"You planted the evidence?" Annie questions.

"No, that was me," DI Collins says, and I shudder with the realization that I was alone in Mrs. R's house with him the other night, and that if he'd have caught me he probably wouldn't have been nice about it.

This is a bad dream. This isn't real. This can't be real. This is just a bad dream.

"What about me?" Heather looks crestfallen.

"Maybe we should all go inside, have a nice little chat, princess?" Mr. S says. He reaches, trying to take Heather's hand, but she snatches it away.

Mercifully, DI Collins has lowered his gun. He's more sort of waving it and gesturing at the ground to urge us forward—it's clear he doesn't think we're major threats anymore, considering my knees are shaking and Annie has progressed to the color of cabbage.

The five of us trail down the driveway, and I feel like my limbs are no longer under my control. I wonder if I've finally got my boyfriend back and now I'm about to be killed. This doesn't feel like what I'm supposed to be thinking about now, though. Nothing seems to be registering in my brain, and all the films I've watched and contingency plans I've made in my

348

life for any dangerous situations seem to be completely useless, because the plan is always to call the police. And the police are already here. They just aren't particularly helpful.

DI Collins points toward the house with his gun.

"In there." He motions to the front door as DI Wallace with Mr. Stevens's gun pointed at him heads through it. "Hurry up. NOW!"

For a second, I think about how funny it would be if someone jumped out of the bushes now and said this whole thing had been a joke. The last week wasn't real at all, and it was all an elaborate prank. The idea bubbles inside of me, and suddenly I find myself holding back hysterical laughter. I don't know if that's the correct response for a situation where I am probably going to die, but let's be honest, when have I ever responded normally to any situation in my life?

We're ushered through the study door and slump down against the wall with DI Wallace at the front. Am I a hostage? Is this a hostage situation? I'm being held hostage by the police and a dead man. It sounds like the setup to a really bad joke.

"*You* did it, then? You killed them?" DI Wallace is asking Mr. Stevens.

"Look, I didn't mean to. I meant to stay away. . . . That was the plan," he begins, but DI Collins interrupts him.

"It was the very carefully worked out plan, and then you came back here, made another huge mess for me to clear up, and when I'd cleaned it up, you were just going to leave again without giving me the money you owe me, weren't you?" he asks angrily. My eyes dart between the two of them furiously.

"I had to come back to tie up loose ends," Heather's dad snaps. "You were supposed to be my man on the ground, but since someone was stealing the stock under your watch, and putting our deals in jeopardy, I had to come back and sort it out. It was supposed to be a quick visit, but then Selena got in the way."

"So you killed her?" Heather shouts at him, and he seems surprised that she's in the room.

"She wasn't your friend, Heather," he says, his voice taking on a sickly sweet tone. "She'd been sending those messages to you from that account with my name, princess. They weren't even for you; they were for me. She knew about Scott, about the drugs, everything. Precocious little madam got some internship working with investigative journalists; by the time summer ended, she thought she knew it all. And she was threatening to ruin everything."

What's with smart women always being called bossy or precocious? I want to trade a glance with Annie about his sexism, but I'm worried this will be considered moving, and even though the guns aren't in our faces anymore, I'm not willing to risk it, so I just telepathically roll my eyes at her.

Mr. S is still monologuing in the hope of winning his daughter back, but I'm struggling to focus with all the stress around me. "She figured out that I had access to your account and was sending me warnings," he says, his voice taking on a pleading tone. "So, I waited until she was on her own in here, when you had your little party, and snuck in to pay her a visit. She started threatening me and shouting, trying to draw attention so people would find me, and I needed to silence her. Your mum must have left one of the new prototype cups on the desk, so I just grabbed it. Shoved it in her mouth to keep her quiet. I hadn't meant to kill her. Just silence her so I could get away. But when I let go,

I realized she'd choked. I guess it got caught. I did try and take it out, but by the time I did, it was too late. I hadn't meant it to happen, but really, it was her own fault she died."

Not only is he a murderer, but he's a victim blamer, too. Finally, I can't take it any longer and switch my eyes over to Annie. I see her struggling to keep in all of her thoughts. Squirming under the pressure. I can only imagine the angry tirade she's trying to keep bottled up. Luckily, Heather doesn't feel the need to keep it corked.

"She was my best friend!" Heather shouts.

But Mr. S just rolls his eyes. "She was a shit friend, Heather. She was having an affair with your boyfriend."

Heather goes completely silent, but all I keep thinking is how awful you'd have to be to do all that and still blame the girl you killed for her own death.

"And what about all the others?" Heather finally asks.

"Look, I wouldn't have bothered killing Adam—waste of space if you ask me; you can do much better than him anyway—but like I said I was here to figure out who stole the drugs. And when I found out it was him *and* he'd been cheating on you . . . I wasn't about to let him get away with it."

"Jesus Christ, you're a monster. An actual monster." Heather's like the angry parent talking to the misbehaving child right now, except the misbehaving child is holding a gun.

"Don't be so fucking ungrateful," he snaps at her. "Look, I'll be gone soon." He turns to DI Collins. "I'll send your cut when I have it so stop getting yourself in a tizzy about it. Heather, this is your chance. You can come with me and live a life of luxury on a tropical island or you can stay here in this tiny town with these tiny people, going nowhere."

I almost laugh out loud. I mean, what a choice: come with me—your serial-killing father—or stay here and lead the perfectly happy life you were having before I showed up back here, just minus some of your best friends that I killed. Does he think he's about to win the Dad of the Year award here?

"YOU KILLED THREE PEOPLE!" Heather shouts at him, almost reading my mind.

"Yeah, I killed three people," Mr. S repeats, his voice mocking. "You're being pretty pathetic about this, Heather. This is LIFE. If someone's going to take you down, you take them down first. Selena was a child playing an adult's game. I never liked you hanging out with her; she was such a bad influence. I thought you were made of sterner stuff than this, Heath." Mr. S shakes his head, as if she's the one that's really let everyone down in this room.

"*She* was a bad influence?" Heather spits out. "Maybe we were better off when you were dead."

The rest of us sit, glued, watching the two of them, our eyes flitting from side to side like we're watching a particularly spicy game of Ping-Pong. I expect her dad to look sad or even taken aback, but it's like nothing gets him; he's made of pure Teflon. I guess that explains how he was able to kidnap his own son and think it was for his benefit.

"You should have gone after you'd killed the boy. You'd fixed the problem," DI Collins tells Mr. S.

"You know I couldn't, though. Not when I saw that cheek of a man that Adam was dealing to. He was the one driving the truck years ago when it crashed, you know. He made off with thousands of pounds' worth of stock. And now he has the *gall* to come back here and live in this village *and* teach my daughter? I wasn't having him disrespect me like that. I bet he thought he was so clever, the smug little dick."

"Mr. C?!" Annie gasps. Then she claps hands over her mouth, realizing she has drawn all the attention to herself. But Mr. S just shakes his head calmly, like there's a fly buzzing near his eyes.

"He was next. I thought I'd made myself quite clear with the period products. We always used to say hear no evil, speak no evil, see no evil—no one ever finds out. I thought he'd have got the message after Adam and disappeared, but he didn't. So I had to stick around to handle Mr. C, give him his punishment. But first you bloody go and arrest him, and then Mrs. R got in the way, accusing me of all sorts of things."

"All sorts of true things that you actually did, though?" Scott offers.

We all turn to stare at him, and Mr. S just grins, this sort of deranged, proud smile that makes me immediately want to vomit.

"Have you met my son, DI Wallace? He's a chip off the old block. That's why I was going to help him escape. Take him with me, teach him the family business," Mr. S says.

We all look shocked at that because smacking your estranged son over the head and tying him up in a weed warehouse, blindfolded, is certainly a weird way of showing your affection for him. I catch Annie's eye, knowing exactly what she's thinking as well. That he's proud when Scott mouths off, but when Heather does it, he calls her ungrateful. A sexism tale as old as time.

"Anyway, Mr. C—as you call him—always was an overgrown child. He didn't have any sense of business; he was just smoking all of it himself. It's no wonder he didn't last long on the money he stole from me." Mr. S shakes his head.

"And then what were you going to do afterward? Just leave? Were you ever going to let me know you were alive? What about Mum?" Heather asks.

Mr. S clucks his tongue and shakes his head, like he's disappointed in the mention of another woman. "Your mum's great arm candy, but she draws too much attention to herself. I need a woman who's quieter, doesn't make such a big impression on people. Your mum's just obsessed with success."

"She *is* successful, and smart, and she doesn't have to live a shady life of crime to get there, either!" Heather says, and I feel bad for suspecting Mrs. S as the murderer earlier.

"Fucking patriarchy," Annie whispers.

"Can't be that smart because she never worked out what I was doing," Mr. Stevens snorts. "Look, Heath, I wasn't about to abandon you forever. I hadn't intended to have to kill this many people, but I guess it got messy."

Heather's staring at her dad like she's never met him before, and I'm willing to bet that with all she's learned today she's going to need a hefty amount of therapy.

"Too right it got messy!" DI Collins is shouting at Mr. Stevens, and his face is twisted in a way completely at odds with the cheery persona he's been trying to fool us all into believing is him. "You messed it up, and now look, all these people know! What are you going to do?"

"Just let me THINK for god's sake." Mr. S starts pacing, and I feel Annie shuffling.

"Um, can I just ask . . . ?" she begins, her voice tight. Oh

354

god, I'm not sure this is a good idea, Annie. "Which one of you put the dolls of us in that locker?"

"I did," Mr. S says, barking out a laugh. "Fucking busybodies, both of you. What were you thinking? You'd solve it like Starsky and Hutch? Nice of you to record everything for us as well." Annie's mouth drops open as she realizes what he's referring to. "Oh yes, smarty-pants, we found your Dictaphone at Mrs. R's place. Very interesting conversations you two girls have been having." He chuckles to himself again—so that's what the Dictaphone was doing there. I guess he hasn't realized that we got it back last night. I wonder if Annie has it on her now?

Anyway we did actually solve it in the end, or at least Annie did. It's not like I'm about to say it to a man holding a gun, but part of the whole reason we're here is because we figured it out.

"We did solve it," Annie says, staring at him. My jaw almost hits the ground. Why does she always do this?

"But I'm still going to get away with it," Mr. S says, snarling at her. "I'll be out of here before you can do anything about it, I just have to figure out how, and my son and I will be off."

I'm so offended that he thinks Scott would have a better life with him than with me. But I'm going to choose to let it slide because I like living and I feel like I won't get to do too much of that if I say anything.

"I'm good, thanks. Better to have no dad than a serial-killer dad," Scott says boldly.

Why do people keep angering the people with the guns? Why are Annie and Scott suddenly talking back? Mr. S looks like he's been slapped, the hurt written all over his face.

"Pity. I always had dreams of us together again at last," Mr. Stevens says sadly. "But I guess Heather's my only real child, after all."

Scott doesn't even flinch at this attempt to hurt him as Mr. S moves closer to Heather.

"Come with me, Heather. We'll go now. We'll get away from all of this. We can live happily. I've found this great island. No one will know us there, and we can just chill without people like your mother ruining everyone's fun." He crouches down in front of her, staring into her eyes.

And just like that, as if she's got no fear, she punches him hard in the face.

"That's for Selena," Heather says. Then she punches him again. "And that's for Mrs. R."

He staggers back, holding his jaw, the look on his face is of shock and pain. I notice that she didn't punch him for Adam.

Mr. S shakes his head, like he's trying to knock off the clear sting of the punch. He's got nothing to lose now. No one seems to matter to him anymore. He looks between both of them, clutching his face.

"Right, well, I guess that's that, then. I'm off. None of you'll ever have to see me or my money again. There's no way anyone'll find me," he says.

"Hold up!" says DI Collins. "What do we do about this mess you've made? All these people know now? After everything I did for you. I faked death certificates and a cremation. I've got half of the drug smugglers in the Western Hemisphere asking me what the hell's going on. You're not the one who has to deal with their anger; you just go off-grid pretending you're dead and go on a nice little murder spree. You've not even given me the money!" DI Collins says.

Mr. S grins, looking truly terrifying now. "What do I care? These people will never find me. That's your problem. Pin it all on the boy for all I care. That was your plan anyway, wasn't it? Get rid of all of them." His eyes coolly slide over us, not even pausing on Heather or Scott. "They're no use to me now."

The room starts blurring, my head pulsing with fear, and I realize that unless we can get the better of both of these people with guns, there's no way we're getting out of this room alive. I hold Annie's hand on my right, and Scott grabs my left.

"I'll tell everyone. I don't care. I'll tell them all." DI Collins turns, pressing his gun against Mr. S's head.

"What now? You're going to shoot me?" Heather's dad asks mockingly, his face so smug I almost wish Heather would punch him again. "You'll definitely go to prison, then. There'll still be witnesses, and it'll be worse. You'll be done for murder, not just holding up hostages with a firearm."

Heather's got her hands over her face, and I can feel her shaking through the floor even though she's on the other side of the room.

DI Collins still has his gun pulled on Heather's dad, and Heather's dad has his gun trained on DI Collins. And then it bangs.

One of the big windows shatters, raining glass down on us, and I dive across Annie instinctively. I'm not sure what I'm doing or what I'm trying to achieve because it just happens naturally. I feel a pressure on my side and realize that Scott's ducked over both of us, and the three of us lie in a pile on the floor.

"That was your fucking warning," Heather's dad says as I see the bullet hole in the paneling across the room. He must have shot to the side of DI Collins's head. DI Collins stands completely still, his gun down, sweat beading on his forehead.

I'm shaking, and I feel like I could vomit any second as the three of us sit back up and I grab Scott's hand. I can't believe he did that. He was going to save us—both of us.

"I totally pissed my pants," Annie whispers, blinking rapidly.

"SHUT UP!" DI Collins shouts.

All of us sit in silence. I look over at Heather, who is crying so much that she looks like she can barely breathe, and I feel terrible. The three of us got each other, but there should have been someone there to get Heather.

Next to me, Annie's started shuffling weirdly, setting me on edge. It's like she wants us to get killed. Sit still, Annie. But she carries on squirming, her hands behind her, like she's stretching.

"What's that noise?" Mr. Stevens rushes over to the window, his gun still pointed at DI Collins, making us all flinch. His face is suddenly bathed in blue and red flashing light. "Your colleagues appear to be outside my window. Please tell me how this is possible, DI Collins?"

"What?" DI Collins squawks, bristling. He takes a half step over to look out the window himself, but Mr. S gestures at him and he freezes. "I don't know. We didn't tell anyone we were coming here. DI Wallace there wanted all the glory for catching the murderer himself."

Next to me, Annie's stretched up as if she's doing a yawn, while the two of them are busy at the window. Whatever she's doing, she'd better not get caught.

"And doesn't pride come just before a fall." Heather's dad smiles smugly at DI Wallace, sitting with his head in his hands, sweating, against the wall. "Okay, well, whatever you *say* you did or didn't do, they now appear to be in my driveway."

I crane my neck to look out the window and see that there're loads of them, more police than I've ever seen in one place. For a wild moment, hope surges through my chest, the weight of my heart almost crushing me.

Annie shuts her eyes next to me, and I feel her start to relax a bit. Then she grabs my hand behind my back, and passes me something. My fingers trace the plastic edges and roundness. It's a tube of something.

"Mr. Stevens, come out with your hands behind your head," a voice booms through the shattered window. Mr. Stevens ducks and runs back through the study door.

I can hear him swearing under his breath as he runs through to the rest of the house, while DI Collins slumps down against the wall, his head in his hands. I can practically feel his brain whirring as DI Wallace tries to plead with him.

"Please think about what you're doing, son," DI Wallace says. "You can head out there and confess to everything. Help them out and it might not be so bad. Or you can stay in here and things could end much, much worse for you. I know what I'd do. This doesn't have to be the end."

"Doesn't it?" DI Collins stands up and heads over to him, gun tipping into DI Wallace's head.

"Okay, we're surrounded; they're in the back, too." Heather's dad comes racing back into the study, eyes bright with something like excitement or wildness.

"What do we do now?" DI Collins sounds panicked, and

his hand holding the gun shakes so it clacks into DI Wallace's scalp.

"Just shut up and let me think, is what we do now," Mr. Stevens says, and I feel Annie stick her hand up next to me.

She's got a plan; I knew she would. I keep my sweaty hand clasped firmly around the tube in it, trying to make sure that no one sees it, whatever it is.

"I have an idea," Annie says. "If I may?"

"It can't be worse than anything that he's come up with," Mr. Stevens says, head jerking at his coconspirator.

"What about down in the cellar?" Annie offers, talking faster and faster as she goes. "Is there a way you two could hide down there that no one could find you and we can just say everything's fine and nothing's going on? That the four of us accidentally shattered a window, just a little game we were playing? You can hide down there?"

"She might not be completely crazy with that, you know?" DI Collins says, and I wonder why it is that men think we need their judgment on whether or not we're crazy.

Like, why is their first judgment always that we're insane? No, this probably isn't the time, but if I'm going to die, at least I'm going to die thinking about the important shit, you know?

I shut my eyes because whatever happens next can go one way or the other. I take Annie's hand, the tube of whatever she gave me still nestled in between our two palms and keep hold of Scott with my other hand. The tube's small and plastic. I think I know what it is; I can picture it in my head, shaped like a small hand cream tube, travel size. Heather looks tired, and next to her, DI Wallace looks like he's given up.

"Not actually a bad plan," Mr. S says, heading for the study door and hovering before he opens it. "Stay here and hold the fort." He gestures to DI Collins. "Make sure no one moves a muscle."

"Move and you're dead," DI Collins says, as if by way of confirmation.

Heather's dad grabs the doorknob but then hesitates and looks around him.

"I need to make sure none of you squeal. I'm going to have to take someone with me, for collateral." He points at me and Annie, and I feel my blood turn to ice. "STAND UP!"

I try to get to my feet, but my legs feel heavy and unstable. I can't quite bring myself to let go of Scott's hand. He kisses it as I loosen my fingers.

I've still got the tube Annie gave me clasped in my fist, but I'm scared they might see it.

"Ahh, love's young dream. COME ON!" he shouts at me, and I see Annie out of the corner of my eye, her lip trembling. I think I know what her plan is though, and we're in this together.

He opens the door and steps out onto the marble floor of the hallway. The second we're alone, just the three of us out of view of DI Collins, Annie nods at me, and I at her. As he strides through the grand hallway toward the kitchen, unaware, the two of us squirt what's in the tubes across the floor behind him in a flash, and then Annie takes one for the team. Always the bravest person I've ever met.

"Hey, over here! What's this?" she says, pointing to something in a plant pot. "Is that some kind of police bug in the plant? Have they been listening in?"

A noise comes from her pocket as she stands next to the flowerpot.

"Yeah, I killed three people," Mr. S's recorded voice echoes through the hallway. "You're being pretty pathetic about this, Heather." Mr. S snaps his head up, staring with wide eyes at the plant that Annie's pointing to. She continues playing the recording of him on her Dictaphone.

Immediately he turns back on himself and starts rushing over.

"This is LIFE," the recording continues. And in that moment, he slips on the contents of our tubes, falling over, shouting.

"If someone's going to take you down, you take them down first," his recorded voice echoes. His gun falls from his hand and goes sliding across the floor, zooming to the side of the hallway, well out of his grasp.

"GOTCHA!" Annie shouts, clicking her Dictaphone off so the only noise from Mr. S is his quiet groaning from the floor as he tries to scramble up but keeps slipping. "V-Lyte Lube! Your wife's newest initiative! Kerry's mum always said lube was a lifesaver!" She chucks the empty tube at him. "Kind of her to leave it all lying around the office for us, to be honest."

I can't believe I just saved my own life with lube. As Mr. Stevens struggles to get up from the slippery lube on the marble floors, the two of us run to the door and freedom.

"GET THEM, GET THEM!!!" Mr. Stevens is shouting, trying to get DI Collins's attention while he fumbles around on the floor trying to get to his gun.

The run from the kitchen to the front door feels longer than ever. But when we get there, we open the door to a sea of armed police, ready to enter the house. We raise our arms like they do in the movies, but by the time we do that, they've already put their guns down—they can see we don't have anything.

We're ushered past the armed police onto the safety of the driveway, where we can stand back from a safe distance and watch as they storm into the house.

Around me, everything seems to be swirling as someone puts something crinkly around my shoulders and directs Annie and me to some waiting ambulances. The world's hazy and strobing with the emergency lights and I can't stop shaking, but I'm relieved. I look at Annie, the two of us staring at each other for a couple of seconds. Then we both start laughing.

"Lube saved the day." Annie chuckles, and the two of us collapse into a fit of giggles.

And then the air fills with the noise of an almighty bang, making everyone stop. One person stays with me while everyone else seems to pile back through the house, and I hear a noise. A high, bone-rattling scream.

I stand back and stop, staring at the front door, willing Heather and Scott to walk through it.

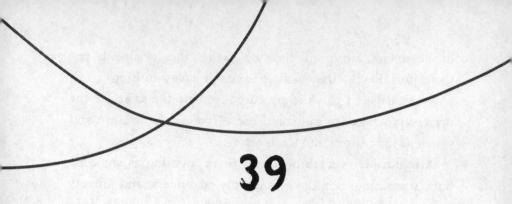

39

Outside, the driveway's floodlit as they wheel the stretcher onto the ambulance. I can feel the foil blanket scrunching around my shoulders in the wind as the paramedics try to calm DI Collins. Since shooting himself quite literally in the foot, he's been making a noise similar to that of someone giving birth.

The police kept asking me questions, and I could hear them but I couldn't answer them because I can't quite piece together everything that's happened. It's as if I watched a TV show while playing on my phone. I feel like I've blurred over major bits of the plot and now I need to rewind to work it out, but the thought of reliving any of what just happened terrifies me. I think they've given up now, and probably realized they'll get more out of me when I've had a chance to decompress. Annie's thrilled that they've taken her Dictaphone for evidence. I almost feel embarrassed about what they might hear on there. Only almost, though, because we did actually figure it out before the police in the end—well, one of the police.

If this is what going to parties and being a high schooler's all about, I'd rather go back to preschool.

"You okay?" Annie comes and sits next to me on the bench in the driveway, rocking her matching foil blanket.

"Yeah, I'm good. The only thing I don't get, though, is how did the police get here? Like how did they know what was happening?" I ask as Annie rubs her hands together, and I prepare myself for whatever ridiculousness she's about to tell me.

"Well, I phoned them from my pocket; before we had to drop our phones, I dialed 999 and just left it on so they could hear everything. And then they came." She looks pretty proud of herself, and I don't blame her.

"You are a queen," I say, doing a bowing-down motion.

"You know," Annie says, pursing her lips in thought. "I always thought things would be easier for us if we were popular, but it turns out things have been anything but ever since Heather noticed our existence."

I try really hard not to respond with anything similar to an "I told you so."

"HEATHER HEATHER HEATHER?!" I hear the unmistakable panic of Colin and Audrey rushing through the crowd that's gathering outside the farmhouse.

"She's over here," I say, getting their attention as the two of them emerge, looking flustered, Audrey with half a head of curling noodles in and Colin with the remnants of a mud face mask on.

"I'm here!" Heather shouts from the ambulance next to us.

"THANK GOD!" Colin screams. He rushes into the ambulance despite the paramedics protestations that they couldn't come in while they are still checking Heather over.

"Oh my god, WHAT HAPPENED?" Audrey gasps, as if Heather looks hideous or something. "You weren't replying to our WhatsApps?"

"Yeah, I was being held at gunpoint. I didn't have my phone. . . ." I can hear Heather rolling her eyes from here as the three of them come out of the ambulance, Heather having been discharged by the paramedics to sit with us.

"We literally always miss the excitement," Colin huffs.

"I had the *perfect* outfit for being held hostage. I can't believe I missed my chance," Audrey says. There's no acceptable answer to this, so we just sit in silence for a bit, on the bench in the driveway among the topiary animals that surround the house, an autumnal breeze coming through as we stare at all the action going on around us.

"Hey, where's my brother?" Heather asks me, making Audrey and Colin look like she's just thrown up.

"Your who?" Audrey questions, looking around.

"Just talking to the proper police over there." I point at where DI Wallace and some other people in detective suits are talking to Scott.

"Ah, cool," Heather says.

"Where's your dad?" Annie asks.

"SORRY, BACKTRACK? WHAT IS HAPPENING HERE?" Colin shrieks.

"Over there." Heather points to where he sits in the back of a police van, his hands in cuffs.

"Oh, my fucking Gucci," Audrey gasps, staring at him.

"What the hell?" Colin looks like he's seen a ghost because, let's face it, right now they're looking at one.

"It's a long story, but he's still dead to me," Heather says as Scott comes over to join us and Audrey's and Colin's eyes pop out of their heads.

He perches on the arm of the bench next to me, his arm around my shoulders while they ogle.

"So, what's everyone doing this weekend?" Annie asks. "Any cool parties?"

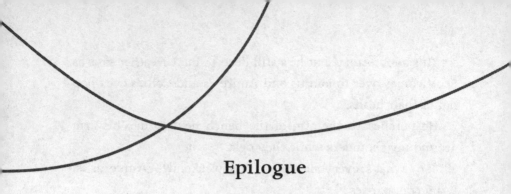

Epilogue

Two weeks later

Annie, Scott, Heather, and I are in the graveyard visiting old friends. I'm at Mrs. R's grave with Herb, when Scott taps my arm, pointing at Mrs. R's gravestone, and starts giggling. Herb's cocked his leg, and I'm pretty sure I know what he's about to do next.

"HERBIE, NO!" Annie shouts, trying to shuffle him a respectful distance away from the dead, but unfortunately he's already started pissing on his owner. "We don't pee on our friends."

Heather comes walking over from Selena's and Adam's graves. They've been laid to rest next to each other, so at least they can be together.

"What's going on?" she asks.

"Herb's just saying hi to Mrs. R in a very unique way," I say.

"Ew! Gross," Heather says. "He should do that over there."

She points to where her dad's previous memorial stone stood, with his "ashes" on top. They've dug up the stone now and taken the ashes for analysis to see exactly who was in there. DI Collins would know, but he's refusing to speak to anyone about anything. In fact, since shooting himself in the foot, apparently he's been completely silent.

"Can you believe that all this time I thought he was dead? He actually let me grieve him?" Heather asks.

"Can you believe that you've got a brother now?" Annie asks.

"Still very much getting used to that," Heather says.

"Me too," Scott says.

"Mum meant it, though, the other day—you can come and live with us at the house," Heather says to him.

"Nah, I'm good. I've got the place I rent with mum's insurance money; I'm cool," he says uneasily.

"Are you SURE?" Heather presses. "We both hate the thought of you there alone. Your girlfriend can come over whenever you like?"

"Oh," I say involuntarily, and squirm, my cheeks burning.

"Erm," Scott echoes.

"Oh my god, have you not defined yet? Come ON, guys, you had a near-death experience together. You're sucking each other's faces off every two seconds. You're totally a couple. Even your mum says so, Kerry." Heather gets her phone out and shows me Mum's latest Instagram story about her daughter having her first boyfriend.

Oh, dear god, the shame.

"Errr, well, I guess. I mean . . . I guess we just haven't talked about it yet," Scott says.

"Yeah, we will," I say confidently. "When we're ready."

The two of us smile at each other shyly.

"What about you, Annie? Have you defined your relationship with Herbie?" Heather asks.

"Oh yeah, one hundred percent besties for life," Annie says as Herbie pees slightly on her shoe. "That's love right there."

At least something good came from all this. Annie's now got an internship at the Ministry of Justice. When we were telling the police everything we'd found out, they were really impressed. It turned out that DI Wallace had some friends in pretty high places, and he recommended her for it. We were all quite shocked considering we thought he hated us.

Heather's dad goes to court next week. It's not likely that he'll get bail because he's a flight risk. The sheer amount of drugs that they found in the greenhouse alone should be enough to put him in prison. Before you've even started on the whole murdering-Mrs.-R-Selena-and-Adam-and-then-holding-us-all-hostage-with-a-gun business.

Heather refuses to go and see him.

Annie and I have been reading through Mrs. R's notes. We're compiling a list of kids that could possibly also have been fathered by Heather's dad. Colin and Audrey are for sure on there because it would appear that their mother was often spotted around the village with Mr. S. Until we've come up with a conclusive list, Heather's decided not to date anyone.

Mercifully, Adam's parents didn't move here until he was five, so she no longer feels quite as sick as she did when we first started this project.

Heather's a bit busy spending most of her time hanging out with us and getting to know her brother Scott, though, at the moment. So, I guess our friend group has gotten a bit bigger and Annie's finally in with Les Populaires, although she frequently asks when we can hang out just the two of us again.

Turns out it wasn't all she thought it would be, being popular.

I always wondered whether Heather was telling us the whole story about why she suddenly wanted to be friends with us. She told us after what happened that it wasn't just because she wanted us to investigate but also because she realized she needed more padding in her group. If they were going to be killed off one by one, she needed to expand, and quickly—give the killer more options. (I can still hear Annie's reaction when she told us. "Padding?! You mean HUMAN SACRIFICES?!")

She tried to make it sound better by telling us that once we started hanging out with them, she realized how great we were. Especially considering how smart we are and how quickly we figured everything out at her party. She swears now that she's friends with us because she really likes us and not because she wants to use us as protective "padding" in case of another serial killer. I guess I believe her—after all, she willingly invites us to parties now.

We actually went to one last week where there were no deaths, no hiding in closets, and no police interviews. Now we're heading to go and watch Audrey in a chess tournament. She told everyone her secret shortly after everything else came out. And Colin told everyone his, too. He and Trey are official and officially Audrey's biggest chess supporters.

And that's everything, I think.

Oh! Except for one thing. We found something in Mrs. R's papers. A file labeled "Kerry and Annie"—inside was just one piece of paper. It said:

If anything ever happens to me, I know you girls
will figure it all out.
Mrs. R x

P.S. Annie, check the drawer next to my bed.
You'll see I really was liberated all along, dear.
GOOD VULVA TO YOU!

Acknowledgments

My first and biggest thank you really must go to my agent, Chloe Seager. I'm so incredibly lucky to have an agent who gets me so well, has such an excellent sense of humor, and is so encouraging. I don't know what I'd do without you! And, as ever, thank you to all at Madeleine Milburn—a wonderful team of wonderful people.

Secondly thank you to my hugely talented editor, Sara Schonfeld—I'm so lucky to work with you, and I have frequently spat out my tea laughing at things you've said. For that I am very grateful, and I feel I really hit the editor jackpot. Also, thank you to all at Katherine Tegen.

Thank you to my friends for your support: Anna, Sarah, Tal, Maz, Abi, James, Debora, Liz, Jo, Theo, Ben, Frances, Victoria F, Victoria G. My fellow writing buddies: Ben D, Julia T, Amy B, Mia K, and Lucy C. And my family: Mum, Dad, Jo, Max, Paul, James, Viktor, and Emma.

Thank you to my husband, Nick, for being so supportive, hilarious, patient, and, of course, incredibly handsome.

And finally thank you to my cat, Angus, for waking me up really early every morning to write (because you were hungry). I couldn't have done it without your help.